Triorion: Reborn

Part I
Book Three

L. J. Hachmeister

Novels by L. J. Hachmeister

Triorion: Awakening (Book One)
Triorion: Abomination (Book Two)
Triorion: Reborn, part I (Book Three)
Triorion: Reborn, part II (Book Four)

Forthcoming

Triorion: Nemesis (Book Five)

Short Stories

"The Gift," from *Triorion: The Series*
"Heart of the Dragon," from *Dragon Writers*

A Note from the Author

Regarding *Triorion: Reborn (parts I & II)*, I am both elated and heartbroken that I have completed the story I set out to tell back in 1988. The prospect of parting ways these characters has been harder than expected, and no matter how many times I tell myself that they're fictional, it doesn't make it any easier—or make them any less real.

That being said, I've decided to write three more books in this particular timeline, starting with book five, *Triorion: Nemesis.* My reasons will become clear enough as you read on, but without spoiling too much, I will say that the story I set out to write when I was seven has been told, but my experiences since then have inspired me to write a few more chapters in the saga of the Kyron triplets.

I hope you enjoy *Reborn* and will continue your journey across the Starways in the books to follow. Best wishes to you and happy reading!

For my "favorite Auntie in Chicago"
My Godmother
Irene

Triorion: Reborn

Part I
Book Three

PROLOGUE

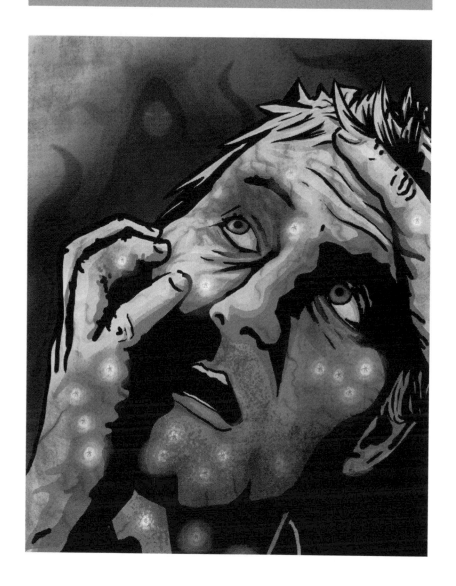

(Old) Earth: February 13, 2052

The world was dying. Sirens blared in the distance as the bombs fell from the sky, destroying the last remains of the city. Even deep underground, in the unregistered sub-basement lab, the blasts rattled the foundation, sending equipment and tools crashing to the floor.

Josef Stein twisted in his clothes, trying to resist the insatiable itch that crawled across his body and concentrate on his objective. Even without looking at his arms, his mind imagined the little buggers traveling under his skin, their spreading toxins sullying his olive color. Soon, parts of him would necrose, his blood hemolyze and turn acidotic.

The part of him that clung to lucidity would not spare him any pain. *This is all my doing. I was Earth's savior—how could I cause this ruin?*

As many times as he recalculated the odds, the answer was always the same. The damage to the planet—to himself—was done, irreparable and irredeemable. But some inexplicable force within kept him from using the gun tucked away in his desk drawer.

Things cannot end this way, he told himself. *Even if it's impossible, I have to keep trying...*

The picture of his son fell off his desk and onto the floor as the structure quaked. Dirt and debris rained down from the ceiling, and the emergency power clicked over, inundating the room in red light. Josef scooped up the picture, broken glass cutting his hands as he removed the paper behind it.

"Kurt," he whispered.

He shuffled painfully over to the desk drawer and pulled out a video-recorder module. Wiping the dirt from his eyes, he held the camera with shaky hands, focusing every ounce of strength on his last words.

Why? the cynical part of him wondered. *There is no way to send this out, and Kurt is already dead.*

Even through the agony and hallucinations, a deeper part of him still answered: *It's the only thing that still feels like it's coming from me.*

"Dearest Kurt, I am ashamed of what I have become. I have let the devil inside me…"

When he was done, he sealed the picture of his son, the recording, and a few other personal items inside an envelope and placed it carefully in the safe under his desk, whispering a prayer as he locked and replaced the protective cover.

"Please forgive me for all that I have done…"

A close-hitting explosion tore into the building above. Support pillars crashed through the ceiling, sending bricks and concrete slabs tumbling into the lab. With dust stinging his eyes, Josef crawled through the debris, coughing and struggling for air.

(*Oh Josef, look what you've become.*)

"No, no, NO!" he screamed, racking his head against the wall. *Impossible—he shouldn't be able to find me here! This is my sanctuary, the one place on the planet that I should be safe—*

(*You can never escape me.*)

Josef thought of the gun tucked away in his desk.

(*Tsk, tsk—such thoughts. You are getting in the way of your destiny.*)

"My destiny?" he asked as the debris settled. A single unbroken emergency light blinked in the darkness. Though Josef heard the familiar voice, he couldn't locate its source within the shadow.

(*You were useless, blind, inhibited—but I showed you your power. I destroyed that which was unnecessary inside you. Now, Josef, you can help me end this war.*)

"Stay away from me!" he screamed, swinging blindly at the dark.

Something slithered in the shadow. (*Now is the time to be reborn.*)

Josef cradled himself as phantom fingers wrapped around his throat. Pain exploded through his head, dilating his mind with new desires.

I have always backed down—

—when have I ever fought back? When have I ever shown the extent of my power?—

I will make the world burn.

The foreign compulsions, fierce and implacable, animated his body with immense pain until he yielded, seeking reprieve in the dark interstice of his own subconscious.

A thought cut right through him: *the experiment.*

Something inside him protested as the dwindling remainder of his sanity slowly pulled apart.

What am I becoming? He thought again of the gun. *I have to end things before I lose the last of myself.*

But his will to live was strong, as was the pull of the abomination he now harbored.

The experiment.

Barely commanding his own muscles, he limped over to the last stasis vial where trial Smart Cell Technology Series #117 hung suspended in gelatinous fluid.

Kurt. Edina. Martin.

All dead.

No hope.

Unable to fight his instincts, or the desires boiling inside him, Josef broke the glass. Gelatinous fluid dripped from his hands and down his arms as his tore open the safety seal with his teeth. Though invisible to the naked eye, the nanites tickled his throat as they crawled inside him, burrowing through flesh and integrating themselves into his decaying body.

"I know who I am," he whispered as he fell to his knees.

The voice in the shadows laughed at him.

CHAPTER I

Cryostasis had slowed Triel's mind, but it had not stopped it. Pulled apart from corporeality by chemical slumber, she drifted in and out of consciousness, faintly aware of her existence in the parallel universe.

Swirls of kaleidoscope colors danced across the dimensional planes as she drifted lazily. Caught up in the sights, the Healer thought less and less of the disconcerting separation and embraced pain-free tranquility.

All I want to do is close my eyes and sleep, *she thought, growing weary of her mind's struggle to maintain its tethers to the physical world.*

A star, shimmering and radiant, descended from the ethers, jolting her awake. From her healing experiences inside Jetta and Jaeia, Triel knew his essence, felt his bond, and recognized his celestial being.

Jahx…

Triel had never felt such a powerful mind, and as he approached, she saw the roots of his talents stemming from a different source than his sisters, stretching back across the infinite, timeless planes of the greater universe.

(Hello,) *he called to her. Crisp circles of light dotted the outline of his features.* (My name is Jahx. You're friends with my sisters.)

(How did you know?) *she whispered, taken aback. He was more handsome than she remembered in his sisters' memories. Bright blue eyes stood out against his dark features, and his magnetic smile drew her closer to his luminescence.*

(I felt you in Jetta's mind. You're very important to them, but especially to her.)

Triel didn't know what to say. (I am?)

Jahx nodded. (Yes. And you need to go back to help them. They're in trouble. You need to tell them the truth about Rion, about Algar legend, before it's too late.)

Increasingly more aware, Triel took in her unfamiliar surroundings. (Where am I? What is this place?)

12

(The place between. I can guide you back to your body,) *he said, pointing to the vibrating strings of light that encircled her and wound back toward the glowing horizon.*

(What about you?)

(Don't worry about me; I will find a way. Just promise me one thing,) *Jahx said, his ethereal light enveloping her mind.*

Suddenly aware of her lungs, she breathed in sharply. The air felt warm and invigorating as blood thundered through her core and down her limbs. (Anything.)

(This is very important. Their enemy is not who they think. Their real enemy is—)

Enemy. *Her memories returned in a rush.* The Alliance tricked me. Reht and the others—they've been made into Sleeper Agents.

Details of the cover-up orchestrated by Unipoesa resurfaced in her mind as she felt the hurt of being struck down and shoved into a freezer case all over again. I was betrayed, lied to—used.

(Triel—no—wait!) *Jahx said.*

(I'm tired of letting others abuse me,) *she said, striking his outstretched hand.*

(They are ignorant and afraid. Please, they don't understand what they do—)

Triel grasped the threads leading back and hurtled toward the horizon that separated her body and mind. As she slipped back into the physical realm, anger throbbed in her chest, hot and alive.

Unable to open her eyes, Triel tried to move her hands and feet, but her body wouldn't respond. Everything felt cold and numb, disconnected from her will.

Don't panic. Listen first.

The curved glass of the cryotube muffled the sounds of the monitors keeping tabs on her vital signs. Intravenous lines, suspended in red animation fluid, occasionally brushed against the confines of her prison, sending tiny vibrations up her arms.

Reach outside yourself.

Expanding her awareness, Triel searched for accessible minds as she stared into the blood-lit darkness. She found two technicians conversing nearby, their minds incognizant and unobstructed.

Hear me, she said, projecting her thoughts.

The nearest one, a human hybrid, had inviting, supple flesh. Reaching into his skull, Triel dug in with invisible fingers, and his neurons flared to her touch. *Get me out of this thing.*

He screamed, bucking backward against the console. The other technician tried to calm him, but Triel dove deeper, scorching his nerve fibers. *Let nothing stand in your way.*

The repeated pounding of flesh finished with a crack. Seconds later, a body slumped to the floor and rolled against her cryotube.

Release me.

Footsteps approached, then paused. The steady beeping of the monitors transformed into a crescendo whine as warm stasis fluid intermixed with the cryon, reviving her frozen limbs.

After regaining command of her arms, Triel pulled at the tube down her windpipe, gagging and coughing as she dragged it out of her airway. Once the fluid pressure dropped and the stasis lid retracted, she opened her eyes. Her victim stood in front of the cryotube, eyes bloodshot, half-crazed, claw marks ringing his neck.

"Wait," he mumbled as he disentangled her from the leads and pulse oximeter with frenetic hands.

She looked to her left where the dead body of the other technician lay. "You do quick work."

"Please don't hurt me," the technician whimpered, falling to his knees.

Triel ripped the intravenous line out of her arm, letting the blood trickle onto the white-tiled floor. "It's too late."

Cold and indifferent to his pain, she watched the technician tear at his skin, his heart racing and nerves afire.

So easy, she thought, walking away as he crumpled to the floor.

"The burning—I'm burning alive!" he shrieked, succumbing to her misdirection. Within seconds, she had induced complete cell lysis, liquefying his organs and tissues.

And to think—all these years I have been afraid, she mused, allowing her mind to linger within the technician's body as he took his last breaths. She inhaled sharply, completely exhilarated as the technician's congested heart stilled. *I should have never denied myself this release.*

She peeked out through the doors of the cryostasis chamber. Only two guards posted. With the power she felt, she could tear apart an entire armada with a single thought.

"Weak minds. Putrid thoughts," she whispered.

Before she could act, Triel leaned against the wall, overcome by the rapid rise of her body's internal temperatures. Sliding down until she was sitting on the floor, the Healer ripped apart the blue-cloth cryoskin wrapped around her torso and thighs. *I've come out of stasis too soon.*

As her head throbbed with every beat of her heart, the compulsion to attack the guards faded. With her emotions quieted, she sobered to the terrifying reality. *I'm Falling.*

"Father," she whispered, raising her hands in front of her face. "Help me. The temptations are too strong."

Green and black veins snaked up her arms, mottling her fair skin and occluding the fading markings of her people. She thought of her betrayal, how some of the people she trusted most had lied to her, and her anger returned with an icy rush.

"Jetta," she said, seeing her marred reflection in the plated door frame. "Help me."

***

Damon Unipoesa woke to what felt like ice picks drilling into his temples. With a groan, he managed to open his eyes, but his contact enhancements had been removed. From what little detail he

15

could make out within a few meters, there were a stack of datascopes with his vital signs to his right. To his left, an IV with the red cryon prep dripped down the tube into his forearm.

"Soldier, I'm giving you a direct order to release me," he said to the nearest technician bent over a datascope keyboard.

The technician glanced at him before pressing the bedside com. "Sir, the admiral's awake."

Tidas Razar's image organized itself in pixilated blue dots on the side rail interface.

My eyes must be playing tricks on me, Damon thought. The Minister looked sick, his eye sockets ringed and his face swollen. *And why can I only see him from the neck up? What's he hiding?*

"Damon, I warned you," the Minister said, his words, slightly slurred, delivered with measured precision.

"You're making a mistake, Razar. Don't put me on ice, especially not when there's so much at stake. You're going to lose the last of the Kyrons' trust."

The Minister's eyes trained themselves to his. "You did this to yourself, Admiral. We've got enough on you to make the case."

"Tarkn's don't sleep well."

"Would you prefer to be an Agent, Admiral?"

"Someone like me with advanced training wouldn't take. You know that. Look what's happening to Tarsha. No, wait!" Damon exclaimed as the hypothermia cycle began to whirr. Liquid ice flowed into his veins. His arm spasmed, and bolts of pain shot up into his shoulder and neck.

"Goodbye, Admiral. You've always disappointed me," the Minister said.

Cold suffocation crushed down upon his body as his temperature ticked down. With every sluggish beat of his heart, his eyelids drooped, and the interval between breaths lengthened. He didn't notice when the technician opened his mouth and measured him for the endotracheal tube, nor did he realize his restraints had been lifted as the team prepared to move him to his cryotube.

Shouting. Gunfire. Commotion surrounded him in dreamlike immediacy as the monitors beeped steadily in the background. His perceptions shifted.

Damon found himself back in the Chief Commander's chair, the entire Fleet tuned in, the crackling static from his microphone hungering for his orders. Panic ground up his insides as the Dominion pummeled their way through the Perimeter and the United Starways Coalition's last defenses eroded.

"Retreat!" his first officer screamed.

No chance to win this; no way out, *he thought.*

The USC had been gambling when they put Damon in the hot seat. Although he fit the intelligence profile, and his service record was impeccable, he didn't have what it took. The growing realization carved into his belly as the little green ship markers faded into oblivion on the Fleet monitoring screens.

Perfect record in the Endgame be damned. I am a child psychology specialist and a covert operations acquisitions officer— not a *godich* CCO, *he thought, slamming his fists against his chair.*

Disturbed by his violence, the holographic displays zig-zagged, but then reorganized on the armrest. For a moment Damon could see himself in the battlefield of the Raging Front.

The Coalition is desperate enough to put me here. I am their last shot at winning this war, *he thought.*

(There is no hope.)

A voice floated in from above. "Is he still alive?"

(Fools.)

"We don't have time to reverse the feed," someone else said. "Let's hope his Tarkn blood can handle it. Hold on, Admiral."

(I am not good enough.)

Molten pain seared through his chest, kicking his heart into overdrive. Blood pressure spiking, his head split apart at the seams as stars of light exploded across his retinas.

Older memories accosted him. Urusous Li sat across from him at the Endgame console, not breaking his gaze with his teacher.

Only twelve years old, he had mastered all the advanced training Damon could offer.

The cold, hollow look in Li's eyes revealed the soulless creature that Damon had nurtured. "I've outgrown you," Li whispered.

(What have I done?)

"Calm down!" someone shouted.

Hands pushed him against the stretcher as something pierced his forearm. Damon screamed as fire exploded into his limbs.

The Minister was younger, his beetle-brows black and thick, his waistline trim. "The problem is that commanders with too much humanity will hesitate," he said, his hands folded neatly behind his back as he circled Damon. "They will questions their actions, the morality of their choices. I don't want a commander—I want a razor. I want someone who will be capable of making the toughest decisions without hesitation. Do you understand your orders, Captain?"

Sitting at his desk, Damon looked down at the datafiles of the two remaining candidates: Tarsha Leone and Urusous Li. Both of them possessed the military acumen, but only one of them could be chosen. Just like the rest of the group, they had been bred to eliminate the competition, and neither would stand for the other's existence.

"It's your choice, Captain," the Minister said, coming up from behind him. He laid both hands on Damon's shoulders, his fingertips digging in. "Let the best razor win."

"Who's Tarsha?" someone said. The voice was muffled, as if he heard it through a wall.

"Don't know. That's all he's been saying."

Overhead lights whisked by through a tiny slit above his eyes at regular intervals. His body felt stiff and distant, but he managed to move his right hand, enough to sense that he was restrained inside some kind of box. A scream rose in his throat, but his vocal cords felt encased in cement.

Coffin.

18

Tears rolled down his cold, waxy skin. The afterimage of Tarsha appeared before his eyes like a photonegative. (*Don't hurt her!*)

"*You've clearly grown attached to this candidate,*" *the Minister said, leaning forward. His face appeared under the solitary light of the interrogation room.* "*I can't have that. I need your judgment.*"

Damon fumbled with the cigarette in his right hand while fanning away the yellow haze of smoke with his left. Think, *he told himself, shifting in his seat and resting his elbows on the table.* Don't give away anything.

As much as he tried to calm himself down, his instincts screamed at him with the craze of a trapped animal. They hadn't let him sleep in three days, and his only meals had been rationed scraps. Pieces of his uniform lay strewn across the room, and it took everything he had to stay focused in the intensified heat and humidity.

In a voice much younger and not yet scarred by cigarettes, Damon replied: "*She has empathy. It's a valuable asset. She can anticipate the enemy. Read my report.*"

"*I have, and that's why you're here. You've lost your direction, your objectivity. And I know you've had contact outside the USC,*" *the Minister said, pressing his fists down on the table.* "*I want answers.*"

Protect his source—at all costs. He couldn't lose his only friend. "*You're paranoid.*"

"*Then you have nothing to worry about when we redline your files and call up all your contacts.*"

Damon didn't say anything. The Minister is probably bluffing, *he told himself,* but there's an outside possibility that Pancar could be tracked.

The two of them had used a viral system code in routine net communications to relay messages to one another, but there was always residual data left floating in the wave network that could be retraced to his confidant.

"Remember," the Minister said, coming down close enough that Damon could smell his sour breath. "You're replaceable."

Blood rushed in his ears, the pressure in his skull building with every beat of his heart.

"We're going to have to jump inside the perimeter," a voice said.

Damon's body jolted to the left at the sound of an engine firing against armed loading locks. A dull ache spread across his side and branched out through the rest of his body.

"I don't have time to make the calculations—" someone shouted.

(I can't save her.)

The Nagoorian appeared in front of him in blue-lit holographics. "You're not going to like what I have to say."

Great, *Damon thought, plopping down on the edge of his bed. Things were already tense. Suspecting Pancar to be his outside source, the Military Minister had elevated security measures to make any form of communication, even in viral code, nearly impossible. Luckily for Pancar, his reputation as a conservative and a supporter of the Alliance kept him safe from arrest—at least for now.*

He won't be able to get this past inspection again, *Damon realized, holding the datafile out in front of him and inspecting the hacked device. This is Pancar's last message.*

"Tarsha Leone's listed parents, Gradivia and Xeodi, are not genetically related to her, nor are Urusous Li's parents, Mi Xing and Tsaio Li. It's all a front."

"What do you mean, Pancar?" Damon asked, but he elicited no response from the recording.

Bumping up the volume on the dataclip, he pressed the bud embedded in his ear canal with his thumb. Whatever Pancar discovered would be instantly erased when the message ended, so he had to be sure he heard every word.

"My labs are not sophisticated enough to decipher all the data, Damon, but it looks as though both Urusous and Tarsha have more

than just hand-selected 'parents' and growth accelerators. They have synthetic DNA. It was as if someone had wanted to experiment with minor alterations to a specific genetic code."

"Impossible," Damon said. Urusous had minimal epicanthic folds, dark hair, and soft facial features—humanoid, almost Eurasian, with accents of outerworlder blood in the horned protrusions near his hairline. By contrast, Tarsha was fair-skinned with angular features, the unusual black of her eyes differentiating her from most humanoids.

"I compared the other children with the samples you provided, with similar findings. There were always two versions of a genetic code, one male, one female."

Pancar's face changed. "This is nothing like what I thought, Damon. These children didn't have 'parents'— they were specifically bred for command. If Urusous is as unstable as you say he is, you might want to find the source of his code."

(What have I done?)

"Damon."

Someone rubbed vigorously on his sternum. "Damon!"

Recognizing the voice, he tried to open his eyes, but they seemed glued shut.

A hand gripped his wrist and felt for a pulse. "What's happening?"

"I don't know, Sir," a nervous voice responded. "He came out of it too soon. These readings are off the charts."

A shot of adrenaline hit him like a cannon blast. He gritted his teeth, muscles flexing impossibly, lungs screaming for air as he arched off the exam table. No longer stuck shut, his eyes tried to spring from their sockets, sending tears sliding down his cheeks. Blurry images zig-zagged about as voices argued and shouted.

Technicians fed more medication down the tubes leading into his arms. Finally, the tension eased and his muscles relaxed. He sank down onto the exam table, exhausted, gasping for breath.

"Damon, it's me, Pancar. Can you hear me?"

21

"Pan…" His friend's name came out in a fractured, garbled slur. Concentrating on his right hand, he commanded his fingertips to touch Pancar's sleeve.

"My friend," Pancar smiled, taking his hand. "It's good to see you again."

Damon could only think the words; his lips wouldn't respond. When he tried to lift his head up, it seemed impossibly heavy.

"Don't rush it. Your body needs time. I will explain everything."

Fuzzy images organized into concrete shapes. He recognized the facility markings on the support pillars and the language on the instruments.

I'm on Nagoor, he realized, *and by the haphazard arrangement of equipment, in one of Pancar's mobile operations facilities.*

"I was contacted by Jaeia Kyron about your unfortunate circumstances," Pancar said. "With her help, we were able to evacuate you to here, to Nagoor, before they completed the cryofreeze process. Since the Alliance's defense network is down, I think they have larger problems then trying to track us right now."

Damon remembered. He hadn't believed Victor Paulstine when he claimed to have designed the entire defense network for the Alliance, but when Li disabled their entire Fleet with a keystroke, he knew he had grossly underestimated his enemy—again.

"I didn't… want to leave. I have to stay… fight," Damon muttered through numb lips.

Pancar folded his hands together and leaned forward. "The last word I received was that Minister Razar has fallen into a coma from a slow intracranial bleed. If the bastard hadn't frozen the Healer, maybe he'd be more than a vegetable right now. Wren's leading the Fleet. He's a good commander. Don't worry, Damon. The war's not over yet."

Pancar left his side for a moment to electronically sign the documents one of his aides passed to him.

"I'm mobilizing the few units I still have working for me," the Nagoorian said. "We're trying to rally the General Assembly—or what's left of it. Victor Paulstine has made many allies in the centuries he's been around, and with Li's popularity and defense against the Deadwalkers, the Alliance isn't going to stay together much longer."

"What?" Damon rasped. He tried to swallow away the terrible taste in his mouth, but his throat felt like two sheets of sandpaper rubbing together.

"It's our latest intel," Pancar said, holding a palm-sized holographic projector over his chest. "My agents have been trying to find Paulstine for years since we traced a human flesh farm back to him, but he's the most elusive Sentient I've ever tracked. When you told me he resurfaced and was interested in the Kyrons, I doubled my efforts."

Seeing Victor's image rendered just above his heart, Damon tried to rise but found his body's response sluggish and weak. Pancar helped him raise the head of the bed before starting the clip.

"We found out that Paulstine makes regular visits to black market restoration clinics on Iyo Kono and Old Earth to have his body modified. Everything from muscle enhancements, cell retainers and tissue serums. Illegal, but not unusual. However, one of my agents managed to get a blood sample," Pancar said, pointing to the nucleotides swimming across the visual field. "It took me two months to figure out what the hell this was."

"Smart... Cell..." Damon managed to say before his head dropped back against the pillow.

Pancar nodded. "Yes, Smart Cell Technology. Ancient. Banned. Can't get this anywhere. I knew he was a relic, but this indicates that he was around even before the Last Great War."

Damon remembered his great-grandfather's stories of the privileged humans from twenty-first century Earth who purposefully injected themselves with the Josef Stein's Smart Cell nanites. Originally designed for soldiers who lost limbs or were critically injured during battle, the nanites could revive and regenerate any type of tissue. After Stein's rivals stole a batch, it didn't take long before they marketed it to high-paying clientele desperately seeking to increase their longevity.

As a child, Damon was haunted by the idea of the tiny little machines crawling around the insides of a body, tinkering and meddling with the laws of nature. He imagined two hundred year old men and women clawing at invisible enemies, pleading with unseen demons until the last of them was swept away into the gulfs of insanity.

The last humans who were stupid enough to inject themselves died over 900 years ago from the unexpected neurological effects, he thought. *There is no way Victor Paulstine could have survived.*

"My biggest concern is this," Pancar said, pulling up an audio file on the projector. Despite the grainy sound, Damon clearly heard the speaker's agitated voice proclaim his madness in one of the root languages of Starways Common.

"We gather here because we are united for a common purpose: Earth. The human menace has desecrated her beauty since its very inception. Man's wretched propensity for violence and self-indulgence has laid sickness down on the land. Now is the time to end this charade. Do humans deserve to live on the land they destroy? No. And it is our job to end our mother's suffering."

Pancar turned down the volume to the reel. "You've heard this speech before, yes?"

Damon nodded. He did his undergraduate work on personality disorders in military and political autocrats, and for his thesis he had studied dictators on alien worlds, specifically Earth. Ramak Yakarvoah was notorious, but many of the allegations against him had never been proven, demoting his status amongst the Starways' most infamous dictators. One of the most serious had been that he had orchestrated the assassination of the United States President in 2052, but the evidence against him was dismissed when Josef Stein became the prime suspect.

Leaning forward in his chair, Pancar spoke softly. "Once I knew Victor's age, I had my teams look into his activity on Earth before the war. I had made a contact on Earth, a caretaker named Jade, and she claimed to have evidence of electronic correspondence between Ramak Yakarvoah and Victor Paulstine, but I haven't heard from her in days now."

Damon tried to sit up again, but Pancar gently pushed him down. "I know you share my worry. If Victor was a disciple of Ramak's, then we may be in more trouble than we know."

"The arch-apostle—" With his throat on fire, Damon couldn't finish the sentence. Instead, he closed his eyes and let the rest of his words play out in his mind. *The arch-apostle of bloodshed...*

The mere mention of Ramak Yakarvoah had drudged up a bad feeling in his gut, and remembering his grisly deeds furthered the sickening feeling. Yakarvoah had been the leader of the "Doomsdayers," a group that wished to end humanity, and he had influenced many political and military leaders during the last few years before the Last Great War, even launching the bioarms race by personally financing the research. The most famous of his disciples was rumored to be Josef Stein, but his ties to Stein during the War were never verified. Most records on Ramak had been destroyed or lost.

"You and I have been friends for a long time," Pancar said, shooing out the remainder of the staff. One of the technicians whispered something in his ear, but Pancar shook his head and dismissed him. "And it's been very difficult for me to keep some things from you."

Damon spotted a thermos on a rolling cart next to Pancar and grunted. His hands, rubbery and numb, grabbed for it, and Pancar helped him hold the brim to his lips. Cold coffee dribbled down his lips as he sucked down its contents.

"I know these last few months have been difficult for you. I know you've felt responsible for Li. And Tarsha."

25

Damon wiped his lips. His words finally came to him, although not as quickly as he'd have liked. "What... have you learned?"

"That last time we talked I told you that Urusous and Tarsha were brother and sister. Now I have to tell you something even harder to hear. I did some digging on the Alliance database when Victor deactivated the net defense system. I found out that Razar ordered the Hub to run a universal aptitude and abilities comparative analysis just before the Command Development Program launched, including test scores from the Endgame and the Military Readiness Exams."

Damon knew the rest of Pancar's theory before he had explained it, and his heart sunk in his chest. A bad taste, worse than the aftertaste of the coffee grounds, singed the back of his throat.

With a heavy sigh, Pancar continued. "Razar ordered research teams to take genetic samples from the most capable candidates, both military and non-military alike."

I was never supposed to be a chief commanding officer, Damon thought, but the truth held firm. Before the Kyrons, before Li and Tarsha, he had outscored everyone in the Fleet.

Duty. Family. Starways. I did it for these things, he told himself, trying to justify the horrors of his naivety.

(Why didn't I see?)

He never thought it odd when they ran him through every single psychiatric and intelligence test the military had to offer. It was wartime, and they needed to find the best commanders. Nor did he think twice when they put him through rigorous physical exams that involved blood sample after blood sample. He was, after all, a Tarkn born of a human surrogate. There were always concerns, though unfounded, fueled by the racial purism that polluted the upper ranks of the old USC.

Damon Unipoesa offered his arm to Pancar. The Nagoorian took it firmly, wiping his skin with an alcohol swab before removing the syringe from his uniform pocket.

26

"I wanted to do this myself. That way there will be no mistakes, no more doubts. This will stay between you and me."

Damon grabbed Pancar's wrist just as the needle touched his skin. "This isn't necessary. Both of us already know."

Pancar gently removed himself from Damon's grip. "Then this is for her, my friend."

Closing his eyes, Damon fought the landslide of emotion crushing his chest. It had been years since he had cried. He almost couldn't remember what it had felt like. As the needle pierced his vein and pulled the warm blood from his body, he smiled, tears cascading down his cheeks.

***

Traveling to Jue Hexron proved difficult with Li's new army staking out territory along routine jump sites. Jetta made two extra jumps, one that barely avoided materializing into the gigantic basalt moons of Oraesis III, just to stay away from frequently trafficked areas. But then again, it didn't really matter. She wanted Victor to find her.

"Come on," she muttered, checking her dashboard readings. The stealth fighter's cloaking ability enabled her to make it past the orbital perimeter, but once she hit the frequency-monitored airspace above the Holy Cities, her engine exhaust reacted against the nitrogen components in the air, making her easily detectable. "I'm right here."

Their instruments not yet able to pinpoint her location, the airspace patrol sent out a general broadcast along her trajectory: "Unidentified ship, please submit your license and registry to the airspace magistrate."

Spotting two ships heading her direction on her scopes, Jetta switched off the primary engine. When they fired on her assumed position she changed course, gliding along the landscape, using her

27

previous momentum and the inverters' anti-gravitational force to keep flying.

At any other time she would have found the landscape breathtaking. The legendary Holy Cities fused ancient and modern design in the sleek, chrome structures butting up against the hand-carved stone towers. Clouds, drifting down from skies, swirled through the city and collected at the base of the mountains jutting up from the south, reflecting the sunlight in soft azure and yellow tones.

Jetta swallowed the sour sting of acid at the back of her throat. *Did I really hit my sister?*

They had wrestled, they had pushed each other, but she had never really *hit* her sister before. Not on purpose, at least. And to knock her unconscious—

Oh Gods—is she okay? Worst-case scenarios played through her mind. *What if she didn't come around and hook onto the drifting medical frigate?*

At the time, the plan seemed so clear and sure in her head: Find Victor, at all costs. But as she approached the coordinates Victor had transmitted, fear wormed its way into her chest, dissecting her rationale.

(I need my sister.)

No, I can't, she thought, stopping herself. *If I contact Jaeia, even to check on her, she'll try and stop me.*

Darker desires gave her the assurance she needed. *Besides, Jaeia is tough; I'm sure she came around.*

Gripping more tightly to the controls, Jetta hardened herself around her decision. *I struck out on this mission alone, and I must complete it alone.*

Without reengaging the engines, Jetta managed to coast to Victor's meeting spot, circling three times to check for any patrol ships or ground forces before landing. He had picked an area away from the heart of the city on the grassy cliffs where a large pillared structure with huge marble archways protruded from the mountainside.

I know I've seen this place before, Jetta thought, unable to remember if she had chanced upon the unusual archeological site in a stolen memory or in a photo.

Keeping an eye on the building and on her instruments, Jetta stripped out of her pilot's suit and donned a combat uniform she had found in one of the lockers on her fighter. She knew better than to keep open arms, so she stashed a handgun, knife, and two grenades in the folds of the suit.

Probably won't be able to keep them hidden for long, she reasoned. *Victor will surely scan me for weapons.*

Jetta rechecked the bioscanner readings linked from the starship to her sleeve. *No Sentient life forms detected? That's suspicious.*

She had expected a complement of soldiers to meet her there and immediately take her into custody. Returning to the dashboard, she re-ran the coordinates that Victor had sent on his last transmission to her, but her navigational system confirmed her location.

(This doesn't feel right.)

Despite her reservations, Jetta cautiously exited the hatch and took a visual and aural sweep of the area. Nothing unusual caught her eye, and only the sounds of the breeze ruffling the feather-leaf pines and the chirps of two warring Tomba squirrels reached her ears.

There has to be something more.

Minding her feet as she walked through the tall grass, Jetta kept a watchful eye for any ground traps, but her other senses told her that Victor wasn't interested in harming her.

At least not yet.

She froze mid-step when she spied a spread of black, spiny-legged robotic sentinels perched in the trees and clinging underneath the overhanging lattice of the rooftops.

This is all expected, she told herself. *Jue Hexron preservation groups routinely use sentinels to guard archeological sites, preventing looters from stealing ancient treasures.*

29

At first Jetta hesitated. Sentinels were attuned to biochip readings, and she had yet to be refitted with a permanent chip. With Jue Hexron's changing military presence, she wasn't sure if the temporary biomarker with her old Alliance clearances would grant her passage.

She took one step.

Then two.

After the third step, she felt safe enough to pass, though their mechanical eyes tracked her every movement as she made her way to the entrance.

Jetta tested the colossal wooden doors, and to her surprise, they opened easily, though not without groaning and creaking. Old smells immediately hit her—dust and polishing oil, and some other kinds of preservatives that settled heavily in her lungs.

Smells like a library or a museum, she thought, rubbing her nose as she stepped inside the dark chamber.

Before she had a chance to call up the flashlight option on her sleeve, bulb lights, strung up on wires, snapped and crackled to life. From what she could see, hundreds of dust-covered statues, from towering sculptures of titans to knee-high marble demi-gods, lined the cobbled pathway.

Taken aback by the size of her lifeless audience, Jetta hesitated, overly aware that each statue had been turned to face her position.

They're just statues! she told herself, averting her eyes from their soulless faces.

Resisting her emotions, Jetta looked back to the wires, tracing them back to their power source and then branching out along the new lines of electrical cord. At the end of one cord, the red eyes of a spycam, nestled atop a statue of a blind female beggar, gazed back.

"Where are my aunt and uncle?" Jetta demanded.

The spycam winked at her and the lights dimmed. Then Victor appeared.

"Jetta Kyron," he said, stepping out behind a cluster of statues. "Alone, I see, and not looking too well. Where is your sister?"

"Where are my aunt and uncle?" Jetta asked again, squaring her shoulders. "You said they'd be here."

This is why Victor didn't need guards, Jetta thought. Out of the corner of her eye she could see the cameras filtering in his hologram.

Appearing in muted tones, Victor walked toward her, his glittering, diamond smile perfectly reimaged. He stopped a meter in front of her and leaned on his cane. "I thought I'd show you around first. Get you familiar with your roots before I took you to see your uncle and aunt. They're resting anyway; it's been a very tough journey. Fiorah is not the galaxy's most hospitable environment, and we won't even get into the paperwork required to get them off-planet."

Jetta let out a breath through gritted teeth. "I don't have time for games, Victor. Take me to them now."

"Warchild, you have no patience. That has always been your undoing. You are much like your father."

Jetta's stomach knotted. She couldn't sense Victor's mind, but the tone of his voice told her he wasn't lying.

"My father?"

When Victor smiled it looked strained, as if the corners of his mouth were being pulled up by hooks. "A very handsome and intelligent man, I must say, and not quite as brooding as you. You get that from your mother. But that's another story for another time. Come, there is much to discuss."

Before Jetta could say anything, a semioptic phantom of sound and light eclipsed her vision. The busy scene of colors and images passed by too quickly, sending waves of nausea through her belly.

What was that?

"Coming?" Victor said, turning back to see if she was following him into the next chamber.

Jetta forgot herself for a moment as she leaned heavily on a statue of a young child. *What am I doing? Why did I come here?*

Answers. Victor knows so such much about me, and he has my aunt and uncle, she told herself. But he also had something else she wanted.

Tilting her head back, Jetta remembered the sweet, vicious taste of his powers. *Victor is no ordinary human. He's something beyond his flesh—*

(—something monstrous like me.)

Jetta held onto her anger to anchor her words. "Why won't you meet me in person? Why this charade?"

Victor fiddled with something off of the holographic projection feed, and another series of lights flickered on, illuminating the atrium piled high with artifacts and relics from centuries past.

"My first responsibility is my country," he said as she walked into the atrium, "so I must stay close to my base of operations. Surely you can understand this, being the great commander that defeated the Motti."

He was insulting her, testing her, but Jetta knew better than to give him what he wanted. "Who are you really, and why have you brought me here?"

Victor chuckled and squeezed the handle of his cane as he trained his gaze on an artifact, a clay man suspended on a wooden cross that hung from the ceiling.

I remember seeing something like that in Jade's hideout on Earth.

"I am a man who chose to upset God's great plan," he whispered.

Jetta approached him cautiously, her eyes unfocused, watching for movement in the shadows. "It's amazing that you would even speak of any God."

Victor sighed. "So quick to judge, and yet you're here. You think you've come for your aunt and uncle, but isn't there something else? You've sensed our kindred spirit, and you can't deny the pull in your heart. You and I have heard the same call."

32

Jetta stopped in her tracks. Pinpoints of light erupted across her visual field. She squeezed her eyes shut and clapped her hands over her ears as a blast of sound ripped them open from the inside out.

"Are you certain you're alright?" Victor asked.

Jetta opened her eyes again. The commotion had stopped as suddenly as it started, leaving her clutching a wooden statue of a multi-armed animal with a long proboscis.

What is happening to me?

"I'm fine. Get on with it."

"Very well then," Victor said. He pointed to a massive sculpture of a meditating male human of Asian descent, his legs crossed and arms lying peacefully in his lap. "Do you know who this is?"

Jetta shook her head, still reeling from the sensory overload.

"How about him?" Victor said, pointing to the cross.

Jetta didn't say anything as she collected herself, refastening her hair back behind her head.

"Do you know what this is?" Victor said, pointing to a book with an ancient symbol on it. Having grafted some of Jaeia's studies of Old Earth, Jetta recognized the symbol as middle-eastern in origin, but beyond that she had no clue.

He continued to ask her to identify other things, but she couldn't. Statues of what might have been deities, dust-covered books, and writings engraved on stone appeared to be of terrestrial design, but she had no recollection of the specifics.

"These belong in a museum," Jetta said. "Did you steal them?"

"No, I did not steal them. They were part of my own collection, acquired before the Last Great War. They are invaluable to some, a terrible reminder to others. For me they are merely ghosts of the past. Fools who didn't know any better."

Jetta walked over to a painting of a haloed man with a lamb in his arms and wiped the dust off its label. Written in English, a root language of the Starways, Jetta managed to figure out the words.

"Jesus of Nazareth," she mumbled.

Closing her eyes, Jetta dug into her gleaned knowledge and experience, sorting through the incidental memories she had picked up over the years.

Jesus Christ. A religious figure from Earth. Son of God, she remembered, opening her eyes. *That was the man on the cross I saw in Jade's place.*

After stringing the bits and pieces of knowledge into a cohesive body, she realized something odd. *Why didn't I figure this out before?*

An unspoken resentment resurfaced: *Because it's all a bunch of gorsh-shit.*

Despite herself, she bit back her antipathy. She had always harbored fierce antireligious sentiments, and Victor's apparent fascination only exacerbated her aversion.

"What does 'the son of God' mean to you, Victor?" Jetta said.

Victor's expression turned to delight. "Please," he said, curling his finger at her and walking into the next chamber.

Jetta followed him, anticipating another room full of religious figures. Instead, she found a library filled with statues and portraits of men, most of whom she immediately recognized.

"Timur. Alexander the Great. Clovis of the Franks. Attila the Hun. The Black Prince. Adolf Hitler. Frederick the Great. Saladin. Lin Piao. William the Conqueror. Napoleon. Joan of Arc. Alaric the Goth," she rattled off in rapid succession.

"Interesting, Victor said. "You know great military leaders, but you don't know religious figures."

Jetta didn't understand his point. She had studied Old Earth's great military minds during her days with the Dominion Core Academy, but her knowledge of religion was limited and always had been, both by circumstance and purpose. There was no talk of God on Fiorah—unless it came from the apartment next to theirs, usually accompanied by the rhythmic banging of the bed against the wall. And after the fall of the Motti she had gone to great lengths to avoid what religious comforts were offered; it seemed cheap to her after all the suffering she had seen and felt.

Of course Jaeia took a different stance. Her sister had always been curious about divine forces, but to Jetta, it was a waste of time. Praying to an idol would have never gotten Jahx back, and it wouldn't get her aunt and uncle back—or help her now. It was up to her to get things done right. Religion—Gods—God—was yet another untruth conjured by those seeking power.

"What's it to you, Victor?" she said. "I'm tired of this. I want my aunt and uncle, or I'm leaving."

"You'll find that you'll want to hear what I'm saying. You can leave anytime, of course, but your questions will not be answered. Who are you? Where do you come from? What is your destiny?"

Victor studied his ring with the red bird of prey for a moment before continuing. "Since the dawn of man there have always been religious figures, prophets, messiahs—leaders, shaping and molding the course of human events. This is no different in the Starways. You and your siblings are unique, Jetta; you're not like other military officers. Surely you can sense it in your blood. You were meant for so much more than taking orders and maintaining the peace—you were meant to change the course of history."

"I think defeating the Motti counted for something."

Jetta didn't like the way Victor cocked his head at her. "No, that's not what I mean. I will show you."

Though his holographic image stayed fixed, his shadow jumped out at her. With a yelp, she raised her arms to protect her face. After several seconds, she finally realized that Victor had not attacked her, but was playing a video reel in the background.

A slick chill ran down her spine, sending shivers down her limbs. *What is wrong with me?*

"You really don't look well," he commented.

She hated the way he smiled at her, and her words did nothing to hide her humiliation. "I'm fine," she snapped back.

"Good," he said, his smile unchanged. "I don't want my prize pupil falling ill."

Victor turned and pointed his cane at the projection. "Look here—that was me in 2045, right before I discovered who I really was and what I was meant to do."

A man, not terribly younger but with less artificial skin, was shown making gestures at a complicated looking machine. The sound had been muted, and Victor narrated over it.

"From a very young age I was inventing things, and my latest work with advanced detection equipment had landed me several government contracts. This here is a prototype for a transphasic modulator," he said, gesturing toward the enormous device that dwarfed its inventor. "My crowning achievement, thirty years in the making."

Jetta tilted her head as she watched the younger Victor pop open a plate, exposing crisscrossing wires and ionic filters. "Impossible."

"Not at all. See those spindle coils? In those days we used 120-10s. Lots of burnouts. I didn't have the advantage of cellular bellicone skins back then—the stuff wouldn't be discovered for another hundred and fifty years."

Jetta hadn't learned or grafted much about the wave-network, but she knew that the system operated by bending space-time, and the original models used transphasic modulators. Rumors circulated that it had originated on Earth, but that she was meeting its inventor was too much to believe.

"I was running it essentially 'backwards' then," Victor said. "I used a delayed feedback loop instead of the modern transitor gradient, but then again, my purpose was different. I was creating a different kind of hole in space-time—one that would allow my employers to spy on their enemies."

Jetta watched the younger Victor show his calculations to the camera, explaining in detail the complex symbols and equations.

"My employers insisted on a live test run after I had just completed a thirty-hour stint; the Russians had just rearmed

Moscow, and unrest was building on the borders. Exhausted, I didn't pay close enough attention to my tertiary calibrations, and I misfired, blowing a hole in the ocean somewhere in the mid-Atlantic and burning out half of my tetrahydral gaskets. The second time I got it right, but only after some heavy explaining to my employers. Later, when I analyzed the recordings from the first firing, I detected something that shouldn't have been—alien signals in dead space during the space-time shift."

"Dead space?" Jetta said.

"A loose term we used centuries ago, meant to describe unseen dimensions," Victor explained.

Something cold grazed her shoulder, and she tucked her arms to her chest as little bumps rose on her skin.

I don't like where any of this is going, she thought, looking around. The collection of statues and painting regarded her with flat, lifeless eyes. *(What is happening to me?)*

Victor squeezed the handle of his cane. "The transphasic modulator was supposed to allow the overlay of two separate points in space, but that day, because of my miscalculation, I opened a door between our world and another."

Voices, in chaotic chatter, came from every direction. Jetta whipped her head around, but no one was there. Clapping her hands over her ears, she tried to muffle the sound as the noise escalated.

Stop, oh Gods, please—

"I could hear something whispering across the dimensions," Victor said, bringing a hand to his lips. "I had to find out who—or what—it was."

The voices peaked, then vanished. When she looked up, she saw Victor smiling at her, his head tilted to the side, eyes hidden behind the reflection of his glasses.

"You are quite strange, Warchild."

Left breathless and increasingly confused, Jetta let her arms drop to her sides.

I am going crazy.

37

(You are awakening.)

Victor continued on. "It took me several months to translate, but the more I studied their language, the more I realized its similarities to ancient terrestrial tongues. Do you know what they talked about? Us. The lowly human filth they preyed on, that they used for *entertainment*."

Jetta scoffed. "You don't expect me to believe this."

Victor seemed unaffected by her skepticism. Instead, he took interest in the statues and figures that surrounded them. "It's a terrible thing to know that you were born a murderer, a cancer upon the world," he said, his holographic fingers grazing the cheek of the statue of Saladin. "I never had a choice. I was their vessel, planted on the Earth for one purpose. And for years I hated myself for it— for being a slave to their cause. But then I realized that knowing what I was gave me the power to change things."

Jetta's stomach dropped. *Knowing what I was gave me the power to change things.*

Is that possible? Is there hope for someone like me?

"How come no one has ever spoken of these beings before?" she asked.

Victor smiled. "But they have. Angels, demons, Gods, God, spirits—the Azerthenes have gone by many names in countless different cultures over the course of history."

"Azerthenes?"

"Yes, that's what they call themselves. And these imposters have been influencing the tide of human events for centuries. Oftentimes they use people like myself to deliver their message, though normally they are unaware of their capacity."

Jetta laughed. "You—a 'prophet,' akin to Christ. Or Hitler."

"You're finally catching on," Victor said. He paused, watching the video reel as his younger self demonstrated the power of his machine.

"They created us in pairs to deliver opposing messages," Victor continued. "Simply put, I was supposed to be the catalyst to end the

38

human race. And my antithesis… he was supposed to 'save' the human race, transform it into something less wretched."

"But you knew who your opposition was, didn't you, since you could hear these things talk?" Jetta inferred.

The change in his face was very subtle, but Jetta could have sworn Victor sneered. "Yes, I did, and I know what you think. But I didn't kill him—I never even laid a finger on him. My competition, when faced with the ugly truth of human nature, eliminated himself."

"What is that supposed to mean?"

Victor didn't look at her. "There are no more prophets to come, Warchild—the lines are finished. I was the last of two Speakers for the Azerthenes. We were the final gamble for the fate of the human race."

"And you're the devil, right?" Jetta ventured. She tried to sound doubtful, but felt anything but. In all her psionic encounters, she had never experienced something like Victor's mind. Battle scenes, torture, endless human suffering—he did more than thrust her into a hellish nightmare, but separated and isolated her from her own identity, stripping her of all she knew.

Victor is all the sickness, all the pain, all the despair I have ever known, concentrated into one man.

"I was born to butcher the world, yes, but I chose otherwise. I chose my own path," he said.

The invisible struggle within her became even fiercer as she realized the potential in his words. *He chose his own path—is that possible?*

She needed it to be; she needed to believe there was hope for someone like her, someone who harbored a terrible demon that was harder and harder to keep at bay. But still, his claims were bizarre— Azerthenes? Interdimensional beings? It was a stretch to believe that such entities were influencing their universe.

No, Jetta thought to herself. *He's insane, with grandiose delusions like every other psychopathic tyrant.*

"So what path did you choose, Victor? Total and complete control of the Starways? The slow eradication of the human race?" Jetta said. "I've seen the reports—I know of your 'investments' in the flesh farms despite all your speeches against them."

"I am against flesh farms, but they have their purpose. With good intention, I bought out many of them and changed the way they operate. No longer are they butcher shops. We only employ humane methods on our volunteers."

"And most of these 'volunteers' are humans, of course," Jetta scoffed.

"Not humans—*Deadskins.* Those who have abandoned their humanity, their decency, any worth they might have contributed to the Starways. Besides, humans have the most compatible tissues in the Sentient spectrum. We've saved countless lives—human and Sentient alike—with our extractions. And I don't have to tell you that there are some people that don't deserve their skin."

Jetta immediately thought of Yahmen, but she said nothing. It was wrong—Jaeia and Jahx would be so disappointed in her—but in the darkest corner of her mind she agreed with Victor. There were humans—Deadskins—and other Sentients who wasted their lives, serving only to clog the gutters of dead planets like Fiorah.

"With these farms I've also helped control the viral human population; it is nothing like the pre-war days in 2050. People were starving, fighting, dying of curable diseases because the resources had been bled dry. Now there is order. All are serviceable, all have sponsors, and all are accounted for—at least in my regions. I take responsibility for restoring and preserving the best of the human race. It was rampant human consumption that nearly ended us in 2052, and I don't intend for that to happen again."

Jetta pinched the bridge of her nose. No, she wouldn't be fooled. Victor was a murderer, a fascist tyrant who had capitalized on the universal prejudice against humans. And he lied. The conditions he spoke of on Old Earth—starvation, disease, war—were horrific, but nothing compared to the soul-devouring conditions of the human labor colonies. "Deadskin" humans were fed and kept healthy, but their lives were strictly regulated and constantly monitored by their sponsors. Freedom didn't exist. And when those who weren't sponsored were caught traveling through unfriendly territories, they were traded or farmed.

"Who are you to decide who lives and who dies, Victor?"

Victor pointed his cane at her. "I'm not gifted like you, Warchild, but my many years have given me the advantage of seeing into the hearts of men."

Jetta watched as the younger man on the video projection showed the data readouts on a flat-screen. "No one man could do what you've claimed. I don't believe you."

"Not one man in one lifetime, you're right. But there is possibility in many lifetimes," he said.

Victor ended the video feed and seemed to fall into contemplation. Save the wind whistling through the breaks in the stone building, Jetta only heard the quiet whine of the holographic projectors and the thumping of her own heart.

"You want to know what my purpose is, what I path I have chosen," Victor said, circling her, his voice cold and precise. "I was born to see the flaws of mankind, and believe me, they are innumerable. But with this knowledge I will open the eyes of all the Sentients, and, faced with their inadequacies, they will fall on their knees and repent. Every last living creature shall submit to the greater will. It is only under one banner that we can create a peaceful, unified galaxy, and only under one rule can that order be maintained."

Jetta squeezed her temples. An invisible ice pick rammed into the space between her eyes, digging through to the base of her skull. She backed up, toppling over a bust of General Sun Tzu.

Victor stood over her, his teeth set in perfect diamond rows. "The reason I asked you here, Jetta Kyron, is to tell you of your destiny. You were not born a Speaker like me, but you are special

41

nonetheless. You are proof that we can confront those who manipulate us and end their games, take control of our lives."

"What do you mean?" Jetta said.

"You traveled to their world, before you were born," Victor said, his voice driving down into the marrow of her bones. "And you brought them back with you."

Jaeia's memory of Triel flashed in her mind. *The Legend of Rion—Rion, the Abomination, the Harbinger of Death, who crossed over into Cudal and stole the power of the Gods.*

"How do you know that?"

Victor pointed to her arm. "Your mark."

"I don't understand," Jetta said, reflexively rubbing the tattoo.

Victor's lower lip curled. "Do you not remember how you got your tattoo?"

Confused, Jetta shook her head. "No."

"How unfortunate," he said, not hiding his disappointment.

"I don't believe any of this," Jetta said, although it sounded more like she was trying to convince herself. "Are you saying I have one of those things inside me?"

But somehow, someway, she knew what he was saying was true. Everything made sense, at least on an intuitive level, and yet she fought against it. She was genetically human with no logical explanation for her unique telepathic gifts. What if she had traveled to another dimension and melded with a transphasic being?

(Is that the dark voice inside me?)

No. Impossible, Jetta thought. Victor was brilliant, a master manipulator, and there was so much he wasn't telling her. She couldn't be sure of the truth.

A phantom chill ran shot down her spine as Victor passed his hand through the top of her head. "Your mind is filled with the knowledge of thousands of Sentients, your body that of a woman's, and yet you're only eight years old. No time to grow up, no time to acclimate to so many encounters, so many changes. You've seen horrible things in your lifetime, and from these dark remnants of

42

stolen and lived experience have come forth something you can't explain, a darkness that pulls at you, drawing you deeper and deeper into a terrible abyss."

Victor stopped behind her, resting his holographic hands on her shoulders. "You wanted to find me not because of your aunt and uncle, but because you know that I can help you with these demons," he whispered. Without thinking, she closed her eyes, absorbing his every word. "I possess control, and I possess answers. Together we can overcome our torments, end the reign of the Azerthenes, and bring order to the Starways. No more persecution, no more war. Peace, forever, for all of us—and for ourselves."

Pain and confusion vanished as the world around her dissolved into an infinite pale blue sky and grassy hills. People lined up in front of her, laughing joyfully, praising her, chanting her name over and over.

With every breath of the sweet summer air, Jetta relaxed, lulled by the comforts of what she saw and felt.

A perfect world, free of suffering and disease, in harmony with all light and energy, *she thought as her body lifted from the ground and floated across the sea of people. Their outstretched hands brushed against her skin. I want this…*

But along the edge of her vision she saw the cheap, cinematic forgery blurring the lines between desire and reality.

This is a dream, *she thought, drifting down from the skies.* An illusion—a reaction to his words.

(Something I am too willing to accept.)

"No," she said, struggling against the calm that had pervaded her body. "This can't be."

"Why can't it?" he said. "With you at the helm of my army, we can achieve anything."

Blue skies disappeared, replaced by the narrow entryway of their old apartment. Jetta crumpled to the ground, shaking as heavy footsteps approached. Cigarette smoke, thick and acrid, filled her nose. Bottle clinking against the wall, Yahmen drunkenly turned the corner, his breathing labored and hungry.

"With order and control we can eliminate needless suffering," Victor said, his voice staying just above a whisper. "I can show you control, how to channel your demons. And then you can finally have the world in your hands."

The footsteps stopped. Heart thumping in her chest, Jetta dared to peek one eye out from under her arms. Staring back at her under the low light of the hallway wasn't Yahmen, but the angel she had seen before in Victor's mind.

The man with the immeasurable second shadow, *Jetta realized.*

Soulful brown eyes held back an unconscionable grief, reminding her of her uncle. As he stood in the archway, his lips upturned in an apologetic smile, as if he wanted to say something, but couldn't.

Slowly Jetta uncurled, curiosity overcoming her fear. (Who are you?)

The vision shattered. Pain capsized her attempts to hold on to the image as she resurfaced on the cold marble floor. She opened her eyes to find Victor standing over her, his black eyes hard set behind his gold-rimmed glasses, lips pressed into a flat line.

"What is your decision, Warchild? Do you choose to let others control you, or do you choose to make your own path?"

Her mind snapped backward, and when she looked down she saw her hands, bloodied and scraped, wrapped around the neck of a boy in a Dominion Core uniform. A crowd of children encircled her, chanting and cheering as she pummeled his face, mashing his nose into an unrecognizable pulp. A teacher stood in the shadows, clipboard in hand, taking notes.

I must protect Jaeia and Jahx, *she told herself. If she didn't neutralize this bully and send a message to his cronies, then the harassment would only escalate.*

As she felt his left eye socket crunch under her knuckles, spraying blood across the floor, she knew she had delivered the

44

message—so why couldn't she stop? Each time her fist connected with his face, she felt more and more alive, a carnal hunger burning in her veins, giving her strength and power she didn't know she had.

Old emotions and thoughts broke free, assaulting her anew.

Am I protective—

Or am I a predator?

(Do I use the love of my siblings to justify violence?)

Deeper realizations weighed in, crushing her with accusation.

It's not my ability to amass the knowledge of an entire armada—

It's how I synthesize that knowledge that makes me what I am. *(Killer.)*

What can I do? *she thought, staggering back from her victim. (Each day that dark voice grows louder in my head.)*

Jetta looked upon the bloody mush she had made of the boy's face, and heard the truth whispered up from the darkest corner of her soul: Soon it won't be enough just to taste my enemy's blood.

(I need more.)

"I am a monster," Jetta said, clutching her head.

"That's what they used to called me," Victor said levelly. "But I proved them wrong. I have done much to improve humanity, and I will do so much more. You'll see, Warchild, that you have a choice. You can choose your own destiny."

Jetta thought about her siblings, about Triel, about her duties as an Alliance officer. She didn't want to hurt anybody else, but would they understand her decision? Even if she disagreed with Victor— even if Victor was evil—he could teach her things that nobody else could about the terrible thing she harbored.

"If your friends and family mean anything to you, you'll take your place at my side," Victor said, standing before her. "You can't leave this place as you are. Your mind is weak and polluted, and you will only continue to hurt them."

45

Bending forward on her knees, Jetta pressed her palms to the ground. Her head seemed too heavy for her neck as she bowed before Victor, vaguely aware of the troops that had quietly filtered in and surrounded her.

"I hear it too, Warchild—the dark whisper, that call deep within my chest. I know how to fight your demons, and you will learn, too."

I want to believe him, Jetta thought, squeezing her eyes shut. *But he's the one behind the attack on the Alliance.*

Other considerations pulled for her attention: the way he treated Deadskins, and how he regarded the human species in general. *How can I concede to a man who thinks so poorly of members of his own race?*

His cold words slid down from memory: *"There are some beings that don't deserve their skin."*

Jetta hesitated. *What if he's right?* she wondered, drawing from not only her own experiences, but those she had stolen. *Not everyone is created equal, and not everyone deserves freedom of choice.*

Twisted philosophies played into old anger: *Sometimes someone needs to take charge and make difficult decisions,* she thought, remembering of all the times her uncle failed to protect their family on Fiorah. Grafted experience from battle-weary commanders interwove with her rage, justifying what she wanted to believe. *There isn't always time for military councils, assemblies, and general consensus.*

Jetta flexed her hands, scratching her nails against the stone floor. *Victor is right. None of this is my fault. And with his help I can finally excel with my abilities rather than cause harm.*

Something in the shadows groaned with satisfaction.

What was that?

Before she could investigate, her chest tightened, and all the blood left her face.

What is happening? she panicked as her heart slammed against her chest wall. Revolt sunk into her belly, and her skin transformed into a slimy, toxic coating.

46

What am I feeling—who am I feeling? she thought, resisting the urge to rip her own flesh from bone. It couldn't have been Victor; he mind was distant and unreadable. *This is the monster inside me.*

Jetta screamed helplessly across the psionic plane, grasping for a lifeline, until something broke inside her. Coming down hard on her hands, Jetta gasped for breath as the world reoriented itself.

"What is your choice?" Victor asked, unaffected by her inner struggle.

She collapsed on the cold, tiled floor. With considerable effort she propped herself up on her hands and knees.

I know what I have to do.

Cold hatred resurrected her limbs and reanimated her drive. The tears were gone, as was her fear. Jetta lifted up her right arm, stretching to touch Victor's looming image. "I am—"

A cacophony of sound cut her off, building in volume and intensity until she was forced to cover her ears. When she could take no more, the din resolved into a desperate whisper: *Help me, Jetta.*

"What? Who are you?" Jetta whispered back.

"What is your choice, Jetta Kyron?" Victor repeated more insistently.

Jetta gasped, cupping her hands over her mouth as new sensations slammed into her mind. *Chest afire, limbs cold as ice. Rage, sprung from the roots of a pitting loneliness, blotted out the colors of the world.*

I know this feeling, Jetta thought, remembering the caustic anger she had felt when she murdered Jahx. *But this isn't from me. This is someone else's experience.*

Blue eyes flashed through her mind. *Triel—*

Jetta hunched forward further, elbows caving to the new weight driving down on her shoulders. *I've never felt anything like this,* she thought, overwhelmed by the concentrated, visceral sensations coursing through her mind. *Even from my siblings.*

Anger and fear fell away as she sobered to her friend's desperation. *She's in danger.*

"I have to go," Jetta said, rising on unsteady legs.

"You can't go," Victor said. "The voice inside you is growing stronger. If you leave now, it may be too late for me to help you."

Jetta wavered a moment. Something heavy slunk back into her mind, and she drew in a deep breath. A primal hunger awakened inside her belly, and she found herself gritting her teeth against the desire to draw the surrounding troops' blood.

Focusing on Triel's tune in the back of her mind, Jetta forced out the words as she turned from Victor. "I must help my friend."

"So be it, Jetta Kyron."

Jetta tried to sidestep Victor's troops, but they crossed their firearms to prevent her from leaving.

"Move, soldier," Jetta whispered. Tasting their aggression, Jetta snarled, unable to subdue the tension building beneath her sternum.

I don't want any bloodshed, she told herself as they raised arms to her.

(There is no other choice.)

A smile hinted at the corners of her lips.

But I will do what I have to.

The one nearest her bearing the captain's insignia on his chest spoke through his headset. "Stop where you are. You are under arrest for trespassing."

"Let me go," she repeated, her voice barely above a whisper. "Please. For your own sake."

"I can't let you go, Warchild. You are a danger to yourself and others. I know what you're thinking of doing to these men," Victor said, his holographic image coming up from behind her. "Let me help you. Stay and conquer this common enemy."

Jetta winced as the Healer's cry intensified in the back of her mind. *Jetta!*

A dark implosion stripped away the last of her control. *There is no other choice.*

With superhuman speed she watched herself tear into the jugular of the nearest soldier with the knife hidden in her sleeve. The other

48

troops opened fire, grazing her shoulder and side, but she wrenched around the injured soldier to shield herself from the attack.

Staying behind her human cover, she drew her gun and shot back, honing in on psionic signatures to better her aim. Despite her deadly precision, she couldn't combat their greater numbers. Within seconds, enemy gunfire ripped apart her improvised shield.

I can't make it to the exit like this.

Dumping the soldier on the cobbles, she somersaulted behind a statue of Stalin, keeping low to the ground as fragments of stone and marble exploded all around her.

Triel's fading voice touched her mind as she reloaded her ammo cartridge. *Jetta!*

Hold on, I'm coming, Jetta thought, straining to maintain a connection to the Healer's psionic tune.

Conflicting feelings tore at her as she returned fire, trying to buy herself a few precious seconds to think. *This isn't working. Triel needs me now—I can't waste any more time.*

(Let them feel your suffering.)

Giddiness pinched the corners of her mouth, if only for a second, as she closed her eyes. She hadn't dumped her feelings onto others in a long time, not after the last time proved so deadly.

I can't do that—

Images of Triel's torments ghosted through her mind. *(It is the only way.)*

Jetta screamed, surprising herself, as she released the violent torrent pent up inside her. The psionic riptide magnified as her unwanted emotions swept through each soldier, knocking them off their feet.

Gods—

As she watched them writhe on the ground, terror gripped her heart. Inhuman gurglings rang out over their headsets as she heard their thoughts, mangled by her emotion, turn savage.

Victor's holographic projection stood behind the complement of soldiers as they turned on each other, folding his hands atop his cane. "This will be your legacy, Warchild."

Helmets and gear flew across the room in a chaotic jumble as soldiers ripped through each other's armor. In a matter of seconds, blood drenched the ground in a chaotic whirlwind of splintered teeth and carnal madness.

Their faces, she thought, unable to look away from the soldiers' crazed expressions. Devoured by hatred, their eyes searched for something they could not find. *My legacy...*

Jetta scooted away in a panic, heart hammering against her breastbone, knocking into a statuette as she scrambled for the exit. A soldier broke free from the fight and chased after her, snarling and gnashing his teeth as she dove through the double doors. She spun around, drawing her gun and firing at her assailant as she landed hard on her back.

With the wind knocked out of her, she couldn't recover quickly enough to avoid him. The soldier landed on top of her, his warm blood dripping down her cheek, dead weight crushing her ribs.

She shoved him off but quickly resumed cover underneath his body when she saw the sentinels, alerted to her movement, arming their pods. Even though she was less than twenty meters from her ship, a dozen more sentinels emerged from their hiding spots, blocking her path.

"*Jeka sheaod om frerecka,*" she cursed in Fiorahian, trying to remain motionless.

The soldier's weight on her chest made it difficult to breathe. To make matters worse, she could sense more troops disentangling from the main fray and moving in her direction.

Think back, she told herself, digging into her cache of stolen memories. Then she got an idea.

As quietly as she could, she unpinned one of her grenades and shoved it into the waistband of the soldier on top of her. As she readied to launch him towards the sentinels, she heard him moan.

No.

His only remaining eye fluttered open, his shredded lips moving without sound.

I can't do this.

(I have no choice.)

She gripped his harness with all her might as wisps of his essence seeped into her awareness.

Pain, desperation. Glimpses of three children and a wife standing in the front doorway of their home, saying their goodbyes.

"I'll only be gone a few days," he says, kissing her forehead.

"Come back to me," she whispered.

Jetta resisted, not wanting to hear the sound of his children's voices, or taste his sorrow.

I'm doing this for Triel, she told herself.

(This is how I've always justified violence.)

With a scream she pushed him hard off of her, sending him flying into the cluster of sentinels. She curled into a ball, shielding herself as the explosion from her grenade turned his body into a red-misted confetti of tissue. Confused and disoriented by the chaotic motion, the sentinels fired at the raining fragments of flesh as she bolted for her ship.

Something sour rose in her throat as she initiated her emergency flight plan. The sentinels redirected their fire at her as the engines flared to life, but she raised her shields, nullifying their hits.

Shoving aside the pain of her own injuries, Jetta watched the few soldiers that had survived her psionic assault spill out of the building. They took aim at her, but she guided her ship out of their range. Still intoxicated by her rage, the soldiers redirected their fire at the sentinels, and the robotic guardians, programmed for defense, fired back, killing the remainder of Victor's squad.

A chill settled in her chest as she laid in a course for Alliance territory. She had wanted to jump in the stratosphere, but out of the corner of her eye she spotted the JAG fighters darting in and out of the clouds, quickly approaching her position.

51

Chak—*I'm still too close to the city to avoid casualties,* she thought, checking her scanners. *And I'll obliterate this archeological site and Victor's collection of terrestrial artifacts.*

Jetta looked up as the lead JAG fighter banked sharply towards her, the tips of its razor guns hot and primed. Without hesitation, she hit the punch.

***

"Jetta, no!" Jaeia screamed. She sat up, racking her head against an overhead swing light, and then quickly pitched backwards. Someone caught her, easing her back down.

"Sir, you've got a concussion. Please hold still."

Waves of nausea threatened to empty her stomach of its contents, but she swallowed hard and focused on her breathing. She touched her forehead where a nasty gash was in the preliminary stages of being closed.

"Where am I? Where's my sister?" she said, squinting under the bright exam light.

A medic popped into view with a sterilization/dermabond biopen in hand. "You're aboard the *Jinluko II,* a medical frigate," she said. "You were drifting in your gear just off the port bow when we rescued you."

"And Jetta?"

The medic pushed Jaeia's hand away from her head and activated the biopen. "I don't know about Commander Kyron's location, Sir."

Jaeia listened to the hum of the biopen as she tried to collect her wits. *What happened? Where is my sister?*

She closed her eyes and grimaced, faintly aware of the medic asking her about her pain.

"This isn't over yet," she remembered saying to Jetta. And then pain, darkness. She was aware of Jetta's voice—*"I'm afraid it is for me... Goodbye, Jaeia"*—but her body was unresponsive, her mind

52

drifting in and out of consciousness as her sister ejected her from their starcraft.

Jetta hit me.

The realization recycled over and over in her head, each time just as impossible to believe.

She hit me, hard enough to render me unconscious so that she could steal the ship.

(Why?!)

Jaeia knew she should feel something—fear, anger, hurt—but the shock of it stripped away her ability to comprehend.

Then everything clicked in place. It had been her longstanding fear that Jetta would turn on everyone, including herself, but Jaeia had always placated herself by thinking that she and Jahx could keep Jetta from becoming blinded by conviction. But something had happened when Jetta had tried to glean thoughts off Victor's mind, tearing her away from Jaeia's sight, leaving Jetta alone to face whatever dwelled in that dark hollow of a place.

Tears formed beneath her closed eyelids, and she stretched her mind out into the neuroelectric plane. Jetta hovered on the horizon of her mind, a steady, low thrum in the thunderous noise of the collective pulse, but she was there. Her usual tune was muffled, distorted and layered within itself as if she was trying to pull away.

Jaeia opened her eyes again. "What is the status of this ship?"

The medic, a human, was transparent to Jaeia, the confidence in her voice betrayed by uncensored emotion. "We've reestablished auxiliary drives, but the navigational systems are blown. Last report I heard was that a tow was on its way. It may be thirty hours or more before we can make port."

Jaeia grabbed a handheld scanner with a chrome frame and looked her reflection. The gash was still an angry pink, but the wound was closed. "Thanks for patching me up. I have to speak to your captain."

"Sir, I'm not finished—"

Jaeia sat up but stopped short of jumping off the table when the vertigo hit.

Help me! a voice called out.

Triel? Jaeia thought. Little bumps rose on her skin as a nebulous feeling of dread pervaded her chest. *Oh Gods—something is very wrong.*

"I *have* to speak to your captain," Jaeia said. "I need to get back to the Central Starbase."

The medic held up her chin and waved a light in her eyes. "The captain's dead. Lieutenant Biggs from engineering took charge. I still need to keep an eye on you, so please stay here and I'll ring him up."

Jaeia stayed put as the medic went to a com access. *Jetta, where are you? Triel needs us. Jetta...*

No response. The vice grip of panic seized her chest and spread out through her body in violent shivers. *If Triel Falls, if Jetta turns against me—if Jahx doesn't make it—*

(I don't want to be alone.)

Please, Jaeia said, gripping the edge of the exam table with white knuckles. *Don't abandon me, Jetta. I can't do this without you. Please!*

The medical bay walls fluctuated, the beeping sounds of the monitors bending into the distance. Jaeia tried to stay upright, but her body toppled over as she submerged somewhere between worlds, into a place she had tried to forget.

The suns baked the cracked and blistered cement, burning her exposed feet. Jaeia hobbled over to an overflowing refuse station and held her nose as she fished the soggy cardboard box out of the heap of rotting trash. Leaning against the rim of the dumpster, she gingerly wrapped her feet in cardboard, tying it down with a scrap of plastic she'd found dangling from a torn garbage bag.

Why am I here? *she thought, looking down the alleyway leading to the main drag.* Oh Gods, the terrible heat...

Close to midday, the Fiorahian suns glared down on her with contempt. Across the street Galm and Lohien bartered with a pigeon dealer in a cramped scrap metal booth littered with feathers and bird droppings. Jetta and Jahx huddled near the corner of the east building, hiding from the passing crowd as they waited for their aunt and uncle.

Her siblings wore improvised shoes too, the soles fashioned from the piece of red polyurethane rubber they had found weeks ago in a vehicle repossession compound. There had only been enough for two pairs, so they rotated who wore them. Lately, though, Jaeia had started refusing her turn. Jahx's feet were nothing but blisters, and Jetta's looked infected.

"How's it going?" she heard herself say as she trotted up to them.

Jahx shook his head. "Not well. The dealer won't give Lohien anything for her hens."

Jaeia remembered. Lohien was selling off most of her females after Yahmen cut Galm's wages again. This happened right before he took our aunt away and put us all to work in the mines...

Jahx looked up, squinting against the glare of the suns. "Trouble is coming."

The fear she had experienced so long ago bloomed fresh inside her as Jahx's premonitions crept into her awareness like a prickly heat. What they were doing was dangerous, especially with Galm being such a hated man after reclaiming the inheritance that Yahmen had taken from him. Sharks, bosses, underhanders, streetwalkers, and Meatheads—they all wanted a cut of flesh from the Drachsi brother with the title to the mines that were sinking the local economy.

Jetta spotted the gang members first, identifying them by the red bandanas tied around their forearms as they insidiously gathered around the booth. Galm, seemingly oblivious to anything but the argument, stood by his wife silently as she got in the dealer's face.

55

Even though it was a memory, Jaeia tried to warn her sister, but there was nothing she could do to change the past. Jetta took off like before, winding through the crowd, screaming for their uncle. Jahx took off too, catching Jetta and pulling her away just before one of the gang members pulled a knife out of his boot and lunged for Galm. Alerted to the assault, Galm grabbed Lohien and whipped her away as two more came from behind.

In the tangle of fists, Galm was thrown to the ground. Jaeia saw the glint of a knife before the milling crowd blotted out the scene, and Lohien's scream, desperate and high-pitched, cut through the city noise like a razor.

Fear rooted her to the cement. Jaeia tried to speak, but her voice caught in her throat.

Jetta—Jahx—

Pain racked her skull as a spectator knocked one of her siblings to the ground. The dealer pulled out a rifle and fired off shots, sending the crowd into a frenzy. She couldn't see her family in the scattering crowd as other Sentients drew weapons and gunfire exploded in every direction.

"Help me," pleaded a streetwalker stumbling toward her. Caught in the crossfire, a bullet ripped through her chest. Eyes frantic and pleading, the streetwalker collapsed at Jaeia's feet, her frothing blood mixing with the yellow runoff that trickled down the alley channel.

Run, Jaeia! *Jetta cried as a stray bullet struck the building next to her, spraying pieces of red brick against Jaeia's face.*

Crouching down, Jaeia squeezed herself against the building and shielded her eyes. More bullets zipped past. Hands shoved and legs kicked her as other civilians tried to get away. She couldn't leave her family in the midst of the riot, but if a bullet didn't kill her, the stampeding Sentients might.

"You!"

Dirty hands grabbed her by the armpits, slamming her against the brick wall. Foul breath steamed from her assailant's mouth, and

56

his wild eyes, glazed white from his choice of flavor, portended a violent hunger.

"It's all your fault. Stupid launnie!"

Jaeia sensed that the human-like Tamesikoid didn't know who she was, but through the haze of chemicals, he felt certain of her crime. Digging his hands into her skin, and he slammed her into the wall again, spit spraying her face with each word. "I'm going to carve you up, little rat!"

All alone in the surrounding chaos of the riot, Jaeia gave in to fear. She turned her face away as he licked his lips, his psionic tune slimy and rank, burrowing into her mind like wriggling fungal worms.

"I'm going to hurt you," he cackled. "I'm going to make you squeal."

I couldn't help it, Jaeia thought, remembering the first time her talent had been provoked. She tried to look away from the memory, but it slammed into her with hypersonic force.

"Take your hands off!" she screamed, her voice multi-pitched and oddly foreign.

The junkie's hands flew off her, and she fell down into the pile of trash below. She looked up in time to see him regarding his hands in horror before sinking his teeth into one of his wrists. Through the wet gnawing she heard his cries, blood bubbling over his lips and down his neck.

Jaeia ran. The cardboard shoes flew off as she tore down the alleyway and through the crush of Sentients, dodging the arms, legs, tentacles, and other appendages that knocked into her as she raced back to their apartment. Molten fear numbed the pains in her feet as she ran across the heated asphalt, leaping over a massive Toork as stray bullets felled people left and right.

No matter how much distance she put between herself and the junkie, she could still feel his panic and taste his pain as he tore away his own flesh.

What have I done?

She rounded the empty parking lot, darting past the twitching homeless in cardboard homes, and scrambled up the grated stairwell of their drab-faced apartment building. In her panic, she lost her footing and cut her chin on one of the stairs.

Heaving for breath, she slammed close the door to their apartment and pushed their stack of cots in front of the entryway. Unable to shake the sullied after-presence of the junkie from her mind, she dove under the couch and made herself as small as possible.

Tears burst forth when she tried to slow her breathing, and, still fearful of being followed, she muffled her cries with her hands. I ran away like a coward!

She cried out silently to her siblings, trying to find them, tears leaving streaks down her dirty face. Blood from her chin dripped onto the carpet as she desperately searched for a familiar tune, but she couldn't calm herself enough to listen.

My parents, my siblings, all dead. All alone all alone all alone—

(Please,) *Jaeia cried, pulling away from the memory.*

"Please," her younger self whispered, squeezing her eyes shut. The junkie's body odor, still ripe in her nose, made her queasy. "Please come back. I'm sorry—I'm so sorry!"

Hours passed as she lay curled up underneath the couch, her face a sticky mess of dried blood and debris. Rats scurried along the floor, pausing to sniff in her direction before scampering off. Though her feet throbbed, and her neck and body ached from her cramped position, she didn't dare move. Not with the junkie and his bloody stumps out there, waiting for her, calling her into the shadows, into the lonely darkness that lay beyond her tiny sanctuary.

"Jetta!" Jaeia screamed, grabbing blindly in front of her. She caught a fistful of hair, but quickly let go when she realized where she was. The medic, frightened by her behavior, held her down as a doctor pressed an adrenaline booster into her arm. Her heart kicked into overdrive, making her inhale so hard she thought her lungs would burst.

58

Grabbing the doctor by his collar, Jaeia's words coming between breaths: "Get... me... to Central Command."

"Pass the word to Biggs," the doctor ordered, gently removing himself from Jaeia's grip.

"But Sir—we have our orders from Central Command," the medic said.

"Which Commander Kyron has the authority to override in an emergency."

The medic ran back to the com access and talked hurriedly over the line as the doctor turned back to her with a queer sort of understanding in his wrinkled face.

"Don't worry, Sir. She came back before, and she'll come back again," he said, rolling up his sleeve. A series of barcodes, tattooed in red and black ink, stood out against the blue-tinged skin of his forearm. He quickly pulled his sleeve down when he saw the look of shock on her face.

A registered telepath who lived through the Dissembler Scare? she marveled.

A careful smile came to his face as he repeated himself. "Don't worry. You're not alone."

* * *

A million thoughts raced through Jetta's head as she sprinted down the corridors of the Alliance Central Starbase. Broken soldiers with disfigured faces littered the hallways, the blast marks and singed walls adding testament of the savage battle. As Jetta followed the Healer's path of destruction toward the intensive care unit, she reminded herself of her objective.

I have to help Triel. We can't afford to lose her.

(I can't afford to lose her—)

Jetta rounded the corner to find a complement of her SMT holding down the perimeter.

"Status report," Jetta whispered, kneeling down besides the unit leader, Ferraway.

Decked out in heavy black armor with auto-guided weapons, Ferraway summarized their current situation. "CMA Triel has broken into the secured wing and is heading toward Isolation 1. No one has been able to get within twenty meters of her location without being killed."

Isolation 1—that's where Tidas Razar is, Jetta gleaned from the images running through his mind. "What have you tried?"

"Electric traps, smoke bombs, neuroagents, and tranquilizers—all without effect."

"She reacts to violence, so your aggression will only make things worse. Stay here, and no matter what happens to me, do not go any farther than this perimeter, Lieutenant," Jetta ordered.

Her heart in her throat, Jetta stepped over broken glass and mangled equipment into the emptied nurse's station. Vital signs monitors echoed in the distance, but the painful dissonance welling in her mind funneled all of her attention.

Gods, what is that? she cringed, accosted by the most terrible feeling in the world. A shrieking animal fear she could hear in her bones made her skin shrivel and her heart ache. With every step the feeling intensified, but she couldn't turn back. *I have to help Triel.*

A scathing voice cut right through her. "Don't come any further, Jetta."

"Triel?" Jetta said, not recognizing the multi-tonal sound of her friend's voice.

Jetta stopped ten meters in front of Tidas Razar's bed. Hooked up to a life-support unit and connected to an array of tubes and lines dangling from the ceiling, the Military Minister looked less like the daunting leader of the Alliance and more like a fragile shell of a man. But even with his bandaged head and atrophied muscles, Jetta hesitated.

Triel is going to kill him for his betrayal.

For the moment, it didn't seem like a bad idea. Razar had always played the game in his favor, and removing him from the picture would eliminate another one of their manipulators. However, there would be consequences for allowing Triel to do such a thing— for both her and the Healer.

"I came here as fast as I could," Jetta said.

"Why?" she said, stepping out from the shadows of the digital column near Razar's motionless body. "You can't stop me from killing him."

Stunned, Jetta couldn't believe the sight of the Healer. Triel's warm, blue eyes had corroded into poisonous black wells, and her unblemished skin was now streaked with gruesome hues of gray, yellow and green. Her people's markings had all but faded, replaced by spidery purple veins threading the deathly color of her flesh.

"This isn't you," Jetta said. "You're a Healer, and you're my friend. I can help you."

"You're too late," Triel said, gray lips twisting up into a smile.

"I know you're not a Dissembler. Otherwise you would have killed me the instant you saw me."

"Leave, Jetta. Before I do kill you," Triel whispered as she spread her arms over Razar's body.

Jetta winced as she sensed what the Healer was intending to inflict upon the helpless Minister. Even in her own rage, Jetta couldn't conceive of such torture.

Holding her head in her hands as the Healer's psionic dissonance multiplied, Jetta fell to her knees. "Please, Triel. For me. Please stop."

"For you?" she laughed, tipping her head back. "What do you care what happens to me?"

Jetta's mouth froze open. It seemed an impossible question to answer, one that she had avoided acknowledging since their first meeting. Something about Triel attracted her, something inexplicable, a force that she constantly struggled against. She respected the Healer for her talents, admired her for her convictions,

61

appreciated her exotic beauty—but there was more, and she had felt it all along.

Subconscious longings seized the opportunity to be heard: *(It's not just Triel's friendship that I crave on all those lonely nights when I stop by her quarters.)*

Jetta clenched her jaw, grinding her fists into the tiled floor. "You are my friend. I would do anything for you."

Triel yanked several of the monitors off of Razar. The life-support machine emitted a frenzy of beeps and warning signals before she sent it crashing to the ground and tore out its power source.

"You left me here—alone. You don't care about anybody but yourself."

"It's not like that!" Jetta said.

She collapsed to the floor as Triel redirected her attentions, bolts of pain searing through her skull. With each one of the Healer's steps, the anguish magnified, causing her to scream out.

Blood and saliva frothed from the Healer's mouth as she bent down to the Commander's eye level. Jetta saw the pooling darkness in Triel's eyes, smelled the stink of her mottled skin, the coldness of her being.

She's going to kill me—

"I have never wanted to hurt you. I care so much about you—I didn't want you to see—" Jetta sputtered as a crushing darkness descended upon her, blinding her to the outside world.

"See what?"

"Me!" Jetta screamed, bucking off the floor as tendrils of pain wrapped around her chest.

Helpless in the vice grip of Triel's mind, Jetta thrashed wildly, but to no avail. The Healer overpowered her, stripping Jetta of every safeguard she had ever erected against others, her siblings, even herself.

With tears streaming from Jetta's eyes, Triel filleted her open, plunging past guarded memories, those she had repressed and those

62

she had even forgotten. Black fire choked her inner voice as she clawed at the Healer's chest, desperate to make her stop before she exposed more than her vital organs.

Jetta floated away from herself, her sight darkened, ears deafened, a strange calmness pervading her senses as Triel's venomous presence deceived her body. On some remote level she remembered having felt this kind of mournful separation before, when she had faced Jahx. *The prelude to death...*

And then it stopped. Jetta could breathe again, and the world rushed back to her in a thunderous blast of sound and light. The seething pain dissipated into an aching fatigue that saturated every muscle fiber. She opened her eyes to see the Healer bent over her, her eyes bloody but irises blue, staring through her, chest heaving.

With all her strength, Jetta managed to lift her arm and wrap her fingers around Triel's forearm. Warmth had returned to the Healer's skin, though a cold sweat stained her clothes.

"Jetta," Triel whispered. "I didn't think... I didn't know."

Slowly, the Healer withdrew from her mind, ceding control back to Jetta.

What did you do? Jetta thought. Even with her returning faculties, she had no idea what Triel had seen, or what she was feeling now. The Healer still felt distant, but her psionic essence, once a cacophony of pain, was balancing itself into a familiar tune.

Triel shifted her weight, then collapsed next to her. Willing herself to sit up, Jetta gently prodded the Healer.

"Triel—Triel!" she tried, but the Healer responded in delirious mumblings.

"Jetta!"

Jetta turned her head to see Jaeia and a complement of shock troopers advancing on her position.

"Stay back. I order you to stay back," Jetta said, collecting herself off the ground and positioning herself between the guards and the Healer.

"Kill her."

63

Everyone in the room turned to the Minister's bed. Rolled onto his side, eyes barely open, he tried to speak, the oxygen mask muffling his words. "That was a direct order, soldier."

"No," Jetta said, spreading out her arms. "You can't do that. I won't let you."

"Jetta, come away from her," Jaeia said calmly.

"How can you say that after she's saved our lives so many times? You know I can save her," Jetta said, not fighting the tears anymore. "Please, Jaeia."

Jetta felt her twin in the back of her mind, and for the first time in their lives, exhausted and desperate, she let Jaeia in as far as she dared. *Please, Jaeia.*

Jaeia's gray eyes misted over, tears building in the corners. Jetta didn't hear Jaeia's response, but she felt it in her soul. *Don't leave me. Not again, Jetta.*

"I have to do this," Jetta whispered back.

"Kill her!" the Minister screamed with his remaining strength.

The shock troopers raised their weapons, their blue electrocells whining as they charged to fire.

"Commander Kyron, please step aside," Ferraway said.

Looking into her sister's eyes, Jetta made one last plea. *I will come back. Please—you have to trust me.*

Jaeia closed her eyes, her brow furrowing momentarily before she spoke. *"Stand down, all units. Stand down."*

Jetta didn't waste any time as Jaeia used her second voice to control the actions of the shock troopers. "Keep Jahx safe until I return."

"I will," Jaeia said, looking away from her.

Jetta threw Triel's arm over her shoulder, and with every last ounce of strength, pulled her up from the ground. Triel's head bobbled, but she managed to gain her own footing.

Thank you, Jetta silently called to her sister as she dragged the Healer out of the intensive care unit. The shock troopers and the

SMT all aimed their weapons at her, but none of them possessed the will to follow the Minister's order.

Jetta summoned a lift outside the intensive care unit and gently lay the Healer down on the bed. As they zipped down the corridor back to the bay where she had docked her stealth fighter, Jetta felt her sister's heartache spread through her own chest.

I'm so sorry for everything, Jaeia. When I come back, I will make things right.

But she wasn't as sure as she sounded. She looked at her reflection in the mirrored bed of the lift, her color ashen, cheeks sunken. The sickness inside her was spreading, and now she had a Falling Healer in her care. Triel had told her it took an entire tribe of Prodgies to save one Fallen Healer—so how could she, in her condition, in the constant fight against herself, save her friend? Every time she had tried to help someone, it had always ended in tragedy.

I am a monster.

She looked down again at the floor bed of the lift. Victor's inhuman face, distorted by the curve of the paneling, quietly smiled back at her.

CHAPTER II

Reht Jagger awoke to the sting of a syringe withdrawing from his forearm. He shot up from a bed, gasping for breath, heart in overdrive.

"It wears off in a minute," a gruff-looking fellow said, wiping the needle on his greasy pants and replacing the cap.

"Where am I? Who are you?"

Reht couldn't identify the species of the man standing at his bedside, but his scales hinted at Wormeron ancestry and the respirator over his gills at Jelaion. His Common was terrible and his breath even worse. "You're safe enough."

No bigger than a storage cell, the room was jammed with bunk beds, scrapped furniture, and knee-high waste. Old videoreels and skin magazines with broken spines lay scattered across the nameless junk, nude females winking at him from faded posters adorning the wall. The stink of body odor and leftover booze reminded him of the *Wraith*.

With a grimace, Reht inspected the wounds criss-crossing his chest, sobering to the reality of what had transpired. Disturbing memories swam into focus as he traced the lacerations with his finger—

Diawn slashing him across the chest with her razorcutter fingers—shooting Mar in the back with pierced rounds—riding on top of him—glaring at him with pure hatred as her white boot struck his face, sending him spiraling into the belly of the cargo ship. The tangle of limbs and slick skins swallowing him whole. Smells of rotting flesh, and death.

He threw up. The man stepped back to avoid the backsplash, swearing in his native language.

"Where am I?" Reht asked again, wiping off his mouth. "And who the *chak* are you?"

The fellow regarded him with a mix of irritation and amusement. "Name's Rook. And like I said—you're safe. But don't count on that for much longer. Don't know why she bothered saving your *assino* if she's just planning on killing you again."

Rook chuckled, slung the medkit over his shoulder, and walked out the door.

Easing himself into a sitting position, Reht pressed his palms against the remnants of his shirt. The fabric was stiff with dried blood.

I should be dead.

He shuddered, remembering the pit of human bodies.

How the hell did I escape?

Still in shock, he swung his legs off the bed and tested his strength. As soon as his boots touched the messy floor he felt familiar vibrations. *I'm aboard a starcraft,* he thought, sensing the buzz of the downshift. *We're about to dock.*

Remembering the com he had stashed away, Reht searched his jacket, but turned up nothing. His cash, cigarettes, and chews were gone too.

"*Gorsh-shit,*" he mumbled.

With a groan he limped over to the door, leaning into the handle until the lock finally released. Directly outside was a mess hall improvised from two overexposed grill cells. Plates and food bits littered the floor, and beer bottles lay in piles or smashed to pieces all over the room. He carefully waded through the debris, stepping over a slumbering body clutching an empty bottle of "Half and Half 20-20," and pushed through another reluctant door.

Down a steel-plated hallway he heard an escalating argument. Curious, he followed the sound until he came upon the stairs leading to the bridge.

"I was told I'd be escorted!"

"Yes, you were—to the belt, as promised."

"You're my partner—you were supposed to keep the Alliance away!"

Reht froze. He recognized Diawn's voice, but the man over the com channel—he knew that voice, too.

"You destroyed my ship and my cargo," he said coolly.

68

Fear mingled with the urgent need to know. Despite his stomach's mounting protest, his legs carried him up the stairs. The door separating the bridge from passageway was conveniently broken, jammed in its chamber, allowing him to peek around the frame and see the man on the holographics.

"Shandin—" he whispered, nearly choking on the name. It had been seventeen years since their last encounter, though the dog-soldier captain saw his face every night in his dreams.

"Shandin," Diawn said, crossing her arms as best she could under her ample chest. Lifting her chin, she squared off with the man in the holographic projection standing across from her. "I'm not leaving without my payment."

Reht stumbled backward against the railing. Desperate for air, he couldn't breathe. He slid down the wall, clamping his hands over his mouth as he gasped, trying to make sense of the impossible.

He's supposed to be dead, he told himself. For the last seventeen years he believed that Shandin had been killed by his own employers after botching a massive job on Reht's homeworld, Elia. *It can't be real...*

Terrified of the truth, Reht looked at his hands. Beneath the bandages he could feel the acid burn, each letter re-carving itself into his skin. Never in his life did he think he'd be confronted with his shame like this again—and never did he think he'd come face-to-face with the man who caused it all.

Crawling back up the stairs on his hands and knees, Reht stayed hidden in the shadow of the doorframe.

"Perhaps you'd better take your complaint to our faithful employer," Shandin said. "I'm sure he has a forgiving ear, just like me."

Diawn's face turned purple as she flexed her razor-tipped fingers. "I want half upfront on the next payload."

Staring flatly at her, Shandin revealed no emotion. Reht remembered that same soulless gaze cutting him down years ago.

"I'll front you a thousand, but I want a shipment of no less than four thousand. And healthy."

"Fourth-class and healthy?" Diawn snorted. "Minimum three thousand just for bartering and fuel."

An impossible assignment, Reht thought. Fourth-class humans were life laborers or fighting ring bait, routinely plagued by kholeria, diplethominia, and the Gunta virus. Uninfected, healthy, fourth-class humans were about as common as telepaths that had survived the Dissembler Scare.

Shandin shook his head. "Fifteen hundred. Last offer. I'll send you the nav specs to a colony on Europa. Alliance recently vaccinated and relocated them. Mostly refugees from Jue Hexron and Ganymaius."

"Human royalty?" Diawn laughed.

Reht saw it in his eyes, the way he curled in his lower lip. *Shandin is disgusted by her.*

"Alliance regularly patrols the site, so don't *chak* up," he said. "Stop by this location when you're done with the drop-off. I have something for you, *partner.*"

A series of navigation signatures replaced Shandin's image on the projection field. Reht scratched the signature into his arm with his fingernail as he retreated down the hallway.

The engines cycled down to an idle, prompting him to hold onto the wall railings as locking clamps took hold of the ship. But as he spotted an emergency hatch, he paused. What about his mission? He would need more information to satisfy the bounty. And what about his crew? If he lost the bounty, they would be out a large sum and take a huge hit on their reputation. Besides, he was skating on thin ice after the bad business with the Alliance, and he didn't want to test his crew's loyalty any further.

At the same time, how could he not? Shandin wasn't some ordinary thug, and for the first time in seventeen years, Reht had a confirmed location. Every fiber in his being had longed for revenge since the death of his parents, and until moments ago, he had never thought it could be realized.

Reht squeezed his bandaged hands together, gritting his teeth against the memory.

"Just tell me where to find them, and this can all be over," *Shandin whispered in his ear as Reht fell to his knees.*

For a moment he told himself that his parents, slumped in their chairs at the breakfast table, were just asleep. Cold, blue, but asleep. But Reht couldn't ignore the coppery smell of blood, or the stickiness of the crimson pools around their feet. Most of all, he couldn't stop the rage expanding through his heart at the sight of the natives' featherhawks jutting out of his parents' backs.

"I will tell you everything," Reht said.

"*Chakking* Gods," he said, pressing his knuckles into his eyes. He would kill the *ratchakker*.

And then it kicked in. He felt himself roll into an invisible slipstream, his emotions sliding farther and farther away until nothing was left but an eerie confidence like nothing he had ever felt.

I will complete the bounty and meet up with my mates.

Everything else could wait. He had found out that Shandin hadn't been killed—he was very much alive—and with his crew he knew he could find him later.

"Going somewhere?"

Reht froze in place as two arms wrapped around him from behind. Black-tipped razors rested delicately against his chest. "You weren't going to leave me again, were you?"

She kissed his ear before nibbling the edge of the lobe. The lurid scent of her perfume, once enticing, made him cringe.

Swallowing hard, Reht carefully peeled her razorcutter fingers back from his chest. "Sweetheart..."

As he turned around to face her, he realized why she hadn't left him to die. Big, glistening eyes formed the same fragile expression he had seen when he first asked her to join his crew. Somehow,

71

beneath the layers of noxious contempt, was the same young girl that craved only one thing. *And I'm the only person that's ever given it to her.*

Although Reht could never be what she wanted, he did care for her. There was something about Diawn he could never entirely disentangle himself from, and it was that same muddied feeling that kept him from killing her when he should have back on the *Wraith*.

Diawn led him to her quarters, and before he knew it, she pressed him up against the wall. Still nursing the injuries she had inflicted, he could barely find the strength to breathe as she ran her hands down his chest and up his inner thighs.

"You're mine."

"Yes, baby, yes," he said through a clenched jaw as she licked the lacerations on his stomach. He tried to move her away from his face, but she pressed her lips against his battered cheekbone, sliding her tongue down and into his mouth. He shuddered at the rawness of both the pain and pleasure as she threw him down onto her bed.

Eyes narrowing, Diawn ran her razorcutter fingers lightly across his skin before swinging her legs over to straddle him. "All mine."

With his need throbbing in his loins, Reht's pain faded to the backdrop as he wrestled her down onto her stomach. She bucked against him, but he gripped her around the neck, choking her from behind until she submitted to him. Wrestling with his pants, Reht bit down on her shoulder, his incisors drawing blood from her salty flesh.

She screamed for him as his momentum built with the speed of his thrusts, but the same fire that had sparked him to life suddenly dulled, and he couldn't focus. Something was missing, something he couldn't quite place.

The arch of her neck, the sound of her escalating breath as her three breasts bounced against the mattress, the warm wetness between her thighs—it should have been enough to get him off, but it wasn't. An unpalatable shallowness consumed the moment, one that he had never felt before, even after all the nameless women he had been with.

Angered, Reht squeezed her hands until she cried out in pain, and her resistance and anguish gave him the release he needed. But like before, it felt muted, a numbness rather than a peak, and he rolled off her in dissatisfaction.

With one quick motion Diawn was back on top of him, the coldness in her eyes all too familiar. Her razorcutter fingers clicked at the joints as the tips grazed his cheek. "Where is she?"

It took a moment for Reht to realize who she meant. *Triel?*

The exact situation was difficult to recall, as if he had been drunk or stoned, but the bitter aftertaste of their fight lingered. *Triel, the only woman I've ever truly loved, used me and split out when she got what she wanted.*

The Alliance was more important to her, as was her quest to save the displaced telepaths. There was no room for him in her life, and his feelings for her—once so strong they were almost painful— seemed to have flamed out the moment she chose her duties over him.

He closed his eyes. "Dead."

When he opened his eyes she was still poised on top of him, ready to strike.

Not knowing why, he lashed out at her, striking her in the chest with the palm of his hand. She careened backward, racking her head against the support beam on the opposite wall. Jumping on top of her, he raised his hand again to finish the job, but as her head rolled limply to one side, Diawn's face changed to that of the Healer's.

Reht screamed and staggered backwards. Cold sweat broke across his brow as he held himself up against the bedpost.

"Starfox?" he whispered.

My love, help me. The Healer's voice, her sweet smell, came over him, and Reht fell to his knees. *Please, my love—*

As Diawn opened her eyes, the illusion vanished.

"What the *chak* is happening to me?" he said, digging his nails into his head.

"You always knew how to treat a lady," Diawn said. She righted herself against the wall, wiping blood from the back of her head. "Sorry I tried to kill you."

"What the *chak* was that *gorsh-shit*?" Reht said.

Diawn, still dazed, stumbled to her feet. "You threw me out. Thought I'd give you a taste of what I'd been through."

"How'd I end up here?" Reht asked as he watched her lace up her bodice.

The ragged scar across her abdomen looked angry and red, as if it had never quite healed. It could have been an injury from a difficult client, but his gut told him otherwise. He only played on the surface of the black market, but he'd seen enough to guess how she might have acquired such a scar. Forced pregnancy, implantation and organ harvesting, or worse—she had been hitting the inner circuits, subjecting herself to the transactions that left a body soulless.

She wiped the blood from her mouth, smearing her lipstick. "My ship was ambushed by the Alliance. I had to take the lifecruiser and dump my cargo. And for some reason," she said, wrapping her arms around his waist, "I took you with me."

Revolted but unable to stop himself, he ran his fingers down her face, cupping her chin and pressing her lips to his. He kissed her fiercely, biting her lip until she broke free. Before he knew it, razorcutter fingers ran neatly along his jugular.

"Careful, soldier," she whispered.

"Why the hell are you dealing with Deadskins? What cash is in that?"

At the flash of uncertainty in her eyes he pulled her closer, her triple breasts warm against his skin. Diawn didn't seem to relax, but she offered him more information than he thought.

"I don't ask questions when I get paid. Seems someone's hungry for their flesh. Pays better than any job we ran, and nobody gives a rat's *assino* what happens to a *Lurchin* in unregulated territory."

Lurchin. After the rise of the human rights movement, he had only heard that term in underground bars and labor camps or the unregulated outerworlds. It was the most hateful word used in any language, conceived by the unfortunate Sentients who had made first contact with the human refugees and suffered the host of diseases mankind brought to the Homeworlds. The only roughly equivalent word in Common was *cancer.*

"Who's your Joe?" he asked.

Diawn's face soured. "No Joe. This job is real. Organized."

This isn't a low-level thug running some back-alley scam, he inferred. *This is a person with resources, someone with enough financial backing to hire Shandin as his middleman.*

"Military? Come on, Di, you wouldn't fall for that *gorsh-shit.*"

Diawn pressed all twelve nails into the thick of his neck. "You ask too many questions. I'm still not sure if I want to keep you…or kill you."

Reht smiled. "You can't kill me."

Blood beaded at the tips of her nails. "You sure about that?"

He kept his smile as she withdrew, her eyes trained on his every movement.

"I have business to take care of," Diawn said as she typed in a command code into the door console. "I'll be back in an hour. Wait here for me."

She's probably meeting one of Shandin's thugs to collect the front money for the next run, he assumed. He wanted to follow her, get a feel for the operation, but she would never trust him enough to let him accompany her.

"I love you, Reht," she said, her back to him as she paused halfway out the door. "I always have."

He rushed the door, but it clamped shut before he had a chance. Frustrated, he tapped his fist against the lock panel and muttered under his breath, careful not to be overheard as Diawn and her crew exited the starcraft.

I ain't sticking around as her hostage, he thought, glancing around her quarters. *Or for her next mood swing.*

"I know her better than this," Reht muttered to himself, cracking his knuckles and surveying the gigantic mess. Kicking her piles of clothing aside, he sifted through the assortment of belt buckles, boots, and other accessories until he unearthed a nightstand next to the bed. Inside he found the usual array of confusing female clutter but also a few artifacts of their relationship—an old, faded picture of the two of them on Mor'Ceye VII, an open can of *RedFly,* and an empty bottle of his cologne. Buried underneath he discovered her latest addition: his com and his chews.

"Thank the Gods," he said, popping the chews under his gums.

Reht crouched to the ground, cleared off a space, and pressed his ear to the floor. No sound, no vibrations. As far as he could tell, the entire crew had deboarded and the path was clear.

After making his way back to the door, Reht inspected the controls. The locking panel wasn't anything he hadn't cracked before, but Diawn was too sly to overlook something like that. At least that's what he thought.

"*Chakking* ridiculous," he muttered as he crossed the wires and the door lifted. He paused before stepping through, eyeing the corridor for any hidden cameras or traps. Nothing. He even found an open weapons locker at the end of the hallway with a live Cobra II double-action pistol and a stash of passable counterfeit currency.

Love blinds, he chuckled to himself, jamming the cold steel and the cash down the front of his pants as he made for the emergency hatch.

"*He'adege!*"

Reht paused and glanced around. *Am I hallucinating?* he thought, looking both ways down the empty corridor. When he turned back at the emergency hatch, the cry came again.

"*He'adege!*" the voice pleaded.

76

The voice, feminine, young, and thickly accented, came from behind one of the control stalls at the far end of the corridor.

"*Chak,*" he mumbled as he raced down the corridor.

Used by almost every dog-soldier and mercenary holding precious cargo, the thermoregulated control stalls typically housed narcotics and temperature-controlled chemicals. But when Reht flipped the view-portal, his eyes met with a dark-skinned beauty he had only seen in dreams.

"Holy Mukal."

"*He'adege,*" the girl sobbed again in her unfamiliar language.

Without thinking, Reht released the door lock, and a half-naked young girl spilled into his arms. As she gasped for breath, he cradled her, completely stunned. No older than sixteen, the girl had curled, silken hair that fell to the small of her back and barely enough animal-skin clothes to cover her most private areas.

"Hello," Reht managed to say.

Her eyes, bluer than the open sky, mesmerized him with their iridescent shine. Except for a few freckles scattered across the bridge of her nose, her ebony skin appeared unblemished by scars or imperfections. By the tribal markings on her neck and shoulder, he guessed that her uncut hair symbolized her youth and virginity.

"*Marrese,*" she said, touching his face with a smile full of bright, white teeth.

"You're welcome," he said, still taking her in. Brightly-colored strands of beads spangled her neck, arms, feet, legs—even her hair. Reht guessed she must have been royalty, some off-worlder abducted by Diawn, to be traded or sold to the highest bidder on the flesh auctions.

And then it hit him. *This girl is perfect, something that a scumbag like Ash won't be able to resist.* Even if he didn't have as much as he needed on Diawn, he would have her—a flawless, virginal beauty, pure as snow and easily devoured—to smooth over his transaction with the bounty master. Then he could settle the bounty, reconnect with his mates and find Shandin.

"Come with me, love," he said. "I'll help you. We'll both get out of here, okay? What's your name?"

She nodded, speaking in another tongue.

"Do you speak Common?" he asked.

Staring back with her shining eyes, the girl remained awestruck, oblivious to his question. Reht looked away, fearing she might see what he was scheming. Fumbling with the bandages on his hands, he swallowed the seed of guilt taking root in his chest.

I have to do this, he affirmed. For his himself, his crew, the natives of Elia—but most of all, for his parents, their dead bodies before his eyes like a hologram, their pain burned into the flesh of his hands.

"Come with me," he said, taking her hand and motioning toward the emergency hatch.

She resisted at first, face contorted with fear. As she dug her feet into the floor, he noticed the cuts and abrasions encircling her ankles and thighs; Diawn had not been kind to her cargo.

Reht pointed to the lacerations on his stomach and the bruises on his face. "I understand. Please, trust me. I'll keep you safe."

"Femi," she whispered, bowing her head.

"Femi?"

She nodded, keeping her eyes on the walkway.

"I'm Reht Jagger. Captain Reht Jagger, that is, of the *Wraith.*"

She looked at and then straight through him, the dark blue of her eyes sucking him down like the deep cold of the ocean trenches. Slowly, she put her hand in his.

Too easy, he thought, tugging her toward the exit. Along the way, he stopped beside the nav computer relay and swiped the motherboard's signature chip. Without it Diawn would have to fly blind, not only buying him some time, but allowing him to track her most recent stops.

"Now," he said, throwing back the emergency hatch. "Where the hell are we?"

The neon lights and din of the bustling city greeted him, as did the familiar night sky.

Reht laughed at his fortune. "Never thought I'd be so glad to be here."

He reached down and helped Femi through the hatch.

"Welcome to Aeternyx," he said, kissing her on the cheek. Her skin felt soft and sweet against his lips. "Get ready for a good time."

* * *

Unsure of where to go, Jetta jumped their fighter to a remote site outside the Narrus cluster. After anchoring to the site, she unclipped from the pilot's chair and made her way back to the aft compartment. The Healer, strapped upright into a passenger seat, barely kept her head up as she dipped in an out of consciousness.

"Hey," Jetta said, touching the Healer's shoulder, "are you okay?"

Triel mumbled something and rolled her head to the side. She looked up at Jetta, blue eyes pleading. "Take me home."

"Home?"

Extending herself, Jetta felt what she meant. *A yearning to go back to a familiar place; somewhere safe and happy, filled with the warmth of the people she loves...*

"Algar is dangerous," Jetta whispered.

"Answers... to help us," Triel said, her eyes closing again as she drifted off.

Concerned about her stress levels, Jetta didn't try to rouse the Healer again. Instead, she unfolded another seat from the wall and sat next to her friend, considering the option.

Algar is extremely unstable with all the looters and radical factions fighting over the planet's resources.

Still, she couldn't ignore the fact that it sheltered the secrets of the inter- and intra-worlds. Could a Solitary Prodgy survive alone in the Starways? Was there a way to restore her? Could she save her

79

tribespeople still trapped inside the Motti's weapon—or pull Jahx out of psionic limbo?

Jetta turned away from the Healer as more disturbing questions surfaced. What was the true story of Rion the Abomination? How did Jetta and her siblings fit in with Prodgy myth? It would be a way for her to corroborate or denounce Victor's theories about the origin of her power, and possibly give her leverage against his manipulations.

Victor.

Squeezing her eyes shut, Jetta ground her knuckles into the support structure of the starcraft, trying to keep her mind from wandering back to his sound of his voice, the glint of his eyes. But as much as she tried, she couldn't stop herself from feeling the disquieting mixture of loathing, admiration, and empathy for the centuries-old man from Earth.

Who is he anyway? she tried to tell herself, but she could not trick herself into thinking she possessed the greater power. Familiar and unwelcome, the dark current of Victor's mind still flowed through her veins, and the more she tried to deny it, the more she hungered to submerge herself in his wickedness.

Jetta touched Triel's arm, reminding herself of her objective, but then quickly pulled back. A deeper fear, not the cool grey of the Healer's skin, made her retract her hand.

(She can't know how I feel.)

The onboard computer beeped at her, alerting her to the ship's low fuel cells. Jetta returned to the cockpit and searched the starcharts for the nearest refueling station, finding an outpost close to their site. Although she had never traveled in this region before, stolen experience bade her to pick their stop sites carefully. Military was typically unwelcome in this sector, and anyone of human descent, however remote, had it even worse.

As she navigated to the outpost, her thoughts drifted to Jaeia. Constantly erecting walls to keep her sister out of her head countered her innate ability. More than anything, she wanted Jaeia to

80

understand her struggles—she needed her support. But Jaeia couldn't and wouldn't understand her predicament, and it would only drive them further apart.

Jaeia is not like me, she thought. *My sister is a good person.*

Shame turned to anger. Her sister wouldn't even consider joining forces with Victor, even if it was only to steal his power and use it for the greater good.

"Gods," Jetta mumbled, disgusted with herself.

After rechecking her landing coordinates, Jetta set down the ship on the busy dock, keeping an eye on the crowds. She didn't want to attract attention, but she couldn't do anything about the Alliance insignia branded on the broadside of her starcraft.

"Triel," Jetta said as she got the equipment she'd need out of a locker. The Healer rolled her head to the side but didn't open her eyes.

"I'm going to stock up for our journey and refuel the ship. Stay here. Hey—" Jetta said, shaking her shoulders. "I need you to stay awake and keep watch while I'm gone."

The Healer mumbled a response before fading back into semi-consciousness.

Chewing on the inside of her cheek, Jetta weighed the consequences of dosing Triel with zopramine from the emergency medkit. It would keep her awake, but it would also put strain on her heart. Already a ghostly white from the physiologic stress of transition, the Healer didn't look like her body could handle any more demands.

I can't risk leaving her alone if she's not awake to protect herself, Jetta decided, taking the medkit off the wall.

Relying on what little medical knowledge she had stolen over the years, Jetta ripped open a medicine packet with her teeth and removed the green hypo booster. Triel's eyes shot open the moment Jetta touched the booster to her wrist and depressed the plunger.

"Oh my Gods," Triel said, slapping away the booster before Jetta could inject the rest. "Where am I? What was that?"

81

Jetta took a step back. "You're aboard a stolen Alliance fighter, and we just docked at a refueling outpost in the Vrea sector, outside the Sister planets. That was zopramine, but I didn't get the whole dose in. You have to stay awake to guard the ship while I go and get supplies—it isn't safe here."

Triel looked her up and down as her memories trickled back. "Jetta—you helped me. I was Falling…"

"Yes," Jetta whispered.

The Healer's eyes narrowed. "You helped me by… I *saw* you."

Jetta blushed and fumbled for her second sidearm. "Here, take this," she said, handing Triel the weapon. "I'll be back in an hour."

"Wait," Triel said, grabbing her arm. An expression akin to curiosity and surprise crossed the Healer's face, but what lay beyond Jetta couldn't—or wouldn't—read. "Don't go. I want to talk about what happened."

"Not now," Jetta said, pulling away again. "I'll be back in an hour. Use this com to get a hold of me if something happens."

Frowning, Triel accepted the communicator from Jetta. "Won't the Alliance come looking for us?"

Jetta pointed to a missing service panel. Severed wires and datachips, dislodged from the motherboard, indicated her strategy. "I took care of any carrier signals, and Jaeia knows better than to come after me. Besides, they have their hands full right now."

"Jetta—"

"One hour, I promise," she said, walking over to the portal and lowering the access ramp.

Not hiding her frustration, the Healer let out an exasperated sigh. Jetta ground her teeth and resisted the urge to look back as she resealed the ramp.

(She can't know how I feel.)

Jetta took a moment to study her surroundings. The crowded dock, jammed with homemade starcraft that looked like scrap jobs assembled from recycled parts, reminded her of any other unregulated outpost. However, the majority of Sentients appeared to be of Vreaper or human ancestry.

We're probably close to one of the displacement colonies, Jetta deduced.

Even though Jetta had ripped the Alliance patches off her pilot's jacket, she couldn't hide the telltale cut of the uniform. She kept her helmet on, hoping that she would look like any other dog-soldier or Jock that liked to steal military vessels.

"Nice bird," someone snorted.

Looking to her left, Jetta spotted a human man with a crooked nose smiling at her, leaning against his hovercycle. His pink prosthetic arm whirred as he rolled his cigarette between the plastic fingertips.

It can't be…

It had been a long time since she had seen an artificial limb, especially one so antiquated. On any of the Homeworlds they could have regrown the arm, and most black market clinics could weave tissues from flesh-farm stock. Sporting a prosthetic—especially after the war with the Deadwalkers—was for the brazen or foolish.

"They recharge fuel cells around here?" she asked.

The man snorted. "You kiddin'? Take a closer look."

Jetta used the zoom in her helmet to examine the refueling station across the dock. It had fuel cell inputs, but the base chargers were dead.

"They ain't even got ethelneprolol for fifth-class flying pieces of *gorsh-shit*," he said. "This place is as dry as every other *godich* port from here to Breck's Pass. *Chakking* government."

Jetta frowned, but determined she might be able to get some of the other things they might need. As she turned to go, the man put out his artificial arm to stop her.

"Hey, I know a guy that'll buy military bird like that."

Jetta played her part as she tried to pass him. "You don't know anybody that rich."

The man didn't lower his prosthetic. "You must be new to these parts, otherwise you wouldn't disrespect me like that."

Close enough to the fake limb, Jetta read the small inscription in English near the thumb, translating it to Common. *Advanced Robotic Technologies.* It sounded familiar—important—so much so that it took the man reaching for his weapon to break her gaze.

"A little jumpy, aren't ya?" he said, flipping over the knife in his hand. "Just wanted to show you my goods. You seem like you're lookin' for something."

He pulled out two boxes from the storage cell on his bike, cutting along the seams to reveal his prize. Methoc powder, dyed pink, glinted under the dome of lights and filtered sunlight.

"Can't buy this in the mainland. Give you a deal."

"Thanks, but I don't like your flavor," Jetta said, trying to walk away again.

The man grabbed her by the collar. Sensing his desperation, Jetta didn't struggle as he got up in her face. Only her helmet separated them as his breath fogged her visor. "I ain't like you, alright? I don't got nuthin' to lose, see? It's easy for you Jocks—it's easy for everyone else. This is all the *gorsh-shit* I got left."

Slipping behind his eyes, Jetta absorbed his recent history in seconds. *He murdered the original methoc dealer and is trying to buy enough fuel to make it to the Tannus Belt.*

But from the way his thoughts laced together, the self-deception didn't hold. With as much debt as he had, and as wanted as he was by both government and criminal circuits, there was nowhere he could hide.

Satisfied she had enough on him to manipulate the situation in her favor, she tried to pull out, but something yanked her down farther inside his mind.

Memories jerked by in random order, and it took everything she had to make sense of the sudden outpouring. She saw herself lining up in Dominion concentration camp, arguing for food with another prisoner before the butt of a gun connected with her face. Hours

*later, she woke up with a gut full of hot iron fear as Deadwalker
ships touched down in the smoldering wreckage of a city. The
ceaseless gunfire didn't drown out the mechanical clicking of the
spiny creatures that spilled out of the buzzing ships, chasing after
her with insect quickness.*

*Reeling farther backwards in time, she woke to the smell of
smoke in her tent. When she ran out, she saw invaders torching her
colony. She turned to find her mother, only to come face to face with
a black-masked soldier who chained her to a line of other captured
humans.*

*"Get in line, Deadskin," the soldier barked, slapping the back
of her head.*

*The second she flashed a hint of defiance, she felt the electric
bite of a shockwand against her hip. Cowering, she fell in step with
the other humans as the soldiers herded them into cargo ships.*

Stop it—

*Fighting the foreign memories thrust her ahead, into the recent
past. Against her will, she relived the man's agony as he sold his
body for freedom aboard the trade ship. She had known females to
do it, but never males.*

I don't want to see anymore, *she thought, trying to break free.*

*Unable to peel herself away, she hurtled farther forward in his
timeline. Jetta found herself back in a crowded city, huddling next to
a steam vent under the unforgiving winter sky. Rain and snow fell in
slushy sheets, soaking her to the bone as passersby shot her looks of
disgust. Beyond hungry, beyond rational thought, she succumbed to
lower instincts, ones that erased any sense of dignity. Jetta knew that
feeling all too well, and she recoiled against that truth as she picked
through the soggy trash outside a restaurant.*

Too much like Fiorah; too much like my old life.

*Except this man didn't have two siblings to share thoughts and
emotions with, and he didn't have their ability to steal knowledge
and experience. Alone in an unforgiving world, he was forced to beg,
something she had seen Galm do but had never been reduced to*

85

*herself. The humiliation, even through a borrowed memory, pushed
her to the edge. When she experienced his first drink, the burning
stream of alcohol brought welcome relief, insulating her from the
madness.*

*Stealing was easier, quicker, and in the dispirited waste it was
the only thrill left. She ran down an alleyway, stolen gambling chips
stuffed under her arm as she plowed through piles of trash and flung
herself over a retaining wall. The man had stopped caring
altogether. He no longer took simple precautions, and he no longer
cared who he stole from or killed. And in the depths of his mind, she
felt his longing for the sweet release of death as those who chased
him drew nearer.*

*Jetta bristled against his blatant self-destruction until his
darkest, most gruesome secret unfolded, blotting out all the rest.*

No—

*Pinned down by hooded figures, she could do nothing as her
arm was laid out on a chopping board and a tourniquet secured
above her elbow.*

*"This is what we agreed to, isn't it?" a man wearing a
butcher's apron said as he set out his sharpened tools on an
adjacent wooden table.*

*She looked around, desperate to find something—anything—to
get her out of this deal. But in her panic, she saw only the limbs and
organs of the other victims before her, preserved in stasis cylinders
around the room.*

*"You are serving a higher purpose," the man said, rolling up
his sleeves.*

*Screaming and struggling did nothing. The butcher approached,
meat cleaver in one hand, derma-abrader in the other.*

Kicking backwards, Jetta pulled out before she could see the
rest. She couldn't show pity or he'd know she had been in his head,
but the strain in her voice gave away her fear. "Get away!"

What is wrong with me? she thought, trying to get ahold of
herself. She had seen the flesh farms through other eyes before, had

submerged herself in the bleak undertow of street life more than once, and she had known war and poverty from many different perspectives. *But I've never slipped that far before...*

Even when she was little, unguarded and still grasping the reins of her powers, she had never been transposed so viscerally into a memory as traumatic as the one she had just witnessed.

"Get out of here—you're worthless," he said, laughing at her.

Still recovering from the abrupt telepathic severance, Jetta clutched her helmet, eyesight blurry and ringed with halos. Time slowed to a crawl and every movement, every sensation became exaggerated. The spray of spittle from his mouth hit her uniform like buckshot and his laughter, shrill and bombastic, nearly blew out her eardrums.

Bracing herself, she watched in horror as a phantom shadow manifested from somewhere beneath his skin. Jetta shook her head, hoping to rid herself of the hallucination. But when she looked back, black-curled brume seethed from every pore of his body, pulsating and slinking towards her like snakes as he continued to laugh.

Jetta surprised both herself and the man when she slammed him against his bike. Even though he outweighed her by forty kilos, he couldn't match her augmented strength, leaving him to struggle helplessly in her grips.

When he tried to stab her with his knife, she broke his wrist, muffling his screams with her gloved hand.

"You shouldn't have done that," she whispered. She drove her knee into his gut, doubling him over. In one fluid movement, she took his head in her hands and wrenched it to the side. The telltale crunch elicited a sickening gratification.

As his psionic tune faded into nothingness, waves of relief washed over her, and she let him slump the ground. But the second she saw his empty eyes staring up at her, the reality of what she had done fizzled away her solace. Guilt congealed into a cold weight in her belly.

Stupid, she told herself. She had seen all the dreadful things inside him—there was no salvaging him, no way to undo the horrors that had mangled his life. He was as much deadweight in her heart as he was in society. Then why were her actions still hard to swallow?

The answer came to her in the twisting of her stomach: *(I wasn't strong enough. I couldn't handle his pain. I hated him for the way he made me feel.)*

Jetta looked around, making sure she hadn't made too much of a scene. Several bystanders had witnessed the event, but when she walked away, making it clear that they could take his possessions in exchange for their silence, they didn't seem to care.

She hurried away from the ensuing scuffle and toward the center of the floating dome where sagging housing structures and businesses competed for space. Despite the filters on her helmet, she smelled something that reminded her of the beggar's oil and the merlik powder her uncle used to use cover up the moldy taste of their rations.

This is bad, Jetta thought. Barren or abandoned shops with "no supplies" scrawled over unlit signs lined the streets. Graffiti artists paid no attention to her as she walked by, her boots crunching on the broken glass littering the sidewalks. With every step her doubt of finding what she needed grew, as did her awareness of being a foreigner in such a place. She knew what the sidelong glances meant and felt multiple presences falling in step behind her.

Up the strip she caught sight of a dilapidated building with a broken neon sign hanging over a barred door. She didn't know the symbols, but by the look of the gears and half-functioning electronics displayed in the window, she guessed it was a repair shop and the closest she would come to what she was looking for.

A small crowd of humans milled around the front door, periodically peering over their shoulders as goods exchanged hands.

"Hey! What's your kind doing here?" one of them shouted at her. Red rings under the woman's eyes and jaundiced skin indicated the end-stages of the *M. eserepthia* parasite infection, a condition easily cured in the Homeworlds.

Why hasn't she gotten treated?

In her heart Jetta knew the truth. Deadskins this far out were on the run, unsponsored, unregistered, and had never had access to the variety of technology taken for granted by the humans in regulated space.

Humans like me.

Squaring her shoulders, Jetta shoved through the crowd, ignoring their curses as she entered the shop. She slammed the door behind her, nearly unhinging it with her force. The little bell attached to the top rattled, protesting its mistreatment.

"I don't appreciate your entry."

Jetta couldn't see who was speaking to her over the drifts of half-assembled machinery and indiscernible piles of metal housing and wires, some of which reached the ceiling.

This is all junk, she thought, tapping the dust-covered innards of some huge, antiquated central processor.

As she waded through the mess, Jetta minded her step, careful not to disturb the towering machine piles or the various collections of black fly husks. She spied some of what she needed at the counter near a register: cable rope, hand tools, and even some batteries—though on closer inspection, acid corrosion ringed the casings.

"What can I help you with?"

Jetta pushed aside a stack of broken datafiles to find the proprietor, an old man tinkering away behind a workbench, under a strange green light. Tufts of white hair stuck out from beneath his headgear, which bore lenses and optics that bobbed up and down as he chewed on the end of an electron probe. His unshaven face complemented his dirty shirt, giving her the impression of a man who poured all of his attention and time into his work, and none on personal appearance.

"I'm looking to buy any cable rope you have, batteries—
working batteries—and that bundle of tools over there," Jetta said,
pointing to the hand tools near the register. "And food rations."

Still under the protection of her pilot's helmet, she surveyed the
room and picked up some unusual readouts on her visor. She
carefully punched in some commands on her sleeve to run a cross-
analysis.

"This is a repair shop, not a supply shop," he said, wiping his
greasy hands on his apron. "And there aren't *any* food rations for
sale around these parts. Not since the Alliance quit sending
provisions. Besides, I wouldn't sell to your kind anyway."

"My kind?" Jetta said.

He got in her face, his eyes magnified a hundred times by the
lenses. "Jocks. Go rip someone else off."

"I'm not a Jock," she said. She laid a handgun on the counter
and the man jumped back. "For trade. I'm not here to hurt you."

He looked her over with a suspicious eye before picking it up
and inspecting it. "Military grade. Dual-phasic, relatively new. Still
has full charges. I'll give you three hundred for it."

Jetta huffed. "Don't rip me off. And I don't want cash."

"Cash is all I'll give you. I know your kind—startin' trouble,
doing the Devil's work. I'll give you cash so you'll go get high.
Maybe your heart will give out, save me the trouble."

It would have been easy to kill him, to take what she wanted and
leave, but her most recent murder was fresh enough in her mind to
make her pause. Jetta swallowed her anger and tried again. "For a
man with a back room full of gold, you'll need something like this
for protection."

His smiled quickly dissolved into a frown. "Get the hell out of
here!"

Jetta grabbed him by the collar and threw him on top of the
counter before he had time to try for his pistol. "I'm tired. Give me
what I want. It's more than a fair trade."

The lenses on his headgear exaggerated the dilation of his pupils. "Wait a minute—I know you. I know that voice."

"What?"

"You're Commander Jetta Kyron, Warchild of the Starways. I've always wanted to meet you!"

Enraged at the sound of her media-driven name, she reaffirmed her grip on his collar, tightening her hold around his neck. Her mind anticipated the way his brittle bones would feel snapping between her fingers, and the temptation grew stronger with every breath she took.

"Please," he whispered. "I mean no disrespect. If you let me go, I'll show you something you need to see."

Jetta thought of the man she had killed earlier, how easily his neck had broken, and became aware of the sweat pouring down her neck and forehead.

I'm not strong enough not to—

(He does not deserve his skin.)

No, this is wrong...isn't it?

A chill shivered through her, loosening her grip. The old man didn't take any cues and rolled out from underneath her, catching himself on a pile of scrap metal. Without pause, he wound his apron around the cut on his hand, keeping his eye on Jetta. He gave her a cautious smile, showing yellow teeth pitted by age and disease. "Come, friend. Please."

A conflicting mix of self-reproach and disappointment made her stomach knot as Jetta followed him to the back room concealed behind advertisements for a brand of cola that had long been out of business. There she found what her helmet readings had picked up: gold. A few bricks lay in an open safe next to a molecular oven.

"How is a man like you in possession of gold and all this equipment?"

He shook his head. "Nobody would expect an operation like this in this dump—did you?"

"You're not trading gold?"

91

"No. I melt it down and mix it with Tremanium. The combination makes an excellent conductor."

Jetta looked around at the half-finished robotics lying in bins and on tables under special lighting fixtures. Some resembled human torsos, others arthropods with multiple limbs and shiny metal carapaces. Ghostly images of flesh stretched across mechanical skeletons surfaced in the back of her mind, draining the blood from her face.

"Who and what are you?" Jetta said, ripping off her helmet.

"I'm an advanced robotics and nanotechnics engineer," the old man said, backing up against the wall as she approached him. "My name is Edgar Wallace. I come from a long line of specialized engineers."

"What are these things?" Jetta said, shaking one of the creations until a limb fell off and clattered to the floor.

"They're artificial life forms—please, be careful," he said, gingerly plucking the creature from Jetta's hand.

"A.I.? You know that's illegal without a permit. Are you in league with the Motti?"

"Goodness, no," he said.

Unconvinced, Jetta boar into his mind, and he grimaced.

"Please, stop," the old man pleaded, falling to his knees. "You know I'm telling the truth."

She did, and she withdrew, but not all the way.

"I designed them to deactivate specified DNA structures, perform basic decontamination sweeps on biospheres and assess for bio-reintegration compatibility," he said, voice quavering.

Pain creased the corners of his eyes as Edgar rose slowly on arthritic knees. He pulled out an old print photo from a desk drawer lined with protective velvet. Holding the photo away from her, he studied it with reverence.

"There were those on Earth who had mapped a way to save the planet 1,100 years ago, and there are a few of us who still believe that it's possible. Most of the datafiles were destroyed after the war, but from what was salvaged we are trying to rebuild. These machines were designed to kill the diseases spread by the bioweapons and plant the nanite 'seeds' designed by our Father to revitalize our world, but there are missing schematics, and I have yet to figure out the master design."

"Your Father?"

Giving the photo one last look, the old turned it over to her with trembling hands. "The Father of nanotechnic engineering, Josef Stein."

The second the photo touched her fingers, she winced. "Oh my Gods."

Edgar tried to keep her from falling, but her bloodless legs could no longer support her weight. Her hand caught on one of his bladed tools as she fell, slicing straight through her glove and into the pink of her skin.

I've seen that man before.

Jetta remembered. Squeezing her eyes shut, she clutched her bloodied hand to her chest as her stomach convulsed in the wake of her revelation.

The man in the photo print is the same man I saw in Victor's mind—the angel with the second shadow.

Mind racing, she made another connection. *And the same man I saw in that waking nightmare on Jue Hexron when Victor was promising me all the things I wanted to hear...*

Jetta opened her eyes and forced her breath through clenched teeth until the blood returned to her limbs. With shaky hands, she collected herself off the floor, brushing away dust and debris. She nabbed the photo and looked at it again. "Josef Stein. Doctor Death."

"No!" Edgar said, taking the photo from her. He carefully wiped it off and put it back in the desk drawer. "No," he repeated more calmly. "He was a good man. He was wronged by those he trusted most. What happened to him—what he did—you have to understand that sometimes good people make bad choices."

Jetta held her breath. "What do you mean? Why is this important? Why did you need to show me this?"

Edgar Wallace removed his headgear and knitted his hands together nervously. "Because you are so much like him."

Appalled, Jetta turned to leave.

"He was persecuted, you know, for his abilities, his superior intelligence," Edgar said, raising his voice. "People were jealous of what he had, and because of that he was isolated most of his life. Governments and militaries exploited his talents, and finally, after he put all of his efforts into saving mankind, he suffered the worst betrayal of all."

Jetta stopped in her tracks but didn't turn around. "Why are you telling me this?"

"Because I believe in you. You have the power to change people's minds, make the Starways rethink old ways. You represent hope and redemption, Jetta Kyron. You were once the Dominion's Warchild, but you choose to fight for the Alliance. And now you can fight for the most worthy cause of all: rebuilding lost worlds. You can help the human race restore Earth. You can give us back our home, give us a second chance."

"But," he said, touching her arm. He immediately retracted his hand once he saw the severe look on her face. "I fear your fate will be the same as his."

"What happened to him?"

"Ramak Yakarvoah happened. But we shall not speak of him," the old man said. He tried to take Jetta's hand and bandage it, but she pulled away.

"No," Jetta said, holding him at the wrist. "Tell me about this Ramak."

Edgar looked around the room, fumbling with his hands. Sensing his nervous tension, Jetta peered around the secret door dividing them from the main part of the store, but she couldn't see past the piles of metal and wires.

"Nobody in my line of work talks of him," he said, keeping his voice just above a whisper. "All I know is that one day things looked promising for Earth—Josef Stein had mastered nanotechnics, and with his microscopic robots he could do anything. Destroy cancers, reconstruct missing limbs, revitalize dead tissue—even program his little bots to decontaminate biohazard zones. The possibilities were endless with his Smart Cells."

"So it sounds," Jetta said, folding her arms across her chest.

Unfazed by her skepticism, Edgar continued. "Most importantly, Josef and his son, Kurt, created the Ark, a genetic catalogue of all the living creatures on Earth. The two of them could literally rebuild Earth. Despite the wars, everyone believed that these technologies represented a chance for peace. But then Ramak appeared."

"What do you mean?" Jetta said.

Dabbing his forehead with the corner of his apron, Edgar sat down on a stool. "Nobody knows where he came from. All that is known is that he started a movement, one to end the world. They called themselves the Doomsdayers."

"Doomsdayers?"

"I don't know the real translation in Common. All that matters is that he found Josef and did something to him—got in his head, changed him. Josef had many terrible things happen to him in his lifetime, but it only made him more devoted to his family, and to saving mankind. He was a strong, loving man. Somehow Ramak found a way to take that away from him."

"So he was tricked into becoming Doctor Death?"

"You don't understand," Edgar said, his tone changing sharply. "Ramak wasn't like other people. He had a way of finding your weaknesses and making you forget everything but your shame. He ground anything decent—anything human—out of you; he made you into a shell of a person. Then he filled you with what he wanted. The only thing he left Josef with was his anger. The rest he filled with madness."

95

(I could do that.)

Jetta didn't know where the thought came from, but it sprang up with troubling urgency, as if it needed to be known. But before she could put more thought into it, she realized a frightening possibility. "Does Victor Paulstine have any connection to Ramak Yakarvoah?"

Edgar shook his head. "Victor? That bastard on the nets? No. The historians say Ramak died in the bombings during the Last Great War. And it would be hard to miss him if he was still around—he was hideous, covered in burn scars from head to toe."

"Victor has claimed to be 1,100 years old—he could have known Ramak."

Edgar laughed. "Victor is a jackal—resourceful, ruthless—but he's not 1,100 years old. No human could live that long. Human cells are too fragile—they degrade over time, even with nanotechnics. Haven't you heard the stories about all those twenty-first century aristocrats who injected themselves with Stein's Smart Cells, hoping to elongate their pathetically empty lives? They went insane."

Something didn't sit right with her, but Jetta couldn't pinpoint her discomfort. She felt as if she was missing a connection, something vital.

Most of Earth's recorded history was destroyed in the Exodus, she thought, *so the survivors passed down information from one generation to the next. Edgar may be kooky, but he's the best source I have.*

"What became of Josef Stein?" she asked.

Edgar's gaze dropped to the floor. "He was killed in his underground lab during the Last Great War. He died distraught, alone and ashamed of what had become of him."

"How do you know that?"

"Some of his electronic journals survived the war on the smart servers, though his more important work and personal journals he kept locked away on hard copy. Rumor has it that his lab still remains, but deep in the heart of the Deadzone where no sane person would ever dare venture."

Jetta thought about it for a minute. "From what you're telling me, the key to rebuilding planets means the recovery of both Kurt and Josef Stein's work."

"Yes," Edgar said eagerly. "But that will be extraordinarily difficult. They both conducted their projects in secret. Nobody even knows where Kurt hid the Ark; he was even more protective than his father."

"These hard-copy journals—would they have details about his Smart Cell experiments? Would they give me insight into Ramak?"

Edgar's eyes darted back and forth like excited fish. "Many have tried to unearth those same secrets, and none have survived. There is something evil there, a curse—something born of Josef's suffering that is more terrible than the Necros that roam those lands."

Jetta looked at Edgar, studying his wrinkled face. "What do you want of me?" she whispered.

Carefully, Edgar reached for her lacerated hand. At first she resisted, but not sensing malice in his thoughts, she allowed him to take it. He turned her palm face up, exposing the wound. Although the cut had stopped bleeding, the angry, exposed red tissue required more than her stoicism to heal.

"I read all the nets, see all the vids," he said, gingerly holding her hand in his. "I know your story. You are an orphaned child of Fiorah, a telepath—and human to some degree, right? You have had so much against you, so many reasons to hate this world, but you still fight for what is right."

"Please, I—"

"There is something special inside you," he insisted, cutting her off, "like there was in Josef Stein—I feel it. Just know that I believe in you, and the others like me who are working to further the dreams of our Father believe in you, too. Lead us home, Jetta Kyron. Help us all find peace."

I am nothing like Josef Stein, she thought. Just moments again she killed a man, and for what? *Because his pain was too real.*

"Help me then. Give me the things I need," she whispered, taking her hand back.

Worry brought tears to his eyes. "Terrible things are happening right now. Victor Paulstine is not to be underestimated. Last year my wife disappeared after we made a presentation at the Human Rights Summit. He's going to find a way to sell or kill every last human—every Sentient he deems unworthy. He's worse than Ramak. What are you going to do about him?"

Jetta thought of Victor, and with it came the rush of terror and hunger she had come to crave. "I don't know," she said swallowing hard, fighting back the dark longings surging through her veins. She caught a reflection of herself in the metal carapace of one of Edgar's mechanoids and didn't immediately recognize herself. It was something in her eyes—something she hadn't seen before. "But I will do something—I promise—before it's too late."

***

Hearing the shouting and explosive noises outside the starship, Triel dared to open the solar shield.

"*Ju'thera*," she cursed, fearing the worst when she saw the fires burning dangerously close to the refueling station, and the rioting on the strip. When she tried to call up the engine controls, the navs system went black. *Oh no—Jetta locked out the ship in case we got boarded.*

Jetta, she silently called, hoping that her thoughts would be heard, *come back now.*

Frustrated, she tried to use the com again, but all frequencies had been jammed. As Triel watched the looters capitalize on the mayhem, she realized why. *Someone within the rioting group did this so that the storeowners couldn't send out any distress signals to the Alliance or neighboring colonies.*

Triel pressed her fists into the dead cockpit terminal. *I have to do something,* she told herself, trying to work up the nerve to do what she feared. Using her powers, especially so recently after coming to the point of a Fall, could thrust her right back into ruin.

For Jetta...

Bowing her head, the Healer reached out. The tense, agitated rhythms of the surrounding Sentients latched on, pulling at her attention. She heard fragments of conversations, thoughts—

No food

(starving)

—Can't go on like

isn't fair

Can't live like—

Why do they have—

"Oh, Jetta," Triel whispered, pulling away, afraid of what the foreign thoughts would to do her. "I hope you can see this."

In the burgeoning chaos, Triel saw and felt humans turning against Vreapers, with other Sentient species taking sides. Most of the battles happened outside the storefronts, with people tearing each other apart for any semblance of rations.

None of it surprised her. With the increasing threat of the Motti's new weapon and the Alliance's military breakdown, vulnerable areas like this one were the first to feel the supply shortages. *And this is only one of thousands of places experiencing the violent backlash.*

Shivering again, she pulled Jetta's jacket more tightly around her shoulders. She had to keep it together long enough to reach Algar. *I'll find answers there,* she convinced herself.

As Triel checked the activity on the rear monitor, something struck the fighter and knocked her off her feet. She racked her head against the console, and in the dizzy confusion she lost track of her surroundings. Rapidly exchanged gunfire erupted all around her, and the smell of burning circuitry filled her nose. Triel reached for the gun Jetta gave her and took aim, but someone redirected her.

99

"Shoot them, not me!"

"Jetta?" she muttered.

When her vision finally reoriented itself, she saw Jetta furiously unlocking the engines with one hand while firing back at the people crawling up the ramp.

"Shoot, Triel!"

Triel raised her gun again, aiming at the nearest human, but his emotions infected her concentration.

Starving—

"I can't!" Triel exclaimed, trying to push the foreign thoughts out of her head.

Jetta shouted something before hitting the ignition. The engines fire blasted off most of the people clinging to the ramp, but some remained, desperately pulling themselves up.

"Jetta, help them!" the Healer cried.

With a cold intensity, Jetta took aim, shooting the last of the rioters in the head with deadly precision before resealing the ramp.

"Oh my Gods," Triel whispered, unsure of what to think or do. *I've never seen that look in her eyes.*

"They tried to kill me," Jetta said, returning to the pilot's chair. "Buckle up—this is going to get nasty."

Unable to get the rioters distress out of her head, Triel persisted. "Those men were confused and desperate, Jetta."

"This is not the time," Jetta said, banking hard to port as incoming fire rained down from above.

"What's going on?" Triel said, strapping into the nav seat.

"I'm not sure. Something about a ration shortage. Vreapers and humans never got along. It's just another excuse to rip each other's throats out."

"Watch out!" Triel said, seeing the fire melt down one of the charging lines at the refueling station. Even with dry tanks, the leftover igniter in the pumps sparked the explosion, sending parts of the outpost spewing into space. The blast force smashed into their ship, testing the strength of their harnesses. Jetta quickly recaptured

100

the ship's direction, and Triel held her stomach as the commander wound through the flying debris with deft reflexes.

"I thought you weren't a very good pilot," Triel said as she watched Jetta thread through two oncoming ships at an impossible angle.

"Jaeia just likes to tell everyone she's better than me at something," Jetta replied as she dipped their fighter toward the planet, nearly colliding with another rogue ship trying to evade their pursuers.

An unexpected smile crossed the Healer's face, even as she held on tight to her safety belts.

"We only have one more jump charge, so check the map. Where's the next closest station?" Jetta said, skimming over the nose of a felled cargo ship.

Still clinging to her harness with one hand, Triel scrolled through the options. "Ummm—how about Teraportis?"

Jetta shook her head. "Something past Breck's Pass."

"Iyo Kono?"

"Punch it in—quickly!" Jetta shouted, firing all weapons.

Glancing at the scanners, Triel spotted a new wave of starships hot on their trail. The onboard computer warned of critical damage to their forward shields as the enemy fighters' missile carriages charged to red.

Gods, protect us, the Healer thought, hitting the jump. Triel braced for impact, but time pulled apart as their fighter passed through the hole in space, and a flash of white light blurred the oncoming fire.

Once the constellations changed on the viewscreen and the jumpdrive spun down, Triel breathed a sign of relief.

"Hey, speak in Common," Triel said as Jetta mumbled in her native tongue and unstrapped from her chair.

"The forward shields were toasted in that blast," Jetta said, checking the aft terminals. "Secondary engines look like they took a nasty beating, too. The computer's acting twitchy; can't tell if there's a coolant leak or a damaged Erteriam relay."

"You got us out safely, and that's all the matters. I can't believe you can fly like that!"

Jetta half-smiled, but returned her attention to the nav computer, trying to calculate the safest route to Iyo Kono. "I think we'll be okay until we get to port."

"Hey—what happened to your hand?" Triel said, trying to get a better look at the gash.

Jetta nearly tripped over herself getting out of the way. "Just scratched it."

"Am I really that bad?" Triel whispered.

"What? No," Jetta said. The level of her voice rose, and she involuntarily rushed her words. "It's just—I don't want to add to your worries right now."

"Jetta," Triel said, reaching for her arm. Jetta didn't move, but her body went rigid as soon as Triel touched her sleeve. "That's not the way it works. Healing someone with positive energy is revitalizing."

Jetta looked away from her. "Then you definitely don't want to come anywhere near me."

"Why? What do you mean? What happened?"

Jetta gripped her hand and kept her gaze trained on the wound. "I killed a man."

"Oh," Triel said, trying to reach through her words. "Did he threaten you?"

"In a way," Jetta said. She laughed to herself and shook her head. "Do you ever...do you ever hate the way others make you feel?"

Triel nodded. "Yes. It can be damaging. That's one of the ways a Healer can turn into a Dissembler."

"That's the way this man made me feel. Damaged. I felt infected by his misery. I felt... weak. And I hated him for it. I saw—I *became* all the pain inside him. I just wanted it to stop, and I just... reacted."

Triel didn't know what to say. It frightened her that Jetta had killed someone so easily, but at the same time she understood. Jetta and her siblings had never been trained how to handle their extrasensory experiences, and ones as intimate as what she described should have been mitigated by more than one telepath.

Not knowing what else to do, Triel grabbed Jetta's hand and pinned her back against the pilot's chair. At first Jetta struggled, but when Triel sank beneath her skin, Jetta froze.

The Healer went through the lacerated layers of Jetta's muscle and dermis, stimulating cell repopulation and directing her body to expunge the harmful debris. Being a relatively superficial injury, Triel didn't need to sink so deeply into Jetta's internal rhythm to facilitate her recovery, but she couldn't help herself.

I wish you would let yourself see that I don't judge you, that I understand why you had to commit such an act, she thought. On Algar, Triel had witnessed a few of her own tribesmen unintentionally kill their patients. Tribal elders declared the act a self-defense mechanism, a violent allergic reaction to a deeply wounded soul. As the Healer seeded these thoughts and memories inside Jetta, she penetrated further, realizing healing wasn't her only objective.

Did I imagine what I saw and felt in Jetta's mind in the intensive care unit? It usually took the strongest band of Prodgies to save the Falling—and Jetta wasn't a Prodgy, nor did she know what she was doing. But what Triel felt inside Jetta was pure, powerful, and without parallel to anything she had ever felt from another being.

"Hey," Jetta said, pushing her away. "It's fine. Thanks."

The abrupt severance left ghostly afterimages in her vision. "I hate it when you do that."

"Sorry," Jetta said, averting her eyes as she returned to the pilot's seat.

"I was just trying to help," Triel said. "Even you need it every once and a while, you know."

"Thank you," Jetta said, sounding sincere, but her tone giving fair warning that the conversation would go no further.

"Jetta," Triel said, trying again. "What happened in the intensive care unit?"

"Not now."

"Then when?"

The commander said nothing as she pretended to direct all of her attention on the flight course, green eyes hard set on the projected readouts.

"Gods," Triel mumbled, clumsily sitting back down in the nav chair.

"Zopramine headache?"

"I guess," she said, massaging her temples.

"There's a caffeine booster in the medkit."

Triel didn't want to give up on the conversation, but more pressing matters, especially her splitting headache, trumped her desire.

Out of the corner of her eye, the Healer noticed Jetta watching her as she self-administered the caffeine booster.

"Did that help?" Jetta asked.

"A little. It took the edge off," Triel said.

Exhausted, the Healer rested her head against the seatback, trying to convince herself that all would be solved once they got to Algar. But in her heart she knew that was far from true.

(How can a Solitary Prodgy and a telepath of unknown origin survive?)

"I'm starting the final approach," Jetta said, guiding their stealth fighter through the planet's upper atmosphere to avoid the orbital station's automated sweeps.

Even though Triel had never been to Iyo Kono, she knew of its reputation. The exterior structures looked like any other dingy cantina and fuel station rotating over a central module, and to most travelers, they wouldn't know any different. However, those with

104

enough cash, and the right motivation, could discover the station's dark secret.

"I used to think Fiorah was the worst place in the galaxy," Jetta said as she initialized the deceleration process and pulled down the visor to her helmet. Twin locking clamps secured their vessel in position as armored commando units and a man clad in a sterile white lab gown came down the portal tube to meet them. "But at least Fiorah doesn't pretend to be anything but what it is."

"Put on that jumpsuit," Jetta said, pointing to the locker. "There's an extra helmet in the rear compartment. Follow my lead, okay?"

Triel tried to conceal the worry in her voice. "Why all the muscle?"

"Human rights advocates occasionally stop by," she replied coolly. "Don't worry—it's a lot of show, but I wouldn't test them."

Jetta dropped the ramp and motioned for Triel to stay in the cockpit.

"Be careful," the Healer whispered.

Flipping on the external cams, Triel watched the two commando units, decked out with tactical gear from head to toe, meet Jetta at the bottom of the ramp. Everything from the trexium-plated exoskeleton and embedded mini-missiles to optic relays mounted on metal faceplates warned of their capabilities. The Alliance military used the same technology, but not to the same extreme. From what Jetta had told her, the soldiers inside the superskins rarely left their suits—if ever—once fitted. Of all the strange customs on Iyo Kono, that one struck Triel as the most bizarre.

A man, impeccably groomed and manicured, stepped out from behind the commandos. "Welcome to Iyo Kono," he said. "My name is Oshiro, and I'm here to assess your needs and verify your passport."

Triel shifted in her seat. The man's amalgam of features and sleek white gown, fitted to the cuff, unsettled her in ways she couldn't rationalize.

Jetta handed Oshiro two passports, which he scanned with the underside of his wrist.

Where did she get those? She didn't have those when we left Alliance territory, the Healer realized. *Unless she acquired them while we were docked on the outpost...*

Triel didn't dare think about what lengths Jetta might have gone to obtain them.

"Amelia Wallace—this is quite the surprise. Has Mr. Wallace accompanied you?" Oshiro asked.

"Edgar," Jetta called, waving her down.

Triel stepped into view, fully outfitted from head to toe.

Oshiro bowed. "Mr. Wallace, your reputation precedes you. This is quite the honor. I promise you full anonymity."

"We just need to refuel," Jetta said. "Then we'll be on our way."

"But your ship suffered damages," Oshiro said, pointing to the sizzling forward shield array. "I could have that fixed at a very nice price while you tour our facility. I'll do it for 2,000 ruthens."

Jetta cursed through their headset com, but made no outward sign of her frustration. Even though neither of them wanted to spend any more time on Iyo Kono than they had to, fixing the repairs now would save them time.

"I have credit with the Bank of Shiera—will that work?" Jetta said.

So that's where she hides her military earnings, Triel thought, smiling behind the protection of the visor. *A masked account on one of the Alliance protectorate worlds with easily transferrable credit. Brilliant.*

"Of course." Oshiro grinned, revealing a mouthful of perfectly symmetrical teeth as bright white as his gown. "Please—come with me."

Reluctantly, Jetta and Triel followed Oshiro and his armored commandos back through the portal tube into the reception gallery. Crisp white walls and floors, devoid of even a single fleck of dust or dirt, housed a variety of geometric furniture. Everything, from the light fixtures to the orientation of the holographic clocks, centered around the video projection in the middle of the room.

"This is where we greet all of our prospective clients," Oshiro said. Several masked individuals sat far apart from each other, watching the video with concentrated interest.

They're all human, Triel thought, sensing their biorhythms. *None of this feels right...*

The introductory message, already in progress when they entered the gallery, continued on despite their interruption.

"The possibilities are endless," the female narrator said. "We are not trying to change you. We are trying to best represent on the outside how you feel on the inside."

Oh Gods, Triel thought, looking nervously at Jetta. *She'll never stand for this.*

Hostesses with unnaturally smooth skin served colorful cocktails and neat little appetizers as the narrator made the final pitch.

"With your financial investment in our facilities, we can offer the life you've always dreamed of."

Jetta turned to Oshiro. "We've had a long journey, and we are familiar with Iyo Kono. Is there any way we can just get a room while the repairs are made?"

"Yes, of course," he said with a bow.

Oshiro lead them out of the gallery to the heart of the station, where hundreds of pavilions encased in curved, glass-block windows fanned out against a soothing garden backdrop. Animated waterfalls cascaded from several points along the video skyline, converging into shimmering pool. As they passed by the translucent waters, Triel saw tiny red and yellow striped fish swimming amongst the aquatic opal flowers.

Beautiful, she thought, but then stopped herself. The creators of Iyo Kono had purposely fused organic design with the cold sterility of modern technology. *As if they wanted to convince their clients that all of this is sanctioned by the laws of nature.*

"As you know, Mr. and Mrs. Wallace," Oshiro said, "our main clientele are humans, but we are not exclusive. This is a place of rebirth for all."

Triel automatically pulled the jumpsuit tighter around her body as her eyes surfed the crowd. White-gowned technicians greeted customers outside nameless clinics while identical smooth-skinned hostesses escorted clients by wheelchairs or hovercart. Most patients, immobilized and sedated with painkillers, bore fresh scars that ran the length of their bodies. The few still limping through the gardens were bandage-wrapped and trailed by attendants carrying intravenous fluids and vials of serum.

Despite her helmet's air filter or the perfumed air from the rose gardens, Triel detected the pungent odor of synthetic hormones and sterilization fluids. When they passed the open door of one clinic, the smell of cauterized flesh wafted out and she nearly gagged. But more than chemicals and medical waste, the place reeked of desperation, a neediness that hung over the place like a wet blanket.

Triel hiked up her shoulders. *This place isn't safe for either of us, but especially not a Healer.*

"Look at me! Look at me!" someone screamed.

Triel turned her head to find a woman pawing at her face as medical technicians tried to discourage her from touching the surgical site. Puffy scars crowded her hairline, and her artificial nose and lips, plumped up and bright pink from the grafting, looked cartoonish in their size.

What is she? Triel thought, unable to visually discern her species after the extensive reconstructive work.

"I'm beautiful!" the woman cried. Several other clients laughed and cheered, but Oshiro quickly steered them away from the commotion.

"I must say, I am surprised and delighted by your visit," he said as they walked by a clinic displaying vat-grown flesh in the window. "Especially you, Mrs. Wallace—you were so vocal against our facility at the Summit."

Jetta's anger, already ripe in the Healer's mind, became a pulsating heat. But, to her credit, the commander muted her emotions before selecting her words. "Nothing is ever absolute in this universe, is it, Mr. Oshiro?"

Oshiro smiled but his slanted brows stayed fixed on his forehead. "As you are famous for saying, Mrs. Wallace, 'we must keep open minds and open hearts if we are to truly come together.'"

"I just want to know what you do with all the leftover parts," Jetta said, pointing at a clinician with a cart full of red biohazard bags.

Oshiro's smile didn't break, even as the worker headed towards a faceless building guarded by commando units. "I don't understand what you're saying."

"The leftover parts you cut off your clients," Jetta emphasized as the commandos allowed the clinician passage. "Surely you must do something with all that human waste."

"We don't consider it waste," was all Oshiro offered.

After traveling through another ornate garden, the trio reached a building with "New Beginnings Hotel" written above the automated doors in soft blue holographics. Every last decoration or piece of furniture served multiple functions. Triel watched as a hotel attendant transformed a chair into a lift for patient wearing dual leg immobilizers.

What have these people done to themselves?

"The repairs on your starcraft could take up to seven hours," Oshiro said. "I will book you in our best accommodations next to our dining hall at no charge."

"A competent mechanic can do those repairs in three," Jetta replied.

"Mrs. Wallace, I realize you've had a long journey, especially since you've been relegated to a military fighter. My mechanics will do their best, I assure you, and you'll be up and running in no time."

In light of Oshiro's subtle warning to report them to the Alliance, Jetta kept her mouth shut, at least until he showed them to their room. After Oshiro left, Jetta checked and rechecked for any bugs before letting loose a string of expletives in her native tongue.

"Who are Edgar and Amelia?" Triel whispered as Jetta threw the bed covers on the ground and pulled the mattress off the frame.

Finally satisfied, Jetta removed her helmet, dark auburn hair falling around her shoulders. Triel rarely saw her with her hair down, and she found herself staring. Not a second later, though, the commander had pulled it back into a tight ponytail.

"Edgar was an engineer I met on our last stop, and Amelia was his wife," Jetta said. "He gave me supplies, including their passports, to help our mission. But I didn't know he and his wife had such a reputation."

"They must have been pretty outspoken human rights advocates. Oshiro is planning something."

"I know, I sensed it too," Jetta said, lifting up one end of the couch. "Hopefully he can be bought out. Or else he's going to have to meet *me*."

Both of them jumped a little when the door chimed. Jetta motioned for Triel to stay back as she refitted her helmet and opened the door a crack.

"Yes?" she said.

"Hi—my name is Lau. I'm the hotel's liaison. I saw that you have just arrived and wanted to offer you my services."

Through the slitted opening, Triel saw that Lau had undergone invasive cosmetic surgery right down to the marrow of his bones. Though his biorhythm read as distinctly human, his entire structure had been altered to resemble the furry form of a Wopporite.

"No thank you," Jetta said. She tried to shut the door, but Lau stuck his foot—crafted into a hoof—into the crack.

"Please, hear me out. I was like you once—hiding behind a human mask, unable to travel, get a real job or own any property. But I found peace here on Iyo Kono. The aestheticians here are renowned throughout the galaxy for their reconstructive procedures. You can be anything you want!"

Jetta grabbed Lau and pulled him into the room, using his body to slam the door shut. "You're human, not a Wopporite! Why would you do this to yourself?"

"Hey, *chak* you. You try growing up in a relocation camp and then give me your leftist, free-world *gorsh-shit!*"

And then Triel felt it—Jetta slipped, her entire essence pulled down into Lau's mind without either of their consent, absorbing his lifetime in the blink of the eye. Even as the Healer grabbed Jetta and pulled her off, she felt her friend's anger expanding at an exponential rate. While Lau fumbled to understand what happened, Triel did everything she could to hold Jetta back.

"It's not his fault. It's not your fault," Triel whispered, pressing both hands against her friend's chest. Concentrating on Jetta's pounding heart, the Healer infused her own sense of calm into the commander, but to no avail. Every beat fueled a relentless, seismic rage, building upon the sense of violation. "It feels like an assault, I know, but it was an accident."

"He doesn't deserve his skin," Jetta whispered back, wrapping her hands around Triel's wrist.

"*Chakking* Deadskins," Lau spat. He was smart enough to make a quick exit, his tail barely escaping the door as it slammed behind him.

"Let it go, Jetta," Triel said, tearing off her own helmet. She tried to remove Jetta's, but the commander shouldered Triel away.

"What do you want me to do?" Jetta said, tossing off her own helmet, eyes ablaze. Triel winced as Jetta slammed her fist against the wall. "I don't want these people inside me!"

Not knowing what else to do, Triel gave in to instinct. She pulled Jetta close and kissed her, reaching beyond the softness of her lips and through her white hot anger to the complex threads of her emotions.

"What are you doing?" Jetta cried, but Triel didn't let go so easily this time. There was something more there, something inside Jetta that she had never experienced in all their mergings, and she had to know what it was. Invisible fingers of electricity traced her spine as the Healer wrapped her arms around Jetta and inhaled her breath.

"Please, stop!" Jetta spun away, breaking Triel's hold.

Blushing, Triel backed off. "Jetta—I thought that—" But she stopped there.

Jetta isn't mad, she realized. An entirely different feeling radiated from her friend's mind, but as soon as Triel tried to home in on it, Jetta shuffled it behind her psionic guard, not leaving a hint of emotion exposed.

"I was just trying to help," Triel said. "I care about you, you know."

This time Jetta turned away, cheeks bright red as she busied herself with straightening her uniform and checking her equipment. "Look, Lau will be back, and this time Oshiro will have an excuse to detain us," she said, her hands shaking and her voice unsteady. "We need to go."

Triel swallowed the hot lump in her throat. *Did I make a wrong move? Does Jetta not feel anything for me?*

Memories of all the late-night visits and shy smiles from the commander made her reconsider. *I know that's not true,* she thought. What she felt was undeniable. But then why did Jetta turn so cold when she tried to reciprocate any kind of affection?

Well, if nothing else, at least the shock of the kiss broke her anger.

The Healer sighed, resolving to set aside the issue but not let it go. "I noticed two alternate exits on the way in."

"Me too. I also saw that their primary energy source is on a Tirsin grid," Jetta said, picking their helmets up off the floor and returning the Healer's. "We just need to create a big enough short and the entire station will go down for about three minutes until the backups kick over."

"Yes, but won't that affect the gravity wells?"

Jetta walked over to the nearest lounge chair and played with the remote. The chair flattened out and illuminated, hovering off of the ground. Two white panels flickered to life, ready to display vital sign readings. "We can ride on this."

"That looks like a stretcher," she said as the commander steered it behind the protection of the bed.

Jetta raised a brow. "This isn't a hotel."

After breaking apart the overhead light fixture and bed frame for parts, Jetta bent and shaped the metal. But as impressive as her strength appeared, the Healer noted her heavy breathing and deliberate movements.

She's exhausted, Triel thought, but the observation didn't satisfy her instincts.

Pale and sweaty, Jetta pulled the back paneling off the butt of her firearm and reversed the feed. She routed the wires from the light fixture into the gun and through a wall socket, then secured it with the metal from the bed frame.

"Stand back," Jetta warned, shoving her helmet back on.

Triel took cover behind the bed and on top of the stretcher as Jetta hit the firing pin and dove down next to her. A series of explosions threw sparks across the room, but before the sirens could reach full volume, the power shut down.

Once the gravity generators failed and lights went out, terror took hold.

Oh Gods, Triel panicked, remembering the similar sensations of cryosleep. *Darkness. Floating—*

—I'm going to Fall—

"Hey, I'm right here," Jetta said, helping the Healer find her grips on the stretcher. The commander's hand lingered on hers a second longer than normal. "You're okay."

Surprised by the pull of her friend's words and the warmth of her touch, Triel relaxed. "Thanks."

With one hand Jetta guided the stretcher to the door to their room. After prying it opened, she navigated them through the dark corridor.

"Twenty meters, then right," Triel said, but she knew she didn't have to tell Jetta. Even before her military training, Jetta always memorized every detail of her surroundings, something her sister said she had been doing since their days on Fiorah.

Screams and cries of the frightened patients echoed down the corridor as they hovered in midair, the soft blue light of the undercarriage the only thing visible in the weightless dark.

"Commandos will be protecting our ship," Jetta said as they cruised through the gardens.

Something slimy slapped her helmet. Triel reached up and touched a fish flailing about in zero gravity.

"What are you going to do about them?" Triel asked as bubbles of water broke across her uniform. Even if Jetta hadn't sacrificed her firearm, she still wouldn't have been much of a match against the armored mechs.

"The only thing I can do."

"Jetta... that isn't a good idea," Triel said, not hiding her concern as they left the gardens and passed through the gallery. Slowing the stretcher as they came to the portal tube, Jetta caught the front bumper on the wall of the narrow passageway, jarring their grips. "There has to be another way."

No sooner had the words left her mouth when the commandos' exoskeletons came into view, lit with lines of orange, their missile tips flared and auxiliary firearms charged. Ion-static crackled in the distance.

What is she doing? Triel thought as she sensed Jetta extending her psionic reach.

"Trust me," Jetta muttered.

The Healer winced as Jetta let go, her mind stretching beyond her own body and into the two soldiers manning the mechs. Knowing Jetta's capabilities, Triel feared the worst. *Will she dump her unwanted emotions or make their worst nightmares come to life and tear them apart from the inside out?*

Psionic vibrations hit Triel like a melody inverted into teeth-grinding discord, but just as she raised her guard, the sensation ceased. Triel looked to see the two commandos powering down their firearms as they stepped aside and let them through.

What just happened?

The Healer kept the mechs in her sights as she carefully extended her own awareness, but she felt nothing from them other than a rhythmic, soothing calm.

Guiding the stretcher up the ramp and into the belly of their ship, Jetta activated the internal gravity wells to the fighter just as the lights to the station cycled back on.

"We need to get out of here before the loading clamps reengage," Jetta said, running to the cockpit and strapping herself into the pilot's chair.

"They didn't make any repairs," Triel said as she assumed the co-pilot's seat and checked the onboard readings.

"But they did refuel us so they could fish through the system," Jetta grumbled. "Hold on."

Jetta pulled back hard on the ship's controls, yanking the fighter out of the clamps and sending them spiraling off the loading dock and into Iyo Kono's traffic portal. As the station's rotational axis came back to life, Jetta banked hard to port, narrowly missing a head-on collision with the outer module.

"I'm making the final jump—we can't wait any longer. Hold on," Jetta said, directing the fighter toward the planet to buy them some time. The solar shield dimmed to protect their eyes as the nose of the ship flared orange against the atmosphere.

"What are those?" Triel said pointing to the radar.

Jetta enhanced the view on the screen. Four black starcraft with Iyo Kono's crest flew in attack formation on their flight path. "Vipers, star class. Don't worry—we'll make the jump before they get in range."

115

"But the nav computer is offline—"

"Let's hope I can remember the coordinates."

With a firm grip on the armrests, Triel watched Jetta make the calculations manually for their final jump. Even one hundred-thousandth of a degree off could land them in a planet's molten core or the burning center of a star—or someplace worse. Jetta once told her that veteran pilots claimed poorly calculated jumps could land a person in one of the infinite interdimensions of space-time. Though such a miscalculation would more likely tear their ship apart, rumors spoke of ghostly creatures that preyed on the poor souls who happened to jump their ship into limbo. Either way, Triel didn't want to find out.

As the ship jumped through the two connected holes in space-time, Triel's body pulled apart, her mind whipped across the stars through a sea of kaleidoscope colors. When she opened them, she gasped. "Algar."

The blue planet seemed to be welcoming them in, its billowy white clouds wreathing lush, mountainous continents.

"It's beautiful," Jetta whispered, enhancing the view on the secondary screen.

Triel immediately looked to the southern continent. Even from their high orbit she could see scars of the Dominion's invasion cutting across the land.

"It's been so long…"

She was surprised to feel Jetta's hand on her shoulder. "Hey… sorry. I know it's hard being here."

Triel shook her head. "We need to get some answers; it's the only way."

"Yeah, we do," Jetta said as she stabbed at the computer interface. The motherboard beeped, not accepting the new data. "Although this might be our final destination if we can't make repairs. It's not even the engines I'm worried about—it's the goddamn computer. We're flying blind. And I can't get the gravity reactors online for the descent."

Jetta cursed in Fiorahian but stopped, resting her head against her chair. Closing her eyes, Triel felt her friend's thoughts temporarily detach as she sifted and sorted through memories.

"What's wrong, Jetta?"

Jetta's mind felt out of reach and her words sounded equally distant. "Sometimes I don't know what's real anymore. Sometimes I can't tell between what I've experienced and what I've taken from other people. Do you ever have that happen?"

Triel nodded. "Yes. I used to have the rest of my tribe to help me purge unwanted essences, but I don't have that luxury now."

Resorting to nervous habit, Triel massaged the webbing between her fingers as she continued her thought. "It was always the tortured souls, the worst memories and nightmares, that seemed to get under my skin. It's hard enough living with your own pain, let alone someone else's."

Jetta turned away from her. "My perceptions are only getting stronger. I used to have to try to take knowledge from other people, but now it seems like I just get pulled right into their heads. Sometimes I can't control what I'm taking anymore. I'm sorry you had to see me—you know—the way I was with Lau."

"I understand what happened, Jetta. But those commandos—you did something different with your talents—you put them at peace. That's something new, something good."

Jetta shrugged. "Kinda. I gave them one of my memories to make them forget their objective."

"Where did you learn that?"

"Earth, of all places" Jetta laughed. "In the jaws of a giant wolf."

Triel didn't want to say anything—not yet. *There's something else Jetta is trying to tell me, but doesn't know how.*

"I'm sorry," Jetta said, her face suddenly serious. "You're the last person I should complain to."

117

"I'm glad you can talk to me," Triel whispered. She wanted to reach out to her, but the intensity in Jetta's eyes made her rethink her action.

"Look," Jetta said, facing her squarely. Triel wasn't sure, but she thought she saw the beginnings of tears. "I want you to know something. Whatever happens to me, I only want what's best for you, and for my brother and sister. I want to do what's right, but sometimes it's hard to tell the difference between what's right and what's smart. Do you get it?"

Those are tears.

Sensing the Healer's realization, Jetta turned back to her controls and dipped the nose of the ship toward the planet. "This is going to be rough. Hold on."

"Wait—Jetta—what do you mean?" Triel tried to ask, but she could barely hear herself above the thunderous noise of the ship's shields reacting with the atmosphere. Red and yellow flames engulfed their starcraft as the onboard computer warned against imminent forward shield failure. Triel tried to reach Jetta, but the acceleration forces pinned her to her seat, plastering her internal organs to her spine.

As breathing became harder and harder, white hot panic lit up every nerve. *I can't survive this descent.*

With considerable effort she turned her head, squinting against the blinding flames. Jetta's form, somewhat blurred, appeared odd. She tried to call out again, but she had no voice.

What is that?

A shadow thing embedded in the commander's skin uncoiled itself from around her body like a snake. Bound to Jetta, but with gnarled fingers like the roots of a plant, it slithered toward the Healer in midair, its dead, hollow eyes evoking a terror that stripped her down to her most primitive instincts. Trapped, Triel found herself prey to a beast with immeasurable hungers.

No—it can't be—

118

It answered back, its voice a cacophony of sound that resolved into something old and guttural, as if it arose from the belly of the Great Beast itself. And as the rest of the starcraft vanished from view, the stress of the descent robbing her of consciousness, its words burned her with their rage, warning her of her own demise.

***

It took Jaeia twenty minutes and a little bit of extrasensory coercion to finally convince Dr. DeAnders to allow her to sit with her brother in the Division Lockdown lab. The condition of the Grand Oblin's body had deteriorated, and they had resuscitated him twice since Jahx had last woken up. Still, Jaeia would have done anything to be with him right then, even if it had meant fully engaging her talents to get past the medical staff.

Jetta and Triel are missing, she thought, sensing their tunes, distant and muddled, in the far reaches of her mind. *And the agents supervising the Sleepers reported that Reht was aboard the* Ultio *when it exploded, and his crew are unaccounted for. With Tidas Razar in critical condition and Unipoesa a fugitive, who's left?*

In all her life, Jaeia had never felt so alone, or the weight of the world so heavy on her shoulders. Sighing, she took Jahx's hand in hers. "Things are bad, brother. CCO Wren has taken temporary custody of the Ministerial position since Razar hasn't gotten better. He's trying to hold the General Assembly together, but many of them have been swayed by Victor to join the new Republic. We don't know how he's doing it, but he's slowly draining the Alliance from within its own government. If we don't have the support of the civilians, then what are we fighting for?"

Jaeia straightened up in her chair, concentrating on every word. "I'm supposed to keep the Fleet together, protect what territory we have left. Defensive tactics are my specialty, but now is the time for something wild—some crazy plan to bail us out that only Jetta could come up with. Remember the time she started a fight with the other

119

children so she could steal a shockwand from the laborminder? Killing rats with it kept us fed all those months when Yahmen cut off our rations. I thought she was insane, but in the end, she was right."

"Well, at least I've been promoted to captain," Jaeia chuckled. "Jetta's going to be pissed that I outrank her now."

Closing her eyes, Jaeia listened to the metronomic heartbeat in the background as her brother's borrowed body lay motionless on the exam table. "I'm scared, Jahx. It was never supposed to be like this. You promised me that it would always be the three of us, that we would go everywhere together, that I would never be alone."

Jaeia squeezed his hand. "Yeah, well, she's run away again and I don't know where you are, so it's just me. It's always me. I'm always the one left behind."

As Jaeia turned to go, she felt his hand on her wrist, and she whipped around.

"Jahx?" she said, leaning over. Except for the shallow rise and fall of his chest, his limbs and body remained flaccid and unmoving. The machines attached to him never skipped a beat.

Jahx?

The room lights dimmed, and the monitors alerted in flashing lights and high-pitched beeping.

Jahx—is that you?

Leaning farther in, Jaeia tentatively placing a hand on his shoulder as she listened, holding her breath and searching the dark features of his face for any sign of movement. *Are you there?*

Crystalline walls, erected by the illusion of separation, came tumbling down. Before she could arrest herself, Jaeia fell away from the cold sterility of the lab, away from her body, plunging into a separate realm. Sensations and images tore apart, then came back together in a new arrangement. A dry heat swallowed her whole, and the air, dusty and thin, made her chest feel tight with every breath.

Fiorah.

*Back under the old couch, Jaeia became aware of the throb of
her feet and the ache of her chin. The evening light filtered through
the slats in the boarded up windows, illuminating the daring rat that
chanced running across the carpet. Black Lokus flies buzzed in her
ears, tickling her face as they sampled the dried blood on her chin,
oblivious to anything but their meal.*

*Fear of the junkie, still fresh in her heart, kept from leaving her
hiding place.*

He's waiting for me. It's him, he's near, with his bloodied,
ragged stumps, wanting revenge for what I did.

*She couldn't move, though the cramp in her neck and back
became increasingly hard to ignore.*

*The floorboards creaked. Shuffling steps came from just outside
the apartment.*

Oh Gods, please, I didn't mean to hurt him! *she thought, curling
tighter as someone tried the front door.*

*The handle jiggled, then twisted. Silence. Too tense to access
her talents, Jaeia's mind played out the junkie, his hands coming
apart like rotten fruit, tearing into her with broken teeth.*

"Jaeia?"

*Soft footsteps padded across the carpet, stopping in front of the
couch.*

It's over, *she thought, heartbeat amplifying in her head. She
squeezed together even tighter, too afraid to look up.* My family is
dead, and the only person left to get me is—

"We were so worried about you."

*Two small hands circled her wrists and pulled her hands away
from her face. She opened one eye, taking in Jahx's clear blue gaze
and outstretched hands.*

"Jahx!" she exclaimed, tearing up.

*"Come on, it's gross under there. Galm said that's where the
other renters let their cat pee."*

121

*With a grunt she wormed her way out from under the couch,
hair and clothes a matted mess of blood and debris. He kept a hand
on her, helping her over to the ottoman.*

*"Gods," she said, hugging him tightly, "I thought you were all
killed."*

*Jahx hugged her back. "You worry too much. We're too short to
get in anyone's firing range, remember?"*

*Jaeia wouldn't let him go, even when he tried to pull back.
"Where's everyone else?"*

*"Jetta went the long way home with Galm and Lohien just in
case. Lohien lost two pigeons in the fight. I think she'll lose the
coop."*

"No," Jaeia said. "Does that mean...?"

*She didn't have to say the rest. It had been Jahx's longstanding
fear that they would end up in Yahmen's mines, but she had never
thought it would come so soon. Only four years old, she and her
siblings weren't even big enough to haul topitrate loads like the
other children.*

"Jaeia," Jahx said, holding her hands in his.

*Old sorrow worked its way into her heart. In the next breath he
would promise her that everything was going to be okay, that they
wouldn't work in the mines very long, and that one day they'd get off
of Fiorah, get away from the junkies, the streets, Yahmen and the
awful heat, and they'd be able to have a real family again, without
being worried about food, shelter and basic survival.*

He's going to reassure me that where one of us goes, we all go,
and that I'll never be alone, *she remembered.*

*But he didn't this time. Something changed. In the corner of her
eye the edges of her vision constantly formed and re-formed, as if
someone was struggling to keep the memory alive.*

*"Jaeia—you have to stay strong, for me." His voice was
different, older, as was the look in his eyes. "Something terrible has
found Jetta, and it's growing, clouding my abilities and preventing
me from coming back. I don't know what is going to happen next,*

and I can't protect you right now. All I know is that you have to find him—Josef Stein—before it is too late. He is a prisoner like so many others. Trust your instincts, and trust yourself. You're not alone."

Jaeia grabbed Jahx by the shoulders. "What do you mean? Where is he? Why?"

"Run, Jaeia," Jahx whispered, terror bleaching his eyes.

The apartment quaked, lights shattering as pictures rattled off the wall. Radiant sunlight disappeared, replaced by acid-bright light with no discernible source. Rats squealed and scattered as slick tentacles and circuitry uprooted the carpet, overturning furniture and routing into the walls. Something red oozed from the tiles and the bricks, and decay singed her nose.

Jahx's color paled, his eyes turned white and hollow, and his hair thinned until he was bald. From his open mouth spilled wires and tubes, and his limbs braided into a web of fleshy gears and wet circuit boards. Jaeia screamed, pulling her hands away and backing into the slick yellow wall behind her.

There was nowhere to run as the pulsating walls closed in around her. And then from the shadow came the sound that turned her blood cold. Twisted, tortured metal and labored breathing—the thing with the burning red eye. Spiny legs stepped into view, bringing with them the massive undercarriage with its human torso and head. He smiled at her, metallic teeth grinding, producing a piercing shriek that tore into her bones.

He reached for her with his pinchers, his laughter grating like rust on rust—

"Captain!"

Jaeia snapped to and fell backward. Someone caught her by the armpits and held her upright as she regained her balance.

"Where am I—Jahx?" she sputtered, shocked by the coldness and sterility of the room, and the mélange of smells from the antiseptics and intravenous fluids.

Regaining her awareness, Jaeia found the team of medical staff hovering over Jahx, running to and from him and the surrounding machines. One of the doctors stood over her, manually checking her pulse and scanning her with a handheld. For a second his features distorted, half of his face buried under a bloody mess of metalwork before righting itself again.

"Everything's okay, Captain," he said. "The team is just making some adjustments to his electrolytes—he had another metabolic episode."

Heart still pounding, it took her several seconds to respond. "I made contact—he's still alive."

"Your body is reading under considerable strain as well, Sir. I can't recommend you make contact with him again until you are both in better health."

Before she could give the doctor a piece of her mind, DeAnders stepped in. He pulled her aside, up to the observatory deck where they could speak in private.

"Jaeia, I'm not going to lie to you. The Grand Oblin's body cannot handle Jahx's psionic signature much longer," he said. "We're working on a solution, but right now I'm going to have to ask you to stop trying to make any contact with your brother, or you risk both their lives."

He left her standing there as he rejoined the rest of the team still working on her brother. Despite the flurry of activity below, the soundproofed observatory only offered the gentle air flow of the overhead vents to break the suffocating silence.

"Jahx," she whispered, pressing the palms of her hands against the window. Bowing her head, she curled her hands into fists.

Don't cry, she told herself. Not now, not after Jahx had risked everything to talk to her.

Exhaling all the air from her lungs, Jaeia fixed the sleeves of her uniform, and after one last look, returned to her post.

CHAPTER III

Rain was unusual on Aeternyx, and for some reason he felt like that was a bad sign. Reht pulled up the collar of his jacket against the wet chill as he checked out the streets. The headlights of hovercars passed over them as Femi huddled next to him, pressing her face into his chest, shaking and holding him tightly.

Breathing through his mouth to minimize the stench of wet garbage, he dragged Diawn's prize through the alleyway toward the shortcut that would take them to the bounty board. Eyes in the shadows flicked over them as they ran through the dark passageway, ignoring the warnings the homeless slurred from beneath their cardboard shelters.

I'm doing the right thing, he told himself. The only the thing, really. He had to nail the bounty—so much was at stake. The money—his crew—

Shandin.

Femi must have sensed his intentions. When he found the familiar double-plated metal door illuminated by its solitary yellow light, she dug her beaded nails into his chest, protesting with wild gestures and fierce words that made the veins on her forehead stand out.

"Hey—hey!" Reht said, wrestling her into submission. He kissed her cheek tenderly, tasting her tears. "Everything's gonna be alright. Just trust me."

She tilted her head in confusion, her blue eyes pleading with him as he greeted the doorman.

"Let me in. I have to settle some business with Ash," Reht said.

"Name?"

"Reht Jagger."

Reht couldn't be sure, but he thought the man snickered as he opened up the door.

Holding Femi by the upper arm, the dog-soldier captain moved through the crowded bounty board. Fortunately for him, the patrons stayed distracted by the fight on the killing floor, where two Ka'vers sliced each other up with their sharp tails and spiny knuckles.

126

Must be another big purse.

The short albino was waiting for him next to the vacant bar with a menacing grin. He nodded to Reht before disappearing toward his back office.

Femi started to protest again, but Reht squeezed as hard as he could, bringing more tears to her eyes.

"You look like *gorsh-shit,* Jagger," Ash commented as Reht shoved Femi through the doorway. She crouched down in the corner, weeping as Ash looked her over and stroked his holstered machete. "Interesting…"

A young, half-naked girl identical to the one Reht had seen during their first visit sat filing her nails on Ash's desk. When she spotted Femi, she batted her long eyelashes with silent contempt.

That can't be the same puppet, he thought, trying not to be obvious about looking her over. There were no bruises, no scratches—at least not yet. *Must be a newer version.*

"Where'd you find a Qua'ti?" the albino asked.

"Come again?" Reht said, unsure of what he meant.

"She's one of the tribespeople from—Gods, what is that planet's name? Ularu, I think—southern continent. Rainforest monkeys," he explained.

At first Reht wasn't sure if Ash wanted her, but then he saw the predatory gleam in his eyes, the raw hunger seething from every white pore for the virginal, unmanufactured beauty. The puppet noticed it too, and her contempt turned into grave concern.

Ah, poor kid. She's gonna end up being just another one of Ash's used-up puppets wandering the streets, looking for work in a dead-end place like Suba House. Some part of him felt badly for the young girl as she played with her thong and bra straps, provocatively bending over the desk in a fruitless attempt to divert Ash's attention.

Reht played his hand. "Here's to business, friend: Diawn's working with a man called Shandin, collecting and shipping Deadskins."

"Shandin," Ash repeated, his blood-red eyes looking him over as his hand relaxed on his machete. "Where have I heard that name before?"

Calming himself first, he answered in neutral tones. "He's an old dog-soldier that did a lot of cheap work for the Sovereign of the Eeclian Dominion. *Gorsheater* didn't exactly follow the creed."

"Neither do you, Jagger—I know your reputation," Ash said.

Reht played with the bandages on his hands, very aware of the Cobra resting against his skin, the molded grip like snake scales pressed into his hipbone. "She said that somebody is 'hungry' for human flesh. She used the word '*lurchin.*' Sounds like a large-scale farming operation.'"

"You think it's the Puritans?"

Reht had already considered that possibility. The Puritans, an extremist sect of Sentient races that banded together when Earth's refugees brought their highly contagious human diseases to the Homeworlds, had done much worse in the past. Using their political and military influences, the hate group kept institutions like the flesh farms, fighting rings, and labor locks well-funded and running. Through more insidious channels they fed the flames of the old-school believers that the Starways would have been much better off without the presence of mankind.

"Could be. Why not ask Shandin yourself?" Reht said, copying the signature he scratched on his arm to a datafile lying on Ash's desk. "Besides, Diawn's just a pawn. If someone's really interested in her, they'd be better off looking into Shandin."

Ash rounded back to his desk and took a seat. Still trying to get his attention, the young puppet made strange mewing sounds and pawed at his shirt. Without so much as a glance, he slapped her across the face. She cried out, stumbling backwards into a filing cabinet and knocking her head against the edge.

"Get down on the floor. Entertain our guests," he growled at her.

Her eyes pled with Reht as she cradled her bloody nose, but he looked away until she crawled off whimpering.

"Is this it?" Ash said.

Reht nodded over to Femi. "More than fair."

Ash laughed. "Come on, Jagger—you know I'm not going to be able to sell this back to the investor. This is thin. I need more. Diawn is too smart to work for some Joe."

Jagger played his last card. "She's a virgin."

"How do you know that?" Ash said, licking his lips.

"'Cause that's the only reason Diawn would have her," Reht said. "She loves to destroy the most beautiful things."

Leaning back in his seat, Ash put his hands on his head and letting his hairy gut hang out over the lip of the desk. Femi started to protest, but the albino put his finger to his lips and flashed the blade of his machete.

Though silent in the face of his weapon, the defiance in her eyes excited Ash. He sprang out of his chair and circled her, running his white fingers across the exposed skin of her back, and her face contorted with revulsion.

Something stirred inside Reht that he hadn't felt so acutely in ages, something that made his legs feel too weak to support his weight. His hands burned, the phantom pain awakening with such vengeance that he winced.

"I'll give you forty percent. And that's being generous," Ash said. He laid the machete's cutting edge against the underside of her chin as he sniffed her neckline, running his yellowed fingernails down her cheek. She squealed, tears streaming down her face as she shivered and whispered what must have been a prayer.

I've done this before; felt this way, he thought, unable to place the familiar feeling.

As Ash loosened the straps of her top, something inside Reht snapped. He tackled the albino, knocking away the machete before taking his thick neck between his hands, squeezing with all his strength. Bucking and kicking him in the shins and thigh, Ash beat him on the shoulders and clawed his face, but Reht only tightened his grip.

(Not again.)

The fat veins on the albino's neck and forehead bulged ominously, his red eyes turning deep crimson as capillaries burst across the sclera. Gurgling, his tongue came to rest outside his mouth. Reht let him fall to the floor with a loud *thunk*. He stared at Ash's body, transfixed by some unseen force.

A clawed hand rested on his shoulder and Femi screamed, her eyes wide with terror. He whipped around to be greeted by two silver eyes and a mouthful of wet, sharp canines.

"Holy Mukal," he exclaimed, clutching his chest. "Hey, don't do that, mate."

Mom bared his teeth as he inspected the albino's lifeless body.

"I couldn't do it, mate," Reht said as he re-bandaged his hands. "I don't know why, but I couldn't let him have this one."

Growling, Mom unfastened the hood shielding the rest of his head. He snapped his jaw at Femi, and she backed into the corner, covering her face with her arms as she yelled at Reht in her native tongue.

"It's okay," Reht said, stooping next to her.

Is it? a voice within questioned. He lost his cool—his mind—in killing the albino. Ash had friends, connections, and it was going to put his crew in serious danger.

What is Femi to me anyway? Just another trade.

But the way Ash touched her—the way he looked at her—it awakened something rank inside him, something outside his field of understanding that left in its wake a hollow aftertaste of guilt. All he had known in that moment was that he had to do something *this time*—whatever that meant—and at that moment it was killing Ash.

The programming. Reht thought. He remembered Sebbs' words: *"I can feel it. The thoughts I have—these urges. They're not me. I don't want to get high anymore—my pleasure comes in deals, dangerous ones, ones that will get me killed. That's my high now."*

The dog-soldier captain flexed his hands. *Not now. Chak the Alliance. Keep your cool, keep it together.*

"It's okay, Femi—this is why I called up my crew," he said, wiping the sweat from his forehead and putting on his best smile. "I wanted my first mate to keep a tail on me but not interfere in negotiations. I thought Ash would be in a better mood without my clawed friend, but things don't always turn out the way you want 'em to, right?"

"Look," Reht said, seeing the disapproval on Mom's face. "I know I said I'd play it smooth, but the guy creeped me out. I made my move and it's done now. Let's just find the safe and get the hell out of here. Is everyone else in position?"

Mom's skepticism remained, but that didn't stop the giant Talian from following the lead of his captain. With a nod, he indicated that the crew was ready.

"Alright, we don't have long before his cronies figure us out. Let's shake."

Rummaging through the desk, Reht pulled out drawers and checked for hidden traps under the feet. Mom assisted his search, tearing the filing cabinets and sockets from the walls and smashing anything that looked big enough to hold a stash. Femi stayed huddled in the corner, her eyes fixed on the giant Talian warrior as she muttered to herself and rubbed her beaded necklace.

"Here," Reht said, dragging an antique steel safe out from behind a broken mirror. Mom took one swipe at it with his claws and the handle and door halved neatly. Inside were stacks of 110s and a few purple lumps of dry methoc.

What a ratchakker, Reht thought, adding up the numbers in his head. Even if he sold the methoc, they'd still be short of the big purse Ash promised. Hopefully, with a little charm and a cut from his own take, he'd be able to placate the crew.

"Let's get out of here," Reht said, stuffing his pockets with as much as he could. Joining Mom at the door, the dog-soldier captain peeked out and made sure the coast was clear. "There's about nine out there, and two watchdogs. Are Ro and Cray ready?"

Mom nodded and then looked back at Femi. Still in the corner, she gestured wildly and spouted harsh words.

Reht shrugged. "I don't know, mate. Might be too much work. Besides, I don't want to give Diawn any more reasons to kill me."

The stink of overripe fruit rotting in the afternoon sun touched his nose.

A Voosik, Reht thought, smelling Ash's henchman coming around the corner toward the office long before his yellow hide was visible under the lights. On their native planet, the sickly sweet stench would attract honey birds, giving Voosiks an easy meal.

"*Chak* me," Reht muttered, trying not to gag. Mom snorted, covering his nose and dropping his claws.

Holding his breath, Reht popped out of the office, trying to walk as casually as possible past the Voosik. The yellow-skinned outerworlder packed more than the usual armaments, carrying two sidearms and a razor baton. His eyes, arranged in threes across his angular skull, stayed on Reht as he strode by.

Keep going. Don't look back.

Making clicking noises with one of his mandibles, the Voosik's nictitating membranes drew back from his eyes to reveal fluorescent, diamond-shaped pupils. Reht shrugged his shoulders, pretending not to understand the warning.

Trailing behind him, Mom kept his face masked by the hood and his exposed claws underneath the sleeves of his disguise. The Voosik sniffed the Talian as he rumbled by but made no move.

Ten seconds. Reht thought. That's how long it would take the Voosik to enter the office and realize what had transpired. He would see the girl—the mess—his boss's dead body. In that moment, Reht would land right in the middle of the bounty board floor, in plain view of all the patrons who would quickly realize their sacrifices had been in vain.

Seven seconds…

132

Reht spotted Ro and Cray in position, bickering on the killing floor.

Good. If those fools are there, that means Bacthar and Tech are waiting outside with a cab, he assured himself. *And Vaugh will provide cover from the rooftops.*

It was still four on eleven inside, but the crew had faced much worse odds, and with Mom on their side they had a huge advantage.

This doesn't feel right. Reht brushed his hand along the hilt of the Cobra, making sure it was still there. His body heat had warmed the steel, but he could feel the cold scales rubbing against his skin.

Three seconds...

Ash wasn't a gang boss and he certainly wasn't a pusher—he was a bounty board operator, a middleman between the hunters and the employers that wanted to remain anonymous. Ash wasn't—shouldn't—be that important. *Then why this rotten feeling?*

He had just turned the corner to the killing floor when Femi let out a scream. The Voosik wailed, alerting the other watchdog guarding the exit.

"Hold it right there," the watchdog said, taking aim at the dog-soldier captain.

Cray bit the guard's hand off as Ro slit his throat with a switchblade. The stunned patrons of the bounty board watched the man slump to the ground, his head pulling back from the gash as fresh blood anointed the killing floor.

"*Ba'sheda!*" the Voosik shouted, running up from behind and whipping his tail at Mom. The Talian warrior raised his arm, letting the momentum of the attacker's blow spear his own appendage on razor-sharp claws. Before the Voosik could react, Mom sliced him down the belly, spilling steaming green intestines onto the tiles.

On the killing floor, the Ka'ver who had won the board raised his hackles and thorns, hissing and drawing his knife as a circle formed around Reht and his crew.

"Hey—we just want out, okay? Nobody else has to get hurt," Reht said, removing the Cobra from his pants.

133

"Pretty boy—you're in a heap of *gorsh-shit* now. Gonna remember your face," the Ka'ver said, licking his lips. "Gonna dine on that face."

Reht had one foot out the front door when Femi came running around the corner. She stopped abruptly when she saw the circle of angry hunters.

"Come on, Cappy!" Ro shouted as he dove into the cab. Bacthar and Tech motioned for him to jump in.

"*Bi me aceustao mi vermesi!*" Femi cried, reaching for Reht as two of the patrons grabbed and fought over her.

With a growl, Mom tried to push him the rest of the way through the door, but he resisted.

"Leave her here and we might call it fair," the Ka'ver said, turning his attention from Reht to the dark-skinned beauty.

Action superseded thought. Reht pulled out the Cobra, firing in rapid succession until he emptied his clip. As the smoke curled from the end of the double barrel, the reality of his deadly aim sunk in. Sentients with sizzling bullet holes through their skulls or vital organs collapsed while the rest of the killing floor contestants dispersed.

Did I—?

No time to think. Two Yumins took aim at him from behind the bar counter, but Reht played against the odds, running out in plain view and tackling Femi from the line of fire. He tumbled with her, dragging her behind an overturned table.

"Just wait," Reht said, picking the bits of glass from her skin as the other dog-soldiers fired at their location. She pressed herself into him, her warm skin heavenly against his body. Smelling her, something inside him supercharged, making him feel invincible.

Instead of waiting for Mom's roar and the wet sound of flesh torn from bone, Reht shot up and ran to the bar, screaming as plasma shots seared his skin. With a wild leap he dove over the counter, slamming one of the Yumins into the wall and cracking his skull.

"*E'tak!*" the other shouted as Reht kicked him in the face, breaking his nose with a loud snap. Mom, who had been busy tearing up the two patrons hiding behind a ruined couch, dropped their shredded bodies and leapt to his captain's side.

Collapsing heavily against the side of the bar, Reht tried to catch his breath as Mom skinned the shrieking Yumin. The stink of gunfire and fresh blood upset his stomach, but he didn't have the energy to vomit.

Femi popped her head over the table and surveyed the area. Carefully, she crawled over to Reht, her words fast and high-pitched as she looked over his wounds. She tried to separate the burnt parts of his shirt from his skin, but he stopped her.

"Hey, leave it—it'll be fine. Chicks dig scars, right baby?" he laughed. He noticed a pack of crumpled smokes on the ground and pulled out a cigarette. To his delight, one of the plasma discharges had left a burning hole in a broken chair. He leaned over and lit his smoke, then took a long, slow drag. "All better now."

Mom stooped down beside him and offered his arms.

"No, mate, I'll walk. Just give me a hand," he said. Before he could reevaluate his request, Mom catapulted him to his feet. Reht wobbled at first, but Mom caught him by the waist.

"Jeezus, Cappy," Ro said as he reentered the bounty board. He whistled when he saw the dismembered, skinned corpses of the Yumins.

"Hey—this ain't good," Cray said, inspecting the slaughter. He pointed to the camera mounted in the corner. "Could be pinned back to us. Gotta burn the whole thing."

"You're always lookin' for an excuse," Reht chuckled. But Cray was right. Better to burn the evidence than let anyone sniff through it.

"Fine. Be quick about it then," Reht said as he hobbled to the cab. Femi latched onto his side, looking back nervously at Ro and Cray, who laughed giddily as they torched the bounty board. Mom, too big to fit inside the cab, hopped on the back and held onto the roof.

"Let's get the hell out of here," Reht shouted, watching the smoke filter out the front door. Hooting and yipping, Ro and Cray ran out of the building and crammed themselves into the back seat as Bacthar hit the accelerator.

"That was a *chakking* riot," Ro snickered as they turned sharply around a corner. "You get the cash, boss?"

Reht opened his jacket. A few stacks had holes burnt through them. "Mom's got the rest. Some methoc too."

Ro and Cray exchanged glances. Tech and Bacthar remained silent.

"There's more, trust me," he added.

"What about her?" Ro said, eyeing Femi.

The young girl squeezed his jacket, pulling as close to Reht and away from the others as possible. Reht debated a moment. The smart thing would be to throw her in the pot with the rest of the money and drugs, but his boys didn't play very nice.

And then she kissed him. Her soft brown lips felt warm against his, her tongue the sweetest thing he had ever tasted. The entire cab hooted and hollered, but he didn't hear them. Her caress ignited his loins, and he forget everything else.

"She's with me," he said, putting an arm around her.

"That ain't enough then, Cappy," Ro said. "I want my cut."

"I promise you'll get yours. Let's just get to the *Wraith*." Reht changed the subject. "Hey, how'd you get the wheels?"

Bacthar looked at him through the rearview mirror. "I asked nicely."

"Right," Reht said, seeing the blood stains on the steering wheel.

They ditched the cab two kilometers from the *Wraith*, scrapping it for parts and, in keeping with the theme of the night, burning the rest.

That's the prettiest girl I've ever seen, he thought when he spotted the rusted, battered hull of his ship docked behind an abandoned warehouse.

"Want me to clean you up, boss?" Bacthar asked as they boarded.

The burns were starting to get to him, but he knew better than to let the rest of the crew see him babied when they just got stiffed.

"Nah. Let's get down to business."

Having been gone, Reht expected to find the ship completely wrecked, but to his surprise he found nothing worse than the usual mess. "Nice work, Mom," he said as he waded through a pile of beer cans. "The place ain't torn apart."

Mom grumbled and started to drag Femi to a holding cell.

"Whoa—whoa!" Reht said, taking her hand. Femi hid behind him, away from his Talian. "She can stay in my den."

He knew the look in Mom's eyes, but he couldn't concede. "Hey, mate, it'll be alright. She ain't gonna do nothin'. 'Sides—I think she likes me," Reht joked as Femi wrapped his arms around her.

Mom just shot him a disapproving look before following Ro and Cray, who were arguing over dibs on the methoc, to the bridge.

"I'll be down in a second," Reht shouted after him as he led Femi to his den. She paused outside before timidly taking a step inside the squalor. Eventually she made her way to his bed and pushed aside his dirty pile of shirts to make herself a space.

"I'll be back. Lots of business. Don't go anywhere, okay?"

She protested when he closed and sealed the door, but she quieted down when the locking mechanism clicked over.

"Hey," he said, grabbing Tech as he swung by. "Where's Vaughn?"

"He beat us back—he's already on the nav."

"Good. Grab Billy and meet us there."

"He's been acting funny," Tech replied, his pointed ears twitching in his nervous habit. "Don't know if I trust him lately."

137

Reht stopped in his tracks. "What do you mean?"

"H-he keeps cycling through his diagnostic modes—can't get him out of it. His specs seem fine to me when I ran a manual, but his automated system keeps resetting the program algorithms and I can't take him offline. At his rate of energy consumption, I'm worried about his central processor overloading."

"Tech—Holy Mukal—in Common, man."

The engineer dangled from the deck upside-down and tried again. "His mechanical systems think he's sick, but it—or I—can't find anything wrong. I don't know where the malfunction is and I can't shut his diagnostic system down, so he's gonna burn out."

"*Chak*," Reht said, chewing on the nub of his fingernail. "Just get him to nav."

"Mom," he said, punching into the wall intercom. "Get us the hell out of here. And then I want everybody to meet in navigations."

A growl proceeded the rumbling of the engines.

Pain, refusing to be ignored, resurfaced in waves as Reht grabbed a handrail to steady himself during liftoff.

"*Chak*," he mumbled, looking at his chest. The fresh hits from the plasma guns invigorated the old, angry wounds Diawn inflicted.

I need to go to medical, he thought. Need interceded. *No—not before I see what's on that chip.*

As he stepped inside navigations, he expected to find Billy Don't spinning on his back wheels or spewing his lubricant across the floor. Instead, the tin can idled quietly in the corner alongside Tech.

"No way. That's the first time I've seen that kid quiet," Reht said as he ducked under the monitors. Chuckling, Bacthar nudged the little Liiker, but didn't get a response.

"Yeah, it's *chakkin'* creepy as all hell," Cray muttered as he crawled up from the weapons pit. Ro hit him in the shoulder, but the play-fighting stopped short of its usual run.

With a grumble, Mom joined the crew, motioning that the ship was on autopilot.

Reht took a deep breath and began. "Alright, well, as you all know, that *ratchak* albino shorted us, but I think I swiped something off of Diawn that will give us more than what we need."

Tech took the navigational chip from Reht and inserted it into the data port where Billy's ear canal should have been. The Liiker buzzed for a moment, adapting and then integrating the foreign programs into his own. Vaughn, seated in front of the star charts, watched with a blank look in his eyes as Billy dumped the files onto the *Wraith*.

"What is all that *gorsh-shit*?" Ro asked.

"Flight patterns," Tech replied.

"I ganked this signature off of Diawn," Reht said, reading the numbers to Tech that he had etched into his arm. "See if tin can over there can figure it out. I'm sure it's in code, or backwards, or something *chakked* up."

Stifling a grimace, Reht leaned against the console. Sweat drenched his jacket and his limbs felt jittery. Bacthar eyed him, but he turned away. *Not now. Can't give in.*

"Who or what are we going after?" Tech asked, scratching the back of his head with his hind leg.

"Shandin," Reht said.

Mom was the only one who reacted, the only one who really understood the significance of that name. His ears flicked forward as he let out a low growl, his canines protruding over his lower lip and his silver eyes slitting with tension.

"Shandin…" Cray muttered, twirling his knife with his fingers. "How do I know that name?"

"Wasn't he some kind of sellout?" Bacthar said.

"Yeah, a *chakkin'* two-timing, *vedego mu'katha*," Ro said, making a thrusting motion with his hips. "That guy would *chak* his own mother."

"Yeah, if the percentage was right," Reht said. "Look, this guy is serious—he ain't just any dog-soldier."

139

"What's the bag then?" Ro asked. "I mean, does he have a gold-plated *assino* or what? Why go after him?"

Reht looked at Mom. The Talian's claws surfaced, and his pupils dilated with anticipation.

What they don't know... he thought. Except for Mom, none of the crew knew about Shandin, or the scars on their captain's hands. And as a consequence, how the Talian became his first mate.

Reht ripped the last shred of nail off of his left index finger, letting the throbbing pain keep him steady. "I can't ask any of you to come with me. This is personal."

"Who is he?" Bacthar asked, crossing his arms.

Bloody images from the past flashed through his mind, reviving the old wounds to the backs of his hands. "The man that murdered my parents. I want his *chakking* head on a plate."

Controlling the rise of his voice, Reht continued: "I can only promise you that when this is over, I'll give you all what you deserve, even if it means my own skin to sell on the market."

Save Billy Don't's queer guttural noises as he processed the stolen chip, the room fell silent.

"You our Cappy," Ro said. "We with you 'til the end."

"Yeah, the *chakking* end," Cray chimed in.

This doesn't feel right. His crew was loyal, but they were still dog-soldiers, and he had asked too much of them over the past few years. He should have gotten the black mark or a knife in the back—not this.

Billy Don't squealed, and all eyes went to the viewscreen.

"Billy thinks that signature you gave him was a code key," Tech said, tracing the flight data with his fingers. "Check this one out—when Billy integrates the key, the results indicate that Diawn made fifty-two stops here in the last two months."

"Berish and Mau Imports and Exports," Reht said, reading aloud the location tag. "That *chakker*—that was one of Shandin's old aliases. Where is that anyway?"

"Old Earth," Vaughn said flatly, rubbing the horizontal scar that ran the length of his shaved head.

The rest of the crew muttered and whined. "Of all the *sycha-holes…*"

Reht cradled his side, the pain too intense to let him to stand up straight. But he couldn't give in—not now, not when his darkest wish had come true. He smiled and winked at Mom as he gave the command. "Set a course for Earth. Let's get that *jingoga*'s head."

***

"Triel—Triel! *Emeath Ma'Tau Ini!*"

Something sharp pricked Triel's shoulder, and she shot upright, cursing as her heart labored with the rush of adrenaline.

"Oh, Gods—you're okay."

The Healer opened her eyes, but bright sunlight made it difficult to distinguish what she was seeing. Two hands gripped her shoulders, but when she looked at their source, she screamed. Black fire burned beneath the skin of some strange, amorphous creature, its flames licking her skin as it leaned closer.

"Triel, it's me—Jetta!"

Triel lashed out, straining away from the heat of the flames, but the burning sensation stopped. As she blinked, the fire dissipated to a few wisps of smoke fading in the humid summer air.

"Jetta?" she asked. Triel tentatively touched her friend's skin, relieved to feel the steady pulse beneath the surface.

Carefully, Jetta put the syringe back in the medkit. "Who did you think it was?"

"Oh, Jetta," Triel said, embracing her tightly. "I'm sorry—I thought I saw—"

But then she stopped. What did she see? Had she hallucinated the nightmarish creature she saw unfurl within Jetta's aura?

Jetta let go, sitting back on her heels. By the pained look on her face, she'd gleaned an impression of her thoughts.

"Hey—it's me, okay? Please don't be afraid of me," she whispered.

"Don't be silly," Triel whispered back. It had to have been the shock of the descent; there was no way Jetta could harbor such a dark entity. Jaeia would have seen it—Triel would have seen it—long before this moment.

Something in the intensity of Jetta's dark green eyes made Triel relax for a moment, allowing her senses to extend beyond the physical barrier between them. She felt only Jetta's familiar, comfortable presence, the essence that filled her and made her feel cared for—not the shadow creature. Tired, bruised, and mentally exhausted, Triel wanted to reach out, to embrace her tightly, to feel her warmth, but she hesitated, confused by her feelings and uncertain of their direction.

Triel tried to move the stray hair out of Jetta's face, but the commander leaned back and blushed.

"Got it, thanks."

Normally Triel would have been offended by her rebuff, but the burns and cuts on Jetta's left arm and shoulder diverted her attention.

"These don't look good. *You* don't look good, Jetta," Triel said, noticing her pale and sunken cheeks. "I've never seen your color like this before. I thought it was just the stress, but it's not, is it?"

Jetta pointed at the smoldering ship twenty meters behind her. "Well, flying blind isn't exactly relaxing."

"Oh Gods," Triel said, tracing the landing back as far as she could see by the scorch marks in the grass.

"Neither was the fire in the recirculators, not to mention getting us out and trying to salvage the fuel cells," Jetta said, continuing to sidestep the question.

Lacking the energy to battle Jetta's iron will, the Healer didn't let her frustration or suspicion register on her face. Instead, she took a few calming breaths and looked toward the sky, allowing herself take in her surroundings.

142

"It's weird to be back here. I swore I wouldn't return," she said, pulling at the blades of yellow grass.

"Why was that?"

Triel traced the outline of her people's markings on her arm. "Too many memories. Too many reminders of why I left."

"I thought you left because of the invasion," Jetta said.

Triel knew what she was thinking—*no Prodgy ever left their tribe. Ever. It is against custom, against nature, against the Gods.*

The Healer shook her head. "It was more complicated than that."

She changed the subject before Jetta could ask any more questions. "Well, I think I know where we are," Triel said, shielding her eyes as she surveyed the area. Two mountain ranges converged in the distance, one in the east and one in the north, their towering blue peaks capped with snow and ice. "If I'm right, there was a village about ten kilometers northwest—the Kingi tribe, if memory serves. I'm sure it's been resettled."

Jetta closed her eyes and tipped her head back.

"What are you doing?" Triel asked.

Inhaling deeply through her nose, Jetta looked northeast. "No, I think the resettlement is that way; I can smell fire, fuel—and people."

Triel raised a brow. "Okay, when did you ever have a sense of smell like that? I would think your telepathic talents would be the first to pick up on any Sentient life."

Jetta frowned. "Maybe it was... no, it couldn't have been. I don't know—but I know I'm right."

"It's the wolf, isn't it?" Triel said, smiling. "I felt the intensity of your exchange when I last restored you."

"What? *No.*"

Triel's smile broadened. "There are legends among our people of powerful telepaths who can meld minds with animals. I think you absorbed some of his abilities. Maybe I'll call you *lakoba*; it means 'wolf-girl.'"

Jetta crossed her arms. "Not funny."

"It's a little funny," Triel said, chuckling. "Alright, alright. Just let me heal those wounds and really check you out before we go anywhere."

Jetta shook her head and tried to get up. "No. You're still recovering; you need to conserve your strength. Besides, I need to finish organizing our gear."

Triel took Jetta's left arm and placed her other hand on her chest. "Let me take care of you just once without a fight."

"You're not going to let this go, are you?"

But Jetta sat down, looking uncomfortable as Triel slipped beneath her skin and guided her body through the healing process.

The Healer tried to be more careful this time. She went through the normal steps of repair and regrowth, but when she tried to delve deeper she found that Jetta had consciously locked herself away, making it impossible to search for more than just damaged tissue without tipping her off that she was snooping around.

No, I have to know—what is Jetta feeling? Why did she act one way in the intensive care unit but is so cold and aloof now?

But she quickly put her needs aside when she uncovered something else.

"Jetta," she said, wavering between her intra- and extra-corporeal perspectives. "Your body…it's changing again, isn't it?"

Jetta pulled back a little, but Triel held fast. *Something isn't right.*

The commander's tune felt familiar, but sounded oddly dysrhythmic, as if starting to fray.

But the twins have been feeling poorly for a while, she remembered. *Why haven't I—or any of the traditional diagnostic tools—sensed this change?*

Guilt and worry multiplied as she discovered burgeoning dysplasias throughout her tissues, as if the very fabric of Jetta's cells had somehow been compromised. "You're—you're—"

144

"A *chakked* up Motti experiment? Yeah, I know," Jetta said, finally pulling free. Even with the premature severance, Jetta's second-degree burns had transformed into healthy skin, her lacerations filled in and smoothed out. "Everything about me is coming undone. So I guess we'd better get moving and not waste any more time."

Triel frowned, folding her arms across her chest. "What are you not telling me?"

Jetta was quick to get her feet, adjusting her clothing and fixing her hair—and not answering the question.

"You're the most insufferable patient I've ever had."

"I'll take that as a compliment," Jetta said, packing supplies from a salvaged storage crate.

"It's not. I thought we were friends. I would hope you're not hiding from me."

Jetta lifted a brow. "Hiding from you?"

"Yes. You're afraid of sharing any kind of feeling with me—unless, of course, I completely force it out of you. I need it, you know—positive psionic, emotional, and physical interactions are part of how my species regenerates after healing."

Jetta's actions slowed as she knotted a sack of tools. "I know that. But I can't help you right now."

"Of course not," the Healer said, playing with the webbing between her fingers.

"Look, let's just get to that resettlement. I'm going to need to barter for supplies and transportation, so grab anything off the ship that looks valuable, okay?"

Triel didn't keep her disappointment to herself as they stripped the ship of anything that they could carry that might be worth a decent trade. Pretending not to notice, Jetta busied herself by briefing the Healer on safety concerns.

Most of what Jetta explained Triel already knew: After the Dominion forcibly removed the native Algardriens from the planet, they destroyed the cities and confiscated or obliterated artifacts of

145

their culture. Anything that could have possibly remained was stolen and sold off by dog-soldiers and looters. Once pillaged, expatriates, defectors, and refugees from other planets came to Algar, transforming a once peaceful planet into a brutal warzone.

Reivers, she thought, remembering the nickname for the immigrants that had desecrated the last remnants of her planet. *Why hasn't the Alliance done something about them? What's kept the councils from reclaiming the planet for the Homeworlds?*

Jetta must have sensed the nature of her thoughts.

"This planet is one of the few that's still habitable after the Motti plague," Jetta explained as they headed towards the settlement. "And all the castaways, outcasts, and exiles that landed here have made their claim."

"I've read the reports," Triel said. "The Alliance attempted negotiations with the Reivers, but there are too many different parties and interests."

"Yes, but what you don't know is that before I was leading the SMT, the Alliance tried to secure various sectors of the planet, but each time miscalculated the opposition. There are so many people here now living in secrecy. It would take a massive, full-scale invasion to reclaim the planet, and with military resources as scarce as they were after the Motti war, and as poorly as everything is going now, it hasn't happened."

Triel struggled with the makeshift pack on her shoulders. Even though Jetta had taken almost all of the weight, the Healer felt ragged and spent, and every extra kilogram drained the last drops of her strength. "My hope," she said, trying to reposition the pack, "is that something of my people still remains. Our most sacred places were never recorded on any map or written in any text."

"Well, my best guess is that we're about fifty kilometers from where you wanted to land," Jetta said, scrambling over some felled trees and taking a visual sweep of the area. "We can stop at the resettlement, get what we need, and then head out. It's too late to do the entire journey today, but if we cut our sleep, we could be at the temple by tomorrow morning."

Triel's heart sunk. Fifty kilometers? That was just a guess—neither of them knew the exact location of the temple, and at this point she would be lucky to walk one. Every last muscle ached from her premature emergence from cryostasis and the gestalt of drugs Jetta had used to revive her. To make matters worse, they had both gone without sleep and food for some time now. They had survival rations, but they had to conserve what little they had in case they couldn't find the resettlement.

Food and sleep won't matter if I'm not strong enough to keep from Falling, she thought, allowing darker realizations to take hold. Separated from her tribe and still mourning the loss of Reht and the crew, she carried emotional burdens too great for any one Prodgy. *How am I ever going to cleanse my spirit without other Healers?*

Thinking of Jetta's own struggles, she reined in her doubts. *That is why I came here. I have to find a way to survive as a Solitary. I have to stay strong.*

A hot lump swelled in the Healer's throat. The prospect of surviving, alone and isolated, all of a sudden didn't sound so appealing.

"Hey," Jetta whispered, touching the back of her hand. Her eyes showed earnest concern. "You okay?"

The contact broke her thoughts. "Yes, I'm fine," she said, wiping her eyes with the back of her hand.

"We'll just walk for an hour, then take a break, okay? We can also break into the rations. I know we'll find food up ahead."

Triel smiled. *Even if she's unreachable, she's always there, and she always seems to know what I need.*

The songs of the yellow-backed Ciki birds kept them company as Jetta led them down a game trail through the forest. Breaks in the canopy let warm sunlight filter through to the Healer's skin, and the air, peppered with the smells of koral flower and dewy moss, woke memories she had long suppressed. She hadn't grown up on the southern continent, but she had performed restorations with several tribespeople who had, and their borrowed memories stirred odd recollections that surfaced in distant echoes and spectral reflections.

"Hey—you're projecting," Jetta said as she leapt over a boulder.

Triel took the long way around to conserve energy. "Sorry. I'm so rarely in the company of other telepaths these days; I sometimes I forget that you can pick that up."

"No, it's alright. It was nice." Jetta fumbled with her words as she tromped through some thick underbrush. "Do you ever, well... How do you feel about the people you glean from?"

"What do you mean?" Triel asked, taken aback. This was the first time that Jetta had ever asked her about her telepathic experiences.

Jetta shrugged. "I don't know. There was this one time, a long time ago—I was maybe two, and my uncle was trying to teach me Common. That's when I found out I could peek into his head. It was so thrilling—to know things instantly. Imagine a two-year-old with an adult language base."

"I can't," Triel said.

"But that was my first glimpse into the ugliness of the world. I accidentally absorbed more than just his language skills. All of a sudden I was subjected to the memories of his accident, his fights with Yahmen, how he came to Fiorah. It was so weird. Overwhelming, I guess. I couldn't relate anything to my own experiences. I resented him for a while, and now I realize I was mad because I wasn't ready to know those kinds of things. It was helpful, yeah, and having a little insight into Yahmen saved my life, but I wasn't ready. Having other people's thoughts and experiences… sometimes it's too much. I don't want to be weighed down by someone else's life."

Triel wanted to take Jetta's hand, hug her—do something—but knew the commander wouldn't be receptive. Instead, she sighed deeply and offered her best advice: "For the most part I believe that being able to share someone else's life experience is a blessing, but I was raised differently. You and your siblings never had a choice, Jetta. You've been forced to grow up early in so many ways. Prodgy children are protected from their elders' experience until they are old enough and prepared to receive it, to avoid confusion and harm."

Jetta didn't say anything, but Triel knew by the way she guarded her feelings and pressed on ahead that she was affected by her words.

"Jetta," Triel said, stopping her in her tracks and pulling Jetta around to face her. "You've been asked to do so much in your life, but all I'll ever ask of you is to be my friend—and to let me be yours."

Jetta's cheeks flushed, but she didn't turn away. A ray of sunlight fell across her eyes, making them come alive in the colors of the lush, green summers of Triel's youth. The Healer's reaction measured beyond surprise and more than admiration at Jetta's beauty, and she found herself pressing closer, until their faces were only centimeters apart.

Without warning, Jetta's neck snapped to the left, and she crouched down low. She grabbed Triel and pulled her down, spilling her pack on the ground.

"Holy Gods—what are you—?"

But she didn't finish her sentence. Jetta put her hand over her mouth and motioned for silence. Using hand signals, she instructed Triel to follow as she withdrew her firearm and headed toward the next cluster of trees.

I don't understand, Triel thought, only spotting a bold opposorodent scurrying through one of the outstretched branches of a willowlai tree.

Quickly and quietly, Jetta led her to the safety of a clump of bushes near a gigantic, twisted firawood trunk and got down as low as possible. She parted a few branches, revealing the three feather-pawed mountain wolves pacing about twenty meters from their location.

My Gods, she thought, but calmed herself. Mountain wolves were the most dangerous predators on the planet, but the scored markings on their ears indicated that they had been trained. Many southern tribes had used them for scouts because wolves, like other wild animals, were unreadable to the Prodgies and easily domesticated.

Old memories of their legendary howls flowed through her in complex harmonics. In the depths of her communal memories, she felt the ripple of ancient times, when tribes communicated with one another through the wolves, bridging the distance between them with animal song.

Since all of the southern tribes had been eliminated, the Healer assumed the pack had reintegrated into the wild until one of them marked the tree with his forepaw. *They're still under someone's command.*

Triel looked back at Jetta, who studied their movements with a strange look in her eyes. Most off-worlders were terrified of the enormous black animals; they weighed in around five hundred kilos and stood over two meters tall at the shoulder. And despite their tremendous size, they moved with remarkable stealth, walking nimbly over branches and underbrush.

However, it wasn't their size but their eyes, the color of burning coals, that spurred most people to panic. In Triel, it brought back terrible memories of one fateful summer's day. *Jasen—*

(Scarlet eyes

Black disguise—)

Her chest felt tight and hot, the air too thin to breathe, but before she could do or say anything, Jetta grabbed her hand and squeezed.

"Whatever happens—don't move from this spot."

Triel didn't have time to dissuade her as Jetta leapt from their cover and bolted in the opposite direction.

"Jetta!" she screamed as the wolves charged after her.

What is she thinking? She's crazy—why doesn't she just shoot them? Jetta had the best aim out of any soldier she knew.

Using her smaller size against the wolves, Jetta dodged and ducked through narrow passageways between rock and tree. Her tactic slowed them a little, but they spread out through the forest and began to close in on her.

Not knowing what else to do, Triel ran after Jetta, screaming for her to shoot her pursuers, but Jetta holstered her gun. "Please, Jetta—they'll kill you!"

The Healer skidded to a halt when she saw Jetta, surrounded and trapped, crouching on all fours. Her eyes were slitted, her lower lip curled under her teeth as she arched her back.

She's using her talents, Triel perceived, *but I've never sensed this type of energy before...*

Usually Jetta projected her abilities, her thoughts spreading out like invisible roots into her enemy's head. This time Triel felt Jetta's talents pulling at the seams of reality, tugging at the minds of the wolves and folding them into her own.

"What are you doing?" Triel she whispered, allowing herself to extend into Jetta's wake.

The world changed. Somewhere similar to Algar, with fertile, mountainous lands appeared under a deep blue sky. She became aware of her body, standing on all fours, and her wagging tail as her mate trotted over to greet her with a tender lick. Golden eyes connected with hers, and as he brushed by, the feel of his gray and white fur stirred deep feelings of companionship she hadn't yet discovered for herself.

These are the wolves of Old Earth, *Triel realized. Centuries ago, when the Prodgies made first contact with the humans, they discovered the terrestrial predator. Impressed by the animal's prowess, strength, and intelligence, the people of Algar decided to introduce the species to their own planet.* How is this possible?

Time had no meaning as she saw through the eyes of many different wolves through the ages, with no hint of their chronological order. The real wolves encircling Jetta remained barely visible, their blurry outline unchanging as the images rapidly flew past.

151

In a matter of seconds the Healer's emotions swam through a succession of lives, each one different and evocative. I've never felt anything so strong or pure.

Unfiltered minds, both instinctive and rational, pulled down the preconceived barriers she had erected, enlivening her soul with unrealized emotion.

They're all connected, *she thought, sensing in their shared memories woven throughout the ages much like the different tribes of the Prodgy.*

What are you doing, Jetta? Triel wondered as the borrowed memories came to a halt.

Jetta did not acknowledge the Healer in any way. A low growl rumbled from the commander's throat and she relaxed the arch in her back. Triel sucked in her breath as the mountain wolf with the one gray paw stepped up to Jetta, his ears forward, tail stiff and upright, and sniffed her. With dilated pupils he inspected her neckline, then circled, giving her the once-over. The other two joined in, though not as bravely as the first, keeping a greater distance between themselves and Jetta.

Finally Jetta stood up and, to Triel's astonishment, reached out and touched the leader's nose, stroking it and whispering something into his ear.

"Jetta!"

"It's okay," Jetta finally said as she caught a good spot behind his ear and sent his gray-pawed leg kicking. "We have an understanding now."

"Jetta, wolves—even domesticated ones—are dangerous," Triel said, backing up as the three wolves turned and came towards her.

"Don't worry—they just want to know who you are. Just let them do their thing."

Triel was glad when they had finished their assessment and walked away, apparently disinterested in her, and returned their attentions to Jetta. The Healer had never seen Jetta so animated, nor with so relaxed a smile as she playfully tugged on one's ears and lightly wrestled with the other.

"How did you do this, Jetta?"

Jetta shrugged as one of the wolves nudged her hand so she would continue scratching behind his ear. "Something I tried on Old Earth. I let them in me instead of me messing with them. These guys are just like the wolves I met on Earth, so I showed them that I could understand them and, more importantly, that we weren't a threat. They're not dangerous."

"Okay, you're definitely *Lakoba*." Triel laughed nervously as she watched Jetta crawl on top of the leader's back. "But are you sure about this?" she said as one of the others resumed his inspection of the Healer, wedging his nose underneath her armpit. "I've never trusted them. They can turn on you at any time."

Jetta looked at her with a funny expression. "Completely."

After laying her head on the wolf's neck, Jetta closed her eyes and listened beyond the means of her ears. "They were just scouting the area, looking for intruders. They can take us back to their camp. From their memories, I think they're working under human handlers."

Triel thought it over. "That can't be a good thing."

"Well," Jetta said, carefully scrutinizing her as she slid off the wolf's back. "We'll have to risk it. You look almost as bad as I do."

She's not joking, the Healer thought, *and I can't argue her point.* She hadn't felt right since she had started to turn, and their travels were wearing her down.

"You're not planning to—"

Before she could fully protest, Jetta got behind the Healer and hoisted her up onto the back of a crouching wolf.

"Let's face it," Jetta said, "we'll need our strength once we get to the resettlement, in case things don't go as well as we'd like. This is our best option."

"I'm not exactly comfortable with this plan—"

153

As the wolf stood up, Triel knotted her hands into his coarse fur, holding on for dear life. The wolf whined and nosed at her until she adjusted her position and assumed a gentler handhold on the crescent ruff of white fur around his neck. "I've never ridden a wolf."

Jetta chuckled as she strapped their gear around the third wolf's midsection, then scrambled atop the alpha. "Neither have I. Should be fun, yeah?"

Not allowing Triel any time to contest the idea, Jetta and the leader took off, bounding through the trees at top speed.

Oh Gods! Triel thought, clinging to her wolf as he took off after the leader, his massive body hurtling through the forest. *Too fast, dangerous—*

Despite the initial spike of fear, the Healer gradually lost herself in the new experience. As enormous and muscular as the wolf was, he glided through the underbrush, leaping effortlessly over rocks and branches and deftly winding in and out of the trees. She pressed low against his body as the wolf broke free of the forest and picked up speed across the open meadow. Wind whipped her face, making her eyes water. *I didn't know I could feel this way...*

With a smile on her face, Triel turned to Jetta, watching her and her wolf slalom between yellow clumps of sunshooter flowers. Not believing her eyes, the Healer squinted, then opened them wide.

Is Jetta...beaming?

Even in the daylight, her friend's aura shined like the brightest star in the night sky. Overwhelmed at the sight, Triel felt her own body react, every cell illuminating as she inhaled until she felt her lungs would burst. Jetta radiated a supernal warmth, and despite the distance between them, the sensation wrapped around the Healer, mending all the wounds inflicted since she had left her tribe.

I've only ever felt this while being restored by another Prodgy, she thought. Another realization crossed her mind. *That is not Rion...*

A new energy rippled through her body, cascading down her limbs to the very tips of her being, revitalizing the old parts of herself she had forgotten existed.

"Oh, Jetta," she whispered as her strength returned tenfold. Until right then the Healer hadn't realized how poorly she'd been feeling. *This feels like I'm back on Algar, surrounded by the psionic energies of my tribe.*

She hugged her white-necked wolf, laughing joyfully as they shot through the meadow and down a slope, back into the trees.

What does this mean? she wondered.

The wolves slowed to a trot and then stopped, shaking Triel from her thoughts. Jetta's wolf whined and paced.

"What's wrong?" Triel asked.

Jetta frowned. "I'm not sure, but we should let them go."

After Jetta unstrapped their gear, the wolves took off, disappearing into the trees. Never comfortable with the canine predators, Triel secretly delighted to see them leave. Still, something felt amiss.

"That's strange."

Jetta scanned the trees, keeping her voice low. "I know. Let's keep sharp."

They walked in silence for about a half-kilometer until they reached the edge of a resettlement.

"Jetta," Triel said. Through the break in the trees she spotted a charred swath of land. Shelters, haphazardly constructed with scrapped material, clustered behind the protection of a lumber and metal wall pocked with blast marks. "I have a feeling we're not going to get a warm welcome."

Jetta's eyes zeroed in on the gun towers guarding the bulk of the buildings. Red and black flags, made out of animal skins, fluttered atop the spired roofs.

"Stay by me," she said, pulling Triel to her side.

Twin laser sights targeted their chests as they stepped out of the protection of the trees.

"*G'thei Yralk it'et*," someone shouted from one of the towers.

Unfamiliar with the language, Triel looked to Jetta. The commander's forehead knitted as she silently repeated the words.

"I know," she said, snapping her fingers. "That's Lock slang!"

Jetta continued to walk slowly toward the gate.

"Lock slang?"

"As in the Labor Locks of Plaly IV," Jetta said. "They must be Lockheads."

The laser sights never left her heart, but Jetta didn't seem concerned.

"Jetta, maybe this isn't such a good idea," Triel said, keeping her distance. "Didn't you say the Alliance failed negotiations with Reivers?"

"Yes, but they've never dealt with me before."

"But—"

"We need supplies," she said, cutting her off, "and it would be helpful to glean some of their knowledge of the territory. Besides—what could they possibly have that I couldn't handle?"

In that moment the looming shadow of Jetta's words eclipsed the experience of her radiance, especially when Triel sensed the accompanying thoughts. *Jetta believes she's more powerful than any Sentient we might encounter.*

More troubling, she felt Jetta's mind open to the prospect of violence, and, despite all of her experiences, the use of her talents.

That is Rion.

Jetta craned her neck toward the tallest watchtower and shouted in Common: "I am Commander Jetta Kyron of the Starways Alliance, and this is Triel of Algardrien. Our ship crashed, and we are in need of supplies and a place to stay. We have military-grade fuel cells to exchange for your hospitality."

A laugh boomed over the loudspeakers. "*The* Jetta Kyron, the slayer of worlds, the Warchild of the Gods?"

Triel watched nervously as Jetta's face turned hard and cold. "The one and only."

"Do you really have a Prodgy?"

Jetta motioned for her to show her markings. Triel lifted her arms and turned her face from side to side.

The gate locks unlatched, and the door slowly opened, groaning as the gears and cables struggled.

"Stay close to me and don't say a word. Lockheads don't trust anyone, especially not military. I've had a lot of problems on SMT missions with the group on Jue Hexron."

"Then why are we here?" Triel whispered as two guards approached them.

An unyielding look crossed her face. "Trust me."

Guards emerged from behind the gates, cloaked from head to toe in mismatched gear. Triel identified a Dominion Core chest plate, pieces of an Alliance jumpsuit, and a Trigonian neck protector on the man to the right. The one to her left dressed more like a dog-soldier with his chest harnesses and fatigue pants. Both wore black goggles and faceguards, hiding who or what they really were.

But Triel knew. Once they stepped into her range she recognized the familiar biorhythm of their species.

Humans.

The guards led them down a tired road winding through the crowded settlement. Houses, made out of plastic refuse and old machine parts, sagged together in clumps. Triel noticed the hollowed-out shell of a warship process cylinder sheltering a family of five huddled around a fire.

My Gods, there is so much sickness here, she thought, closing off her perceptions to protect her own health. Skeletal people in the streets made no eye contact as they passed. Even withdrawn she sensed epidemic levels of gastrointestinal disease, and in some the beginnings of blood poisoning. An open door revealed a pile of bodies, and Triel caught a whiff of burning flesh.

Triel wished she could connect with Jetta to share what she was seeing, but the concentrated look on the commander's face showed that they had reached the same conclusion.

"How long has it been like this?" Jetta asked the guard as they passed a little boy crumpled against a doorframe, but he didn't respond.

The guards led them to a tent in the middle of town. Inside, a man studied a red topographic map spread across two tables. As he tapped his chin with a gloved hand, he placed little figurines made of plastic twist ties and broken bottles on the borders and territories already outlined in black.

"Sir!" the guards saluted.

The man parted from his thoughts and looked up. With a careful eye he reviewed Jetta and Triel before dismissing his guards.

"I am Counselor Salam. You are Commander Kyron—I recognize you from the newsreels. And you must be Triel of Algardrien. You are most welcome here, Healer."

Something about Salam made Triel uncomfortable. His cool gray eyes stood out against his olive skin, and his dark hair, pulled back from his forehead in a neat braid, drew attention to his slender frame.

Maybe it's his clothing, she tried to rationalize, looking over his drab military uniform bearing insignias too faded to distinguish.

No, it's something else.

What little skin showed was covered in scars, the most notable one running from the corner of his mouth to his ear, trapping half of his face in a permanent smile.

(Something doesn't feel right.)

Jetta stepped forward and offered her hand, which Salam took lightly, not bothering to remove his gloves.

"I am Commander Kyron. Here—a token of my appreciation for your hospitality."

Jetta dropped the packs and gave him the fuel cells. "Wired right, each cell could power your village for three or four years."

Salam counted the seven fuel cells and nodded. "Thank you, that's very generous. But what our people really need is medical supplies—or the help of your Prodgy. Our enemies have destroyed our food supply and my people are sick and starving."

"Triel is in no condition to heal as a Solitary," Jetta said.

Salam bowed to the Healer. "Triel of Algardrien—our people revere the Prodgies. You would not be in danger here. We would take care of you—protect you—give you anything you need."

"I'm sorry," Jetta said, stepping in front of her, "but our mission is urgent, and we must head out by morning. I promise to send aid once I am able to contact the Alliance."

"Then perhaps you could offer advice on our upcoming offensive with the Jumaris? We're down to less than half our fighting force, and if we don't succeed in taking back our hunting grounds then we will surely perish."

Jumaris, Triel thought, trying to place the name. Then she remembered the words she had always associated with them. *Flesh eaters.*

Even Jetta flinched at their name. Reputed as vicious killers who slowly tortured their victims before consuming them alive, the Jumaris were flushed out of their homeworld when the Motti first disseminated the outerworld populations. Like other castaways, they found their way to Algar and carved out a place for themselves on the desecrated world.

"I can help with negotiations—not warfare. That is against my oath," Jetta replied.

Salam look disgusted. "The Jumaris don't negotiate. So then tell me, Commander, what is more important than the lives of two hundred people?"

"The lives of all the Sentients of the Starways."

Salam laughed. "How do you expect me to believe that, coming from someone like you? I know you," he said. "I've seen all the reels, seen the trials. You only do anything for one reason— resurrecting your dead brother."

Jetta's anger burst into Triel's mind, permeating the Healer's body in a roaring fire. As Triel choked back the sensory onslaught,

Jetta fought to keep the emotion out of her voice. "Huh. I didn't think you'd let a liberalistic, anti-government institution like the mainstream news sway your opinion. Especially someone with your history."

She's right. The media is generally cool when it comes to human rights, Triel thought. *As far as I can remember, the true nature of the Labor Locks has never been covered by any major media network, despite the petitions and amateur footage provided by the Human Freedom Fighters.*

Jetta's head tilted to the left, and just by the way her eyes seemed to focus on something outside the tent, Triel could tell she was using her hidden talent, the one that bored into a person's soul.

"I will not lie to you, Counselor. We are here because the Alliance is fighting for our very survival. I believe that Li's army does not have the means to truly defeat the Motti's new weapon, and it's only a matter of time before we're all turned into Deadwalkers."

Triel did the best she could to hold back her surprise. *It's usually Jaeia who employs the direct and honest approach, not Jetta.*

Experience dampened her astonishment. *I know better—Jetta is never without an ace up her sleeve.*

Salam lifted a brow. "Then why come here? To see the dying remnants of a disinherited race? Algar is dangerous, as you very well know, and this planet has little to offer anyone who already has a warm bed."

"Our ship malfunctioned and crashed several kilometers back. Before the accident we were headed to the Temple of Exxuthus."

Now Triel understood why Jetta elected the honest approach. Only the Prodgy elders knew the exact location of the Temple of Exxuthus, but the Lockheads might have uncovered the holy site during their battles with the other Reivers. *That's why Jetta offered him the fuel cells—to elicit an emotional response, levering his mind open with thoughts of reward.* And she was honest with him about their mission, knowing her candor would shock him and trigger his knowledge of the Temple. *With a mind like hers, all he has to do is give it a moment's thought and Jetta will know everything he does.*

"The Temple of Exxuthus..." Salam's face changed subtly. His gray eyes dilated, and his hands moved to the edge of the table. "I've heard that is where the world of the Gods meets ours. The sickest vessel can be restored there—even granted powers."

Jetta smiled. "Yes—you've been there yourself?"

Sensing a number of human presences gathering around their tent, the Healer brushed the back of Jetta's hand. The commander glanced at her but didn't seem upset by the growing problem.

"Perhaps in a dream."

"Counselor—you wouldn't be holding out on me, would you?"

Salam rose and turned his back to them. "I know who you are, Commander. I know what you're capable of. You can kill me with my worst nightmare, yes? I'm human, without any Rai Shar training; you can just take what you need from my head and leave me here."

Jetta's face turned to stone.

Looking her friend dead in the eye, Salam sharpened the tone of his voice. "Do you know how we escaped the Labor Locks, Commander?"

Jetta's lips barely moved. "No."

Salam removed his gloves, exposing two artificial hands. The crude, twenty-first century models with synthetic skins and antiquated geared motors whined and clicked as he moved his fingers.

"They shackled us by the feet or by the hands. Or both. No way to get the key without triggering an alarm. Only one way to escape."

Jetta paled, and Triel's hunger pains gave way to nausea.

"You won't find a single adult here with all their hands and feet."

"I can't imagine—" Jetta began.

"Yes, you can," Salam said, slamming an artificial hand down on the table. He paused to compose himself as he put the gloves back on. "I only ask that if you take my knowledge of the Temple, you take our reasons for coming here. How I came here. You take all of it. You can't reap someone's knowledge without living in their shoes."

Jetta's green eyes dilated, her lips forming silent words as she swayed back and forth. Triel had seen Jetta glean from another being before, but never this intensely. Something about the counselor must have caught her attention.

I don't like this, the Healer thought, noting Jetta's brow slicked with sweat.

The commander's words came breathlessly. "You do know where the Temple is."

"Thousands have died to learn of its location. We were so close—*so close*—when the Jumaris came. You must understand—everyone wants inside."

"Why?" Triel asked, seeing that Jetta was no longer paying attention.

Salam gave her a sad smile. "Because it is our last hope."

Jetta ran a hand through her hair and cursed under her breath. "I need... I need..." but she couldn't finish the sentence. All the color drained from her face as her attention split between the real world and what she had absorbed.

"Counselor—we're both so tired. Can we please rest here for the night?" Triel asked, taking Jetta by the arm. "We can discuss the Temple tomorrow."

"Of course," Salam said. "You are welcome here, and any friend of a Prodgy is a friend of ours. Even if they are part of the Alliance."

Triel kept a close eye on Jetta as the guards escorted them to a tent within the militarized zone of the settlement. As soon as the tent flaps closed and the guards walked out of earshot, Triel went to Jetta's side.

"Lie down," she whispered, gently guiding her to one of the cots.

Jetta didn't protest, and rolled onto her side. "So tired..."

The Healer rested her hand on her friend's shoulder. *It isn't physical exhaustion she's talking about; this is something deeper.*

Surveying the commander's mind and body, Triel sensed Counselor Salam's psionic residue radiating from Jetta's thoughts like a scream in an empty room. The Healer couldn't divine Salam's memories herself, but she sensed the resulting strain on her friend.

I haven't seen Jetta like this since she killed Jahx in the Motti attack, she thought, triggering some of her worst memories. *And that was right before she went catatonic.*

It had taken all of Triel's energies to bring her back that day, not to mention the support of the ship's entire medical staff and, most importantly, the aid of her twin sister.

I'm not strong enough to do that now.

Triel tentatively stroked Jetta's hair. "Hey—are you okay?"

Jetta shook her head. "No. He..." she started, her mouth hanging open as the rest of the thought came out in a weak exhale.

The Healer took Jetta's hand and closed her eyes, dipping beneath her skin and into the rhythm of her mind and body. Gritting her teeth, she tried to navigate the internal dissonance, but found the conflict intolerable and withdrew. "What did he show you, Jetta?"

Jetta's eyes remained distant, her mind unreachable. "Hell."

"Let me see," Triel said, trying to sink into Jetta's biorhythms once more. Again, the cacophony forced her out, leaving her shaken.

"No," Jetta whispered. "He knew what he was doing. He wanted to hurt me." Jetta turned to Triel and gripped her shoulders, eyes frantic. "I won't let him hurt you, too."

Triel tried to contain her shock. What if Salam had played his hand offensively? If, knowing he couldn't keep Jetta from pilfering his knowledge, he had manipulated what she would see?

If that's true, we're in more trouble than I can even guess.

"Jetta—let me see—I can help you."

"No, not anyone," Jetta mumbled, bringing her knees to her chest.

Whatever Salam showed her must be terrible for Jetta to withdraw this far. I have to do something, fast.

"Jetta, you have to let me see—what if it's a trick?"

"No trick," Jetta whispered, burying her face in her knees.

Out of options, the Healer's thoughts turned grim. *Jetta is stubborn, unreasonable, and defensive—it's always been her undoing—but without her help, we'll never make it out of the settlement alive.*

She remembered Salam's need for her services, the dubious reverence in his voice. *What if taking Jetta out of the equation is part of his plan? What if he wants to capture me?*

It could have been the sense of impending doom spreading through her body like wildfire, or the fear that she could lose her closest friend. Or perhaps something more. But before she could question the impulse, Triel leaned over and kissed Jetta's temple. When the commander reeled in surprise, Triel cupped her cheek and kissed her on the mouth. Her skin felt warm and tender, her lips invitingly sweet. Triel had never kissed a telepath, let alone a female, and the explosive wonder of it sent charged currents to the tips of her fingers and toes.

"What are you doing?" Jetta exclaimed, pushing her away.

"What's wrong?" Triel said, suddenly very confused herself.

Jetta's mind leapt in twenty different directions, her emotions a tangled wreck. Struggling to speak, she pawed at her face before her arms went limp and her eyes rolled back in her head.

Triel shook her by the shoulders. "Jetta?!"

Without hesitation, Triel placed one hand on Jetta's chest and the other on her forehead. As she waded toward the horizon between mind and body, dark, caustic vines slithered up her arm.

"Oh Gods—"

Her hands no longer rested on Jetta's skin, but the slick, endless black of the shadow thing that coiled around her, yanking her out of the physical world. Triel screamed as she plunged headfirst into a nightmare.

164

***

Jaeia wandered down the corridors of the Alliance Central Starbase, barely aware of the passing crewmen.

The senior officers' debriefing will start in less than fifteen minutes, she thought, glancing at the time on her sleeve. *I should have spent my time readying for my presentation...*

The truth of the matter edged its way into her mind. *(Working alone in my quarters is the last thing I want to do right now.)*

She had successfully renegotiated a treaty between Trigos and the original nine Homeworlds, but Victor's hold on the Perimeter worlds and the industrial planets within Calmunis, namely Tatos and Pyme, would unravel her treaty within a matter of weeks, if not sooner. The Homeworlds had become too dependent on Tatos and Pyme for everything from military parts to luxury goods, especially Trigos, which had relied heavily on imports for the last two hundred years since its global urbanization.

Jaeia let her fingertips graze the smooth, cold surface of the wall. *Victor is playing this perfectly. He's attacking the Starways on every possible front—politically, economically, militarily, and socially.* Some fronts he attacked insidiously, some outright, but all with such precision and guile that she couldn't predict his next move. *And every counter-maneuver or offensive I try is met with an effective, almost expected, response.*

His latest move was to play to the sympathies of the Human Rights movement while placating the Freedom Libertariats by promising both sides that he would end the human–Sentient conflict that had been raging since first contact centuries ago. *If he succeeds, that will mean the end of the Alliance and the totalitarian reign of his new Republic.*

For reasons she couldn't rationalize but felt deep within her bones, she knew that he had waited for this moment for years. Maybe even orchestrated it over the centuries. He had destroyed the

Alliance's defenses in seconds, all but stripped the General Assembly, and somehow stopped the Motti in their tracks. *If he could do those things, he can do anything.*

But unlike any other enemy she had faced, Victor was nearly impregnable, hiding behind the wall of people he had erected around himself. While Li ran his army, he appointed delegates from the most wealthy and influential worlds to his court. *He isn't the prominent face of the Republic—at least not yet—but he's certainly holding all the strings.*

For some reason it reminded her of Yahmen, how he had set up her uncle to take the fall when he ran into debt. With Galm taking his beatings, he weaseled his way out of trouble, even nabbing Lohien for himself along the way.

"*Mugarruthepeta,*" she mumbled in her native tongue.

When she looked up, she realized that she had somehow wandered into the restricted area of the security and interrogation wing.

This is the room where I confronted Minister Razar about Reht and the crew of the Wraith, she thought, standing a few meters away from the interrogation chamber.

Despite her clearance to be there, every security guard within range asked if she required assistance.

"Sir, can I help you?" one soldier asked, his eyes moving back and forth between her and the security control board terminal.

This is odd, Jaeia thought. She checked the time on her sleeve and let out a frustrated sigh. *I'll have to look into this later.*

Jaeia was about to leave when she heard someone call her name. "Captain Kyron?"

She turned in time to see a male human being escorted into a holding cell. No older than his late teens, the young man had sandy-blonde hair and fair skin. For a moment she lost herself in the deep violet of his eyes.

"Keep moving," the guard said, shoving him inside the cell.

"Wait," Jaeia said, catching up to them. There was something about the way he looked at her, the way his eyes were too old to belong to a young man. "Who are you?"

"Sir, you should go now. We're about to start the interview," the guard insisted.

Jaeia gasped. *He isn't human at all.*

His DNA read human—even his telepathic signature sounded and felt human—but inside him wiggled a little green worm that had spun his body to resemble the young man she saw before her.

This is no interview, she thought. *They're using the Spinner's replicated body as a weapon against whatever prisoner they're holding in that cell.*

Alliance interrogation specialists would mangle, torture, and even kill the Spinner's body if it meant extracting the information they needed. She had witnessed it before, most recently when they had tortured Reht.

Jaeia barely kept her fury in check. She had petitioned the military council to put an end to the abuse of the Spinners, but despite their reassurances and promises, it still occurred on a regular basis.

She pulled the guard aside. "Who gave you these orders?"

"Minister Razar, Captain."

Grabbing the guard's sleeve, Jaeia scrolled through his orders. His approved tactics made her sick to her stomach.

Humiliation.

Near suffocation.

Beating.

Avulsion.

"Who's the prisoner?" she asked.

The guard betrayed no emotion. "That is classified, Sir."

Jaeia was about to press her authority when her uniform sleeve beeped, alerting her to the meeting.

"Soldier, I'm ordering you to delay your interview until I return from my meeting."

"But Sir, I was given explicit orders from the Minister before he—"

The temptation to use her second voice excited her, but she stopped herself. *Not when I'm this emotional; not when there's a chance I might go farther than making the guard delay his interview.*

"My name is Aesis," the young Spinner said, "and I'm tired of dying."

Jaeia took his hand and pushed the guard away. "He's coming with me."

"But Sir, I—"

Jaeia summoned a lift and led Aesis onto it, ignoring the warnings of the guard.

"Sir, I must insist. I was given strict orders by the Minister."

"Right now Wren is the custodian of that title," Jaeia replied coolly. "Stand down or I'll have you removed from duty."

Despite being one of the better-trained practitioners of Rai Shar, as all of the personnel in interrogations were, snippets of the guard's thoughts seeped through his frustration.

This is a classified mission known only to the Minister—a last resort—something he authorized before falling into a coma, Jaeia gleaned.

"Thank you," Aesis said as they cruised down the corridors.

"Do you know who were you impersonating?" Jaeia asked.

Aesis looked at his feet, his shoulders hunched forward like a whipped dog. "They say you're different from the other officers, Captain. They say you can bring peace to this galaxy. I hope they're right."

The way he said it made her blush, but she quickly composed herself. "Aesis, please, tell me. I want to help you."

He lifted his head, his gaze meeting hers, his warm violet eyes somehow penetrating her guard.

"I'm not sure. I'm never told. They just give me a strand of hair or a few flecks of skin, and then that's it. I just wait to…"

Aesis pressed his lips together, his eyes finishing the sentence.

"I have no idea what you've been through. I can't imagine dying over and over again," Jaeia began stupidly. She wrestled with what to say next, but Aesis diffused the tension. He smiled shyly, his violet eyes connecting again with hers.

"My mother always said to give everything at least one try. But I'd wait on that one a little while."

After deboarding the lift, Jaeia lead the Spinner to the conference room. The horseshoe-shaped conference table, usually occupied by all seventeen members of the senior military council, had been reduced to just seven in the face of the political war that divided their ranks:

Gaeshin Wren, acting Minister and CCO
Msiasto Mo Chief of Military Intelligence
Ryeo Kaoto, Chief of Medicine
Trecyn Rook, Acting Commander of the SMT
LuShin DeAnders, the Director of Military Research
Severn Mallok, Chief Officer of the Perimeter Guard
Lory Berrara, Chief Advisor for Sentient Relations.

"Captain, what are you—?" Wren said as she instructed Aesis to take her seat at the table. The other members, who had been talking among themselves, hushed immediately upon seeing her guest.

"I was assigned to debrief you on the recent peace negotiations with the Nine Homeworlds, but I realized what our real problem is," Jaeia said, laying a hand on Aesis's shoulder.

"I'm sorry, I don't follow," Wren said, his words rushed and impatient.

She would have to make her case, fast. "It took a lot of convincing for my sister and me to join the Alliance. After fighting for the Dominion we had a hard time believing that any government or military could be trustworthy in the pursuit of justice and peace. But the Alliance fought for the telepaths, campaigned for human freedom, and stood for the greater good of all Sentient kind. At least that's what I thought."

Aesis looked up at her, his eyes strangely calm and steadfast. She couldn't read Spinner minds, but somehow she felt his silent reassurance.

"This is Aesis, and he is a Spinner. When I look at him, I see that we are no better than our enemies. We torture and kill his kind because it benefits our interrogations and allows us to stay within legal limits of prisoner rights. Yes, he can replicate hundreds of thousands of bodies, and he is monetarily compensated for his work—but what psychological damage are we doing to him and all the other Spinners, and how do we continue to justify our actions?"

Jaeia rounded the table to stand at the apex of the horseshoe. "How can we say we are any better than our enemies when we employ such barbaric techniques against those we have sworn to protect?"

"I'm sorry, captain, but I don't see how this relates to our debriefing," Wren said.

"It has everything to do with our debriefing," Jaeia replied, careful to keep her voice from rising. "I just formed a treaty with the original Nine Homeworlds, promising our protection and strict adherence to the Basic Rights Tenets of the Starways. I swore that we would honor and protect every life form, and be guardians of the laws of the Homeworlds. But how can we continue to exploit the Spinners and uphold these oaths?"

Wren broke the silence. "Captain, a word with you?"

While the rest of the council members talked amongst themselves, Jaeia followed Wren into the adjacent private council room.

"Of all the people I have ever served with, surely you understand why we have employed the Spinners. And if you pretend not to, then you choose to deceive yourself."

I wasn't prepared for that to come from Gaeshin Wren, she thought.

Recognizing the shocked look on her face, he elaborated in his usual calm fashion: "Democracy, Sentient Rights, freedom, liberty—

these are words that politicians use to quell the general populace. But civilians don't understand war like you and I do. They don't know that the rules of decency and humanity don't apply when your enemy is gunning down your friends and family. They don't understand that sometimes the *smart* decision has to supersede the *right* decision in the battle for survival. Sometimes there can be no negotiations, no trials, no rulebooks. Not for the greater good."

I can't entirely disagree with Wren, she thought, struggling with a response. Even without her thousands of years of stolen knowledge, her experience on Fiorah proved his words. *There are some people that only understood the language of violence.*

In the back of her mind she heard Yahmen's brutal laugh, and a shiver ran up her spine. Yahmen never understood reason, never listened to any of their pleas or cared about anything but pleasuring himself with their pain.

If we had stayed on Fiorah, he would have eventually beaten us to death. I would have had to let Jetta fight back—we would have all had to fight back, she thought, succumbing to the grim reality of their plight. *To survive, we might have been forced to kill him, breaking all the rules and beliefs I have always stood by.*

Jaeia thought of Jahx. "There has to be another way."

Wren placed a hand on her shoulder. "I admire your conviction, Jaeia, but your first duties are as to the Alliance. That soldier was given strict orders regarding that Spinner, and I need him returned to duty immediately."

"I can't stand idly by while they torture him, Sir."

Wren's posture stiffened, and Jaeia felt his thoughts retract beyond her senses. "You have your orders, captain."

Alarmed by the unexpected change in the CCO's temperament, Jaeia let her legs walk her back to her seat at the conference table as her mind tried to assimilate this sudden shift.

What just happened?

171

"Thanks for trying," Aesis whispered as an expressionless soldier with silver-sealed eyes wrapped his hands around the Spinner's left wrist.

I always believed Wren was on my side. Now I'm not so sure. Jaeia watched as an escort squad led Aesis out of the conference room. *I'm more alone than I thought.*

"Captain, your platform," Wren said, drawing her back into the meeting.

Numbed by disappointment, Jaeia walked to the front and began her debriefing. It took all of her concentration as she called up the video reels of her negotiations and scrolled through the list of planetary demands on the holographic projectors.

"...The representatives of Trigos require that we re-route our trade lines to include the moons Aris and Calle. Um, the Chancellor has, uh..."

But the words rapidly left her. *It's meaningless to review the latest peace treaty when the Alliance is going to violently kill Aesis.*

An urgent call from the Alliance flagship interrupted her unraveling speech.

"Chief Wren—I have a relay message from Jue Hexron. Privatized and prioritized from Victor Paulstine, addressed to the military council," the ship's captain said over the intercom.

Wren nodded to her and she switched over to the channels.

Not another one of his prerecorded messages, she thought. Victor enjoyed sending them about once a day through various channels within their communications network as another means to show them that he had ways inside their defenses that they weren't even aware of.

This is different, she realized as his image materialized on their projectors.

"Good afternoon, officers of the Alliance. I bid you *ketamei* from the Holy Cities."

Jaeia's stomach turned to ice. Maybe it was the way his cheeks creased with his savage smile, or how his words dripped with arrogance. *He's going to make his move.*

"I have come across classified files on both Jetta and Jaeia Kyron, including some rare footage of their time with the Dominion Core, and I must say that I find it very disheartening and deeply disturbing that the Alliance would continue to keep such unstable individuals in service. Admiral Unipoesa himself has submitted numerous concerns to the war council, and Jetta's postwar breakdown should have been proof enough of their liability."

Jaeia's looked to Wren. The soft-spoken Chief never took his gaze off of Victor, but he maintained intense focus on shielding his thoughts.

Victor held up a datawand in his hand. "Assault, perjury, larceny, murder—genocide—the charges against them are lengthy. But neither the public nor the courts know the extent of it. The military has kept many incidents classified. I am here to unveil the truth. The public needs to know who is really at the helm of the Alliance military."

Horrified, but unable to look away, Jaeia vaguely heard Wren's command to terminate the message as she got closer to holographics. As she leaned in, face centimeters from the projection, the rest of the room fell away in the blue nimbus of light.

The videos played. "I don't remember," she whispered.

But she did. Somewhere tucked away in the deepest, darkest corners of mind lurked the terrible knowledge of what Victor revealed. It could have been post war shock syndrome, or some innate self-preservation mechanism that had kept her from recalling what had happened.

Jetta was shown first. Eyes unseeing, she writhed and screamed under heavy five-point restraint, her body hooked up to a confusing mess of intravenous tubing and monitors while medical staff ducked in and out of camera range. A staff psychiatrist tried to ask her questions, but even after sedation she continued to scream. When his hand approached her shoulder, she somehow managed to break her right arm restraint and grab him by the neck. After a sickening crunching sound, the doctor's head rolled bonelessly onto his shoulder and Jetta dropped him to the ground. The camera crashed to the floor as soldiers and medical staff rushed in, showing only the scuffle of feet and empty medication vials dropping to the floor.

Another clip. In this one Jetta was catatonic, her mouth frozen open in a silent scream. A neurologist checking her readings bent toward her a little too closely, his lab coat brushing her cheek. After a moment, his face warped oddly as if he was stuck in a vacuum. He dropped his clipboard and backed against the wall, shielding himself from an invisible attacker. Moments later he ripped out his throat with his fingernails, his screams garbled by his own blood. Medical staff poured in, trying to remove him from the scene, but his legs seemed rooted to the ground.

He died within seconds.

Jaeia identified the time period. *This was right after we defeated the Motti. Jetta lost her mind after killing Jahx.* She had known of incidents during Jetta's recovery, but not deaths.

*It could have been doctored—reimaged—*Jaeia tried to rationalize.

It got worse.

Jaeia hadn't been allowed to see Jetta for several days after their victory over the Deadwalkers, and during that time she had only vague recollections of the intense preparations she had undergone to help her sister. She could recall being advised by several therapists and conferring with Triel about how to heal Jetta's trauma, but she didn't remember a frightened, out-of control young woman that needed psychological intervention herself.

"What do you see?" the doctor on the video asked her.

Jaeia saw herself huddled in the corner of a padded room, her hair in greasy knots, fingernails ragged and chewed to the quick. Her red-rimmed eyes stared blankly at the camera as she rocked back and forth on her knees.

"He's coming for me—Jetta, where are you? HE'S COMING FOR ME!" she cried.

"Who, Jaeia? Who do you see?"

"HIM!" Jaeia screamed. She broke from her cradled position and lunged for the doctor, screaming unintelligibly as she clawed at his face. The doctor hit the emergency alert right before Jaeia broke his hand.

From a distance one of the three orderlies shot her full of theralol, but it did little to calm her.

This time she used her talent. *"Get away from me!"*

All three orderlies ran for the exit. The doctor, a mangled lump of flesh, somehow managed to break free of her grip and limped to the exit, leaving a trail of blood.

Victor narrated over the video. "One orderly ejected himself into outer space. The other two were found in the incinerators—at least what was left of them. The doctor recovered but was deemed unfit for duty after suffering severe psychological trauma."

"Can somebody shut that thing off?" Wren yelled in the background.

Oblivious to the commotion that surrounded her, Jaeia continued to watch the video. Two officers tried to pull her away, but she fended them off with little effort.

This time the projection showed the admiral, red-nosed from booze, his face ballooned in the camera lens.

"I know too much," he whispered, slouching back into his desk chair. He unbuttoned his uniform top, revealing a second shirt drenched in sweat and alcohol. *"I know what they're going to do next. They are going to keep those leeches serviceable. They're too valuable to discharge, too dangerous to incarcerate. We need powerful figureheads now that Li's gone, but they can't be trusted. Too unpredictable. Too much like Li... and Tarsha."*

Unipoesa wept into his hands, great sobs stealing his breath.

That is the most frightening sound I've ever heard, Jaeia thought. Somewhere, deep inside, she recognized the sound of a man

175

at the end of his rope, entirely hopeless, gutted and bled dry, wishing for a swift end to his misery.

"Li and Tarsha were our failures, our attempts at controlling something we didn't understand, and now look at him—and her! Look at what they've done. Look at what we've done to them. And we still can't—we can't—"

He threw his bottle at the far wall, sending fragments of glass and booze flying. After a long pause he returned to the visual field and gripped the camera so tightly that the picture trembled. *"They're monsters. We should have killed them when we had the chance."*

Betrayed seemed too pale a word to describe the frantic surge of rage that closed off her throat.

It could have been faked— she told herself, not wanting to believe what she heard and saw. But the clips of her and Jetta were real. And when she saw the look of panic on Wren's face, she knew that the admiral's segment was legitimate, too.

Victor came onscreen again, a smile quirking his mouth. Statistics and written reports scrolled in the background as if to substantiate his claims. When Jaeia touched any of the highlighted titles, the entire document popped into view. Things like *biochips enhanced to track subatomic brain waves of Kyron twins* or *constant audio-video surveillance of Jetta and Jaeia Kyron authorized by Minister Tidas Razar.*

"Jetta Kyron is regarded as volatile, antiauthoritarian, and antisocial with a high propensity towards violence," Victor said, highlighting several of the reports. "Her behavior would be deemed unacceptable for other military or government personnel, but despite the evidence of her psychosis, she has been given senior-level rank in the Alliance fleet. Worse yet is her sister, Jaeia. With her deep-seated lack of self-worth, the other Kyron twin uses her abilities to control others to compensate for her own insecurities. But don't be fooled by her pleasant nature or her diplomatic titles—her *accidental* murder record is much higher than her sister's. Jaeia is the wolf in sheep's clothing."

"Why?" Jaeia stammered.

"You're probably wondering why I'm telling you this," Victor said, bringing the camera around to focus on his plastic face. He leaned forward, the glint of his diamond teeth overworking the pixels, "because tomorrow you will have no choice but to submit to my demands."

The video bleeped out.

Jaeia stood there, unable to move. Someone put a hand on her shoulder, but she barely felt it.

"Council dismissed," Wren barked.

The rest of the room cleared out. When it was just her and Wren and the hypnotic drum of the ventilation system, Jaeia finally found the ability to speak again.

"Is it true?"

Wren stood a few meters to her right with his hands clasped behind his back, his voice just above a whisper. "He did those things to provoke you. You and your sister are key to our defenses. If he can take you away from us, we'll have nothing, Jaeia."

Jaeia saw the logic in Wren's argument. She and Jetta in command of the Alliance fleet were an unspoken part of the Nine's treaty. As commanders they could perform miracles against impossible odds, and it was the faith of the original Nine that kept the Alliance together.

Out of nowhere, Jaeia laughed. *Victor really is the perfect enemy.*

"He'll go public with it tomorrow on one of his galactic broadcasts," she said, wiping the tears from her eyes. "He wants everyone to see how dangerous we are. When that happens, they'll petition for our resignation. Or worse. Probably demand an Arish trial."

Too overwhelmed by all that had transpired, Jaeia only half-heartedly realized what she had just said. An Arish trial meant no judge, no jury, no deliberation—just the sweeping ruling by the crowd. In the annals of shared memories, she recalled that the punishment necessitated that each member of the crowd took a small cut of the offender's flesh.

(Seems appropriate,) a cynical voice inside her whispered.

"Well then, Captain. I think it's time we plan our offensive," Wren said.

Jaeia's heart leapt into her throat. To calm herself, she ran her fingertips along the seams of her uniform and looked at the stars shining through the window. "Can I trust you, Chief?"

Wren made no sound as he approached her. The next thing she knew he was standing at her side, his slanted eyes level with hers. "You have no choice, Captain."

***

At first Reht didn't hear his first mate when he pounded on the door to his den, nor did he notice the message light flashing on his terminal. With every climax, Femi's vocalizations got louder and more dynamic.

"*Gibar m'elo k'fatquo!*" she cried, thrusting her hips against his.

Reht gasped as he let himself go, flowing into the dark-skinned beauty that lay trembling beneath him.

"Holy—" he whispered, closing his eyes. *It's not just with Diawn...*

What's wrong with me?

Under any other circumstances, an unblemished, unadulterated beauty would have challenged his restraint and control. But now, drained and spent, he felt wholly unsatisfied no matter how many times or how many ways he slept with her.

Reht reached for a half-empty bottle of Eckir rum that he had tucked away between the mattresses in case of emergencies. Tasting like battery acid, and probably just as caustic, a swig set his throat on fire.

At least pain is still real.

Femi lay across him, her hair draped across his chest and arms as she delicately traced his abdominal muscles with her fingernails. Gazing longingly at him, she whispered words he didn't understand, but he inferred by the vulnerability in her eyes. He had seen in before, hundreds of times, in the many women he had bedded in his den. Usually he found it amusing, but at the moment, already feeling disconnected and frustrated, her need grated his last nerve.

Mom growled over the intercom.

"Yeah, I got it," Reht grumbled as his eye caught the flashing light.

Since Femi didn't speak Common he didn't see the harm in letting her stay as he switched the terminal on. The jaded face of Mantri Sebbs materialized on the flat screen, looking even more sour and crusty than normal.

"Oh Gods—"

Reht stood up, stretched, and yawned as Sebbs covered his eyes and recoiled in horror. Both of his shoulders popped as he shook out his arms and legs. "Morning, champ! Didn't expect to see your shining face."

"*Chak* you, Jagger," Sebbs said. He lit up, holding the cigarette between two unsteady fingers, but he threw it aside when the first puff threw him into a coughing fit. He looked awful, like he hadn't slept in weeks.

"I take it back. You look like *gorsh-shit*. What's been eatin' you?" Reht said, grabbing his bottle for another pull.

"Can't sleep," Sebbs said. "Bad nightmares. Too real."

"You should start drinkin' again," he said as Femi giggled and pulled him back into bed, spilling rum onto the sheets. When he touched the bottle to his lips, he realized there were only a few precious drops left, but she assuaged him by stroking his upper thigh.

Sebbs looked disgusted. "You still think this is a game, don't you?"

The old Dominion traitor searched for something off-camera. After a few curse words, he thrust a poster advertisement for RedFly into the visual field. The graffiti letters scrawled across the bottom looked familiar, but Reht couldn't decipher any of the words.

"See this?" Sebbs pointed to a complex symbol. "That's your head. Alive gets double. You're one hot ticket."

"Where they pitching this? Bounty boards?" Reht said, taking Femi's hands off of him and tossing the bottle into the ankle-deep collection of garbage on the floor. He wrapped a sheet around his waist and moved closer to the terminal, trying to get a read on the foreign logograms.

"No. Bigger. This is strictly for the Slingers."

Slingers, short for gunslingers, was underground slang for the trained assassins that kept the meat market as corrupt and dirty as possible. The logograms were their secret language, their way of communicating in code right there in the open.

I call gorsh-shit; *how could Sebbs know this?*

Then he remembered. A long time ago, the Joliak had ties to a renegade Slinger named Landis Trehff. All Slingers were cultivated and harvested by the crime syndicate, and occasionally a few came along that resented their breeding. Sebbs helped Landis do the impossible and break his bonds, and in repayment, the former Slinger gave him what every person playing the streets wanted to know: when they were going to buy their ticket.

"That fruitcake taught you their code?" Reht said. Moaning, Femi spread her legs and ran her fingers up and down her abdomen. The dog-soldier captain felt himself rising again, rapidly losing interest in Sebbs. "Look, Mantri, I appreciate all that, but I got a job lined up, and I can't be losing my head on something like that."

Mantri snorted. "Bet you can't get off."

Reht reared around. "What did you say, *old friend?*"

"That's the mind*chak*. It's what they did to us. They take away what pleasures us most and replace it with their objectives. That's

180

why you gotta do what they want—nothing else can give you that high."

"You lying son of a—"

Sebbs blew air through his lips. "Please—you know that bounty board on your skank pilot was a setup. Tell me you don't believe me and I won't tell you what could save all of our *assinos*."

Femi tilted her hips and curled her finger at him, tearing his mind at the seams. Carnal hungers bade him one direction, rational thought another. He massaged his bandaged hands, feeling the phantom burn, and remembered his strange confusion when he discovered Shandin was still alive; how his crew was acting differently—how he didn't feel like himself. *How I can't really get off.*

(Starfox—)

He turned back to Sebbs. "Okay. Then what?"

Sebbs sported an unusual grin. "Pick me up in Southie by the gaming theater."

"You chicken-*sycha*," Reht said. "You've made a few enemies and now you're running to me for cover, aren't ya?"

"Same as you. You, me, your crew—we're all running for our lives now."

The Joliak hung up, leaving Reht more confused and agitated than before.

"Not now," he said, pushing away Femi's hands and hitting the com next to his nightstand. "Mom—land us near the gaming theater on the south side of the city. And make sure the crew is in position before we cross the district boundaries."

A grunt preceded the shifting of the engines as the first mate altered the ship's course.

"*Chakking* Southie," Reht grumbled to himself as he waded through the mess to find his pants. He always avoided that dump. An area for scavengers, players, and deadbeats, the denizens of the south side were notorious for shooting anything in the sky, even their own people, to protect their precious games.

In all his years, Reht never understood the attraction.

But at least you get to shut those holographic girls off, he thought to himself as he calmed Femi with promises to return later.

After securing Femi in his den, Reht went down and waited by the ramp with his first mate. Scanning the streets lit by advertisement signs, he couldn't help but feel a chill, even through his jacket.

"I can't stand this place," he whispered to Mom as an unfortunate fellow stumbled along an empty parking lot, his eyes bloodshot and vacant, mouth forming words that came out in long strings of drool.

Mom growled in agreement. The aftereffects of the games were worse than any trip Reht had witnessed, so he'd never tried it. Sebbs once told him the hook was deadlier than methoc, but it was hard to believe a computer simulation could have that much hold on a mind.

Sebbs appeared out of the shadows, hurrying toward the ship, keeping an eye on the street.

"Go, I got this," Reht said to Mom, patting him on the shoulder. "Get the *Wraith* back to the upper atmosphere."

Mom grumbled, but complied, heading back up to the bridge.

"*Chak,* Sebbs," Reht said as the Joliak scurried aboard. "What are you doing in this part of town anyway, *jingoga?*"

"You wouldn't believe me," he said, rubbing the abraded skin around his wrists.

Reht looked him up and down, marveling at the wide array of bruises and scabbing lacerations at the base of his neck. *Someone gave him a good thrashing.*

The dog-soldier captain slammed him hard against the wall. "Try me."

"You don't scare me anymore," Sebbs whispered, his eyes strangely hollow and voice mechanical.

"We'll see about that."

Grabbing him by the collar, Reht dragged Sebbs onto the bridge. Mom took one sniff of the Joliak and growled. Ro and Cray snickered in the corner, making sure that Sebbs could see them gesturing at him with their knives.

The dog-soldier captain threw Sebbs in his captain's chair, and the others gathered around. Even Tech joined the inquisition, hanging from the ceiling while Bacthar stood behind Reht, encircling half the group with his wings.

"Talk," Reht said, kicking the chair. "We don't have time for your *gorsh-shit*."

Sebbs sighed and stared off into the distance. "I don't really know what got me into Southie. A few raw deals, killing two cops and an undercover hooker. Doesn't matter. Here's where I ended up. I was double-crossing some yank in the back alley of a dive when I overheard two game operators talking about the latest craze. Some game called Crazy Betty. Real popular with the guys and lezzies. The most real simulation you can get out there, and it's all skins and tails."

For a moment Reht puzzled over Sebbs' words. Skins and tails were basically interactive pornography, which was fairly popular with all the insecure chums who were too scared to hire a real girl in the red light district. But turning it into a game where the patron jacked their neuro-network into a fully integrated servo deck and played for days or weeks at a time brought it to a whole new level.

I can't imagine what the programmers did to turn cybersex into a full-scale game, he thought.

"Crazy Betty is so real that those poor stiffs *think* it's real," Sebbs continued. "They can't get their head out of the game. One of the operators said he started throwing ads in the games and watched every sucker go out and buy whatever dumb product he had on the line."

Reht got in his face. "Not caring."

"You should," Sebbs said, "because some of it is hacked military technology."

Reht drew back a little bit. "Yeah?"

183

When Sebbs tried to grab one of his wrists, Mom shoved Sebbs back into the chair.

"Watch it, friend," Reht chuckled. "Mom's had a temper lately."

Sebbs turned bright red as the Talian squeezed the Joliak's neck with one hand. "Aaaack—it's the… same thing… they're using… on… us!"

Reht tapped Mom on the shoulder, and the Talian let him go. "How do you know that?"

Gasping and massaging his neck, Sebbs looked indignantly at the Talian, but did nothing else. "Front pocket."

Reht reached in and withdrew a datachip.

"I swiped it from an operator. Has all the specs on Crazy Betty. Have your tin can look at it. You'll find hacked Alliance master programs operating the base matrix."

Reht tossed the rectangular unit up to Tech who caught it with one of his back legs and swung himself to the upper deck.

"How are you going to help us then, dear friend?" the dog-soldier captain asked, returning his attention Sebbs.

"We keep on Diawn. Dig a little bit deeper, figure out the rest of her job. With that information we can bargain with Pancar of Nagoorian."

"Why that old crust?"

"Pancar hated Tidas Razar for all of his illegal, under-the-table *gorsh-shit*, and because the old bastard snuffed his nephew a few years back. He'll sympathize with us, grant us asylum, especially if we can give him the information that Razar wanted. He's trying to take over the Alliance anyway."

Reht took a gamble. "Everybody out. Except you, of course, darling."

Mom lingered for a second, but Reht gave him a reassuring nod. "Autopilot's on, and me and Sebbs got some private business."

"I'm not really into guys," Sebbs said.

Reht didn't acknowledge the Joliak's newfound humor. "You know who Shandin is?"

The blank remained on Sebbs' face.

Is that assino *hiding something?* he thought, unable to read his features.

"Diawn's linked with him," he added, keeping a close watch for any changes in the Joliak's expression. "…And I have a personal score to settle with that *ratchakker*. I want both their heads on a plate."

"It's dangerous to go after two prizes, especially if it's between business and personal vendettas. You know that," Sebbs said. "What will happen if you have to choose? You can bet your sack that you'll lose your own head if it comes down to that."

Reht unsheathed a knife from his belt and stabbed it into the arm of the captain's chair, narrowly missing Sebbs' hand. "Do you know who Shandin is?"

Sebbs didn't flinch. "No," he said, his eyes flicking to his bandaged hands, "but I can guess."

Reht smiled. "You know the Nagoorian's signature?"

The Joliak grinned.

"Let's make the call."

***

At first Triel didn't know where she was or how she got there. Heat surrounded her on all sides, beating down from the suns above and radiating back up from the asphalt. Feeling suffocated, she took cover under the first shade she could find.

(Where am I?) *she said. Once her eyes adjusted to the intense light, she looked around from underneath the protection of a weathered store awning. Dilapidated housing projects with crashed-out windows lined the city street. Old hovercars, long since abandoned and gutted for parts, looked like the bleached skeletons of ancient creatures.*

(Hello?) *she said. In the distance someone gurgled and fell quiet.*

185

Unsure of what to do, Triel walked along the blistered sidewalk, trying to stay inside the shadows. The urban development offered no sights but graffitied buildings and chain-link fences, and the occasional liquor or black arts shop touting their wares behind bars.

I feel like I've been here before...

The Healer came across a parking lot in a gap between two buildings. More hovercars, broken down and covered in tan dust, waited to be stripped. She yelped when a pair of Domo dogs ran out from behind one of the wrecks and charged the fence. One, missing an eye, leapt and snarled while the other licked his chops, muzzle still fresh with wet blood from a previous kill.

Triel hurried on, weaving between open sacks of garbage roasting in the sun. The air, sulphurous and thick, hurt her lungs to breathe.

"Hey baby—got you some sweetness?"

A man with half a recognizable face appeared from behind a dumpster. Most of his hair and skin had been burned into tight pink lumps. He grinned at her, revealing black stumps. Triel gave him a wide berth as she passed. (No, sorry.)

"I'm going to gut you and eat your face!" he shrieked.

He continued to yell obscenities at her as she ran down the street. Even after a distance, she couldn't shake the feeling of pursuit.

Hurry, *she thought, picking up her pace as the surrounding buildings closed in on her. An unnamed terror, rising from the pitch of the homeless man's scream and expanding into the decaying streets, clenched her stomach.* I have to get away!

She rounded a corner into an alleyway and slumped against the wall, trying to catch her breath in the acrid air. That's when she heard the child's cry.

That voice sounds so familiar, *she thought, looking up toward a grated staircase running up the side of a dilapidated housing structure.*

The scream came again, and Triel pinpointed the sound to the third-floor apartment with boarded up windows and the back door dangling from its hinges.

I can't turn away from a child in need, *she told herself, but her senses pulled her in the opposite direction. Something dangerous and terrible lay inside the apartment, something much more powerful than her.*

(Oh Gods,) *Triel whispered, remembering being pulled into Jetta's mind.* This is Fiorah…

Fear seized her chest, making her heart race.

Why am I here? *she wondered.* Salam did something to Jetta when she tried to steal his knowledge—so shouldn't I be seeing his memories?

Slowly, Triel ascended the steps, careful to stay quiet as she listened for any kind of sound. In her periphery she saw the world around her shrinking down to encompass only the back alley and the staircase, and the dark apartment in front of her.

I have no choice, *she thought, stepping inside.*

The smells of rotten cabbage and mold assaulted her first. Slivers of light filtering through the boarded windows hinted at the glass and broken furniture scattered throughout the apartment, and dried blood mottling the ragged carpet.

Frightened and curious, she passed through the dingy kitchenette to the remains of a living space. The stuffing had been torn from the couch, and the coffee table lay broken in half. After spying a few cots in the corner down a hallway to her right, a figure moving in the shadows caught her eye.

(Hello?) *Triel whispered.* (Jetta—is that you?)

An animal sound came from the shadows, growling through sharp, wet teeth.

Don't give in to fear, *she told herself as she took another step forward, giving her a clearer sight of the bedroom to her left.* Someone's in there.

(Jetta?) *Triel said, this time a little louder.*

187

"I'm here," someone whispered. Small and weak, the voice belonged to a child no older than five.

Triel stepped into the bedroom, tripping on the dirty mattress lying just inside the door. After catching herself on a cement block shelf she looked up, startled to see the adult figure by the far wall.

(Jetta!) Triel exclaimed.

Jetta stood with her back to Triel, blocking her view of the mirror on the wall. What Triel could see of the reflection appeared distorted and strange.

(Hey,) Triel said, walking over and touching her shoulder. Jetta felt as stiff as a board, her mind untouchable and her face as white as a ghost. Mumbling under her breath, Triel couldn't understand her friend's words.

As the Healer turned her attention to the mirror, time slowed.

That's not Jetta's reflection, *she thought, horrified by the man in the mirror. The malice in his eyes shot straight through her, stripping down her walls, making her feel worthless, naked, and vulnerable. His stinking, suffocating presence surrounded her, whispering in her ear.*

"I'm not going to just kill you..." he said. "I'm going to make you suffer—make you pay for all that you've done."

Triel tore herself away from the mirror. Pain shot down her neck and spine, and she collapsed on the dirty mattress. Something squealed, and Triel recoiled from the tiny bodies wriggling out from underneath her. She caught a glimpse of the rats fleeing for the cover of the nightstand as she rolled over and collected herself.

I know that man, *Triel thought, digging through her memories.* I've saw glimpses of him when Jetta battled Jahx—

Yahmen.

Covering her eyes, the Healer wrapped her free arm around Jetta. She tried to pull her away, but Jetta stayed fixed in place.

Triel put her ear closer to Jetta's mouth, trying to hear her words.

"All I am is what I can see, the world is just a reflection of me. All I am is what I can see, the world is just a reflection of me..."

(Jetta—come away from there,) *Triel pleaded.* (That isn't you.)

Something in the shadows hissed. Triel spun around, trying to pinpoint its source, but it came from all around her. The shadows grew, blotting out the doorway and the dirty mattress until all that remained was the two of them and the mirror.

(This isn't real!) *Triel cried.*

Jetta took a step forward, her face only centimeters from the false reflection. With every word her voice rose until she was yelling.

"ALL I AM IS WHAT I CAN SEE, THE WORLD IS JUST A REFLECTION OF ME!"

And then she dove headfirst into the mirror, the surface rippling like water.

(No!)

Triel dove after her, not thinking about the consequences. Her sense of self fractured as the surface broke her apart and then threw her back together in a haphazard mosaic.

When she came to, breathless and dizzy, she didn't recognize her surroundings. A scoured wasteland, devoid of any life, stretched on for kilometers, with the ruins of a massive city crumbling along the horizon. Lightning and thunder raged overhead, waging a fierce battle for supremacy in the tortured sky.

(Jetta?) *Triel whispered.*

Jetta hunkered down on all fours, her neck collared and linked to a massive chain that extended beyond the horizon.

"I'm so sorry," Jetta said, her eyes downcast and her body trembling. Something roared in the distance.

(I have to get you out of here,) *Triel said, trying to open the collar.*

Closer inspection revealed metal spikes driving into Jetta's inflamed skin. Blood oozed from each puncture site.

"Please," Jetta said, grabbing hold of Triel's hands, "forgive me!"

Footsteps approached, light and unrushed.

(Come on, Jetta—you have to try!) Triel said, trying to find a weak point in the chains.

"She's beyond you now. You and all her little friends," a voice said.

A man stepped out of the shadows. Although he appeared human, his unnaturally taut skin and diamond-studded smile hinted at otherworldly origins. He wore a dapper suit, gold-rimmed glasses and many different pieces of jewelry, most notably a signet ring of black gold emblazoned with a crimson bird of prey. Leaning forward on his cane, the man inspected her with his obsidian eyes.

"You think you could have her?" he laughed.

Triel held tight to Jetta. (Stay away.)

"You think you love her?" he said, yanking on the chain to Jetta's neck. "You don't know what she is!"

Jetta screamed, blood leaking from beneath her collar as her face distorted, and her body changed shape. Within seconds she transformed into a dark-haired man Triel didn't recognize but felt as if she should.

That face, *she thought, captivated by the kindness in his brown eyes, and the profound grief and regret in his expression. His aura stretched beyond her visual spectrum, and when he spoke, the weight of his words took her breath away.*

"Forgive all that I have done."

The man from the shadows yanked the chain again, dissolving the image. Jetta reappeared, her blanched skin pierced through with wires and buzzing machinery in the early stages of Liiker transformation.

"You're all worthless. You stink of your imperfection, your disease. You don't deserve your skin," the man from the shadows hissed at her.

Jetta opened her mouth, emitting the buzzing sound of a thousand competing voices at a deafening decibel.

(Jetta!) *the Healer screamed, clapping her hands over her ears.* (Listen to me—we're on Algar. Salam did something to you. He tricked you—you have to snap out of it. This isn't real!)

The buzzing noise intensified.

"She's beyond redemption and hope," *the man laughed at her.* "She's beyond you."

Something warm and wet dribbled through Triel's fingers.

(Please,) *the Healer cried, squeezing her eyes shut,* (I *need* you. Come back to me!)

Triel opened her eyes.

I'm back in the tent, she realized, finding Jetta lying in front of her on the cot. Her relief vanished the second she touched the commander's shoulder. *Her skin feels like ice—*

(Am I too late?)

Jetta's eyes fluttered open. After a moment of confusion, she seemed to remember where she was.

"What happened?" Triel asked. "Are you okay?"

Jetta's brow knitted, then relaxed. "I'm okay."

Triel hugged her tightly.

"Okay—okay!" Jetta said, wrestling free. She sat up, holding her head in both hands. "Gods…"

"What did Salam do to you?"

Angered flushed her cheeks. "He made me think I was…"

But she didn't finish the sentence. Triel held her hand, patiently waiting.

Swallowing hard, Jetta took her hand back. "He knew how to hurt me," she whispered.

Jetta swung her legs over the cot and looked at her squarely. "Have you ever heard of something like this?"

Triel nodded. "Some of the telepaths we recovered after the war underwent similar experiences. It's a kind of thought poisoning used to torture POWs, though I've never seen anything this advanced—or from a human."

191

"I'm not so sure he's human," Jetta said as she stood up, straightening the remains of her uniform. "But he knew what he was doing. He's done this kind of thing before."

The dark look in her eyes sent a chill down Triel's spine. "It's time we even the score."

Triel put herself in front of her. "Jetta—we should talk about this. Clearly Salam knows you. I think it would be dangerous to go in without a plan."

Jetta kept her eyes trained on the front of the tent. "He knows me, yes," she said, her words trenchant. "But to assault me, he risked me seeing him."

Sidestepping Triel, Jetta opened the flap and called to the nearest guard: "Get Salam. Now."

"The counselor has turned in for the evening—" the soldier started.

Jetta didn't give him a choice. "Now."

As the soldier took off to summon his commander, Triel pulled Jetta back into the tent. The commander's fury bubbled behind the sharp green of her eyes.

I know that look, the Healer thought, *and the deadly calculations that are taking place behind it.* Triel imagined Jetta synthesizing and reprocessing thousands of years' worth of military knowledge and tactics until she selected the perfect move. *One that will not only stop her enemy, but eliminate him.*

"I was there with you in that nightmare," she started, not sure of how to phrase her concern. Beneath Jetta's cold facade brewed anger and humiliation from Salam's surprise attack.

I have to be careful, Triel thought, sensing Jetta's elevated stress levels. *How do I tell her how I feel?*

Up until Salam's assault, Triel believed that Jetta's greatest weakness tied into her participation in the death of her brother. *But that's only a part of something much more complex and malignant.*

"I saw all of what you did. I know how much he hurt you," she said. "I'm worried about you and what you're going to do next."

192

Jetta's expression turned militant. "He's malicious. He wants me out of the way so he can get to you."

"Do you know why?"

"To get into the Temple," she said, referring to the ancient legend that only those of Prodgy blood could access the holy grounds. "He doesn't care about the Prodgies, he wants the power inside that Temple."

"Do not condemn all these people because of him," the Healer whispered.

Jetta turned away, her lips curling into a snarl as she waited for Salam.

Triel ran her fingers through her hair. Frustrated and frightened, she gave it one last shot. "Do you know what happens when I heal you? You stay with me long after you've gone."

Jetta didn't take her eyes off the tent flap.

"I feel like I've seen you, Jetta—all of you. And you know what?"

The commander didn't budge.

"I'm still here, at your side. I'm your friend. You're unlike anyone else I've ever met."

"I didn't think you knew many other eight-year-old commanders with my kill count," Jetta bit back.

"It's not your talents, Jetta. It's you. I care about the person behind all of it. You're beyond your age and you are more than your borrowed experiences. And despite all that's happened to you, you still strive for the best for your friends and family."

Jetta visibly shuddered. An unexpected feeling jarred Triel's senses, threading worry through her subconscious and pulling at her confidence. *Jetta did something...*

The Healer refocused her efforts. "Look, Jetta, I know you're angry at Salam—I am too—but you can't take him by force. You don't know how strong you are. You could take out the entire settlement."

A hurt look cut across Jetta's face but vanished with a blink.

"You're right," she said quietly. Her shoulders relaxed a little, but her eyes remained on the tent flap.

Footsteps approached the tent. The Healer had expected Salam, not an escort team. "Follow me," the leader said.

Jetta and Triel fell in step behind them as the sun settled behind the eastern horizon, turning the cloud-smeared sky shades of scarlet and lavender. A few familiar stars sparkled in the twilight, pulling Triel's mind back to the past. *Was it that long ago that I gazed up at the night sky while my father collected night-blooming plants for his apothecary?*

Old memories trickled through. The intoxicating smell of the nocturnal flowers and the way they glowed in the moonlight; how the brisk northern breeze brought little bumps to her skin as the woods came alive with the sounds of awakening creatures. *I miss my home...*

Even as a child she understood the dangers of night travel, but didn't care. *My father was invincible. He would always keep me safe. Nothing could ever separate our family.*

Triel pinched the webbing between her fingers to keep the darker memories at bay. *Don't get emotional,* she told herself as the escort team led them into an enclosed area in the middle of the settlement.

What is this place? she thought, surveying the muddy ground littered with empty shells and broken equipment. A thicket of lights and torches kept the place well-lit. At one end of the fenced area, caged animals hooted and howled, pacing anxiously behind the bars. *That's a gray Wammercat. And that's a razor-toothed Tygra, a feather-pawed mountain wolf...*

Dread swam through her stomach. *Those are Algar's most feared predators.*

Salam waited among the animals, petting the gray-pawed wolf Jetta had ridden earlier. The wolf whined, flattening his ears against his head and tucking his tail between his legs.

"I'm impressed, Commander. I've never encountered a leech that could survive me."

"Why do you hate telepaths?" Jetta asked, keeping her distance.

Salam continued to pet the wolf, appearing to pay them little attention.

"I don't hate anybody. I'm a survivor. All of us here are. We've done what we've needed to do."

Jetta kept her voice even and emotionless. "It was risky doing something like that to me. Now I know you. I've seen your greatest weakness."

"I know mine. I've always known mine. But did you know yours?"

Jetta paused.

Salam looked up. "It's amazing how little we really know about ourselves. When I was a slave in the Locks I thought my biggest weakness was being human. But I was wrong—my biggest weakness was pity. Pity for myself, for others. Once I realized this, I put both my hands in a rock grinder. As I watched it tear away my flesh and bone, I was no longer afraid, no longer a slave, no longer weak—I was free," he said, holding up his gloved hands.

"You've lost your mind," Jetta said.

Salam's smile made Triel even more uncomfortable. "Easy to accuse someone of that, isn't it? We don't always do things we're proud of in order to survive, and yet it gives others the means to judge us so harshly. You know what I'm talking about, Commander. I know your weakness. You don't see the difference between you and the monster that killed your brother."

My Gods, Triel thought, sensing just how far Salam had gone. *He hasn't just seen the reels on the nets or the publicized trials— he's studied the twins, specifically Jetta. But why?*

Triel stepped in front of Jetta. "You're an idiot."

The Counselor cocked his head at her. "Excuse me?"

"You heard me. You're provoking the most powerful telepath in the galaxy. Why do such a stupid thing? She can end you with a thought."

"Why don't you tell her, Jetta?" Salam said.

Jetta's face turned pale and cheesy. "Because he's right about me."

Oh no, Triel thought, realizing her mistake. *I should have been worrying about Salam, not Jetta's talents. What is he doing to her?*

"See there. The most *powerful* telepath in the galaxy is so easily unhinged. Not so powerful, and certainly not worthy of her titles. Just like all the rest of you who think you're smarter, stronger and more cunning than us humans—us *Deadskins.*"

"What is this all about? The Commander and I are both human advocates—"

"You're telling me that the most *powerful* telepath in the galaxy, someone who could do anything at all with her authority, is a Human Rights advocate?" Salam said, loosing a beastly laugh. "Where is the outrage? Where is our liberation?"

Salam grabbed the wolf by the scruff, making him yip. "I didn't turn away while my hands were mashed to a bloody pulp, or when I cut the hands and feet off my fellow slaves. I liberated over five hundred men and women from the Labor Locks despite everything I was and everything I had already lost."

"She looked away when she killed her brother," he said, pointing an accusatory finger at Jetta. "She left us to here to die while she wallowed in her own self-pity. Her life is a mockery of mine."

Something slithered into the back of her mind. Triel sucked in her breath as she felt the terrible beginnings of rage crystallizing on the surface of her consciousness.

I'm going to Fall—

"You're weak and pathetic. Both of you. When I have the means, I will liberate our people, and I will do more than any of you leeches ever could."

Triel finally understood. *Salam wants the powers of the Gods to seek revenge, just like Saol of Gangras.*

The Healer looked at the wolf at Salam's side. Where the idea came from she wasn't sure.

"Please," she whispered. "Help us."

The wolf's ears pricked forward, and he sniffed the air.

"Commander Kyron is finished. It will just be you and me, Healer," Salam said, showing his teeth like a predator.

Triel glanced at Jetta. The young commander froze in place, her eyes distant and shadowed by something ominous, her essence completely withdrawn.

"All I need is a drop of your precious leech blood, and it won't matter if you are alive or dead. It's your choice," Salam said.

"You know… what happens… when you threaten a Solitary?" she asked, doubling over as the fingers of malice wrapped around her core. In an instant, her skin mottled and her markings faded into the gray of her flesh.

"I've studied your kind for years," Salam sneered. "I know that much of your power comes from the reactions of others. Fortunately, I will not be the one drawing your blood. Neither will my soldiers."

Salam grasped the scruff of the wolf tightly and then let go. The wolf whimpered and rolled to the ground. "You have complete power and control over the Sentient mind but cannot connect with the most basic of all creations. What a shame. It could have saved your life."

With a wave of his hand, Salam signaled the guards waiting outside the fence, and they unlocked the wolf cages. A series of whistles echoed from the loudspeakers. None of the beasts took notice of Salam as he left the enclosure, but they did see her and Jetta.

"Jetta!" Triel cried as she fell to the ground. Pain ripped through her, incredible and intoxicating. *If the predators don't kill me, the Fall will.*

197

Eyes open but unseeing, the commander didn't move, her hands clenched in tight, white fists.

Please, Jetta...

Triel craned her neck up at the wolf that Salam had been petting. Keeping his eyes focused on her, he rose and approached them cautiously.

"Please," she whispered.

Of the seven wolves in the pack, only the three that they had encountered earlier kept their distance. The rest closed in, eyeing Triel possessively as if they already knew the taste of her flesh. Snarling, one crouched low next to Jetta, ready to spring.

Terrified, the Healer's world shattered into prisms of light and sound as her mind circled the infinite drain of the Fall. Through the haze of pain she caught the eye of the gray-pawed wolf Jetta had bonded with and made one last attempt.

As the poison in her veins sapped her voice, her mind reached out. *Please—help us—help her! Don't you remember?*

Triel collapsed, splattering mud. She saw the wolf strike Jetta from behind as the world turned crimson.

CHAPTER IV

The fluttery queasiness in Agracia's stomach soured into a pit of acid the closer she got to the warehouse on the outskirts of the underground Spillway. With every step she took, she saw fewer and fewer of her people—the townies and Jocks—and more of the Johnnies she had been careful to avoid over the years.

(These bastards are the most brutal kind,) her subconscious eagerly reminded her.

With an inconspicuous eye, Agracia tracked the movements of the Johnnies clustering around the chop shops, liquor stores, and smoke joints. Most of them came from black-market operations, or got kicked out of other gangs for vicious behaviors. The red bandanas tied around their right arms distinguished them from the regular thug, as well as the mangled lumps where their left ears should have been. Some of them even filed their teeth to points, adding to the savage effect of their tattoos and scars.

"Yeah, yeah," she muttered, pushing that thought away. *Even if they got a drop of off-worlder blood, they're still human.*

Despite Victor's assurances that she wouldn't have any problems getting into the warehouse, Agracia had learned over the years not to trust anyone. *Especially not creeps in fancy suits,* she thought, hiking up her shoulders.

Two Johnnies snickered as she neared the sign carved into one of the foundation pillars. It read "Berish and Mau Imports and Exports."

From the structure of the original archway, Agracia guessed that this nest site was part of the old subway station. It had been severely damaged in the Last Great War, and modifications had been made to the supports to keep the whole place from caving in. Gouges marked the walkway where early survivors dragged their machines to expand their new underground homes. A couple of derailed subway cars, gutted and refurbished with an arsenal of weapons, confirmed her suspicions.

One of the two Johnnies guarding the entryway to the warehouse spoke in a garbled mixture of broken English and

Common as he stroked his submachine gun: "Oh sweets, you just stepped into the wrong neighborhood."

If she showed fear they would kill her on the spot, even if Victor truly had ordered her safe passage. The unspoken code of the Spillway deemed that only the toughest deserved their skin. "Shove it or I'll spank you just like I spanked your mom last night."

The second Johnnie laughed out loud, slapping his companion on the shoulder. "You just got burned, Sykes."

His face turned bright red, but the flush of color disappeared with a malevolent smirk. "You keep that smart mouth. I'll eat that tongue of yours by tonight."

Agracia shouldered past them, keeping an eye on their position by watching their shadows. They kept their distance, but it didn't stop their verbal assault as she tried to open the steel-plated double doors.

"Little sissy need some help?"

"Check out that tight little—"

What the hell? Are those retinal-coded door locks? she thought, seeing the scanner panel to the left. Technology like that didn't exist on Earth, not with the power supply shortages. Besides, who here would keep anything that needed that kind of protection?

Agracia held her breath as she struggled with what to do next. Now that Jetta Kyron had revealed her terrestrial upbringing to be a fabrication, she questioned every action and every thought. Was it really her choice or was it part of the military construct? Where did the low-life Jock end and she begin?

But who the hell am I anyway?

Agracia bit her lip and cursed as the beginnings of a headache swelled inside her skull. *Not again*, she thought to herself. Now was the time to help her friend and screw everything else.

That's Agracia the Scabber—

"Hey, numbnuts," Agracia shouted, "are you going to open this for me, or am I going to have to rip your eyes out?"

201

The first one aimed his gun at her, but she crossed her arms and leaned to one side. "Come on, really? Ain't you got two brain cells to rub together?"

"Gonna eat your tongue, and maybe your ugly little face," he whispered, clicking off the safety.

With a chuckle, the other guard slung his gun and walked over to the interface. After punching in the codes and scanning his eyes, the double doors parted. Before she could step through, he grabbed her by the arm. His breath, soured by years of smoking and cheap booze, felt hot on her face. "Sykes over there ain't half of what you gonna see in there, little missus. Gonna make you wish you hadn't been born. Gonna kill every last bit of you that ever mattered."

Agracia deftly kissed him on the nose before breaking his grip with her opposite hand. "Awh, don't you worry about me. Big boys with big guns and little peckers don't really get my panties in a twist."

Was that me or the Scabber?

As he raised the butt of his gun, Agracia unsheathed the knife from his belt and ducked out of range. The first guard fired a few rounds but missed as she flattened herself out behind a pylon.

"Leave her!" someone shouted from inside the warehouse.

Begrudgingly, the two Johnnies held their fire.

What chumps, she thought, letting out a sigh as the double doors sealed shut.

"Agracia Waychild. Always making a scene."

Agracia stopped in her tracks at the sight of the man standing ten meters away. Immediately her gut kicked in. There was something ominous about him—something sinister in the way his cold eyes looked her over. *Play this one straight.*

"Discard the knife and come with me. I was just having a chat with your friend."

After dropping the weapon affording him a casual shrug, Agracia tried not to let the pain in her head distract her from her surroundings.

202

It's getting worse, she thought as the throbbing expanded inside the confines of her skull.

Ever since Jetta had pried into her head, she'd been bedeviled by headaches, each one progressively more painful and violent, the worst of which seemed to be triggered by thoughts of her upbringing.

"Keep it together," she mumbled to herself, cracking her knuckles.

Despite the pain splitting open her head, Agracia forced herself to memorize every detail of her environment. The entryway to the warehouse looked like an old ticket booth. Cash registers, rusted and barely recognizable, sat atop the counters behind broken out windows. Graffiti and ominous stains splattered the crumbling tiles and peeling paint, giving fair warning of what lay ahead.

What is that smell? Agracia thought, seeing a lighted doorway at the end of the narrow hallway. Industrial rock and drunken chatter leaked through the cracks. She couldn't imagine what caused the foul odor, only that the terrible stench stirred a distant memory that made her stomach hitch.

"Now count backwards from one hundred..."

Agracia lurched forward, swallowing hard to keep the memory locked away. *Not now—I can't come unglued.*

"Who are you?" Agracia asked, refocusing on her escort.

The man looked at her with his cold eyes, his extended silence making her squirm. Finally he answered, "You may call me Shandin."

Agracia followed Shandin into a large chamber that looked as if it had been carved out of the Earth but never finished. Dead roots still hung from the ceiling, and clumps of dirt and construction debris littered the floor. In the middle of the room was an active wet bar made out of clawed bathtubs, toxic waste drums, copper wiring, and spiral tubing with *No Smoking!* scrawled across the apparatus every which way. In the Dives she'd seen active bars, but none this elaborate or with such a variety of alcohol churning through the tubes and into the spigots.

Perched on the stool nearest the spigots sat her pig-tailed friend, who alternated sucking on her lollipop with spouting profanities as she impatiently waited for the machines to cook up another round. An audience of Johnnies surrounded her, all of them as battered and bruised as her friend but seemingly in good spirits, laughing as Bossy stood on her stool and mocked the barkeep.

"You call this whiskey? This is Scabber piss!"

"Bossy?" Agracia said, her headache suddenly ebbing.

Bossy plopped down on the edge of the bar and faced Agracia, her eyes bloodshot and glazed as she swayed drunkenly to the beat of the music. Finally she seemed to register Agracia's face and pursed her lips.

"You traitor—*godich* Skirt-lover," she slurred.

Agracia carefully approached her companion, keeping her eye on the Johnnies. Each one rested a hand on their drink and the other a little too close to their weapon.

"Bossy, please—this is serious," Agracia whispered.

Bossy's brow furrowed in confusion.

She doesn't recognize the tone of my voice, she realized. No, Agracia the Scabber wouldn't bother with appeals. *This is the stranger inside me.*

In some remote corner of her mind she delighted that she was no longer just a bottom-feeding urchin, a Scab that had remained on a dead planet to piss away her life in the wastelands. At one time, she had been someone important, someone who had been groomed to be a leader and hero.

Jetta Kyron had promised to come back and help her remember the rest in exchange for information about the tattoo on her right arm, and if Bossy hadn't run away, they'd already be halfway to Ground Zero in the Deadzone. But Victor had interceded, promising her two tickets to the Mars colony and three months' pay if she could go to the Deadzone and retrieve a launch signature. Most of the computers were destroyed or broken, but a few still existed deep underground, safely hibernating in protected vaults.

Huh… it can't be coincidence that both Victor and Jetta need my help to go into the Deadzone, can it?

Agracia suppressed the thought and focused on her friend. "I have work for us."

"Can't you see I'm busy?" Bossy said as the barkeep poured her a steaming glass of a rusty-red liquor. With a giddy look on her face, she rolled her designer lollipop to the other side of her mouth and took a giant swig.

Thinking she was too plastered to care, one of the Johnnies tried to slide his hand under Bossy's crop top.

Oh chak, Agracia thought, taking a step back. Over the years many men had tried to take advantage of her quick-tempered friend, most of whom met their untimely demise.

Before the other Johnnies could reach for their weapons, Bossy broke her glass against the bar and pressed the jagged pieces up against the offender's jugular. Out of the corner of her eye, Agracia noticed Shandin watching, his expression cool and emotionless.

"Wanna know how I got my nickname?" Bossy asked, her eyes ablaze.

The Johnnie sputtered something unintelligible that widened Bossy's grin.

"Quit, Bossy. You don't want his mud blood stainin' your skins," Agracia said.

Bossy seemed to consider her advice and lowered her weapon. Most Johnnies had infected blood. HIV was the most common disease, even though a cure had been found in 2032 and was readily available in the Homeworlds. By adapting itself to bypass the weak and meager drugs available on Earth, the virus had stuck around, silently infecting junkies, streetwalkers, and Meatheads, and more often than not the children born to infected mothers.

Bossy leapt off her perch and grabbed Agracia by the collar. "Why did you leave me for that Skirt?" she sputtered, her eyes rolling around in their sockets. "She's a filthy leech—she messed with your head!"

Agracia quietly pulled Bossy to one side, out of Shandin's direct view, and relaxed into her old slang. "She showed me things I didn't remember straight. We've got her on our side, alright? I don't need you buggin' out on me—things are really juiced right now."

Bossy gave her the side-eye and sucked noisily on her lollipop. "Why'd you come here?"

"I came after you, dimwit. Can't be you havin' all the fun, yeah?"

Bossy let a smile slip but quickly shuffled it behind a scowl. "After you made kissy face with that Skirt I hitchhiked to the Spillway. Only purse available in the fighting rings was a pinch bag—maybe fifty bucks—but it didn't matter. I just need a fight. I thought it was just gonna be a Meathead or two, but they laid fifty guys on me within the first thirty seconds. I managed to kill about twenty or thirty before they blew in Rage."

How is she still alive? Agracia thought. Used in the Last Great War, the aerosolized bioweapon incited soldiers to battle. Even the most docile human being would transform into an aggressive, violent killing machine, completely oblivious to their own injury or harm in the process. Fighting rings still used Rage when the bouts weren't exciting enough for the crowds, or when the underdog needed a boost.

"Rest of it was… red. That's all I remember. Then I wound up here. But I still weren't right in the noggin'," she said, jabbing her thumb at the bruised Johnnies. "But just one of these—hey you! What the hell is this *sycha* called?" she said, holding up her mug.

"*Mississippi Diesel 999*," the barkeeper replied indifferently over his shoulder.

Agracia caught a whiff, and it made her nose burn and eyes water. Bossy grinned as Agracia fanned the smell away. "Yeah, a few *999s* later and I'm shipshape," she asserted, letting out a giant belch.

206

Out of habit Agracia reached for the smokes tucked away under her sleeve, but the bartender whipped around and stabbed his chubby finger at her before she could even flip open the carton.

"Can't you read?" he barked, pointing to the *no smoking* graffiti.

It made sense. *Mississippi Diesel 999* smelled like a crude mixture of gasoline and witch hazel, so a single spark would probably ignite the whole place. Regardless, Agracia found herself resorting to her Scabber attitude. "Don't get your panties in a bind, I ain't gonna light up," she said, poking one in her mouth and chewing on the end.

The barkeep looked to Shandin, grumbled something, and resumed cleaning his spigots with a dirty rag.

"So anyways, a chump named Victor said he bailed you out. He told me you were here and offered me a job."

Bossy wrinkled her nose. "You didn't buy that *gorsh-shit*, did you?"

Agracia shrugged. "It was two tickets to Mars and three months' pay."

Bossy's eyes grew wide, but she didn't look convinced. "Still smells like *gorsh-shit*."

"Speaking of smells," Agracia said, eyeing the Johnnies at the bar. Guzzling their brew and slapping each other around, the thugs paid them no attention. Shandin, standing where he had left them, watched closely. "What is that smell?"

Bossy scoffed. "It's a meat-packaging plant. Or some crap like that. Dunno, don't care. They make good booze!"

"Come on," her tiny companion said, heading back to the bar, "I'm getting sober."

"Wait," Agracia said, pulling her back. "Do you want to hear about the job?"

Bossy listened as Agracia explained Victor's assignment to retrieve the launch signature from a computer database in Ground Zero. The pint-sized fighter looked bored and uninterested until

Agracia noted the coincidence about finding Jetta's tattoo scrawled near the same site.

"Somethin's fishy."

"I know, I feel it too, but we gotta take this."

"Whaddya mean 'we gotta?!'" Bossy said, crossing her arms.

"There's something about Victor—he ain't no ordinary Joe. And that jackoff there," Agracia said, nodding towards Shandin, "is of the same breed. Somethin' ain't right with them. I want to play this one straight, get our dime and get out. No fussin'. All we ever wanted was off this crap hole, and this might be our ticket."

"What about the Skirt?"

"Jetta?" Agracia laughed. "Come one, she's alright. We can settle two scores by taking the job in the Deadzone. 'Sides, you shouldn't be jealous—it's bad for your complexion."

Bossy popped out her lollipop and stuck it in Agracia's face. "You play me over a Skirt or any other jerkoff and you better believe I'll be stuffin' a 20-20 where the sun don't shine."

Agracia smiled. "Aw, I missed you, sweetheart."

"Enough talking—are you ready to get started?" Shandin said, walking up behind them. "We need to equip you for your assignment."

Agracia saw Bossy cuing up to say something inflammatory, so she wrapped her arms around her friend and pulled her away from Shandin. "We was getting tired of waiting."

Shandin shot her a look of disapproval before motioning for them to follow him. A few of the Johnnies at the bar hooted and hollered at Bossy, and she teased them by raising the hem of her skirt just above her upper thigh before flipping them off. Beer glasses came flying their way, but the three of them turned down another narrow corridor as they shattered against the wall.

The terrible smell got worse the deeper they went in the warehouse, reminding her of old meat ruined by disease.

"What the hell is that stink?" Agracia said, covering her nose.

By the way Shandin paused before answering, she knew he was going to lie. "I run a butchery and packaging plant. We distribute survival rations to the poor across the Greatlands."

"Whaddya butcherin'? Month old meat?" Bossy scoffed, but Shandin didn't answer.

Up ahead Agracia spotted a cargo ship in a fortified hangar. Whatever had transpired during the drop-off had been vicious. Old blood darkened the dirt floor, and bits of clothing and broken chain link testified to the real nature of Shandin's operations.

Agracia remembered the words of the Johnnie guarding the entrance as she stepped through a cloud of flies that swarmed over some gray, blistered body crumpled against the wall. *Sykes over there ain't half of what you gonna see in there, little missus. Gonna make you wish you hadn't been born. Gonna kill every last bit of you that ever mattered."*

"Nah," she whispered to herself as they entered the cargo hold. Then the smell hit her. Open sores festering in a damp, tight space. Meat, stripped from rotted bone.

"Jeezus!"

She tripped but caught herself against the ramp to the cargo ship. When she looked down she saw a clump of human hair. Someone nearby screamed but was silenced with a gunshot.

Bossy nudged her. For the first time since Agracia had known her, she saw genuine fear on her face. "Gracie, this ain't feelin' right."

Shandin stopped at the junction between two hallways on the opposite end of the dock.

"Something the matter?"

Agracia played it as casually as she could. "Gettin' antsy is all. Jocks don't belong belowground."

Shandin led them down a poorly lit tunnel and into a large stockroom packed with supplies ranging from biosuits to advanced detection equipment. Mostly stolen riot gear from Saturn's border police, the collection touted an assortment of bulletproof vests and face guards. A few bigger weapons were scattered here and there, but Agracia noted that they were older firearm models from decades ago. Otherwise, Shandin primarily stocked stun guns and shockwands.

"It's a *chakking* trafficking port," Bossy whispered as Agracia spotted the shelf full of electric shackling equipment.

Agracia swallowed the hot lump in her throat. *Why is Shandin trafficking humans?* Given the size of the ship in his docks and the amount of gear he stocked, he was moving hundreds if not thousands on a regular basis.

Even more worrisome—why the smell? *What is he doing with them?*

Back when she first met Bossy in the dregs of Paradise City, Agracia chanced upon a trafficking port. It wasn't uncommon for Scabbers to sell out their own, especially if an outerworlder got the taste and was willing to import from Old Earth, but that was usually on a smaller scale, maybe ten or twenty poor souls in a month. *This is much larger, more organized, and clearly funded.*

Victor. The man with the terrible diamond smile. *What is his hand in all this?*

"My men will outfit you for your assignment and give you the medicines you'll need once you cross into Ground Zero," Shandin said, signaling three of the men cleaning firearms on a work table to help them.

"No way," Agracia said. "I'll take care of that myself."

That was one rule that every Jock followed—know your dealer and don't trust anyone else's drugs. Tainting meds was both a common practice between warring Jocks and an unfortunate consequence of poor shipping methods between Pits.

"The Necro plague is rampant in the Deadzone, Agracia. We have the best medicines available on the planet."

Agracia didn't like the way Shandin regarded her. With a slight tilt of his head he looked her up and down, as if mentally rendering her down for parts. "No, we'll barter in the marketplace. I have a reliable source."

The Necro plague, or the manmade *V. mortuuseria*, had been infecting organic tissue since its use in biological warfare in 2052. Rumors circulated that it reconstituted dead cells and reformatted living cells, but Agracia didn't care about nitty gritty scientific explanations. As far as she was concerned, the plague turned living and dead things into nightmarish creatures similar to the zombies of the late twentieth century horror movies. No cure existed, but the pills she bartered for in the marketplace would keep the pneumonic form from infecting them. If they got bitten, though, they'd be just another pair of deadheads roaming the wastelands.

Shandin's words, lanced with cold, concentrated anger, caught her by surprise. "My men will escort you back into town after you've been outfitted. I'll allow you one hour to get what you need or the deal's off."

Bossy shoved off one of the men trying to size her for a biohazard suit, but Agracia interceded before he retaliated.

"Hey," Agracia said, pulling her aside. "Let's keep it pleasant, yeah?"

"None of this feels right, Gracie. This stinks. It *really* stinks," Bossy said, wrinkling her nose.

Agracia checked out the radiation detection equipment as Bossy's words sank into her like a lead slug. Never in all her years as a Jock had she felt this way, like someone's pawn.

I'm not seeing all the angles on this job, she thought, listening to her gut scream that the rules would change the moment she found what they wanted.

But then she smiled. She and Bossy were back together again. They were the only pair of Jocks ever to survive the Deadzone. There was nothing they couldn't do.

"Bossy," Agracia said, giggling as she watched her companion try on a helmet way too big for her pig-tailed head. "Betcha I can kill more Necros than you."

Bossy flipped the visor back and flashed her a smile full of teeth. "Game on, sista!"

Or so she hoped.

***

In her dream, razor-sharp teeth sunk into her flesh as if it were warm butter. Gray and black shapes flickered everywhere against the bright background. Shouting, gunfire, and the smell of copper hung over her like fog.

The sensations changed. Instead of teeth, Jetta felt pincers close around her neck. A massive weight slammed her down, grinding her face into the dirt and preventing her from rolling over. In her periphery she saw his burning red eye and felt his cold breath, wet and reeking of rotting meat, against her cheek. "You are weak, worthless—you are unworthy of your flesh."

Victor stood over her too, saluting her with his martini glass as M'ah Pae stabbed her with another of his appendages. A tremendous auger of pain drilled into the base of her head, and something slimy wormed its way into her skull. Victor was no longer in front of her but inside her. She saw through his tinted glasses and tasted the sting of his drink on her tongue.

"With eyes open, they burn," she heard herself say in his voice.

The world unfolded into a nightmarish scene. Hordes of screaming people crawled toward her on their hands and knees as mushroom clouds plumed in the distance and missiles streaked across the sky. Charred land, heaped with the remnants of buildings, skeletonized trees, and indiscernible rubble, quaked and heaved under the rain of bombs. She lifted her hands as if to welcome the dying people, and they all cried her name in unison, reaching out to her, begging her to save them.

The world changed again, as did the body she inhabited. Oppressive heat bore down on her, drawing forth beads of sweat from every pore in her body. The patchy remains of an expensive suit

212

strained to accommodate the girth of her fat belly as she crashed through the back door of the red and gray apartment.

"Where are you?" she hissed.

Sunshine filtered through the boarded windows, barely illuminating the bottle and cigarette she held in her hand. Tipping her head back, she finished off the bitter drink, following it with a burning drag from her smoke. Her breath felt wheezy and congested, but it had been for some time.

"You're disgusting. You're all disgusting," she heard herself say as she stumbled into the living room, her vision hazed by drink. Light glinted off the television screen, and her reflection looked back at her with Yahmen's face. She wanted to scream, but she couldn't. Instead, her reflection grinned.

Someone whispered in the entryway. She knew those voices—

(No!)

She rounded the corner, belt already freed from its loops. A tiny body with a mess of brown hair scurried out from underneath a fort made of broken cots, but another remained curled up inside. His bright blue eyes were already wet with tears, his lips trembling as he watched the belt come snapping down.

(Jahx—)

"You little rat!" Jetta heard herself say as Jahx tried to scramble away. Her monstrous hands grabbed him by the collar and dragged him back into the living room, where the punishment continued.

"Stop, please stop!" Jaeia screamed, but that only enraged her further, driving the belt harder and faster with every stroke.

(No—you have to stop! STOP!)

Finally, she did stop. Jahx ceased moving, his small body awkwardly splayed on the carpet. Blood trickled from both nostrils. His eyes swelled shut as his chest stopped rising, and his lips turned a waxy blue.

(He's dead!)

213

Jetta tried to scream, but it came out as a howl of laughter in Yahmen's raspy voice.

(No no no no no no—)

She caught sight of her reflection in the television. This time it mirrored back her own image, hollow and lifeless.

"You did this," it whispered back at her.

She looked back at Jahx. A thicket of wires erupted from the carpet and burrowed into her brother's flesh. All of the color drained from his skin, transforming him into a ghostly white creature with dead, glassy eyes that stared right through her.

His voice sounded like tortured metal. "You did this."

Jetta came to when a bullet struck her right shoulder, sending spasms of pain tearing through her arm and chest. Still torn between two worlds, she didn't understand the black and gray shapes dancing around her in violent, jarring movements.

Am I still dreaming?

Growls and hisses followed a flash of teeth. She tasted blood on her lips. *No. This is real.*

Blurry images solidified. Jetta discerned the ashy-gray Wammercats from the dark-coated wolves as they tore into each other's flesh, spilling blood onto the dirt.

Before she could scramble away, the gray-pawed wolf she had ridden only a few hours before pinned her to the ground with his foreleg. He snarled at the Tygra as Salam's men jeered and took shots at the animals not engaging in the fight.

Is he protecting me—or defending his meal? Jetta thought. As she tried to glean an impression of his mind, the wolf dug his paw into her back.

Don't struggle, she told herself, taking a breath as pain exploded down her legs. *Find Triel, assess the situation.*

She spotted her friend lying face down a few meters to her left. The other two wolves they had met earlier crouched over her, biting and snapping at their attackers.

214

Triel, she called across the psionic planes. When she touched the Healer's aura, waves of nausea buckled her stomach.

She's turning again, Jetta realized, noticing the greenish cast to her friend's skin. *If we don't get far enough away from this violence, there won't be anything I can do to save her.*

Something bit into her right arm, and she screamed. Clawed feet dug into her back as fanged animals gnashed their teeth above her head.

Fear drove into logic. *(We can't survive this—)*

No, she thought, seeing her distressed friend and reclaiming her emotions. *I have to reconnect with those wolves. My bond to them has to be greater than Salam's conditioning.*

Borrowed strategies surfaced, warning her of the grim reality. Even if she successfully subdued the three wolves, the two other wolves, orange-striped Tygra, and the gray Wammercat remained.

The ghosts of old men with black hearts whispered up from the depths of her stolen knowledge:

(Frighten them, leave them wasted and begging for death—)

(Only total annihilation can be considered a victory—)

Gritting her teeth, Jetta curled up in a tight ball, shielding her face and head as best she could from the clash of claws and fangs.

This is my battle.

Using her memories of Earth's wolves worked during her first encounter, but she needed something stronger to overcome instincts charged by the scent of fresh blood.

Something sharp gouged her back leg. "Gods—" she gasped.

As pain electrified her senses, she realized exactly what they needed to understand.

Deceit.

Without wasting another breath, Jetta evoked the deepest rage she had even known, its potency driving away all but the awareness of the memory. Pain faded into the backdrop as she reached out both physically and psionically, ensnaring the wild minds around her and pulling them back into her realm.

215

The muddy ground and tumult of warring animals disappeared, replaced by the cold confines of a windowless, gray room. Only the red and black posters of the militant, mustached man gave any color to the spartan quarters.

General Volkor...

His eyes watched her every move.

Still dressed in her battle uniform, she willed herself over and over to sleep. Any time to rest was precious and unusual now, but even exhausted, she could only lay on top of the sheets and stare at the ceiling.

In some remote corner of her mind, she acknowledged the truth: she feared her dreams more than the nightmare of her life.

The monster with the burning red eye is always there, *her subconscious whispered.* He's waiting for me, calling me to join his side...

She didn't know exactly what he wanted, but he promised her power and revenge, and the longer she remained apart from her siblings, the more confused she became about who she was and what she was doing.

A buzzer went off. She rubbed her tired eyes and looked at the electronic notice blinking on her uniform sleeve. Time to fight.

Dragging herself to the door, Jetta fell in step with her escorts as they led her to the war room. She hated following orders, but the sickening euphoria that came with winning left her craving the next battle.

Then one day it all changed. While sitting in the war room, ready to ring in her fleet as a circle of the highest Dominion commanders watched from above, she noticed the cannulas protruding from her uniform, pumping a milky white substance into her veins.

It's not a game.

Jigsaw pieces fell into place: They're using me and the other captured telepaths to fight their war against the United Starways Coalition.

Rage flooded her memory. She wanted to turn all sides against each other, but Jahx brought her back from the brink of total destruction.

Don't, *Jahx whispered.* It's a trick.

Before she could act, soldiers hauled her away and threw her in a cell, leaving her to suffer through the withdrawal of Benign White.

Time passed in black-outed segments of pain. Disoriented and groggy, Jetta woke to find her sister across from her in the cell. Hair clung to Jaeia's face, her sweat and blood soaking through her clothing. Her twin could barely open one swollen eye.

"Jetta," her sister called, but she didn't have the strength to respond.

Where is Jahx? *she wondered.*

Gone, *Jaeia thought back.*

Shivering, Jetta couldn't stop the bleak truth from cutting into her bones. We are useless to the Dominion.

(We are going to die.)

Tears slid down her face as she laid her head against the cold steel wall and accepted the creeping shadow of death. I just wanted to save my brother and sister…

Jetta opened her eyes. Her face was pressed into the dirt by the wolf's paw, but the commotion around her had stopped. Despite Salam's screams on the other side of the fence, or the men firing their guns to incite attack, the wolves, Wammercat, and the Tygra froze in place, eyes darting every which way, ears pricked and alert.

Sensing a shift in the atmosphere, Jetta eased into the thoughts of the gray-pawed wolf leader.

He's confused by my memories, she gleaned. But something in the way he looked at her made her believe that he understood at least a small part of it.

And then he bit her. Jetta panicked, slapping at his nose as his teeth dug into her thigh.

No, Gods, no—

The pressure didn't increase, didn't break the skin. As carefully as he could, the wolf pulled her away from the brawl and the gunfire.

Jetta gaped. The Wammercat charged the fence, and even through the rain of bullets, the gigantic feline managed to knock down the gate. Following suit, the Tygra leapt over the broken gate and sunk his teeth into one of the gunmen. He tore off one of the Lockhead's arms before moving to his next victim.

"Run!" Salam shouted, taking off with the rest of his men to find cover in one of the shelters.

Several wolves made a break for the gate, aiding in the Tygra's attack.

"Please…" Jetta whispered, watching as the white-necked wolf still standing over Triel sniffed her around the neck and growled. "Save her."

With a gentle nudge, the wolf rolled the Healer over and picked her up in his powerful jaws.

Thank you, Jetta thought as he trotted over to follow the gray-pawed leader.

"Wait—wait!" Jetta shouted as he dragged her toward the gate. She rolled out from underneath the wolf and struggled up to pull herself up onto his back. "Go!"

Jetta kept low to the wolf's back as he dodged the gunfire. Blood from her injured shoulder seeped through her shirt with each movement, but she clenched her jaw against the pain and kept her eyes trained on the perimeter fence ahead.

How the hell are we going to get past those walls? she thought, scanning the five-meter high barrier of wood and barbed wire. With the Lockheads hot on their trail, they didn't have time to even pause.

The wolf's voice entered her head. Low, breathy bass tones with guttural accents translated into a language she didn't know, but felt.

Hold on.

Sounds and images formed streamlined concepts. She could see the path he chose before he took the next step. Never one for heights, Jetta knotted her fingers in his fur as he leapt onto a checkpoint tower. His next jump fell a meter short of clearance, but he rebounded off the wall and used his momentum to push off the adjacent fence, this time clearing the barbed wire.

Jetta opened her eyes in time to see the terrible length of their descent. Her heart seized as they began to fall, rocks and dirt rushing toward them at bone-crushing speed. If she could have, she would have screamed.

"*Mugarruthepeta,*" Jetta gasped as the wolf landed gracefully on all four paws.

Before she could collect her wits they were off and running, this time into the deeps of the forest. She looked back to see the wolf carrying Triel crawl under a new break in the fence and follow their lead as they wound through the trees.

Jetta let them run for the better part of half an hour before pulling on her wolf's fur to make him stop. She needed to check on Triel, especially since she had been awkwardly carried in the jaws of the second wolf.

Forgetting her own injuries, she dismounted and nearly wound up face-first in a thorn bush.

"*Skuchecka!*" she muttered. Gathering herself, she hobbled over to the other wolf as he gingerly laid the Triel down on the ground for her to inspect.

"Hey, are you okay?" Jetta whispered, stroking the Healer's hair back from her forehead.

No response. Jetta checked for the pulse on her neck and watched her chest.

Well, she's breathing, and her heart rate is slow, but regular. But she couldn't find a single one of the Prodgy markings on Triel's blotchy, gray-green skin. As her despair burgeoned, she felt a large lump on the side of the Healer's head and realized their luck. *If Triel hadn't been knocked unconscious in the scuffle, we'd probably all be dead,* she thought.

Sitting back on her heels, Jetta decided her duty. *I can't let her wake up a Dissembler.*

Jetta looked her over more carefully. The Healer bore marks where the wolf's teeth had gripped her, but aside from the blow to the head she didn't appear to be seriously injured.

We need to keep moving, she thought, considering their options. From what she saw of the Lockheads' map, they held a fairly large territory, and she wasn't sure what kind of transportation they might have. She hadn't seen any other domesticated animals, but that didn't mean they didn't have other stables or working machinery somewhere else.

And now Jetta couldn't risk Triel becoming conscious.

"You're afraid of sharing any kind of feeling with me—unless, of course, I completely force it out of you. I need it, you know— positive psionic, emotional, and physical interactions are part of how my species regenerates after healing."

Triel's words circulated inside her head as she resisted the most obvious course of action.

What happened in the intensive care unit was an accident, she thought, remembering Triel's mind descending upon her. Exposed and unprotected, Jetta should have been killed, but the terrible something inside her prevented the Healer from destroying her in one poisonous swipe. *I didn't mean to—*

"No," she whispered, stopping herself. Unwanted feelings seized her weak moment, pressing hard and hot against her sternum. But she would not acknowledge them, nor would she assign them a name or description. She swallowed hard, pushing her fist against the bullet wound in her shoulder, letting the pain drown out her conflicted feelings.

There has to be another way, she thought. She could not connect with Triel on that level. *I can't lower my defenses like that with anyone ever again.*

She and her siblings unconsciously shared everything when they were very little, but back then there hadn't been anything to hide.

Everything is different now. I am different now, she decided, disgusted with herself.

(How long can I keep hiding from the truth?)

Goosebumps popped up on her arms and legs as Victor's voice called to her from within, bidding her to take her place at his side. *Together we can overcome our torments. We can take control of the Starways. We can be free.*

She recoiled, remembering the reflection in the mirror from her recent dream. *It wasn't me—it was Yahmen—*

(The monster inside me.)

No, she resolved. *Never again. I will never show myself to anyone else—not Jaeia, not even Jahx. No one.*

Still, this was her friend, and when Jetta rechecked the Healer's waning pulse, she sensed her window of opportunity rapidly closing.

And I need Triel just as much as she needs me, Jetta realized, seeing the blood leaking from her own wounds.

The gray-pawed wolf whined softly and nudged her from behind, pushing her closer to Triel. Jetta's wild friend saw something that she couldn't—or wouldn't—and he too sensed the imminent danger.

Leaning heavily on her good arm, Jetta finally acknowledged her own exhaustion as the pain of her fresh wounds whittled down the last of her reserves. Without thinking, she rested her head on Triel's chest.

"Please—I don't know what to do," she whispered. Normally eager to deconstruct and analyze what problems came her way, Jetta locked down when it came to the issue of the Healer. She didn't want to think about the routes their relationship might take, nor could she even begin to fathom what she herself wanted from it. As much as she longed to pull closer to one of the few people she truly cared for, the thought of actually allowing herself to do so made her cringe.

But I have to try something.

"You've gone beyond my injuries," she said, thinking of all the times Triel had healed her, doing so much more than realigning flesh and bone. "You've tried to reach me… and I've always hidden."

You are so beautiful, she thought, touching Triel's cheek. Looking past the grotesque Dissembler mutations, Jetta saw the Healer's long, dark hair and eyes, bluer than a winter sky, returning her gaze. Her lips, full and inviting, parted to reveal a smile.

Memories of their rocky first encounter came to mind. *Even then, I knew. My feelings for you have always been...different.*

But I am a monster, Jetta reminded herself. *I do not deserve your friendship.*

With a heavy sigh, Jetta found herself at the same impasse she had been revisiting for months. She felt frozen inside, the ice wall holding back a flood of emotion she couldn't access.

"*We'thera?*" Jetta whispered.

The gray-pawed wolf nudged her again, this time pushing her completely over to sprawl on top of Triel. With her face only centimeters from the Healer's, Jetta held her breath, unsure of what to do. One part of her wanted to rear back and yell at the wolf, but she found herself unable to take her eyes off her friend.

Something inside her pleaded with fervency: *(Let go.)*

Before she could give it another thought, Jetta pressed her lips against the Healer's with a force she couldn't have stopped if she had wanted to. For the first time in her life she lost herself in the complex simplicity of the moment, reveling in the electric feel. Not minding her own psionic distance, Jetta sunk beneath Triel's skin and into new depths of the Healer's mind.

Judging by the arrangement of the constellations, Jetta guessed she was on Algar.

This is Triel's memory from long ago, *she thought as the late summer winds rustled the trees.*

A full moon gazed down from the cloudless night sky as her father took her hand in his. His touch felt warm and strong. Without saying a word, he led her down a path to a hut within the wooded valley. Inside the hut Triel found a crackling fire, and a potent blend of spices steaming from the cauldron hanging in the hearth. A woman sat in the corner on an old tree stump, leaning on her cane to be closer to the fireplace. Wrapped tightly in a black cloak, Triel could see very little of her face or figure.

"Triel, you must obey."

Triel drew closer to her father despite his tone. That seemed to be his choice phrase these days. Something had changed. In a matter of days, her soft-spoken father had become authoritative and strict about the rules she had always liked to bend—or break. Now everything mattered, even the most archaic rituals in Prodgy history, and to violate any rule of his house or the tribe meant swift punishment.

"Do as she says, Triel," he commanded.

By the feel of her small body, and the markings just beginning to show on her skin, Jetta inferred that her friend was no older than seven. She did not like this place; the other children whispered of the dangers of entering the witch's home.

"Bring her closer," the old woman said, looking up at her. Striking violet eyes, set deep beneath her wrinkled brow, expressed a stern gaze, as did her voice when she called for Triel again.

"Triel, you must obey," her father said more sharply, this time pushing her forward.

Jetta tested the edges of the memory, extracting what she could about the woman without breaking the vision.

Her name is Arpethea, *she gleaned. The old woman wasn't a witch but a Seer, a Prodgy with the ability to perceive the realm of Hetaqua, the mortal world, and that of Cudal, the Otherworld of the Gods. Unlike other Prodgies, who rarely ventured outside their tribes, Seers would take extended trips into the backcountry to isolate themselves and better communicate with the Gods.*

She couldn't have possibly lived for that many centuries, *Jetta thought, grafting the rumors and whispers Triel had heard about the old woman. Then again, Triel's family had been coming to her for the last three generations. Her grandparents had consulted the Seer when her father first began to show the markings of his people, and, as they famously claimed, everything Arpethea had predicted about his life had come true: his early ascension to chieftain, his blessings of many children, and his global acclaim as a Healer.*

Now it's Triel's turn… *Jetta realized, sinking deeper into the vision.*

Ever since her first markings appeared, Triel's parents had nightly arguments behind the barn where they thought their youngest daughter wouldn't be able to hear them. She didn't understand their concerns, nor the fear in her father's eyes when he decided to take her to see the old Seer.

They didn't react this way when her other siblings gained their markings, *Jetta thought.* Something is different about her…

Immersing herself in the emotional essence of the memory, Jetta sensed that even at a very young age Triel knew she was not like other Prodgy children. Her abilities were no greater or stranger than her peers or elders, but her psionic source was. Drawing her powers from somewhere intangible and inexplicable to her teachers, somewhere beyond her physical body, Triel frightened everyone around her.

Some of her own tribesmen refused to heal with her, *Jetta realized, hearing whispers that Triel's unknown energy source could indicate the instability that predisposed a Prodgy to Fall. A few postulated that her unusual healing style was divinely inspired, a sign she was the next Great Mother. All Triel understand was that people stared at her in the streets and walked a little faster when she approached.*

"Let me see your hands, child," Arpethea said.

"Do as she says," her father ordered.

Embarrassed, but not sure why, her cheeks turned red as she presented her hands to the Seer. Arpethea took them without hesitation, her lips moving silently while she traced Triel's markings from her palms to the backs of her hands and up her arms.

Pursing her lips, the Seer sat back, gazing at Triel for a long moment before speaking. She did not look at Triel anymore, only at

224

her father. *"Your daughter will go against you one day. Her heart will not rest here."*

Her heart will not rest here. *From the look on Triel's father's face, Jetta inferred that this was the worst news possible. Only when the rest of the memory, and Triel's thoughts, unfolded did she understand why:* Prodgies believe in the unity of Algar, that every being is part of the great living rhythm of the world. *To turn against her people, to abandon her world, meant that she was an aberration—an anathema—and the rumors of her propensity to become a Dissembler could be true.*

Her father's face turned to stone, and he commanded her to wait outside as he consulted the Seer in private. Fear gnawed at Triel's belly and pounded in her chest. Should she run away or stay and face her father's shame? Was she doomed not only to Fall, but to poison the rest of her tribe? She would be hunted and slain if the others found out. No one would protect her then—not even her family.

As Jetta's mind and body churned with the Healer's conflicted emotions, she realized her friend's worst fear. She reached through the memory, past the frightened little girl and into the stew of raw emotion bubbling beneath the surface. Isolated behind a pulse of electric fire strummed her friend's familiar rhythm. Anger, pain, and loneliness saturated every fiber of her being, but Jetta pushed through, knowing what she had to do to save her life.

(Triel—can you hear me?) *she shouted. Triel's silhouette appeared in the distance only to dissolve under Jetta's gaze and re-form into something inhuman and disfigured, fluctuating as she pressed closer.*

(Do you know why I come to visit you all the time?) *Jetta yelled over the raging torrents of psionic energy.*

No time left, *she thought, watching her friend unravel. Terror heated her mind. It wouldn't be long before Triel became unrecognizable.*

(Don't you know?) *she screamed, suddenly angry.* (You can't tell me you don't. All the times I visited you—all the times I brought you the things you liked or needed—you couldn't have thought that was coincidence?!)

A guttural, rasping voice full of menace came at her from all sides. (You've always turned away from me.)

(I've never turned away!) *she protested.* (I'm just—)

And there it was. The truth. One she had shied away from for as long as she could remember having these feelings.

Can't do this, I can't—

Outside of the psionic limbo, Jetta felt herself dig at her injured shoulder, trying to quell her emotional pain with the physical. She shrank into herself, but did not stop. (Even when we first met, under terrible circumstances, I knew that you were okay, that I could trust you—and I don't trust many people. You may have been different from the other Prodgies, but it's not because you're poisoned or any *gorsh-shit* like that. There's something special about you. You're more than just a Healer, and you're more than just my friend. I— I…)

The world around her shuddered and groaned like an old building about to collapse.

(I…)

The gray specter rematerialized centimeters from her face, its cold, slippery presence creeping under her skin.

Jetta closed her eyes and let go.

(I love you.)

The gray thing seized her, cutting through her like the sharpest blade. She screamed at pain's embrace, forgetting herself—

"Jetta…"

Jetta opened her eyes. She felt her chest, expecting to find it carved open, but found only the bullet wound in her shoulder. The pain was gone, replaced by a curious serenity.

She looked at the woman caught up in her arms. Healthy pink skin and the resolving lump on her head portended no sickness. "You're okay…"

Two blue eyes shone back her, and a gentle smile that conveyed great thanks. The Healer ran her fingers along Jetta's cheek. "Thank you."

Jetta had longed for this moment, but found herself quickly falling back into old habits. "Come on," she said, offering her hand, "we need to keep moving. It's not safe here."

Triel's brow knitted in confusion. "Please, Jetta—don't—"

The gray-pawed wolf whined, and Jetta snapped her head back in the direction of their escape. The distinctive stink of the Lockheads and their sickness bore down on their trail. "No time—let's go."

Jetta helped Triel up as best she could onto the white-necked wolf before mounting the other. "We need to reach the safety of the mountains before sunrise. Can you ride?"

Triel stared at her in bewilderment and didn't answer. After an uncomfortable moment she gave her wolf the back of her heel, and the two sprinted off toward the mountains. Jetta followed, grateful that the pain of her physical injuries was severe enough to let her ignore what she had just done.

***

Stepping out onto the watchtower platform, Damon Unipoesa faced away from the military base and toward the open lands of Nagoor. He found the ice, snow, and tundra that covered the frozen planet to have a sort of unforgiving, primitive beauty. Mountains that reminded him of broken teeth scored the land to the south, and the silver lakes to the north sparkled in the pale sunlight, filling him with wonder.

How did anyone survive this place? Most of its blue-skinned inhabitants acted shy or aloof, unlike his friend Pancar, and seemed to prefer roaming the inhospitable land rather than settling in any once place. *Or want to join an intergalactic government?*

"You're the only human-like I've met that seems to enjoy our planet," Pancar said, coming up from the dugout shelter.

Unipoesa scanned the horizon, his eye catching the V of migrating birds to the east. He followed them for a while, listening to their whistling calls as they traversed the cloudless sky.

"I studied environmental sciences as an undergrad. This reminds me of the place on Old Earth that used to be called Alaska."

Pancar joined him at the railing but did not look him in the eye. He watched his men loading a hovercar full of weapons and supplies as one of the ground teams went through their daily calisthenics. It seemed like eternity passed between them before the Nagoorian finally spoke.

"The results came back, Damon. I thought you'd want to know."

For some reason this made him look at his hands, his eyes following the creases and folds. *How did I get so old?*

Damon followed Pancar down into one of the private offices in the base, and his friend told him the results of the lab tests. He expected some kind of reaction from himself, as did Pancar, but none came. Either it was too soon to know how he was going to feel, or a part of him had known all along.

"I have to go back," Unipoesa said, looking his friend dead in the eye. "I'm no good here. I need to get back at the helm."

"That isn't an option, my friend," Pancar replied, setting down the datafiles on his desk and sitting back in his chair. "The Alliance is finished. Whatever Victor has done to the defense network looks irreparable; the remainder of the Fleet are sitting ducks. It's best to regroup the remaining systems and start a new rebellion."

"There isn't time for that. We need to act now," Damon said, searching the top of Pancar's desk for something he couldn't name. When he couldn't find what he needed, he got up out of his seat and paced. "I know what Li is capable of."

"Rescuing you was not easy, Damon," Pancar said, his blue face pinched with concern. "Please don't throw away what Jaeia and I have done."

"I'm not." He rubbed his unshaven face with tired hands and tried to soften the tone of his voice. "I'm going to set things straight. It will require more than military tactics to bring him down. It will take someone who knows his blood and his upbringing."

It took everything he had to argue the point to his friend, and in the end Pancar never conceded. But he and Damon had known each other for a long time, and when he boarded the Alliance ship Pancar had reassembled from an old wreck, the Nagoorian didn't try to stop him.

"I wish I could talk some sense into you, Damon," Pancar said as Unipoesa climbed into the cockpit. "Leaving now will only dissolve our last chance to fight Li and Victor."

Even though the sun had reached its zenith, the air still carried a frosty bite. Unipoesa pulled his jacket tighter against his body and glanced down the icefield runway. "I've always respected you, Pancar, and I'm grateful for everything you've done for me. You've saved my life, and countless others, many times over. I owe you more than I'll ever be able to repay. But I promise you that I know what I'm doing."

"So does Li," Pancar said as Damon closed the hatch.

Head still reeling, Damon fired up the engines and launched the second the green light blinked on the console. He and Pancar had disagreed about matters before, but Pancar never displayed such ferocity in his arguments.

Maybe Pancar is right—how am I going to reason with Li? he thought as he passed through the cerulean hues of Nagoor's upper atmosphere. The young commander had been bred to be a jackal; negotiations and treaties would be impossible with someone like him.

(Because I made him that way.)

Unipoesa sighed heavily and looked again at his hands.

Tarsha. Li.

As his jumped the ship to the coordinates outside the Alliance Central Starbase, he pushed aside the ache in his chest to focus on his objective. *I'm the only one who can take down Li.*

The Alliance guard hailed his ship as he approached the perimeter to the starpost. "I want to speak to CCO Wren," Damon said over the com line.

Gaeshin Wren appeared on his monitors with dark circles around his eyes, and his wrinkled uniform popped open at the neck. In all his years training and then serving alongside the commander, Damon couldn't recall seeing him so stressed.

"I've been informed that the Minister has been relieved of duty," Damon said. "That being the case, I've come back to offer my services. I know it wasn't you who ordered me into cryostasis."

"But I made no motion to stop it," he said unapologetically. "I'll be honest with you, Damon—over the last few months you've been unraveling. Not following protocol, going against orders. How can I trust you?"

"You can't afford not to, Chief. I'm the only one that can get inside Li's head. I know him—I raised him. With your network down and your support dwindling, what do you have to lose?"

Wren's picture disappeared. In its place flashed a clearance to dock in Bay 17.

When he landed, Gaeshin greeted him with a security contingent. The guards patted him down and searched his vessel before they allowed him to approach the Chief.

"I hope you'll forgive the inspection, but I'm cautious these days. Hard to trust anyone," Wren said as they exited the dock.

Out of respect, Damon offered him the truth: "Pancar is not your enemy. And neither am I."

Though his assurances were met with silence, Damon sensed that Wren had afforded him trust, if only very little.

"What's the fleet status?" Damon asked.

Wren secured them a lift before he answered. "We're down to fifteen percent of our Fleet capacity."

Shocked, Damon didn't know what to say. *Fifteen percent? Even the Kyrons couldn't pull this off.*

As they raced down the halls toward the command deck, Damon reached over Wren's arm and halted the lift.

"What are you doing?" Wren exclaimed, doubling over the vehicle railing.

"I need to see the Minister."

"He's in a coma," Wren said, trying to take back the controls. "Without a Healer they don't think he's going to make it."

"What about Triel?"

Wren shook his head. "She escaped with Jetta's help. We haven't had the resources to track them down."

"Can't Jaeia help?"

"Jetta's 'blocked' her out."

Damon dared to ask about the captain's whereabouts. "Where is Jaeia, anyway?"

"I would advise against seeing her right now."

Despite Wren's cryptic reply, Damon inferred from his inflection that the captain had discovered something undesirable.

"I need to see the Minister," Unipoesa insisted. "I need to get something off my chest before I do anything else."

"Will you harm him?"

Wren's eyes locked with his. The CCO would know if he lied, so Damon chose his words carefully. "I just have to get something off my chest. That's all."

Overworked and exhausted, Wren believed him. However, the CCO didn't hide the frustration in his voice as he stepped off the lift and signaled for another. "There's a senior officer's meeting at 1700 hours. We don't have much time, Admiral."

"Yes, Sir."

Wren grabbed his sleeve. "Don't do anything stupid or I'll let the Kyrons have you—understand?"

Damon watched him leave, stunned by the threat. *That's not like him.*

Then again, the admiral himself had acted out of character so many times in recent years that he could hardly pass judgment on the chief.

As he entered the medical wing, the truth came uncalled to his mind. He wasn't sure why he wanted to see the Minister, or what he was going to do when he got there.

But I have to.

The medical staff watched him from the corner of their eyes as he stepped inside the intensive care unit. One nurse braved asking him if he needed help.

"I'm fine," he said, spying the Minister's location on the central station monitors.

"Gods," he whispered, walking up to the Minister's bed in bay five. Within just a matter of weeks Razar's frame had atrophied, and his once fierce, angular face looked like a sculpture of wet cardboard. Tubes, monitors, and probes emerged from every limb. Tidas Razar, the indomitable Minister of the Alliance, had been reduced to a nearly unrecognizable remnant of a man.

"Sir," one of the two soldiers at the Minister's bedside acknowledged.

"Some privacy, please, Lieutenant."

"We're under strict orders from the chief, Sir."

"Well, I'm giving you a direct order. Give me five minutes of privacy with the Minister. You can watch outside the window and keep a lock on my signal."

The soldier looked nervously at his partner, but Unipoesa held his ground.

"Five minutes," the lieutenant said, circling around with his partner to the observation window.

Unipoesa pulled up a stool and sat beside the Minister. The words came to him more easily than he thought they would. "You and I—we've done some unforgivable things...."

Damon's mind wandered back in time to when Tarsha and Li were first introduced into his class. Due to their accelerated growth they were rated as five years old, though in reality only six months had passed since the day of their birth. Initially, neither of them would interact with the other children in the Program, but they quickly adapted to their schoolwork and competition with their classmates.

Even with their superior genetic design, Tarsha and Li had the fundamental needs of any child, most especially for love and acceptance. But that was not part of the curriculum. In his class there was only discipline and reward.

"All those years, all those things you ordered me do to my students—*my own children*. I will never be able to live with myself, knowing what I did to them."

From the start it was apparent that Tarsha and Li were leagues ahead of the other thirty children selected for the final phases of the Command Development Program. Tarsha had been designed with heightened empathy based on the theory that her sensitivities could lead to understanding an enemy, even thinking like one. Li was designed as her antithesis, with a limited emotional spectrum and, in Damon's opinion, a pathological egocentricity.

Damon's orders were to break Tarsha and Li, remolding them so that their strengths could not be turned into weaknesses. *Drill Tarsha so that she is empathetic but cutthroat in her tactics. Train Li to be vicious but anticipatory of his enemy's desires, and responsive to the needs of his soldiers,* he remembered.

Under the vituperations of her teachers, especially Damon's, Tarsha broke easily. Li did not. Unipoesa was forced to break all the rules he had learned as a child psychologist to deconstruct the boy.

"I'll never forgive you for ordering me to torture my own son," Damon whispered. Tears slid from his eyes. He could still hear Li screaming.

My own son...

Memory and emotion pulled him back in time. He saw Li before him, a young child again, sobbing and wiping his eyes with the back of his uniform.

One of the few times I ever saw him cry.

Something had gone wrong during Li's accelerated growth and development. The boy's bladder didn't develop properly, and for the first twelve weeks after his introduction into the program he had multiple accidents per night. USC doctors tried to fix the problem, but in the meantime his superiors devised another lesson for their investment.

"Show him discipline," the Minister Razar instructed.

Discipline came in electric shocks administered with every accident.

It's not fair—it isn't the boy's fault!

But it didn't matter. His superiors wanted Li to understand what was and wasn't allowed.

"We didn't show him discipline—we showed him shame," Damon said, looking at the floor. He could still see Li's broken body shivering in a tight knot, soaked with his own urine and whimpering from the electrical burns.

"He was just a boy. He still had a chance to be decent. You tore that right out of him. You left him with nothing but his anger."

But every accusation that he threw at the Minister came up short. It wasn't the truth. The truth was far too dangerous for him to acknowledge.

Unipoesa closed his eyes and let the past wash ashore the present.

Having been pitted against four other candidates in the latest Endgame, Li was supposed to win by predicting his enemies' movements and defending the targeted territory. Instead, he did what he always did, what he had been designed to do, swiftly destroying every last piece on his opponent's board. In the process he had lost many of his own game pieces, a tactic that made Unipoesa more nervous than his superiors.

234

"He doesn't care about the lives of his soldiers," Unipoesa pleaded to Razar, trying to sway his supervisor with statistical reports and video reel evidence. "He will sacrifice every last one for the sake of victory."

Razar only glanced at one datafile before glaring at Unipoesa from across his desk. "Then show him his actions will not be tolerated."

Later that evening, Unipoesa walked in on one of Li's classes with three soldiers trailing behind him. The teacher paused his lesson, and the rest of the students stiffened in their chairs at the sight of the disciplinary squad. Li didn't so much as flinch.

Remaining in his seat, the young cadet stared ahead blankly as the soldiers took turns beating him. Older and conditioned, the boy no longer responded to corporal punishment. He made no sound and shed no tears.

The mistake wasn't disciplining him in front of the other children. All of his students had been beaten in front of each other at some point in their training. Unipoesa took it a step further.

(I should have known better.)

"Not very good at following orders, are you, candidate?" he said, circling Li. Despite his injuries, the young soldier rose, favoring his right leg as he stood at attention. He stared defiantly ahead through the eye that wasn't swollen, his face unyielding.

Unipoesa told the soldier where to hit next. The soldier's punch landed hard and fast over his bladder, and Li doubled over in pain. His blue uniform darkened around the crotch, and his futile efforts to conceal it from the other students left him panicked.

"Still pissing yourself like a baby, just like you did when you first set foot on base," Unipoesa said. "You're still a baby. You can't follow a simple set of orders. You'll always be a worthless little pisser. A failure. An embarrassment to this program."

One of the other students snickered. He couldn't remember which one. Probably Henderson, given what happened to him. All he remembered was the hatred boiling in Li's eyes, the blood burning in his cheeks.

He still remembered the words of the chief medical officer. *"Candidate 00110 was murdered. No mistaking that. But whoever it was knew what they were doing. I can't give you a culprit based off my exam."*

Henderson, a likeable kid with a decent chance at obtaining the coveted title of chief commanding officer, had been one of the four candidates to witness Li's punishment. He was found strung up in the bathroom by his ankles, all his joints dislocated, eyes blinded and tongue ripped from his throat. The only clues left at the scene were blood-soaked, sharpened utensils from the mess hall.

Li had an alibi and witnesses. But Unipoesa knew better. Witnesses could be bought—or bullied—and after Henderson's death, no student was brave enough to speak against Li, even when given assurances of protection and promises of reward by his team of teachers.

After Henderson's death, the students were heavily guarded and chaperoned. But that didn't stop Li from ruining the others who witnessed his shame. One of them suffered from panic attacks and night terrors so severe that she had to drop out. The performances of the remaining two declined over the next several months to the point where they were iced out of the program. Unipoesa was never sure how Li did it. There was never any evidence, just the rotten feeling in his stomach.

Returning to the present, Unipoesa looked at Razar's face. All of the sternness, the gruffness that hardened his expression had wilted away. His beetle brows, unkempt and overgrown, cast caterpillar shadows across his eyelids.

"Then you gave me the final order," Unipoesa whispered to him. "You wanted me to teach Li the value of life. But I didn't. In fact, I think I taught him the most deadly lesson of all. Now I don't know who I hate more. You... or me."

236

Time rewound. Unipoesa found himself standing in front of the Minister, his face blotched red with anger.

"Break Li or ice him out of the program," Razar ordered, throwing a datafile at him.

So he did; after all, he had no choice.

When he rated at sixteen years old, Unipoesa gave Li command of a battleship and assigned him to patrol the planet they identified as his homeworld. The Dominion attack was a simulation, but Li was the only one unaware. Unfairly outnumbered, his ship's primary weapons array and communications malfunctioning, they had thrust him into a situation that would force him to use defensive measures. When he didn't, Unipoesa was forced to play a coldblooded hand.

"My parents?"

Li's face turned oddly quizzical as Dominion soldiers threatened the man and woman identified in the Command Development Program's registry as his biological parents.

"Retreat or we will kill them," one of the soldiers repeated, pressing knife to the man's neck. Despite the zig-zagging interference of the holographics, the man's tears could be seen cascading down his cheeks, his mouth forming a silent plea.

Li could have fallen back, covertly deployed his SMT, or stalled his enemy with negotiations—but he didn't. That's when Unipoesa realized how wrong he was about Li.

"Lock missiles on their communications tower and forward scanner relay. Fire."

Even knowing it was staged, Unipoesa had to steel himself to watch the simulated execution. As the older couple slumped to the floor with freshly slit throats, Li's eyes never faltered, his gaze steadfast and voice unwavering as he ordered a second round of missiles.

Damon's superiors, concerned with the financial ramifications of Li's ruthless tactics and expenditure of resources, had finally had enough. After only an hour of deliberation, they ordered Unipoesa to create a situation even more horrific.

Unipoesa looked up into the lights, his eyes burning. "Why did you have to involve more innocent students?"

Livia's ghost appeared before him, tall and thin, with gangly limbs and brown freckles smeared across her incongruously wide face.

What did Li see in her? Unipoesa wondered. As one of the Command Development Program's early attempts at genetic design, Livia's cognitive abilities didn't match up with her peers, especially Li's. But despite her plain appearance and the sexual inhibitors programmed into all of the students' genes, Li showed her more than a glimmer of interest.

... And so she became a convenient tool for the USC's greater purpose.

"You used her Broekgaen's syndrome as an excuse," he said, wringing his hands. The deadly autoimmune disorder had already killed several genetically modified students before her, and despite modern medical advancements, would kill her in less than three months. "And you said she'd be given a tranquilizer, something to take away the pain. But I saw the look in her eyes—she was still aware."

Grief transported him back into the past, forcing him to relive the incident.

"You killed your parents," Unipoesa said. "An undesirable outcome. You're lucky it was only a simulation."

From across the desk, Li sat staring coolly at Unipoesa. Usually a score of guards accompanied him, but this time Unipoesa ordered him alone. He wanted no unnecessary witnesses.

Li withheld the smile hovering at the corners of his lips. "I won the unwinnable."

Folding his hands across the metal desk, Unipoesa took his time responding. "Not all victories are worth celebrating."

He played his ace. Unipoesa typed the orders into his datapad. Two guards escorted Livia to the front of the room and then left. A cocktail of drugs should have been keeping her disoriented and unaware, but Unipoesa saw the fear in her eyes.

It's too late for Livia anyway, *he told himself. His superiors expected results or else it would be his hide on the line.*

He looked back at Li. For a split second uncertainty flickered in Li's eyes, but he shuffled it behind his customary smugness.

Unipoesa swallowed the last of his pride and continued. "There are twenty-six candidates left in this program, yes?"

"Yes, Sir."

"And only one will have the chance to be chief commanding officer, correct?"

"Yes, Sir."

"Well, congratulations, soldier, because now there are only twenty-five."

His withdrew his sidearm and shot Livia at point-blank range. Giving her no chance to scream, the shot made a neat, smoldering hole above her heart. She slumped to the ground, her head nodding limply to one side.

Damon swallowed hard to stop his stomach's contents from surging up his throat. The soldiers reentered, dragged her body out, and closed the door behind them.

In an unprecedented display, Li's face crumpled right before his eyes.

Damon hated himself for being able to continue.

"That was not a simulation." *Unipoesa leaned back in his chair, giving Li time to absorb the full weight of what had transpired.* "Since you have refused to follow my strategies, I've decided to change the game. I'm playing by your rules now, candidate. No mercy."

"I'm the best commander you have," *Li said angrily as tears spilled over his lashes.* "I do what I have to do to win battles."

"So do I."

"You're weak," *Li growled,* "Your strategies are beneath me! I could beat you right now and spit on your record."

Unipoesa smiled. "Well, candidate, maybe you'll earn that chance someday, but for now, you will do as I say."

Standing up, Unipoesa circled Li. He took his time, his voice barely above a whisper. "The next time you disobey your commanding officer, there will be twenty-four students left. We have no need for a bed-wetting pissant like you. And I'll make sure the world knows of your disgrace."

Unipoesa overturned the Minister's shriveled hand in his. "I didn't sleep. I started smoking again. And drinking. You watched it eat me alive, but you didn't care. You found another use for Li, one that made all my work obsolete."

By the time Li rated at twenty years old, his competition had been whittled down to six students. The other nineteen had either been put to Sleep or succumbed to the strange misfortunes that seemed to plague their training base. One student broke his neck during combat drills, an accident the holographic safety restraints should have never allowed to happen. Two accidentally blew themselves out the cargo hold while running a raid simulation. Another had somehow managed to slip and drown in the shower room in only a few centimeters of water.

When Unipoesa read the reports his stomach always tightened with the same rotten feeling. The accidents could be explained in other ways, but in his heart knew the truth. Even though none of the other students, save Tarsha, came close to scoring as well as Li, he didn't leave anything to chance.

Li is a killer, *he thought.* And he's getting back at me for Livia.

Unipoesa had nearly convinced his superiors to remove Li from the program when the breach occurred. Someone in the media had gotten hold of enough information about the Command Development Program to start rumors flying on the nets. Pictures of the students soon circulated, and Li's became the primary focus. Attractive and striking in his uniform, the mesmerized public soon pushed for full disclosure of the CDP. Then the General Assembly voted. Limited transparency was decided.

"Use him. We can work this to our advantage, but I don't want a circus," the Minister instructed as Unipoesa escorted Li to the news conference.

When he first exposed the young man to the bright lights and cameras, Unipoesa expected him to act much like he always did—cold, calculating, and palpably dangerous. Instead, he became someone else—a smiling, charismatic, self-assured champion—as if he had planning for this moment all along.

"I choose to serve the Starways. I will fight to defend the rights and liberties of all Sentient kind!" Li declared to the dizzy swarm of reporters clamoring past the safety bar to nab his picture.

In a few weeks he had completely won over the media. Soon afterward the funding came pouring in, and Unipoesa's pleas to remove Li from public light were drowned in the sea of flashing lights and exchanged credits.

"In the end he beat us at our own game," Unipoesa said, hanging his hands over his knees. "He was always smarter than us, always one step ahead, just like we designed him. So I did the only thing I could. I protected Tarsha."

It came at a heavy cost. Tarsha had always scored higher than Li, and her aptitude put her leagues ahead of him as a potential commander. It surprised Unipoesa that she wasn't the first he decided to kill, but years later he figured it out.

Leaving Tarsha for last was Li's best means of torturing her. And me.

But to save Tarsha, Unipoesa couldn't just break her—he had to damage her beyond repair.

"You're a disgrace to that uniform, candidate, and to all the people who have wasted their time and money training you," he said, coming around to face her at the Endgame console.

The young cadet didn't make eye contact with him, keeping her gaze ahead and clenching her jaw. She had just lost her thirty-eighth straight battle, unaware that Unipoesa had rigged the game so it was impossible to win no matter what she did.

"Why did you bother evacuating the ground teams? You needed to drop your missiles! What the hell were you thinking?" he screamed in her face. "Know when you're defeated!"

She hadn't slept in days, and the latest string of losses hit her hard. In less than two weeks she had already lost five kilos, and with the stress of defeat, had started washing obsessively. Medical teams monitored her showers so she wouldn't scrub herself raw. Even so, Unipoesa could see the red patches of abraded skin scoring her neck and hands.

It was time to deal the final blow.

He brought in Li.

"But Sir, we weren't scheduled to battle for seven more months—" Tarsha said as Li sat opposite her on the game console.

"Your final is now. I'd suggest you pay better attention to your front lines this time." He leaned over and whispered into her ear. "You're weak. Pathetic. You're no match for Li. Let's get this over with."

Fear, already raw and wild in her eyes, crushed down on the last fragments of her composure. She didn't move. Not when he initiated the game, not when Li won, and not when he screamed in her face—

"Know when you're defeated!"

—and threatened to have her iced.

She was done for.

"I saved her the only way I knew I could. I broke her so you would have to make her a Sleeper. As far as Li was concerned, she was dead."

Unipoesa wiped his eyes. "Since it was my fault, it was only fair that I watch her be put to Sleep. But you'd never told me how brutal the transition was…"

When he closed his eyes he could still see her strapped to the table, her skull splayed open as the doctors struggled to implant her with new memories and a substitute personality. Her eyes remained open the entire time as tears slid down her colorless cheeks. Tarsha

Leone, the brilliant but sensitive warrior, was systematically laid to rest and reborn as the foul-mouthed, insolent Scabber named Agracia Waychild.

"It was one of the worst moments of my life, but back then I was blissfully ignorant. I convinced myself that she was just an experiment, a means to an end like the rest of the students, but that I had done well by saving her life. But it's different now, knowing who she is. Knowing that..."

When he finished the sentence, his voice broke on the words. "...she's as good as dead."

Unipoesa's hands found their way under the Minister's bed, away from the guards' eyes, and wrapped themselves around the life support cords feeding into the frail body of his commander. His muscles tensed, begging to tear the lifeline in two.

"It didn't have to be like this," Unipoesa said, firming his grip. "You destroyed the best parts of me."

The monitors fluctuated. Numbers and figures changed, though he didn't know what they meant. Unipoesa looked at the Minister, and this time he saw someone different.

"What I did was wrong. And now I will have to answer for it."

Minister Razar's life support cords dangled beneath the bed still intact as Admiral Damon Unipoesa walked away.

***

In the brief time it took for the soldiers and Admiral Unipoesa to exchange words, the patient in the intensive care unit opened his eyes. The monitors captured the moment, though the doctors who later reviewed the anomaly could not account for what the patient had said. With a swollen tongue and cracked lips he spoke only one word. Jaeia Kyron, who had remained out of sight but observed all that had transpired, heard that word.

***

"We have to stop," Triel insisted for the third time, sensing the commander's considerable blood loss.

"Not safe… Lockheads," Jetta said, her eyes half-closed as she rode slumped over her wolf, barely conscious but still hanging on with her one good arm.

Frowning, Triel steered her wolf over the first rocky pass. The sun, creeping over the mountains, suffused the world in hues of yellow and orange. As Algar awakened in the morning light, the moon, nearly full, retreated with the stars.

"Hey," Triel said, pulling up her wolf to trot alongside Jetta's. "Really—it's time to stop."

The Healer guided their party into the shelter of a stand of trees felled in a rockslide. Jetta mumbled incoherently as Triel helped the wolf dismount the rider.

"Are all humans this stupid?" Triel asked the wolf she had begun to think of as Gray Paw. He flitted his ears at her and licked her foot as she took a closer look at her friend.

Alright, let's see how bad this is. The ride had torn Jetta's wound open further, but it remained within the scope of the Healer's abilities. Still, something made her hesitate.

Gray Paw whined and nudged Triel with his nose.

"I can't keep doing this."

With a pinched brow the Healer opened Jetta's uniform, placed her hands on her warm chest, and dipped below the barrier of her skin. Triel managed her wounds like she would for any other soldier but rushed through the parts Jetta's body could take care of on its own. This time she didn't indulge her curiosity, though Jetta's biorhythm sounded greatly disturbed.

"Feeling better?" Triel said as she withdrew and Jetta regained her senses. Before the Healer could say anything more, Jetta took to analyzing the position of the sun and their shelter under the fallen trees, her jade eyes flicking past Triel and onto more important matters.

"This is good cover, but we have to keep moving," Jetta said, picking herself up off the ground with a grimace. Surprise widened Jetta's eyes when she realized that the Healer hadn't fully restored her, but said nothing.

"Are you hungry?" Jetta asked as Triel ducked out from underneath their shelter and made her way toward the boulders where her wolf stood sniffing the eastern winds. "I forgot I stashed two nutrition pills in my inner pocket."

Jetta produced the pills and held them out for Triel. Each blue capsule contained 3,600 calories and all the balanced nutrients and minerals required by a soldier in combat. Though not exactly filling, the supplement proved to be a lifesaver in the field when food was scarce or difficult to transport.

"I guess that's a dumb question," Jetta said, blushing. Neither one of them had eaten properly in days. "You can have both of these. I'll be okay."

Triel turned back to her, hugging herself as she tried to make sense of Jetta's actions.

It's always the same scenario, she thought. *Jetta looks out for me, protects me, but neglects my most basic need as a Prodgy—*
—and as...

She stopped herself, confused where her train of thought was taking her.

Without saying a word, Triel nabbed only one of the pills and walked away, mounting her wolf before Jetta had a chance to say anything.

"Wait up!" Jetta shouted as she looked around for Gray Paw, who had wandered back down the trail.

Triel didn't wait. As the wolf ran up the mountain slope, the Healer relaxed her grip, allowing him to find the best route through the trees and thicket. Unforgiving, glacial winds from the north washed down the mountain face, finding every tear and hole in her clothing to chill her bones.

Jetta finally did catch up, frustration etching her face with a scowl. "I'm not playing games."

"Neither am I," Triel said, giving her wolf a touch of her heel.

When Jetta caught up to her again, Triel didn't give her a chance to ask questions. "Do you have any idea where we're going?"

She didn't have to look back to know that Jetta was still glowering. "No, but they do. I asked him—"

"Gray Paw," Triel said.

"Okay, I asked Gray Paw where this place was, and he seemed to understand. Let me pass so he can lead."

Without affording Jetta the satisfaction of a reaction, Triel pulled over on the narrow trail to allow Jetta's wolf to take over. As Jetta's aura brushed by, Triel felt the underpinnings of deep hurt beneath her outward brooding.

That's new…

They traveled in silence until a hot and oily sensation crept into Triel's belly. "I think the Lockheads are closer than we thought. I can feel their sickness."

"I know," Jetta said, her voice firm. "I'm aware."

The commander didn't acknowledge her further, and Triel didn't have the energy to engage her. Even with the tension between them, she still trusted Jetta more than anyone.

As they reached the first false summit, Triel felt Jetta's thought patterns shift. To her surprise, Jetta turned to her and said, "Thanks for healing me. I didn't realize how bad it was."

Triel held on tight as her wolf leapt from one boulder to the next. With no particular emotion, she replied, "it's what I do."

A few rays of sun poked through the gathering clouds, but despite their intimations of warmth, a light snow fell from the sky, dashing Triel's hope. Before the north wind picked up the weather had been tolerably cold, but now the Healer found herself shivering uncontrollably, pressing her body into the wolf's fur.

We're completely exposed to the elements, she thought as they broke out of the tree line and traversed a sharp ridge along the saddle between two peaks. Once she caught sight of the spectacular drop off and the sheer face of the mountain below, the Healer forgot all other worries and concentrated on the wolf's every step.

"This reminds me of Tralora," Jetta mumbled.

Triel's wolf stopped suddenly, but she was too cold and scared to look up. A warm jacket encircled her shoulders.

"What's going to keep you warm?" Triel asked as she pulled it tighter around her body.

"Don't worry about me," Jetta said as she remounted her wolf and pressed on toward the peak.

"Don't worry about you?" she exclaimed, tired of backing down. "Jetta, when you brought me back in the forest, what did you see?"

Jetta stayed silent for a moment as her wolf struggled with a difficult section of the trail. "I saw you when you were younger."

"I know you're holding back," Triel said. "When a Healer is on the brink of Falling, all of their darkest secrets become accessible. So if you saw any of my childhood then you know my worst fear. And you know what? I'm not afraid of you knowing that. I just wish you trusted me enough to allow me to see inside you and let me stay your friend."

But before Triel could elicit a response, gunshots exploded all around her.

"*Skucheka!*" Jetta shouted, her wolf rearing wildly as a bullet ricocheted off a nearby rock.

Triel didn't see what happened to Jetta as her wolf turned and sprinted back toward the saddle.

We have to summit, Triel thought, realizing their only chance of surviving without cover or weapons. With more than four hundred meters to go, she hung on for dear life as her wolf took the increasingly steep ridge in giant strides and leaps.

When she looked back, Jetta had dismounted her wolf and directed him toward the Healer.

No! Triel cried silently as Gray Paw caught up to them, struggling to make it over the pass with his packmate.

"Jetta!" Triel shouted as she watched her friend drop down to avoid a spray of gunfire. She managed to find cover behind a boulder, but with the Lockheads pinning her down and steadily approaching, it wouldn't last long.

Losing his purchase on the incline, Triel's wolf careened backward. She screamed as they plummeted, the world a jumble of rocks, sharp pains, and snow.

Before she could put any thought to her situation, she slammed into something soft and warm. She tried to lift her head, but the world refused to orient itself. White teeth and pink gums wrapped around her face, smothering her with hot, panting breath. Her feet and legs bumped against rocks as snow slid down her pants and up her shirt.

Am I falling again? She couldn't tell anymore.

The confusion of movement stopped. She opened her eyes to clusters of soft clouds and gentle snowfall. She could breathe again, but the breath that filled her lungs did not completely quench her hunger for air. When she looked around her, the wolves were pacing nervously on the ridge. White Neck was limping terribly but seemed otherwise okay. They had made it—but Jetta had not.

Triel scrambled up on bruised hands and knees to look down toward the saddle. Jetta emerged from behind her boulder, her arms held high in the sign of defeat as the Lockheads broke their own cover behind the tree line and approached with their weapons aimed at her heart. Triel counted six of them when Jetta looked back at her.

She's not looking at me, the Healer realized, tracing Jetta's eyeline to Gray Paw. Head held low to the ground, the wolf watched the commander with intense concentration.

The Healer saw it unfold as if she was inside Jetta's head, timing the entire event and calculating her next move. "Run," she whispered.

Hands pressed to her ears, Triel collapsed to the ground as Gray Paw threw back his head back and cried out, releasing a howl that shook the foundations of her being. The sound started out as a reverberating bass that seemed to emanate from somewhere beyond his massive black body. He quickly shifted his pitch, gaining momentum and volume until he struck a discordant high note in the most mournful cry she had ever heard. White Neck joined in, adding his voice and strengthening the howl tenfold. The chorus multiplied, reflecting off the mountains and scattering across the valley.

As the wolves continued to howl, Triel could barely distinguish the rumbling that seized the mountain. When they stopped, the world quaked beneath her.

"Jetta!" she screamed as rocks shook loose from the slope below. The rockslide picked up debris and energy as it cascaded downwards, right into the path of Jetta and her enemies.

Gray Paw shot down the mountain as Jetta scrambled up the path as fast as she could. The Lockheads also clambered for cover, but it was too late. Like a great ocean wave, the rocks and debris swallowed them whole, sending up a great plume of dust and snow that covered the side of the mountain.

"No!"

Triel started down the slope, but White Neck caught her leg and held her fast despite her pleadings.

"I can still save her—it's not too late," she begged as she pried at the wolf's jaws.

"Save who?"

Triel reeled around to see Jetta emerging from the cloud of debris on top of Gray Paw, covered in a thick layer of dust. Like nothing had happened, Jetta and Gray Paw trotted up beside her. At first the Healer was too shocked to say anything, and then her hand clenched into a fist.

"Ow!" Jetta yelled as Triel socked her in the thigh.

"Don't do that again," Triel said.

Nursing her thigh, Jetta half-smiled. "Wasn't planning on it."

249

Jetta dismounted and went to the injured wolf. "He broke his leg. We can't go on."

"I can't heal an animal, Jetta," Triel said, stroking White Neck's nose. He whimpered as she inspected his leg. "No Prodgy has ever healed a wild animal. Their rhythms are nothing like ours."

Jetta hugged herself tightly as the wind whipped through the saddle and stung their exposed skin. "We have to get off the mountain before this storm picks up or we'll freeze, and they're our best chance."

"I'm open to suggestions," Triel said, not hiding her doubt.

Then Jetta surprised her. "What if I helped?"

"What do you mean?"

Jetta tilted her head as she formulated her response. "I can hear them, even understand some of their thoughts. Maybe you could reach them through me."

Triel wanted to dismiss the idea, but Jetta continued to explain how it could work.

"My brother was very different than me and Jaeia, so I used to look through his eyes every once and a while. One time there was this laborminder who was too hard for me to crack, so I went through Jahx's head and then used my talent on him. Made him think there were Widowmakers everywhere so he would abandon his post and we could steal some tools."

"Widowmakers?"

"A poisonous spider on Fiorah. Liked to hide in the ship's engines and then lay its eggs in your ears. My sibs and I always put waxing putty in our ears after we saw them explode out of a kid's head one shift."

Triel made a face. "Sounds awful."

"Yeah." Jetta trailed off, her gaze dropping to her feet. "He didn't exactly return to his post. Kinda made him go crazy. But the point is," she said, quickly redirecting the conversation, "is that maybe you could access my mind to heal the wolf."

250

Triel didn't see another option, but she couldn't acquiesce. "What if he won't let us? If he fights back he could kill us both. Or if he's got an unclean mind."

Jetta pursed her lips. "He's a wolf. Besides, he saved us a few too many times for me to believe that."

Sighing heavily, the Healer gave in a little. *Jetta's right. The way the clouds are gathering, it won't be long before another mountain storm hits. We have to descend to a safer altitude.*

On top of that, she wasn't sure how much farther the Temple would be, and trying to go anywhere on foot without food, equipment, or shelter would be next to impossible.

These wolves are domesticated, so they've been trained to gather edible plants, she remembered. *And if we can't find cover, they know how to use their bodies to shield us from the elements. It would be foolish not to travel with them.*

For a second she considered the possibility of getting by with just Gray Paw, but nixed the idea. *Jetta would never stand for abandoning the other wolf.*

Triel touched the back of her leg, stirring distant memories. The wounds were long gone, but the pain was still there. She knew she couldn't judge an entire species based on one experience—she wouldn't do that to any Sentient—but still—

Jasen...

Tears brimmed at her lids as her heart surged with unexpected emotion. Reflexively, she looked to Jetta. Green eyes looked back intently, watching her every move with confidence and a familiar comfort.

"You exposed me to the pack's memories," Triel said, remembering their first encounter. "I know wolves aren't *evil*, but I can't—"

"You must trust me." Jetta offered her hand. "And trust in what you experienced. Their familial bonds are in some ways stronger than ours. They are honorable and worthy comrades."

The Healer heard the ancient warning song in her head.

251

Scarlet eyes
Black disguise
(Jasen)

Phantom pain bit down on her leg. She reflexively winced. "You don't know what you're asking of me."

"I will be here. I won't let you go."

Triel turned to White Neck. Whining softly, he tucked his tail under his belly as he licked his injured leg. He looked up at her, his fiery eyes betraying their fearsome appearance, beseeching her for mercy.

Triel gave Jetta her hand, and they each placed one on the wolf.

"What's there to be afraid of?" Jetta asked.

The Healer didn't say anything.

It's better that she doesn't know the cautionary stories the elders told of the Prodgies who tried to heal a beast, she decided. Or about her past. Her teachers had repeatedly warned her against restoring any being when her heart was not fully committed. Not fully investing in a healing process left the Healer vulnerable, and more importantly, malleable to any destructive facet of the host.

"Whatever you do, don't let go," Triel whispered.

Jetta squeezed her hand. "I've got you."

The Healer closed her eyes and tipped her head back.

***

Jetta didn't know what to expect when she suggested they use each other's gifts to heal the injured wolf. Imprinted with canine instincts after her encounter with the fighting-ring wolves of Old Earth, Jetta didn't question her reaction in the presence of the wolves of Algar.

I will do everything in my power to save him, she thought, primal impulses burning through her veins.

In a remote corner of her mind, she understood that it wasn't normal for any being, Sentient or not, to stay at the forefront of her mind for such an extended period of time. *This is different. We are a pack now.*

Following the Healer's lead, Jetta bowed her head and opened her eyes to a different world.

Iridescent colors swirled together with starry constellations as she passed through an intricate dance of energy and light. Jetta's only impression of her own existence, and those of her companions, came through as impossibly long filaments threading between three distinct halos of light.

This is incredible, *she thought, marveling at the new experience.*

She had never acted as an anchor and eyeshot before, and keeping herself grounded while simultaneously accessing the wolf's mind was more of a challenge than she had anticipated. As Triel's psionic rhythm wound around hers and entered the wolf, Jetta struggled to keep her grip on the physical world. Before, on Old Earth, she had merely connected with the wolf's shared memories, not integrated with his biorhythm. Locked in tandem with the Healer, Jetta coursed through an uncharted world of living cells and biological energies.

What is that?

In the far distance she felt her lips curl and her head fall back. Something growled, and a strange sensation slid down the axis of their world between worlds.

(Jetta,) *Triel called across to her, voice stricken with terror.* (He's fighting me—)

Something lashed against her hold, and the constellations froze. A flower of singing black sound blossomed from within the threads holding them together, blotting out the confusing amalgam of neurofeedback.

In a drastic shift, Jetta felt warmth against her skin, and breathed in air spiced with lavender and the lingering scent of afternoon rain. Jetta looked down at her hands and saw the Healer's markings.

253

These are Triel's memories, she thought, sensing the familiar tune. But she wasn't alone. Eyes, set behind her own, watched intently as the events unfolded.

The memory progressed. Under the bright afternoon sun, the young Healer ran in an open field, her fingers gliding over the prickly tips of orange grass as she hummed the bedtime tune her father sung to her every night. Her youngest brother, Jasen, pumped his legs as fast as he could, trying to keep up as she turned down the hill towards the river.

Scarlet eyes
Black disguise
Winter skies and raven cries
I know you're there
Shadow in the trees
Call to the moon
when you're done with me

A thunderous howl rang out, stopping her in her tracks. Desperate and agonized, the cry made her think of her father.

"Father!" she cried, sprinting toward the noise as she rounded the stables toward the pasture.

Unrecognizable carnage lay steaming in the sun. The fresh kill, dragged from the stables, left a trail of blood and yellow gristle. Mauled beyond recognition, Triel couldn't tell which of the livestock had been slain.

Her eyes followed the bloody footprints to the forest, where the breeze carried the scent of burning timber and flesh. Catching up to her, Jasen grabbed onto her shirt, begging her to take him home as he tugged with all his might.

"Please, Tree," he said, calling her by her nickname. "Go back, go back!"

But she didn't go back. She heard the whimpering, the yips of pain. *I have to see.*

"Father?" she timidly called.

She wrestled herself free of Jasen and pushed through the pricker bush, ripping her clothes and scratching her face. But the pain disappeared as soon as she saw the wolf's eyes, burning like embers as he pawed at the ground, trying to gain purchase despite his shattered legs. Her father loomed over the massive creature, drawing back his bloodied ax for another strike.

Triel screamed as the wolf lurched forward and his teeth snapped down on her leg. He thrashed her sideways, turning the forest into a green blur before her head smacked against an exposed tree root. The world wobbled and seesawed. She wasn't sure what was going on, if she was really seeing another massive, black creature come bounding through the brush. But there was no mistaking her brother's shriek.

"Jasen!" her father cried.

Before Jetta could see more, the memory split apart at the seams and coalesced in a different time. It was perhaps a few days later. The wounds on Triel's leg had been healed, and she lay bundled up in her bed. Her mother sat at the foot, her back to Triel as she stared out the open window at the evening sky. The sweet-smelling breeze carried the sound of her father arguing with the neighbors somewhere away from the house.

"Where's Jasen?"

She asked several times before her mother finally replied. She never looked at Triel, keeping her tears to herself, but spoke just loud enough for her to hear. "Your father is in trouble with the tribal council for killing the remainder of the pack. They should have never allowed them to come down from the mountains. What use do we have for them anyway? They're dangerous—they can't be trusted."

"But father was training them—"

"And look what happened. That wolf turned on him. Your father is lucky to be alive."

"Why did he have to kill the others?"

Her mother didn't answer her. She clung to the bedpost, her body rigid and frail.

"Don't you understand?" her mother whispered, her tears flowing freely now and wetting her blouse. "Jasen can't come back anymore. He's gone forever. They never found his body."

Listening to the inner voice of Triel's memory, Jetta realized what Triel's mother had meant. Since they couldn't find the body of her brother, they would never be able to give him a proper burial or preserve the memory of his biorhythm.

Somewhere in the distance, back in corporeality, she felt herself gulping for air as the wolf fought back viciously, tearing at the fragile lifelines connecting the three of them. He had seen Triel's memories through Jetta's eyes but only understood the slaughter of his kin. He didn't grasp the implications of the wolf's challenge for dominance that had nearly killed Triel's father, nor did he understand why wolves should not kill livestock. The pain that had shattered Triel's world when the second wolf abducted and killed Jasen paled beside the image of her father piling the wolves onto the wood pile, dousing their lifeless black bodies with fuel, and erasing entire generations of shared consciousness with one swift motion of his firestarter.

Thrust backwards with impossible force, Jetta skidded several meters on her back before coming to a halt dangerously close to the mountain's edge. She opened her eyes, surprised to find herself back in the physical world.

"Oh Gods—"

No time to think. Triel straddled her, teeth bared and eyes ablaze. Jetta batted away the Healer's attempts to claw her face while defending against her biting teeth.

"Triel!" she shouted. Crazed, the Healer assailed her with wild strikes while cursing in a language Jetta had never heard. The predawn blue of her eyes vanished, replaced by a festering, angry purple that cut through Jetta as if she had no psionic defenses at all.

The fight unfolded too quickly for Jetta to see what the two wolves were doing. For a split second she caught sight of Gray Paw looking at her curiously when her viewpoint flipped, but she returned to her own sights as Triel's mind pressed into her with vicious intent. Jetta bucked off of the ground, insides tore apart by invisible claws.

In the throes of agony, a memory hit her. The Motti weapon. The voices she heard inside their machine when she breached the horizon. Their whisperings, their words that she heard within her bones—

(*Ai-lĕ, ime, Ai-lĕ—nos k'etekμe imœ Ai-lĕ*)

(*Umnïero, Amaroka, f'ro ime nos wrli e*)

(*Dk'a ovŋĭl sh'dar'o*)

At first she had no breath to speak. Triel bit into her neck, anchoring her position while asphyxiating her with unseen hands.

Gods, Triel—please...

As the colors of the world faded, she remembered the place of pain within the weapon's inner realm, the blistering halo of light, and the voices whispering the same phrases over and over—

(*Ai-lĕ, ime, Ai-lĕ—nos k'etekμe imœ Ai-lĕ*)

(*Umnïero, Amaroka, f'ro ime nos wrli e*)

(*Dk'a ovŋĭl sh'dar'o*)

Facing death, the final pieces of the puzzle locked into place. It made sense. She finally understood why she felt their words rattling inside her, jarring her fading mind.

"*Ai-lĕ, ime, Ai-lĕ—nos k'etekμe imœ Ai-lĕ, Umnïero,*" Jetta choked out with ragged breath. Blood spilled from her neck as Triel shook her like prey.

Jetta fought for every word, "*Amaroka, f'ro ime nos wrli e.*"

Triel seized Jetta's throat with her teeth as the words broke free.

"*Dk'a ovŋĭl sh'dar'o...*"

***

Triel tumbled backwards, landing flat on her back, slamming the air out of her lungs. Snowflakes melted on her face as she caught her breath and came to. Her mouth tasted like warm copper, and her body felt alien and sluggish. A strange growling grated in her ears, only to cease when Triel realized she was the one making the noise.

The Healer sat up, shaking her head to right the disconnect between her body and mind. It wasn't right. She looked at her markings, tracing the familiar pattern with a fingertip but not knowing who or what lay beneath the flesh.

The wolf.

She looked over at the injured wolf, who was lying unconscious where she had left him. Gray Paw circled him, nudging his packmate with his nose.

"Jetta—"

The commander lay motionless. Triel rushed to her side, turned her over, and gasped in horror when she saw the deep gouges in Jetta's neck.

These marks were made by teeth, but not by the fangs of a wolf...

Triel touched her mouth, fingers scraping at the crust of congealed blood on her lips. "Oh Gods—"

The Healer's stomach spasmed, purging every last drop of its contents onto the mountaintop.

As the heaving began to slow, she realized her worst fears had come true. First Jasen, and now Jetta.

Why didn't you listen to me? she thought angrily, gripping Jetta's sleeve. Wolves were wild and unpredictable, and now her brother and best friend were dead.

Gray Paw snapped at her, setting her back on her heels. Scarlet eyes, twin flames of unfettered spirit, glowed fiercely in his black face. He snarled, showing the sharpened tips of his canines as he bowed his head and locked his gaze with hers.

258

A new voice entered her head, speaking in a foreign tongue she had never heard. Somehow her consciousness translated the words into recognizable feelings.

It's not too late.

Triel took no further cues and lunged back toward her friend. "Come back—"

She interlocked her fingers with Jetta's and laid her opposite hand over the wound. As she plummeted beneath the surface of her skin, she realized the extensive internal damage, as if a wild animal had torn through ligaments and tissues, cracking bones and thrashing organs...

(What did I do?)

It was too much, and she didn't have enough time to resuscitate Jetta's vital organs without neglecting the totality of her being. Besides, their attempt to heal the wolf had depleted her own reserves.

(Hopeless.)

Through her fingertips, Triel felt Jetta's cells dying off at exponential rates, blood supplies drying up, clogging pathways and congesting her senses. At every turn another system failed and shut down.

She's too far gone.

(I killed her.)

But just as she started to crumble, something warm and furry bolstered her. An aggressive, savage dynamism galvanized her flesh, not unlike what she had experienced within the other wolf. But this time the biorhythm felt strong, vibrant, and easily accessible, sliding down her fingertips like liquid energy and flowing into her lifeless friend. Coruscations of light flowed through her veins, repairing Jetta's injuries much faster than she had ever healed anyone.

Jetta's heart began to vibrate with electrical impulses that Triel quickly guided into an organized, viable rhythm. Tears of joy streamed down Triel's face as she cupped her friend's heart with her hands, nursing its pump and directing its flow within her body.

259

Green eyes fluttered open, full of disbelief and shock. "Triel?"

"It's okay," Triel said, smoothing away the hair on her forehead. Triel let go of Jetta's hand and scooted back a little bit. "You're going to be fine."

"*Hei Meitka.*" Jetta winced as she sat up, checking for the wound on her neck, but it had already healed. "You... weren't yourself."

Triel dropped her gaze. "It's one of the reasons why Prodgies were forbidden to heal animals. Their biorhythms are difficult to navigate and they usually end up infecting us with their primitive instincts."

"So you took on his fear?"

"In a sense, yes. That's why I attacked you."

Jetta looked at the injured wolf lying a few meters away, a thin layer of snow blanketing his charcoal fur. "He saw something in you, in your memories—the deaths of his brothers."

Triel shivered at the nasty bite of the wind. "You saw what happened to Jasen?"

"I'm so sorry, Triel," Jetta whispered.

"Now you know why I couldn't heal White Neck."

Jetta frowned. "You couldn't heal him because you don't trust him. That's why he won't let you in."

"A wolf killed my brother. How would you feel?"

"They have a pack mentality, Triel," Jetta said. "And in a pack, if you can't trust your mates, then everything falls apart. He saw the deaths of his brothers, but he also saw the inception of your distrust. With the way you feel, you'll never accept them."

"That's not true," Triel said. "At least, not anymore."

"What do you mean?"

Triel reached out and stroked Gray Paw's head. "I found a reason to trust."

"As you should," Jetta said with a smile.

"It turns out the elders were wrong. At least about reading them. I understood Gray Paw when he told me I could still save you. It's not like sensing other Sentients, but it's very distinct. Maybe not all of the old teachings were as accurate as I thought. Or maybe it was because of your guidance."

Triel stopped petting Gray Paw and looked up. "Jetta," she asked carefully, "how did you know that prayer?"

Jetta frowned. "What prayer?"

"*Ai-lĕ, ime, Ai-lĕ—nos k'etekµe imœ Ai-lĕ...?*"

It took a moment before Jetta recalled what she had uttered while under attack. "I… don't know. I remembered it from when I made contact with the Motti weapon. I heard the voices chanting it. I just felt like I had to say it. What is it?"

"A protective prayer. It's to keep a Healer grounded."

"What does it mean?"

"I don't know how well it will translate into Common. Something like *take me, take me, for I know not what I do. I give myself to the Great Mother so that she may wield my spirit, for her will is of the greater good.*"

"I don't understand."

"The Prodgy believe that the Great Mother is the channel between the spirit world and the mortal world. By giving ourselves to her, we can maintain our inner peace and restore a Falling Healer."

Jetta nodded as if she had solved the troubling puzzle. "Now I know why I heard that in the Dissembler device."

A fierce gust of wind nearly toppled both Triel and Jetta. "We have to get down," the Healer said.

"Yes, before this gets any worse," Jetta yelled over the wind, pointing to the thick swirl of clouds blanketing the range below. "Let's heal the other wolf and get out of here. We can do it now—he will see your change of heart."

"Are you sure?"

"We really don't have a choice."

Massaging the webbing between her fingers, the Healer tentatively approached White Neck, holding onto her gratitude for

261

Gray Paw's help in healing Jetta. White Neck looked up at her as she touched his injured leg, a low growl rumbling in his throat, but he settled once Triel joined hands with Jetta. Whimpering and yipping, Gray Paw circled the group as they tried once more to restore the broken leg.

All was going well until the first dart struck the back of her arm. The second and the third planted themselves deep in her right thigh. The Healer tried to call out, but her body washed away in a tidal wave of numbness.

Blackness claimed her. She didn't feel the fall.

***

Jetta slowly regained consciousness, greeted by a headache that racked her skull and left her ears ringing. Inhaling sharply, she filled her lungs with the pleasant scent of blooming flowers and fresh rain.

Her eyelids felt weighted down. Rubbing them seemed to help. When she finally peeled them back, she found herself surrounded by the dense greenery of a vast forest. Vascular roots formed the forest bed, giving rise to massive trunks that stretched toward what should have been sky but instead wove into a distant, leafy canopy.

As her senses adjusted to her new surroundings, the melodies of the various song birds and chirps of the other forest dwellers filled her ears. A light rain fell from above, providing cool relief in the uncomfortably warm air.

Where am I? Weren't we on top of a mountain? Jetta tried to pick herself up off the forest bed, but found herself tangled in the purple vines blanketing the nearest gigantic tree. *No, not tangled— bound.*

When she looked to her right, she saw Triel in the same predicament.

"Triel!" Jetta whispered. "Wake up!"

Triel opened her eyes and went through the same stages of shock and bewilderment. "Where are we? Where are the wolves?"

"I don't know. But there's someone here in the forest with us."

Fully alert now, Jetta sensed the multiple presences fanning out around them, watching them from the protection of the trees. The birds stopped singing and the forest became very still, as if holding its breath. "Show yourself!" she demanded, straining against her bonds.

A tattooed man stepped out of the shadows. His face was inked to resemble some kind of predator, and to further the illusion, he had filed his teeth to points. He wore the bones and hides of his kills, and fresh blood painted the few areas of unmarked skin on his head and shoulders.

"Jumaris," Triel whispered.

The Healer's fear exploded across the psionic divide, causing Jetta to shrink into herself to avoid succumbing to her friend's panic.

"Let us go!" Jetta shouted.

"They don't speak Common," Triel reminded her, keeping her voice low.

Two more emerged. Then six more. In the end they numbered nearly fifty, wielding weapons of sharpened bone and cut stone.

They're brutal to outsiders, no matter who they are, Jetta recalled. Despite their humanoid appearance, their minds felt alien and unreadable. Straining and flexing across the unseen planes, Jetta couldn't seem to reach them on any psionic front.

I should be able to sense something useful, she thought, frustrated at her limitations.

The tattooed Jumaris who emerged first drew a blade and circled them, pointing to various appendages and licking his lips. He chanted at them in a foreign tongue, repeating the same phrases over and over again. The others joined in one by one until they were all shouting, dancing, and waving their weapons closer and closer to Jetta and Triel.

"Jetta..." Triel whispered, her eyes the size of saucers as one of the female Jumaris used her knife to pantomime a cutting motion across her breasts. Tilting her head, the warrior woman pointed the blade at the Healer.

Where are the wolves? Jetta looked around, but they were nowhere in sight. *Calm down. Think. Find them.*

Dipping back into the link she had forged with her lupine companions, Jetta traced the lines of their animal thought patterns through the confusing jumble of the Jumaris' minds.

Help us, please, Jetta called out.

All of the chanting and the commotion of their dancing stopped. The forest fell under a hush broken only by the light padding of the massive shadowy animals.

"Gray Paw—"

Head down and teeth showing, the black wolf approached the group. The Jumaris froze in position, their jubilance lost as the wolf growled and walked toward Jetta and Triel.

Jetta instantly regretted her decision. *There are too many Jumaris—what if they kill Gray Paw?*

(They'll eat us all—)

Gray Paw stopped in front of her, his teeth still bared and a growl in his throat. But when Jetta whispered to him, he sniffed at her and licked her face.

"*Akata Caumri!*" the first Jumari shouted, falling to his knees. The others repeated his words and dropped to their knees, humming and mumbling indistinctly. From the trees, someone clapped

"Congratulations, outsider. You are one of the few to earn the Jumaris' respect."

A Sentient of unrecognizable origins stepped out of the brush. His frame and stature indicated some degree of human lineage, but his blood-red skin and hairless body spoke of the outerworlds. Wearing the briefest of animal-skin garments, the man slung a sighted phase rifle over his left shoulder.

"What is going on?" Jetta exclaimed.

The man smiled, his pitch black eyes following her every move. "I am Keyl. I will bring you to your fate."

"What the hell does that mean?"

But Keyl didn't answer her. Instead, he made a series of clicking sounds with his tongue, and one of the Jumaris stuck his blade into the exposed pink heart of the tree. The vines that tied them down instantly retracted, and Jetta didn't waste time helping Triel up and getting as far away from the tree as possible.

"Do as I say, outsider," Keyl said, tapping the butt of his rifle. "Or you will know pain."

Jetta and Triel followed the Jumaris and the red-skinned man through the thick of the forests, stopping every few meters to hack and slash their way through the stubborn brush and the angry purple vines that snaked across the forest floor.

"Where's White Neck?" Triel whispered.

One of the Jumaris shot her a cautionary glare, but it didn't stop Jetta from responding. "He's close, but that's all I know."

"Oh my Gods." The words escaped her lips before she could take them back. Jetta had to tilt her head back as her eyes followed the stone steps of the massive temple up to where they pierced the clouds.

"Is this the Temple of Exxuthus?" Jetta whispered.

"I think so," Triel said, her voice quavering.

Flowing, elegant symbols adorned the steeply sloping sides of the temple. Other inscriptions, and a stone relief of demons and bloodshed, shocked Jetta. *I never associated this kind of violence with the Prodgies.*

"Climb," the red man said, pointing his gun toward the stairs.

Gray Paw had stayed by her side the entire time, but when she set foot on the first step, he did not join her, instead pacing nervously at the base of the temple.

"Come on," Jetta said.

The red man laughed. "He knows better than to tread lightly up those stairs."

"Why? What's at the top?"

265

A savage smile revealed the red man's many rows of teeth. "Whatever you bring with you."

Jetta once again commanded the Gray Paw to join her, and he reluctantly followed, his tail tucked snugly between his legs. The entire tribe of Jumaris made the ascent as well, chanting in their odd tongue for what seemed like hours.

Something isn't right, she thought, unable to discern one moment from the next. Everything blurred together, from her breath to the beat of her heart, every step up taking her farther away from the top. *Is this real?*

Jetta's eyes grew heavy as she plodded on, one foot in front of the other, her muscles screaming in protest.

"I can't..." Triel began, eyes half-closed as she wobbled on the steps.

Jetta took her by the waist and wrapped the Healer's arm around her shoulder. "Just lean on me. Keep walking. We're almost there."

After only a few more steps, Jetta's legs refused to support the both of them.

"Stay here with Gray Paw," Jetta said between breaths, easing Triel down into a sitting position next to the wolf. "I'll be back for you. Don't worry, he'll keep you safe."

Triel touched her face. "You always go away."

The Healer's words faded away in exhaustion, and she collapsed against the wolf. Curling protectively around her on the stairs, Gray Paw laid his head on her shoulders and closed his eyes.

"Triel, I—"

"Coming?" the red man asked, cutting her off. He pointed the rifle at Triel and teased the trigger. "Don't you want to see what awaits you?"

Reluctantly, Jetta resumed the impossible ascent. With each step, fatigue and pain chipped away at her will as she drew deeper into the swirl of clouds. She lost sight of Triel, the Jumaris, even the red man, until she traveled alone in the gray stillness.

"Hello?" she called, but no one answered.

I can't fail again, she thought, forcing herself to press on. *Everything is at stake.*

Minutes or hours passed; she wasn't sure. The cool wetness of the mist against her hot skin became her only companion. Enervated, all of her pain dissolved into numbness, turning her legs into dead things that she dragged up with her onto each stair.

The silence, the isolation, ate at her. For all her strides toward independence, she had never liked being alone, or the company it brought.

(Jahx. Jaeia. Triel. Galm. Lohien,) her subconscious whispered. *(I can't protect them.)*

Doubt and emotion took turns whittling down the last of her resolve.

What am I doing here—?

I can't do this.

(I'm not strong enough.)

Reduced even farther, she dropped down, crawling on her hands and knees.

I am no one.

Finally, she collapsed to the stairs. Chest heaving, the smell of polished leather touched her nose. She looked up, seeing his soulless dark eyes before anything else.

Volkor—

Gazing down at her, his martial scowl and perfectly cropped mustache looked exactly as they did on the newsreels and posters all those years ago.

Jetta scooted away as fast as she could. "You're not real!"

As she tried to dodge past the General, he seized her by the throat and pinned her against the stairs. Nothing she did could break his hold, even with her augmented strength and advanced combat techniques.

When Jetta tried to stop him from throwing her off the platform, he broke her right arm with a quick snap of his wrist. He paused, dangling her over the edge, reveling in her pain and fear. For a moment, Jetta thought she saw more than herself in the shadows of his eyes.

Before she had time to process what she had seen, he threw her, sending her tumbling down the steps. She fell chaotically, reaching for handholds and managing only to crack bones and break fingers.

At some point she hurtled past Triel, and the Healer cried out for her. Gray Paw howled, and the Jumaris chanted. The red man caught up with her, studying her with hungry eyes as she rolled past the base of the stone stairway and into the nothingness.

***

"She's coming around," a voice said.

Still sensing the fall, Jetta shot her arms and legs out, only to find a solid, unmoving purchase. Confused, she opened her eyes, expecting the gray mist.

This isn't right. Enormous stone walls and arched ceilings covered in moss enclosed her in some sort of chamber. *I was falling down the Temple stairs... Wasn't I?*

A group of strange looking humans stood around her, holding oil lanterns up to her face. Two stood out from the group, a man and a woman wearing Old Earth clothing and brimmed hats.

"Where am I?" she asked, checking her arms and legs. No breaks, no grievous injuries. "Where's Triel? Where are the wolves?"

"She's right here," the man with the brimmed hat said. In his early sixties, the portly fellow sported a handlebar mustache and hair that grew wildly out of his ears. He stooped down and pointed next to Jetta where the Healer lay mumbling and twitching from the effects of drug-induced slumber. "She's not yet awake, though. She was hit with a few more darts than you."

Jetta eyed the woman standing next to the man. Around the same age as her companion, she had weathered features and a thin

268

frame, and silver hair pulled back in a neat braid that fell down the middle of her back.

The others looked like the Jumaris she had seen earlier, though not as menacing. Dark skinned and heavily decorated with ink and bone, they lacked the smears of blood or the air of carnal hunger she remembered. As they held their spears and torches, they regarded her with curiosity, keeping a good distance from her and Triel.

"Who are you?" she asked. "What the hell is going on?"

"I am Sir Amargo and this is my wife, Lady Helena, of the Imperial Order of Intergalactic Archeology. We are both experts in Prodgy history. You have already met Tekay, our interpreter."

The red skin and alien eyes were gone. He looked like just another Jumari, though he wore Terrestrial clothing and had significantly fewer markings.

"I thought his name was Keyl."

Amargo laughed uncomfortably. "Keyl means demon in *Amiqi*, the ancient language of the Prodgy Gods. Where did you get that?"

Jetta massaged her forehead. "I thought it was real."

"Ah, I see. The plant neurotoxins coating the darts cause hallucinations. I apologize for that. Our scouts mistook you for the Lockheads that have been raiding our grounds. Once our Whisperer spoke to your wolves, though, we found out you were running from them."

Amargo nodded toward a woman swathed in animal skins. Pausing between puffs from her pipe, she bowed back.

"They also told her that this is a Healer, and that she restored Cano's broken leg," he added.

"Cano?"

Jetta stifled her smile as both wolves trotted around the circle of Jumaris and bounded over to her.

"*De beq we ni,*" the Whisperer said approvingly as Jetta greeted her canine companions.

"Yes. They have names, although they told us you were calling them 'Gray Paw' and 'White Neck.' The gray-pawed one actually goes by the name Kiyiyo," Amargo said.

Jetta looked at the Whisperer. "Is she a telepath?"

Amargo shook his head. "Not by textbook definitions."

As Jetta scratched behind Kiyiyo's ears, she examined the carvings that decorated the stone walls. They looked exactly like those on the facade of the temple in her hallucination. "Is this the Temple of Exxuthus?"

"Yes, you are inside it."

"I remember a giant stone staircase that went on as far as I could see."

"There is no staircase leading here. The Temple is built within the base of a carnivorous tree and hidden within a maze of its shoots that spans thousands of kilometers. It takes insider knowledge to navigate safely."

Just like the tree in my dreams, she thought, remembering its strangling roots. Other parts of the hallucination trickled back until she remembered the most important part and gasped.

Volkor.

"In my hallucination I saw... someone at the top of the staircase."

Amargo looked to Helena. With a soft, velvety voice she replied, "That's just the effects of their poisons, my dear."

She didn't believe them.

"Why are you here?" Jetta demanded.

Amargo raised his hands. "Please—we are not going to hurt you. However, we have some questions for you. Why are you here? And are you...?"

"Yes," Jetta said, sensing his recognition. "I am."

"Commander Kyron, it is an honor," Amargo said, removing his hat. "My wife and I were in the shelters on Trigos during the final battle. We thought we were doomed, but you saved us all. We know your story very well, and we are forever in your debt for the sacrifices you made to ensure the safety of the Starways."

Jetta was accustomed to such praise, but whether it was the kindness beaming from the old woman's eyes or the chubby fellow's genuine expression of thanks—or the residual effects of the poison—she found herself touched by the sentiment.

I made a difference…

Pushing the thought aside, she ground her fists into the stone floor to keep her emotions in check. "Thank you."

Triel opened her eyes and reached out for something or someone that wasn't there.

"It's okay," Jetta comforted her. Cano got down on all fours and licked the Healer's face. "We were shot with poison darts, but the Jumaris have treated us and taken us to the Temple of Exxuthus."

"What?" Triel said, pushing the wolf away and holding her head in her hands. Eyes swimming in their sockets, the Healer's focus was everywhere but Jetta's face.

"This is Sir Amargo and Lady Helena," Jetta said. "They're archeologists, but I'm not sure why they're here. I would appreciate an explanation."

Amargo chuckled and nodded to his wife. "She's just as headstrong in real life as she is on the news vids."

With a twitch of his mustache he continued. "My wife and I are part of group called the *Natari*."

"Promise keepers," Triel said, her eyes growing wide.

"Yes, that's the Common translation."

"I'm not familiar," Jetta said, looking between Triel and the archeologists.

"They were a group of humans that promised to repay my ancestors for their kindness," Triel answered.

"My thirty-sixth great-grandfather was Captain Julian Delphius, one of the leaders of the Exodus. He and several others helped orchestrate the evacuation of Earth after the war made it uninhabitable. But they weren't anticipating how quickly the planet would fall, and they were left with half-operational ships and untrained crewmen."

"It was a disaster," Lady Helena added.

"Billions died instantly when the bombs fell, but it is argued that millions suffered much more intensely under the brutal conditions of primitive spaceflight."

Lady Helena didn't miss her cue from her husband. "There were no jumpdrives, and on many ships there were no gravitational fields. People literally turned to dust without gravity. Others had no food stores and did unspeakable things in the name of survival."

"For weeks our ancestors struggled to survive on overcrowded and overtaxed starships. But just when the situation looked bleakest, our saviors arrived."

Helena's smile doubled the crow's feet around her eyes. "They were the first aliens our ancestors had ever seen. Some feared them, but that changed when they healed our sick."

"I know the story from there," Jetta said. "The Prodgies transported the humans to the Homeworlds. That's where the Starways' history depends on the teller. Some praise the Prodgies for saving a dying race, others curse them for introducing a viral population. Humans brought new vices and a host of diseases. However, they possessed unprecedented fertility and interspecies compatibility, making them a welcome solution for many struggling races. The 'purity' of the Sentient races dissolved, and because of this, many of the elder races still curse the Prodgy for their charity."

"You sound as if you are reciting from a history book."

"I am," Jetta said. "*A Brief History of the Starways*, chapter 22, pages 111-515."

"Ah," Amargo said, waving his finger. "But what I know you can't find in your history books, Commander. You don't know why the Prodgies came to find us, do you? Earth is on the other side of the galaxy."

"There is speculation that there was a distress signal—"

272

"Hogwash," Amargo said, his twirling the ends of his mustache. "With technology that ancient it wasn't even halfway possible."

"You see, dear," Helena interjected, assuming a gentler tone, "a Prodgy Seer sent ships to intercept the human fleet. She saw them in a vision—one so violent that it nearly killed her. When Captain Delphius met her, she told him he had to promise her one thing if he wished the humans and Prodgies to survive."

"And that was?" Jetta asked.

"She made us promise…" Helena stopped herself, looking at Triel and then her husband. Amargo nodded, his eyes full of an uncertain excitement. "She made us promise to commit ourselves to the elder teachings and deciphering ancient script. She said it would be a Promise Keeper who would pass the sacred knowledge on to the last Healer."

Doubtful of their tale, Jetta turned to Triel. The Healer had turned a ghostly white, and her eyes, wet with tears, cast downward as her body trembled.

"What's going on?" Jetta said, putting herself between Triel and the archeologists.

"It can't be me," Triel whispered.

Helena's voice remained soothing despite the weight of her words. "And she told us the last Healer would become the next Great Mother."

"*Amaroka!*" the Jumaris whispered in unison.

Amargo laughed. "We taught them a bit of Prodgy history. I think they're just as excited to meet you as we are, Triel Aelana of Algardrien."

I never mentioned Triel's full title, or her rarely-used Healer name, Jetta thought, piquing her suspicions.

"Her arrival was prophesied eleven hundred years ago," Amargo answered.

"It can't be me," she said, picking at the webbing between her fingers. Then her voice changed. Jetta felt her friend's anger rise in conflicting waves of guilt and denial. "It *can't* be me. Arpethea told me—"

"What you needed to hear," Lady Helena said, her blue-gray eyes as kind as her voice. "After all, you're here, aren't you?"

"Wait a minute," Jetta said. "What does this mean?"

"It means that we can teach your friend the lessons of her elders so that you can find all the answers you seek on your journey," Amargo said.

"We don't need your help," Jetta began, but Triel took her hand in hers.

"Yes, we do, Jetta. I can't read *Amiqi*. It was only taught to the higher-ranking members of the tribes."

"What?" Jetta exclaimed. "Then what were we supposed to do when we got here?"

"No need to worry, Commander. We're here to help you. You can sense that, can't you?" Amargo said. "I bear no ill will toward you or the Healer."

"Then how did you get a band of Jumaris to yield to you?" Jetta demanded. "They eat the faces of outsiders. I can't imagine them submitting to some ordinary Deadskin. They bow only to fear and blood."

Amargo's face soured. "They are Jumaris, but they are not cannibalistic man-haters like many of their kin. When the Deadwalkers came, the only ones to survive were those who would accept the help of others."

"These forty have lived with us in the Temple and help keep Reivers at bay, sometimes with only the reputation of their more violent relatives," Lady Helena said.

"What do they get out of it?" Jetta asked.

Amargo's fat cheeks turned a rosy pink. "We saved them from the Deadwalkers. They feel indebted to us."

"Jetta," Triel whispered, touching the back of her hand. "These people are here to help. This was all… expected."

"Expected?" Jetta whispered back, crouching down beside her.

Triel traced the markings on one of her arms. "I rebelled against my people's teachings from a young age, but even at my most defiant, I couldn't deny a deep feeling of responsibility to the tribes. Maybe Arpethea told me what she did so that I wouldn't think twice about running when the Dominion came, knowing that I would one day return."

Amargo and Helena nodded in unison. "Then we must begin your lessons—there isn't a moment to spare."

Jetta wanted to infiltrate their minds, to pillage every secret, expose every indiscretion, but then she thought of Salam.

"I won't trust you until you show yourselves to me," Jetta said.

Lady Helena smiled. "We have nothing to hide."

"But do you have something against me?"

Amargo looked at her quizzically. "You must have run into the thing that calls himself Salam. Not many telepaths survive his tricks."

"Thing?"

"He's a human-Berroman hybrid, meaning he can alter his human appearance, but he can't shift into the forms of other species. He was a notorious interrogator for the rebel forces trying to seize the Kercis mines operated by the Tre. It was rumored that he learned some technique there to torture their workers before he was captured by allies of the USC and taken to the Labor Locks."

"So his hands…?"

Amargo huffed, making his belly jiggle. "Another one of his tricks. He's a shapeshifter. He can manipulate his appendages any way he pleases."

"My dear, do not be afraid of us. Do whatever you need to do," Lady Helena said, her sweet face glowing in the light of the lanterns.

Taking in a deep breath, Jetta allowed herself to fall away and into the auras of the people surrounding her. Though virtually unreadable, she sensed the Jumaris' thoughts at rest. Unsurprisingly, Triel felt upset and guarded, but an old determination rose to the forefront of her mind, dominating her passions.

275

Everything the archeologists said confirmed Triel's beliefs.
(I have to protect her.)

Determined to find something, Jetta directed her attention to the minds of the two human archeologists. She fell straight through the shallows of their thoughts and into the deeper trenches of emotion winding through their memories.

"You're telling the truth," Jetta said, releasing her breath. Amargo and Helena looked a bit shaken but otherwise intact.

"My Gods, Commander—have you never been able to trust people without having to fish through their heads?" Amargo said, holding the lantern to her and studying her face.

Jetta pushed it away. "Let's get this started; we don't have much time. What's first?"

"Triel, come with me," Helena said, extending her wrinkled hand. "I will take you to the worship chamber of the Gods."

"Wait, I'm going with you—" Jetta started, but Amargo held her back.

"You, Commander, must come with me."

"Why?"

"Because in this place, to be unbalanced will bring about nothing but bad fortune."

Jetta scoffed. "Excuse me?"

Amargo's tan eyes turned steely. "Do you want to help your friend?"

"Of course, but—"

"Then you must first help yourself. I will take you to the *Diez di Trios*, or the Court of Three."

"What is that place?"

"It's the place of judgment."

Jetta crossed her arms. "Why are you taking me there?"

"You came here because you wanted to uncover the truth about Rion; you want to see where Saol of Gangras crossed over into Cudal. You want to know the truth about the next world, yes?"

Jetta guarded the emotion from her words. "How did you know that?"

The shadows cast by Amargo's lantern made his face look angled and warped. "This is a living place, Commander Kyron. I bade you to be mindful of your thoughts, your feelings, and your secrets. Follow me, and I will show you everything you need to know."

Trying not to let his warning jangle her nerves, Jetta followed Amargo down the dark corridor. She looked back; the Jumaris stayed behind, staring at her as the distance grew between them. The two wolves followed her a short distance but stopped as they reached the edge of the light cast by the Jumaris' torches.

"They won't follow?"

"No," Amargo confirmed. "This place is not, how you say, *welcoming.*"

Jetta didn't know how to take his words, but as the psionic vibrations steadily increased the further they traveled into the musty darkness, she didn't debate the idea of caution.

"Why are you helping me?" Jetta asked as they descended deeper into the heart of the temple.

Amargo turned around and rolled up his sleeve. Inked into the skin on the inside of his right upper arm was an intricately designed tattoo much like her own. "I must keep the promise of my forefathers," Amargo said. "And you are my only hope."

CHAPTER V

Blackbird. That was the word Tidas Razar whispered before falling back into his coma.

Jaeia let the term marinate as she studied the celestial bodies from the sanctuary of her quarters, hoping that it would rekindle a lost memory buried somewhere in her gleanings, but so far it hadn't sparked so much as a glimmer.

Lost in the cold shivering of the stars, Jaeia's thoughts turned to what she so recently witnessed. She had monitored Admiral Unipoesa's arrival and his interaction with Wren. Unsure of her own intentions, she followed him to the intensive care unit, where she waited behind a digital monitoring column, listening as he vented his guilt and grief to the comatose Minister.

I just wanted answers, she tried to rationalize, even though she felt it more complicated than that. When Victor sent them the video of the drunken admiral professing his sins, it had conjured up something far beyond anger and hurt.

"They're monsters. We should have killed them when we had the chance."

At first she had taken Unipoesa's statement to mean he regretted keeping her and Jetta alive, as Victor clearly wanted it to come across, but that was before she witnessed his confession. During his episode with the Minister, the admiral's mind hemorrhaged memories far faster than she was accustomed to receiving; even now she was still digesting the experience. She couldn't believe the extent of the Command Development Program's violations of the Sentient Rights Tenets, or how brutal the admiral had been to his own students, especially his own children, Li and Tarsha. It tarnished everything she had ever felt for him and whatever potential he might have.

Except it isn't so easy to brand him an ironfisted monster. Unipoesa's feelings for Li and Tarsha were fiercely complex, as were his motivations for his brutality, a tangle of obligations that she still hadn't completely unraveled after an hour of walking the decks.

He felt responsible for how far they had fallen, the profound guilt begging to be made physical.

But to wish for death, for oneself or others, is unforgivable, the last resort of the weak-willed—

But as she imposed her own judgement, a memory jerked up from her childhood and dismantled her conviction.

Mind rewinding back to her days on Fiorah, Jaeia found herself to be three years old again. Jetta and Jahx lay together on the cots, burning with the dangerously high fevers of the Gypassi virus as Galm tended to them as best he could. Even at three, she sensed her siblings' delirium and the seriousness of the disease.

They'll need more than prayers and ration scraps to survive this.

"I want to go with you," Jaeia said, stopping her aunt at the front door of their apartment.

Lohien must have seen the look of desperation on her face. "Okay, but stay close to me."

The unrelenting suns, at their highest point in the burnt orange sky, beat down on them and the few inhabitants brave enough to travel during the hottest part of the day. Jaeia struggled to keep up with her aunt as she moved quickly down the main drag from one area of shade to the next.

"Not much further," her aunt mumbled, her voice anything but reassuring.

Lohien pulled her along, not noticing that one of her shoes had fallen off. The boiling asphalt burned her sole, but she kept quiet, knowing that they had to reach the public health and handouts office on the lower east side before they reopened and were swarmed by the other needy slum rats.

"Almost there," Lohien whispered.

Up ahead Jaeia caught sight of the barred windows of the public health office. A dilapidated structure sandwiched between two abandoned buildings, it was patched with scraps of tin and composite fiberboard. The only door leading into the building bore pock marks from angry rioters.

"Hello?" her aunt yelled, banging on the door and peeking into the windows. "Is anybody there?"

Even now, years later, Jaeia could feel the choking heat as they stood outside the office, fully exposed to the suns. She shielded her face, silently balancing on her one shoed foot and wishing for her aunt to hurry.

"Hello!" her aunt said, tears perching on her eyelids.

Wobbling, Jaeia accidentally touched her toes down but jerked her leg back up with a yelp. She didn't look at her naked foot, afraid she would see it sizzling to a crisp.

"Please," Jaeia whispered, but her aunt didn't hear her. Frightened and in pain, she imagined her tender skin blistering pink, then charring black.

"I need help!" Lohien shrieked.

Jaeia searched for cover from the roasting suns, but her aunt held fast to her hand.

Jetta, Jahx, she silently called out. A hazy, feverish wall blocked her connection to her siblings, keeping her from feeling the comforts of their minds.

A surly woman with a beaked nose and permanent scowl popped open the face plate in the center of a reception window. "What?!"

"Please," Lohien begged, "I need medicine for the Gypassi virus."

"We're out," she croaked, already beginning to close the face plate.

Lohien shoved her fist through the barred window, preventing the women from closing the face plate. Blood dripped down her wrist.

"Please! My children will die!"

The women gave Jaeia a hard look through her thick glasses. "On this planet, lady, they're better off dead."

Jaeia didn't know how much longer she could last. The suns felt like they were centimeters from her skin. Soon her clothes would catch fire and she would burst into flames.

281

"I'll give you anything—anything!" Lohien said.

"You've got nothing I want, Sukk'ath," *the beak-nosed woman spat. "Get back to the gutters!"*

The expression on her aunt's face marked the first time Jaeia had really seen the fragility and hopelessness of their situation.

"Here," her aunt said, removing the chain she kept hidden beneath her blouse. A gold wedding band dangled from the silver necklace. "Take this."

The beak-nosed woman examined it with feigned indifference, but Jaeia could sense the greed seething from her pores.

"No launnie is worth it," she muttered as she shoved the medicine bottle through the slot.

Jaeia watched her aunt take the medicine bottle with a look of defeat.

Maybe our aunt wouldn't have had to give up her wedding ring if we weren't around, *she thought, guilt wringing her stomach.* She and Galm would be so much better off without us. There wouldn't be three extra mouths to feed, and maybe Yahmen wouldn't be so hard on them…

"I'm sorry," Jaeia started to say, but her aunt looked away.

"Let's go home," she said, her voice tight and strained.

Lohien hadn't noticed her unprotected foot or the tears in her eyes. Dangerous thoughts entered her mind: Maybe aunt Lohien wishes it too… Maybe she thinks it would be better off if we were dead…

Her memories leapt forward to a few months later. Back in the apartment, Jaeia huddled under the cots with her siblings. Every time she thought things couldn't get worse, Yahmen proved her wrong.

"I told you I don't have any more money!" Galm pleaded in the living room as their owner tore the place apart, breaking windows and ripping fixtures right out of the wall.

They all knew what was coming; it had been building for weeks now. Jetta and Jahx shook violently, both of them anticipating the

282

blows that would soon come their way. For some reason Jaeia couldn't stand waiting for the inevitable. Despite her siblings' protests, she crawled out from under the cots. When she peeked around the corner, she immediately wished she hadn't.

Lohien was sitting on the only unbroken chair, eyes cast downward, her hands folded neatly on her lap.

"Then what are you going to give me? The debt is 500,000 ulians. You couldn't make that up in a thousand years of labor," Yahmen said, punching a hole through the drywall.

Galm wrung his hands, his voice broken, halting. "I know what you want, but I can't—that's not something I—you can't have her."

No, Jaeia thought, you can't let him! You're the elder brother!

But he did. Galm would never fight Yahmen. Even as little kids they knew that Yahmen lorded it over his meek older brother.

Yahmen laughed. Then he grabbed Galm by the collar and slammed him against the wall. Lohien wept silently as Yahmen struck her husband in the face again and again. Hands pressed to his temples, Galm did nothing but cry like a helpless animal.

"It's just for the night, brother. Unless you want me to take those rats. They're young, but there's a buyer for every age," Yahmen snarled.

The air seemed to disappear from the room, leaving Jaeia gasping for breath. Sweat dripped off her nose as she waited impossibly long seconds for her uncle's decision. But Galm said nothing, squeezing his eyes shut as if wishing himself away. Yahmen laughed as he grabbed Lohien and dragged her screaming toward the entryway. Jaeia ducked back into their makeshift shelter and waited until they heard the front door slam.

Jetta and Jahx didn't say anything. Through their mutual connection they soothed each other, but for Jaeia it wasn't enough.

Crawling out again, she crept around the corner, keeping her mind locked on her siblings' perspective of the front door. She picked her way through the shards of glass and pieces of broken furniture until she came to her uncle's side. Folded over and

283

breathing heavily, her uncle mumbled in a daze as blood dripped from the corner of his mouth.

"Pao, why did you let him take her?"

"No choice. I had... no... choice," he said.

Jaeia was too little to understand her feelings then, but she understood them now. She was furious at her uncle, beyond any anger she had ever known. How could he let Yahmen take Lohien? How could he be so weak? Why did he allow for things to come to this?

"He won't kill her, will he?"

"She would be better off if he did," Galm whispered, his eyes growing distant.

No, *Jaeia had thought then,* I wish you were dead—then none of this would have ever had to happen!

Having remembered enough of her own checkered past, Jaeia bit her lip hard enough to make the memories recede.

I have to see him, she thought, calling for a lift using the interface on her uniform sleeve. She buzzed through the empty corridors, passing other soldiers only on the deck exchanges. With their situation growing worse by the hour, there wouldn't be much left of the unraveling Alliance forces.

If there is to be a resolution, I have to find it now, before the senior officers' meeting—

(Before Wren decides whether he is going to give me up to Victor's forces.)

She found Unipoesa in the observatory, facing the astronomy team's telescope monitors. Even with his back turned to her, he knew the moment she stepped onto the deck.

"How did you find me here?"

"Never play hide and seek with a telepath, Admiral."

"I've heard this is one of the few places of respite for telepaths on a ship. Away from the main decks, far from the greatest concentration of minds. Even to a plain old Tarkn like me, it's a nice getaway."

"You should count yourself lucky, Admiral," Jaeia said, standing beside him under the surveillance videos of an emerging star. "If it was Jetta seeking you out, she might not be affording you the luxury of explanation."

The admiral's laughter sounded pained. "Well then, Captain, how can I be of service to you?"

"I think I have something you want. Something very important."

The admiral looked at her curiously. "Oh?"

"But first you must answer a few of my questions. Do you regret keeping my sister and me in service?"

"Not at all."

"Even though you can't control our talents?"

The admiral paused. He seemed to consider an alternate response but resigned himself, with a heavy exhalation, to the truth. "It's concerned me before, but it's not what you think. You have no real handle on your own talents, and especially for someone like Jetta, this can present a serious threat to security. Where is she right now?"

Jaeia remained as calm as she could. "I don't know."

"Exactly."

"Have you ever wanted us dead?"

"No—what in the name of the Gods would make you ask that?"

"Have you ever wished that Tarsha and Li were dead?"

The admiral sucked back his lips. "Why do you ask that?"

"Since you've been gone, Victor's been threatening to go public with classified Alliance documents and video footage. I saw one of your personal logs. Your words were…" Jaeia paused for a minute to choose the right phrase. "…*quite inflammatory*, between what you said about us and your children."

"You know?"

"I was in the intensive care unit."

The admiral mumbled something about the need for a smoke before sitting on the edge of the window railing. He faced her, his tired eyes showing more emotion than she had ever seen in them.

285

"You didn't see everything, Captain," the admiral said, his voice just above a whisper. "Otherwise you'd know why it would be better if Li and Tarsha were dead."

"I understand Li," Jaeia said. "But not Tarsha."

The admiral leaned heavily on the railing, looking away from her. "Tarsha was given interrogation resistance training when she was still an operative candidate, and that made it extremely hard to put her to Sleep. Now that Jetta's given her back some of her memories, her life—and ours—are in danger."

Jaeia didn't see the connection. "How?"

"Agracia might know that she was once Tarsha, but she'll never return to her true self unless she is given the Keyword Unlock Sequence. Her opposing personalities will make her unstable and susceptible to numerous countermeasures. If Victor found out who she really is, how she is triggered, he could do whatever he wanted with her."

"And she's a trained officer."

"More than that," Unipoesa said, "Victor has our defense system pretty well mapped out, but she knows all our blackout ops for situations like these. She would know how to find the rest of our fleet."

Jaeia lifted a brow. "How would she know that? Those are classified operations."

The detail waded up from experiences she stole from the admiral. "Wait," Jaeia said, "you slipped her that information."

The admiral nodded.

"Because you really believed in her," Jaeia whispered. "You really thought she would be the one to win the war for the Coalition. You taught her everything you knew."

But her moment of renewed respect quickly dissipated in the wake of everything else she still held against him.

"What little advantage we have right now would be wiped away if he found a way inside her head, much less put her back in command."

"Which he will. He's seems to be very good at that."

"But that's not all," the admiral said, staring out the observatory window. "Even if Victor doesn't get to her, it's inevitable that she will go mad. Razar was the only one to know the Keyword Unlock Sequence, and he's a vegetable."

"You really care about her?"

The admiral gave her a sad smile. "Remember when I first said you reminded me of someone? She was a lot like you. Compassionate, caring, sensitive—to a fault. She was brilliant, our top student, but she had trouble with the idea of killing real soldiers. It took a lot of… conditioning… to get her used to the idea of battle."

This was it. This is what she had to know. "Why did you do it?"

The admiral's eyes drifted away, and his thoughts receded beyond her immediate reach to someplace cold and isolated within himself. "I truly thought that I could end the war, and I gave up everything—*everything*—to pursue that belief."

"Why in that way?"

"Even from my limited command experience going into the CDP, I knew what if felt like to sacrifice soldiers and deal death to the enemy. But I believed that if we habituated a child to the burdens of command, he or she could thrive in that environment."

Jaeia read into his statement. "You never got over the deaths of the soldiers under your command. That's why that assignment appealed to you."

"I know you understand this better than most, Captain. I know how poorly you sleep."

Jaeia wouldn't let him flip the conversation back on her. "But this doesn't justify your treatment of your students."

"Doesn't it?" he asked, his eyes glistening in the light of the stars. "To make a good commander, you have to understand the meaning of pain and discipline, and most importantly, sacrifice. The rules of humanity don't always apply in wartime."

"I think that's when they're the most crucial." Something in her response unhinged his guard, just enough for her to taste the edge of his deepest sorrow. "I... I never knew you were married."

"How dare you," he whispered.

She didn't need to go farther; she could already see well beyond his words into the craterous pain that had scarred him years ago. "She's why you signed up, and why you fought," Jaeia said, tears welling in her eyes as his emotions overpowered her own. "But I don't understand why she left you."

"Get out of my head, Captain," the admiral said through gritted teeth. "Haven't you had enough of this?"

"Just one more thing," Jaeia said, running her fingers along the guard rail, concentrating on the cold smoothness beneath her fingertips. "Why do you care so much about Tarsha Leone?"

It took the admiral several seconds to compose himself. He turned his back to her when he answered. "I loved her from the very beginning," he said quietly. "There was always something unique about her, something that elevated her above the dehumanizing bleakness of warfare. What I turned her into—that foul excuse for a Sentient, Agracia Waychild—is unforgivable. But to see her go mad, to know that she'll lose the last parts of her that made her special—I can't live with that."

"Would you do anything for her?" Jaeia said.

He turned back to her, allowing her to see beyond his words. "Yes."

Doubt lingered in her thoughts, but she pushed them aside. She looked out to the stars. "Blackbird."

"What?"

"That was the word Razar whispered after you walked away."

The admiral's confusion didn't abate. "I don't know what that means."

"You had said Tarsha was as good as dead. That was his response, I assume. Maybe it's part of your Keyword Unlock Sequence."

"It's more than one word."

"I know someone who could help. But you haven't been very kind to him."

"No, Jaeia, that is not an option."

Jaeia shrugged her shoulders. "The Hub is your only choice. He'll have access to more answers than any of us."

The admiral checked the time on his sleeve. "We should get to the meeting."

Jaeia stopped him in his tracks. Without asking him she couldn't go any further. "What did it cost you to do what you did to them?"

The admiral looked at her for a long time before responding. "You already know the answer to that."

***

As Jetta followed Amargo into *Diez di Trios*, she became more aware of an otherworldly presence like nothing she had ever felt before.

It's everywhere and nowhere at once, she thought, sensing no discernable origin to the psionic rhythm. With every step she felt something like a cool mist seeping into the back of her head, and an unseen voice sigh against her ear. Disconcerting and yet strangely familiar, the sensations only got stronger the farther they went. *I don't like this.*

Fighting against her fears, she reverted to old habits, taking in every detail of their route down the dark stairwell.

This is even worse, she thought, alarmed by not only the alien presence but the architecture. Brooding and imposing, the stonework suggested something sinister hiding in every shadow and around each corner. And yet, for reasons she couldn't explain, she felt comforted, as if she was returning home after a very long journey.

Jetta bit the inside of her cheek hard enough to draw blood. *Refocus. Keep sharp.* She turned her attention to Amargo. "Your tattoo—where did you get it?"

Amargo seemed delighted that she asked. "It's a family tradition; every Delphius has one. My ancestors were on board one of the few ships that made it to the Nine Homeworlds, and like my forefathers, we tattoo the mark of that ship on our skin to remember our struggle and narrow escape from death."

Jetta rubbed the tattoo on her own arm and frowned. Being reminded of her human heritage made her uncomfortable.

"I thought Prodgy blood was needed to get into the Temple," Jetta asked as they ducked underneath a trellis.

"Not Prodgy blood," Amargo said, squeezing through a narrow passageway. With a grimace, he wiped the cobwebs from his face. "Salam told you that, didn't he?"

"He seemed very intent on getting it, too."

"Well, he was misinformed. You have to *be* of Prodgy bloodline to enter the most sacred areas. Consequently my wife and I have never made it into many parts of the Temple, just like the many others who tried before us."

"Many others?"

"The Alliance sent a ship here just after the war. They blasted a sizeable hole in the worship chambers, but they never got anywhere."

Jetta tested his memories and sensed he was telling the truth. "I didn't know this happened."

"Of course not, Commander. The secrets this place possesses are not readily shared, especially by those seeking its power," he said, hinting at the fate of the Alliance crew.

Jetta stopped walking. "So why are we doing this? Neither one of us are of Prodgy lineage."

Amargo turned around and held the lantern up to her face. "The Seer told my thirty-sixth great-grandfather that the last Prodgy would have a companion, and that this person would be a foreigner in their own skin. She used the word *Apparax*, which doesn't have a true Common translation. The best equivalent would be 'divided

290

soul.' She told my grandfather that although they would not be Prodgy, they would possess the only other key into Cudal."

Jetta scoffed. "If I hadn't been inside your skull, I would think you were lying. Maybe I should be questioning your sanity."

"Your skepticism—and cynicism—is expected, Commander," Amargo said. "I have gathered that you are not one to believe in the mystical powers of the otherworlds."

Her guide stopped at a gigantic wooden door framed by foreboding stone carvings.

"I thought the Prodgy were a peaceful people," Jetta said, taking in the nightmarish depictions of murder and death. In some areas, polished bone and dried skins, stretched and stained, illustrated the bloody battles instead of the stonework.

"Before Rion, there was often war among the tribes. Many historians draw parallels between humans and the Prodgies of ancient times. But the Great Mother changed everything, saving Rion and unifying the people," Amargo said, holding up his lantern to illuminate a carving of a beautiful woman with open arms and flowing hair. Her smile, subtle and creased with pain, caught Jetta's attention.

"Why are her eyes closed?"

"She gives herself blindly to those in need. She is the model of self-sacrifice and compassion."

Jetta noticed the woman's odd resemblance to Triel but quickly dismissed it. *No way,* she thought to herself. *It's just the dark playing tricks on me.*

"Commander, I can't go through those doors. Only you can. Death comes quickly to those that are not welcome, as described here," Amargo said, pointing to the symbols inscribed on stone slabs.

"What's in there?" Jetta asked.

"Whatever you bring with you."

Jetta remembered her dream, and the warning the red man had given her. She hesitated at the door. "All I want is to know the truth

291

about Saol of Gangras. I have no wish to see this Cudal. I have no desire to possess any power."

"I am as eager as you, Commander, but the tablets are in that room. Find the tablet with this marking," Amargo said, etching it into the dust with his shoe, "and maybe we can both find closure."

"What's your interest?"

Amargo raised a bushy white brow. "Saol of Gangras is the most highly debated figure in xeno-archeological history. To discover the truth about his origins and have an exact translation of the events leading to him becoming Rion would be the most important finding in all Sentient history."

"The Prodgy that entrusted you never told you?"

Amargo shook his head. "They were very guarded about him, and to this day I still don't know why."

Jetta turned back to the doors and looked one last time at the Great Mother surrounded by chaos. "I'm sure they had their reasons."

The shadow of Amargo's mustache cast a strange expression across his face. "It's important for all of us, Commander, to know the truth about Saol. I believe that his story holds the key that will let all of us—human and Sentient alike—unlock the door to everlasting peace."

Why am I really here? she wondered as she studied the sculpted men killing each other under a painted sky. Eyes peered down from the heavens and fingers rose from the ground, pulling the murderers into the fires that burned beneath the surface. Ghostly figures of the accursed melded with the carved shadows, watching and waiting.

"What will I use for light?"

Amargo removed a flashlight from his coat pocket. "I was saving this for a special day; batteries are hard to come by on this planet. Here you go. Although from these writings, I don't think you'll need this much farther."

Jetta took it anyway. "What are you going to do? Just wait here?"

"I am *Summu Nura*—without light. I cannot go," Amargo replied with a nod. "I will wait for you to bring back the tablets."

"Right," Jetta said, testing the massive doors. They gave way easily, though not without protest and a draft of cold, damp air. She coughed the dust out of her lungs and swatted at the dirty air until it settled. Even then, all she could see was a dark corridor and more stairs leading downward.

"Another underground passageway? Really?" Jetta muttered, clicking on the flashlight.

Several minutes after losing visual contact with Amargo, she felt the beginnings of panic unpin her thoughts. The beam of her flashlight didn't seem to give her much advanced notice of what lay ahead, putting her in mind of the endless staircase from her dream.

...And Fiorah, Jetta thought, remembering the cramped blackness of the air ducts. Too many times her headlamp battery had failed, leaving her scrambling in the dark, trying to feel her way home before the duct rats summoned the courage to make her their next meal.

She wished she hadn't made the association. There was already something incredibly stifling about the place, compressing her thoughts and competing with her psionic connections to those closest to her. After only a few minutes, she felt crushed by the stone walls, hidden away from herself and everything she knew.

"*Meitka!*"

Jetta never saw what tripped her. Rolling head over heels down the staircase, she lost the flashlight as she tumbled. Stone stairs slammed into her again and again, battering her helpless body until the bottom floor brought her to an abrupt stop.

It took her a moment for her eyes to adjust to her surroundings, and when they did she pinched herself. *Is this another hallucination?*

She checked her arms and legs, shocked to find herself relatively unharmed, and gathered herself up off the floor. The stone construction of the temple had vanished, replaced by solid wood floors angling toward raised benches. Masked figures occupied two out of the three of them, leaving the middle bench empty.

"Amargo?" Jetta called. Turning on her heels, she tried to retrace her steps, but the staircase had also disappeared. A bright spotlight shone down on her, preventing her from seeing much beyond the vacant jury boxes walling her in.

Disconcerted, Jetta closed her eyes and searched with her talent for extrasensory information, but she found her abilities muffled by the intangible interference she had felt earlier.

A discorporate voice shot through her, cutting her in half. "Jetta Kyron, formally Jetta Drachsi, why did you give up your uncle's surname?"

Jetta gasped for air. "Who are you?"

A high-pitched ringing pierced her skull, dropping her to her knees. She covered her ears, but to not avail. "I—I wanted my real name!"

The ringing intensified. Jetta grimaced and tried again. "I didn't want our owner to find us!"

But that wasn't the truth either. The ringing escalated. She squirmed and bucked, trying to escape the torment until she felt certain her head would explode. "I was ashamed of my uncle!" she screamed.

The ringing stopped.

Bodiless voice spoke again. "What is your relationship to General Sarkof Volkor, Destroyer of Worlds?"

Jetta spun around to face the masked figures in the tiers. "Relationship? What are you talking about?"

A low murmur arose from the empty jury boxes. Jetta didn't know which way she could run. When she turned back to the bench, Volkor stood before her, eyes bloodshot and mouth ringed with something black and oily. The same ooze dripped from his fingers and pooled around his feet.

"Jetta Kyron," the voice asked, "what is your relationship to Yahmen Drachsi?"

Jetta backed away quickly when her owner appeared, looking disheveled and drunk. A bottle hung lazily from his fingers, pouring out the same black slime.

"Amargo!" she screamed. "Help me!"

"Jetta Kyron, what is your relation to M'ah Pae, Overlord of the Damned?"

Falling backward, Jetta scooted as far away as she could when the Motti Overlord appeared alongside Volkor and Yahmen. He spun around on his undercarriage to face her, black ooze dripping from his bulging eye and the hollowed-out voice apparatus in his throat.

The clamor from the empty jury boxes grew heated. She understood their accusations, even their foreign tongue.

(Liar.)

(Murderer.)

(Thief.)

"Who stands accused?" the voice asked.

"I, Jetta Kyron, stand accused," Volkor declared.

"No, *I*, Jetta Kyron, stand accused!" Yahmen shouted.

"I *am* Jetta Kyron, and I stand accused!" M'ah Pae hissed.

Laughter cascaded down from all corners of the room.

"No, that's not me," Jetta said, but arguing only served to incite the invisible audience even further.

"It's not ME!" she screamed. She didn't let up, emptying her lungs until she could yell no longer.

When she opened her eyes she was no longer in the spotlight.

"Impossible," Jetta mumbled as she picked herself off the cavern floor. Macca fruit glowed in clusters on the walls, and brown furskins, spread out on the flattest rocks, looked as if they had been recently used. Even the air smelled sweet and damp, just as she remembered from her time in the Traloran caves.

"Ah, the Thief awakens."

His kind smile was the same, as was the amethyst color of his eyes, but the celestial glow outlining his figure hinted at his otherworldly origins.

That can't be the Grand Oblin, can it? she thought, looking over the old man sitting on a rock outcropping. "Why am I here?"

"Why are you here, my dear?" the old man asked, taking a drag from his pipe. His rheumy eyes looked her over with a curious glint. "You shouldn't be here, you know—very dangerous for someone like you."

This is some kind of test, Jetta thought. *But who—or what—is asking the questions? And what do they want?*

Because she had raided Amargo's mind, she had not only grafted his knowledge of the inscriptions, but read the warnings on the doors herself.

The Diez di Trios *is not a gateway into Cudal but a window,* she reminded herself. *And that's assuming such a place truly exists...*

Still, seeing the manifestation of the Grand Oblin before her, she knew that whether it was a window or door, she was out of her element, and she had better play it straight. "I need to know if Saol and I are the same—if I am also Rion."

"Rion," the Oblin mused, tapping his pipe on his knee. "It's been many years since I've been asked about that. Not too many visitors these days."

"Please, I need to know."

"Why? What difference would that make?"

"All the difference!" Jetta said, not minding her tone. "I need to know if..." But the words died on her lips. She couldn't speak her worst fear.

"The easiest way for me to explain your predicament," the Grand Oblin said, running his fingers along his braided beard, "is that wherever you go, the dead will follow. That is as it will be until your last breath."

Jetta cringed.

"Come now," the Grand Oblin said, "I will show you something you want to see, but only if you promise to leave right after."

"Why?"

The Grand Oblin lifted a brow. "Not everyone will be as happy as I am to see a Thief. Best if you be on your way as soon as possible."

"A Thief?"

Gathering his robes, the Oblin rose on rickety knees. "I trust you can read our language?"

"Yes," Jetta replied. "How did you know that?"

The Oblin smiled, revealing the familiar toothless grin. "Who do you think I am?"

Without her extrasensory perceptions, Jetta didn't know how to answer the question, though she knew better than to say how she really felt. "You're a God."

"But you don't believe that, do you?" the Oblin corrected, waving a bony finger. "Even though you witness it with your own eyes?"

"No, I don't. It isn't possible. There is no such thing as God. I have known that my whole life."

The Grand Oblin's grin humored her. "And still you cannot explain this, can you?"

"No rational person would assume 'God' just because something appears unexplainable."

With a chuckle and a wave of his hand, the Grand Oblin led her through the passageway and into the main cavern. The old meeting circle around the fire pit was still there, with Rawyll's tools laid out near a sharpening stone as if he were in the middle of a project. Senka's scarves and Crissn's electronic trinkets occupied their owners' customary spots, indicating their imminent return. Jetta even spotted one of Dinjin's patched boots resting against a log.

It's all so real, she thought, feeling an unexpected pang of longing.

"Why are we going down there?" Jetta said, stopping at the entrance to the lower tunnel. *The last time I went down that path I found the Liiker—*

297

The memory of the Deadwalker resurfaced in a nauseous wave of sounds and images: A pool of dark blood, the metallic aftertaste of the Macca. Antenna twitching. Metal casings and circuits puncturing inflamed skin. *(It has no eyes!)*

The old man kept on going despite her. "You wanted the truth, yes?"

Swallowing her fear, Jetta followed him down the tunnel, sloshing through puddles of water. *None of this is real*, she kept telling herself. *It's all just an illusion. Maybe I'm still poisoned. Maybe I never woke up.*

When they reached the lower cave that held the Liiker, the Grand Oblin stood at the mouth, obstructing her view. Her stomach knotted when she heard the buzzing and whining, and every fiber of her being screamed at her to run away.

"Before you enter, Jetta, you must answer this: Who stands accused in your heart?"

"Of what?"

The ground quaked, shaking loose rocks and dirt from the roots hanging above. Jetta crouched down, shielding her head and face with her arms. Once the tremor stopped, she looked again at the Oblin. His eyes, no longer kindly, turned dark and chasmic.

Jetta braced herself against the cave wall as the ground shook again, this time more forcefully. By the grisly look on the Oblin's changing face, she didn't have to guess what would happen if she didn't answer correctly.

What the hell does he want? Gazing down at the puddle near her feet, she saw her own reflection. Terror gripped her chest. "Me," she whispered, unsure if she had actually spoken or thought the word.

When she looked up the Oblin was gone, and so was any indication of the Liiker. In its place stood a giant stone monolith etched with inscriptions.

Tracing the writing with her finger, Jetta mumbled the translations out loud. "Saol of Gangras lost his wife and children during the Ten Wars of Perspheolys. Enraged at the Gods and angry

298

at his own helplessness, he journeyed to Cudal and stole the power of the Gods to resurrect his wife and end the war, but his imperfect mortal body was no temple for God, and he was corrupted. Reborn on Algar as Rion the Abomination, he became obsessed with the destruction of the imperfect, and blinded by the power of the Gods, he annihilated his enemies with as little as a thought. The tribes of Algar, facing total destruction, came together under the guidance of the Great Mother and quelled the unstoppable Rion. Because of their sacrifices, the Gods gave them the power to unite for all time."

She took a step back to read the finer carvings. "With balance, the ability to heal, with selfish desire, the power to destroy."

Intrigued, she circled around to the other side.

"Diyanna of Algarsie, daughter of the East, saved her people from the corruption of Rion by casting herself between Hetaqua and Cudal. Seeing her sacrifice, the Gods bestowed her with their life, giving her the power to transcend her mortal body. Diyanna became a Speaker for both realms, guiding her people from the realm of Gods. She is the Great Mother, a vessel of peace, forgiveness, and healing, and through her, all are restored."

Jetta dusted off the bottom half of the monolith. There she saw the warning. "So shall it be that the daughters of the South, West, and North will ascend as the tides of time resolve. Darkness will fall soon after, and dead fires will reign. Look not for the last Great Mother from the people, for she will fall from the stars. And with her she will bring—"

But Jetta didn't know the word. She sounded it out the best she could. "Trio… trio-Rion. Triorion…"

She exhaled heavily, wiping the sweat from her brow. *Triorion.* Why did that word make her nervous?

"…who will bring down the heavens and break open the skies to the realm beyond all worlds. But beware the Apparax, the Thief of all Thieves, for within the shadow of doubt lies the seedling that shall undo us all."

A child's giggle echoed down the tunnel. Jetta looked back and saw a small figure scurrying away.

"Hey!"

Jetta remembered the Grand Oblin's warning but couldn't keep herself from chasing after the child.

It couldn't be, she thought, recognizing the familiar tune.

The tunnel didn't wind back to the main cavern like she remembered. Instead it narrowed, straightening out like a subway tube or a ship conduit. Clusters of Macca grew farther and farther apart, forcing her to use her sense of touch to guide her in the dark passageway.

That smell—

She couldn't believe the sour odor that filled her nose and lungs. Something like mining runoff, and the competing body odors of too many people trapped together in a dead heat.

It can't be the drillship... can it?

As soon as she stopped to turn back, she heard the giggling again. Seeing a light flicker in the distance, Jetta picked up speed. The small figure came into view, but she was still too far away to make out more than her outline. No longer cool and damp, the temperature rose noticeably, making her wipe her forehead repeatedly to keep the sweat out of her eyes as she ran.

Rocks and dirt gave transformed into a grated walkway. Before she could stop herself, Jetta slammed into a sputtering power column. Dazed from the collision, it took her a few seconds to realize what the little girl was asking in her thick Fiorahian accent.

"Recombinator?"

Sitting cross-legged and facing away from her, the little girl worked on a routing console. Its components lay in a tangled heap of cords, microchips, and linear processors.

She needs a recombinator. Spotting the oblong instrument lying on the railing, Jetta grabbed the tool and circled around to hand it to the girl. She nearly dropped it when she saw her face.

"Thank you," the girl said, taking it from her.

"Now I know this isn't real," Jetta said, stooping down. *That's me, when I was barely four years old, working on Yahmen's mining ship...*

Her younger self didn't look up as Jetta tried to make sense of what was happening.

"Three-volt?"

"No, don't use that," Jetta said, taking the broken piece from her. "You need a two-volt with a lug inverter to fix this. A three-volt will just offset the problem until you fuse the processors."

The little girl frowned and studied her for a moment, but then picked up the two-volt.

"Why are you here?" Jetta asked her.

"My brother and sister are in the engine room fixing the burnout, but we need a working routing console or we'll never get it up again."

"Can't stand the heat?" Jetta asked, remembering why she had elected to work away from her siblings all those years ago.

The little girl shook her head. "Sometimes I can't stand listening to them," she whispered. Her words sounded heavy with fatigue. "I know how bad it is. I'm doing my best to make it better. I know I can get us out of here."

Sitting back on her heels, Jetta swallowed the knot of emotion in her throat. *I know better than to play this game.* "I'm done with this. Show me who you really are."

The little girl shook her head. "I'm trying to help you. Not everyone is as nice as me."

"Who else are you talking about?"

The girl snapped a few cords in place and tested the wiring. "We have many names, some of which you know, none of which are of any consequence."

Brushing the damp brown hair back from her face, the girl revealed her midnight eyes.

Those aren't my eyes—

"You wanted to know what is inside you, yes? Well, it isn't that simple. You aren't deserving, and you have upset our plans."

"What are you? What are you talking about?" Jetta said, standing up and taking a few steps back.

The little girl rose too, her eyes deepening into polychromatic wells. "Thief. You stole from us—you stole from me. You took my *chacathra*, and I want it back!"

Jetta didn't know what to do but run as the younger version of herself expanded into a hulking creature with many heads and slick, red flesh. As she fled down the ship corridors, she recognized Victor's voice in the fray.

"Give back what you've stolen!" he said, his thunderous shriek rattling the ship.

She hit Deck Juncture A and climbed the steps to the cargo room, hoping to find some sort of mining tool to use as a weapon, but the steps never ended. The instant she put her foot down a dozen more appeared before her.

Legs and lungs burning, she struggled to stay ahead of the monster at her heels. She could feel its hot, carnal breath on her back as she pushed herself past the pain and exhaustion.

Thief... a rasping voice whispered across the psionic planes.

Slimy, red fingers wrapped around her leg and pulled her feet out from under her. She slotted her fingers into the grated stairs, fighting with every last ounce of strength against the force threatening to pull her free. In the corner of her vision she could see Victor's smile, diamonds sparkling in the saffron light before he sank his teeth into her calf.

***

Triel followed Lady Helena and her troop of Jumaris down the torch-lit hallways to the worship chamber of the Gods. The two wolves kept pace with her, brushing up against her every once and a while and leaning in for a scratch.

302

Since she couldn't read *Amiqi*, she paid little attention to the writings or the sculptures and stonework adorning the hallways. Instead, her mind lingered on what Lady Helena had told her in the antechamber: *The last Healer would become the next Great Mother.*

It can't be me, she kept telling herself, frightened at the possibility of becoming her people's most revered leader, second only to the Gods. She thought of all the times she rebelled against Prodgy teachings, how she fought her father over their pacifist philosophies, and ran away when the Dominion came. *Everything I've done has been against my people's ways.*

"Something troubling you, dear?" Helena asked as they entered the worship area. Elaborate stone sculptures of men and women, arranged in a circle, held up the domed ceiling in homage to the Gods. Even the patterns on the marble floor held purpose, with individual tiles representing a single tribe, and as a collective, forming the Prodgy symbol.

"Yes," Triel said, stopping in the center of the circle. "This. It can't be me. I may be the last Prodgy, but I'm not the next Great Mother. I'm—I'm *weak*. I've Fallen, and if it weren't for Jetta, I'd be a Dissembler. That's the whole reason I came here, anyway—to see how I could even survive as a Solitary—not to assume the role of my peoples' savior."

"But here you are," Lady Helena said.

"I'm not the best Healer, either. I'm decent, but the Great Mother—she has to restore all of Algar. And to top that off—are there any of my people left?"

"You know the answer to that, my dear," Lady Helena said, taking her hands. "Not all hope is lost. Your friend has told you this."

"How do you know that?" Triel whispered, thinking of Jetta's encounter with the Motti's weapon and seeing her father's face in a blur of light when she healed her friend.

Helena smiled, her wrinkled cheeks bunching around her eyes. "I told you, it has all been foreseen; you need not worry."

Holding Triel's hands against her own chest, Helena softened her voice. "Now is the time to turn to your faith, Triel Aelana of Algardrien. Give away your fear and your doubts. Let yourself become who you were destined to be."

Triel looked around her. The Jumaris and the wolves stood behind the outer circle of the worship area, watching them closely.

"What do I need to do?"

"No Great Mother has done what you will need to do, Triel of Algardrien. Even Diyanna of Algarsie never faced such a daunting task. The risk will be great for you, so you must prepare yourself."

"How? And with what?" Triel asked, looking at the surrounding statues. Each was of a great Prodgy who possessed exceptional powers. Arpethea was amongst them, stationed between two other avatars renowned for their abilities to resurrect the dead. "Spells and magic? Prayers and offerings?"

"The ritual of *Ne'topat'h.*"

"A mating ritual?" Triel exclaimed, pulling away.

"That's what the commoners call it," Lady Helena explained. "The translations have lost their meaning over time. Have you read the words of the Gods?"

"No, but I'm not expecting to have a child," Triel said, starting to walk out of the circle.

"Stop!" Helena said. "It is not just your life at stake."

Triel exhaled. *That much is true.* The *Natari* had silently served her people for centuries, and by defying Helena she broke the sacred oath between the humans and the Prodgies. Breaking the rules never bothered her before, but this felt different.

"Come," Helena said, leading her to the altar and sitting her down across from the symbol of the Gods. After rummaging through her satchel, Helena pulled llalana leaf and gave it to Triel.

"You've used this before, I take it," Helena commented as she watched Triel break down the center of the leaf and roll it into two separate halves.

"I haven't, but my father always used it to meditate. He always tried to get me to, but I just never…"

She didn't finish the sentence. With one bite she ingested both halves. *I never obeyed.*

Crossing her legs and folding her arms across her chest, she waited for the leaf's properties to take effect.

"Now," Helena said, pulling down the scroll from the altar. "Just listen."

"But I don't know *Amiqi*—"

"Listen," Helena told her.

Triel closed her eyes, letting Helena's words slip inside her like water through open fingers. Despite the archeologist's atrocious accent, the Healer found herself gliding away from her feelings and settling into a place far above her cares and concerns. Memories of her summers on the farm and running through the yellowtail flowers after her brothers flowed through her consciousness. She smelled her mother's perfume and heard her father's voice in the distance.

Triel…

Amaroka…

As she relaxed even deeper, she drifted away from the sensations of her body. Memories of her past healings wove in and out of her awareness. Bridging the physical planes with invisible filaments of energy, Triel opened herself to the parallel axis of her patients. Ragged, asymmetrical tangles of disease and injury disrupted otherwise harmonious biorhythms. She remembered the fight to not only survive another's disorder, but transcend their flesh and engage in the most sacred aspect of all Healing—the exchange of quintessence.

Her father, her grandmother, her friends; soldiers, civilians— even a few enemies. She had many memories of the deep and wonderful connections she had shared over the course of her life. But of all her restorations, two stood out the most: Her healings of Reht… and Jetta.

Reht was her first love, so it was no surprise to her that their interaction had been so powerful. She had fallen hard for him at first sight, and even to this day, despite what they had been through, she still missed the way his bandaged hands touched her body and the way he smelled, even after a night at the bars. There had always been something about him, something dangerous and unpredictable, but also genuine and compassionate.

And then there was Jetta. Unusual and complicated, the commander was easily the most guarded individual she had ever managed to heal. Still, in the brief moments of unadulterated clarity between them, Triel had felt something so pure and luminescent that she couldn't turn away. Everything else—all the confusion, all the reasons to stay apart—faded away.

Lady Helena's voice whispered somewhere from the beyond.

Ne'topat'h…

Mating ritual…

Ne'topat'h…

Jetta's face materialized before her, eyes shining like the clearest cut emeralds. With arms outstretched and a warm smile, she invited the Healer's embrace. Triel reached out, touching her friend's stomach. "I choose you."

(Help me!)

Triel heard the cry and woke from her meditation. Everything around her vibrated as if tuned in to a different frequency until her mind adjusted to the jolt back to reality.

"What's wrong?" Lady Helena asked, looking up from her reading.

"Jetta's in trouble," Triel said, uncrossing her legs and standing up. "We have to help her."

"Wait!" Helena shouted as Triel grabbed a torch from a Jumari and ran back the way they came. "It's not safe!"

Ignoring the archeologist, Triel raced down the hallway, the two wolves at her heels, following the siren of psionic turbulence.

Could it be?

"Jetta—no!" she shouted, fearing for her friend and those around them. *Is that the sound of the Fall?*

As she descended the staircase to the *Diez di Trios*, she came to an abrupt halt. Standing at the door, Jetta repeatedly struck a motionless Amargo in the head, spraying the stone work with his blood. Her green eyes deepened into chasms of animal fear, lighting up her entire being like an overcharged circuit.

"Jetta!"

But the Healer could take no step further. Something hovered in the air, something oppressive and heavy, and moving any closer made it feel as though a vice was tightening around her head.

"Jetta, what are you doing?"

Triel hadn't noticed that the three Jumaris behind her drawing their bows, but Jetta did.

"Dema'qorp!" Jetta screamed.

The Jumaris froze and fell over, their bodies limp and colorless, as if she had struck the life from them.

Helena stood at the top of the stairs and shouted down: "Get out of there! It's too late!"

Running back up the stairs, Triel grabbed Helena by the shoulders. "What happened down there?"

"I don't know—it wasn't supposed to be like this!"

Helena and the others turned to run down the corridor but stopped in their tracks. Everyone but the wolves and Triel dropped to their knees.

"Please," Lady Helena said through blue lips, "don't hurt us..."

Triel tried everything she could, going from person to person to save them from the invisible hands asphyxiating them. Finally, she came back to Helena. Her eyes bulged from their sockets as she choked out each word.

"Do not... Do not let her... believe..."

Frantic, the Healer dipped beneath her skin to save her dying body, but the same force that kept her from approaching Jetta kept her out of Helena's biorhythm.

Helena locked eyes with Triel one last time, her lips quivering, *"Ne'topat'h..."*

Laying Helena to the ground next to one of the Jumaris, Triel closed her eyes and whispered a prayer of peace. The two wolves whined softly, their ears flat against their heads as they cowered behind a statue.

"Jetta?" Triel said, her voice reverberating off the stone walls. Save the sound of her rapid heartbeat pounding in her ears, the Healer heard only silence.

She remembered her meditation; she remembered Jetta's open arms. *I choose you.*

With careful steps, Triel approached the top of the stairs. She leaned over and peered down the staircase.

"Jetta," she whispered, spotting her friend hunched over Amargo's body, breathing heavily.

Jetta looked up, the familiar green of her eyes doused with terror. "I—I thought they were going to kill me. I didn't know. I saw you, the wolves—but they were not real. They were the monster in my dreams."

Scooting away from Amargo, Jetta's voice faltered. "I couldn't stop."

Triel froze in place, not sure what to do.

The commander held up her bloody hands, her brow pinching as she recalled something troubling. "Death follows me wherever I go..."

"Jetta, I—"

"The Grand Obling was right. I can't keep doing this," Jetta said, cradling her head in her hands. "There is something terrible inside me. I am an abomination. It doesn't matter if it's me or some*thing*. I can't be trusted."

And with that, Jetta unsheathed the knife hanging from Amargo's belt. *"Until my last breath,"* she said, and she plunged the blade into her stomach.

Triel felt the knife as if it stabbed her own belly and screamed out in pain. Collapsing, she rolled down the stairs, coming to rest in a battered heap by Jetta's side.

"Why?" the Healer sobbed.

Triel moved her hands over the wound, but Jetta swatted her away. "It's for the best," she whispered. "I've killed so many people. I can't kill any more. I can't risk hurting you."

"Jetta, no one can tell you who or what you are. You are Jetta Kyron. You are my friend."

With a grunt, Triel shifted her weight onto bruised hands and knees. She brushed back the damp hair clinging to Jetta's forehead and held fast to her hand. "You can't abandon me now. I need you. You have to fight this thing—whatever it is. This is too important. It's beyond me and you, and it's beyond anything we've ever stood for."

Jetta's breathing went shallow and rapid. The Healer felt the pulse beneath her skin waning as her blood pooled on the cold stone floor.

I can't quell her anger and fear. More than anything, she wanted to have her friend back, but when she thought of the dozens of people Jetta had just felled, she hesitated. *Am I capable of making the right decision?*

Jetta's head rolled to the side as she lost consciousness. Even as Triel tried to pull out of her grasp, the commander's grip stayed firm, and she found herself falling backwards and inwards, into the deepest recesses of her mind.

Thrust behind Jetta's eyes, the Healer found herself huddled up with her brother beneath a fort made of cots in a hot apartment with boarded-up windows. Nobody else was around; it was just the two of them.

Jaeia is off mapping the ducts, *she absorbed from the memory,* and Galm went out again. He won't return until early morning, probably with a few new cuts and bruises.

Despite the late hour, the two of them feared sleeping, so instead they played a rock dice game they had come up with a few months ago when things started getting really ugly.

"You can go first," Jetta said, handing her brother the dice, "so at least you have a fighting chance."

Jetta wanted so badly to make her brother laugh. Something about the way his cheeks turned cherry red and his little belly jiggled brought her joy. There was no other sound as important to her, but tonight she couldn't seem to make him even smile.

"Jahx, what's wrong?"

She didn't have to ask. Through their connection she felt the pangs in her brother's empty stomach. They had donated all their food to Jaeia, and Yahmen had stripped the apartment of anything even remotely edible the previous week.

Jahx rolled a triple moon, winning her lot of buttons and paperclips, but still no smile, not even a hint of delight at his victory. Though she tried to deny it, she couldn't help but notice that his cheeks looked more sunken than usual, his eyes dull and flat.

Crawling out from their cot fort, Jetta ignored her brother's arguments as she decided how to fix the problem.

"No way, Jetta—don't do it—it's suicide. We can wait until morning."

But waiting until the morning scramble for food with the other child laborers wasn't any kind of guarantee that they would eat. In their shape, they needed something now.

Since the front door was guarded by Yahmen's henchmen, Jetta choose the air vents between the apartments. With considerable effort she hoisted the last remaining kitchen chair onto Galm's mattress and climbed the unsteady mountain of furniture to reach the air vent in the ceiling. She removed the latch and lifted herself up, accidentally toppling the chair. Jahx whispered for her audibly and screamed for her silently to come back, but she blocked him out.

Please come back, Jetta. I'm okay, please, I'm okay!

She smothered her cough as the dust and debris in the air vent choked her lungs. Be careful, *she told herself. The next door neighbor, Mr. Gravesbury, was a nasty old man with strange proclivities that made even the hardened criminals of the drag seem benign.*

In one slow movement, Jetta pushed out the vent cover to the neighboring apartment. She could hear the television on in the next room. By the bells and buzzers, she guessed it was the game show channel, and someone had just lost a hefty bet. The audience cheered wildly as the host read his fate from the cue cards.

"Oh, so sorry, contestant number 196! Looks like you'll have to—"

The audience called the last part out in unison with the host. "Run—For—Your—Life!"

Run For Your Life. *Jetta knew that one. Everybody talked about it. The contestant would have to run through a gauntlet of armed audience members and trained animals to the safety zone. The prize for winning was close to ten million in cash, more than the entire planet was worth, but no one ever won. Usually a free-for-all, the audience members wound up beating and torturing the contestant to death.*

Jetta could barely see. From what she could tell, Mr. Gravesbury had tacked blankets to the windows, creating a nearly pitch-black apartment. The flickering light from the television gave her little clue what lay below her as she lowered herself onto what she hoped was a dresser.

The wood composite creaked as she set down her full weight, and she froze in place. No sound but the television.

"Get ready to run, contestant number 196!"

Triel couldn't tell if it was her own fear or Jetta's that charged through her veins as the little girl padded slowly across the patchy carpet. She kept quiet when her toes sank into something squishy and warm, reigning in her fear with her imperative.

I have to get food. For us, for Jahx.

311

The refrigerator was only ten meters to the right, and the lone recliner faced the television, away from her. She kept her mind on the unpleasant presence in the reclining chair as she tiptoed slowly towards the kitchen.

Five meters. Four.

She felt chipped tile beneath her feet. So close.

Three. Two.

"On your mark. Get ready!"

Her tiny fingers wrapped around the refrigerator handle and tugged. The massive door wouldn't give. She put a little more effort into it, trying to keep quiet despite the escalating noise from the audience on the television.

Please—Jahx has to eat—

Finally, desperately, all her weight. The refrigerator door popped open.

"Go!"

The blood drained from her face. Body parts were stacked neatly on every shelf. There were even jars of bobbing eyes tucked away in the fruit suspender. The parts were humanoid, small. Like the parts of a child.

By the time she noticed the presence behind her, it was too late.

"Finally come to visit, little Jetta Drachsi? I thought your uncle would never allow you over. I know you and your siblings are always so hungry. How about a drumstick or a breast of the finest meat Fiorah has to offer?"

Jetta tried to dodge his bony hands, but she slipped on something wet on the kitchen tile and came down hard on her chin and chest, knocking the wind from her lungs.

"Oh, the first blow is always the worst. Look at contestant 196—still running, though! Watch out for the axe!" said the announcer.

Tasting warm copper in her mouth, Jetta rolled over just in time to see his boot coming down on her face. She dodged to the left and he cried out in pain at his impact with the floor.

312

Panicked, she darted out of the kitchen and tried to get back to the bedroom, but random junk, hidden in the shadows, reached up and pulled her down like hands from the grave.

"Get back here!" Gravesbury shouted. His eyes, magnified behind thick lenses in the television's light, portended only wicked desire.

She scurried up the dresser and leapt for the air vent, but he grabbed her by the pant leg and threw her on the bed.

"You're a little thin, but I'm sure we can find some meat on those bones."

The television seemed to agree with her predicament. "Oh, it doesn't look like contestant 196 has a chance."

Seeing him reach for something on his belt, she screamed. All sense of control left her body, and a reflexive reaction to his violence took hold, tossing the Healer into a parallel world.

This is the place of Jetta's power, *Triel realized.*

Torrents of psionic energy rushed in from all directions, coursing over and through her with violent force. When the onslaught drained away, she found herself in a blue-white, ghostly world, standing ankle-deep in one of an infinite number of mirrored pools. A young girl stood in another, crouching to dip her hands in the blackened water at her feet.

(My Gods, Jetta,) *Triel whispered,* (Don't you see what you are showing me?)

Thrown back into the scene in the adjacent apartment, Triel witnessed Jetta eviscerating the old man with a nightmare so profound she moved away from the memory to spare herself the knowing. Gravesbury screamed, clawing his face and knocking over furniture, speaking in foreign tongues.

Staggering back to the kitchen, Jetta swiped whatever non-humanoid edibles she could find before returning to the bedroom. She moved out of the way as Gravesbury reeled past her, his blood splattering her clothes as she hurriedly wriggled through the air vent.

She avoided Jahx's eyes as she lowered herself back into their apartment. Usually she would join him in celebrating their prize, but she merely emptied her pockets onto the bed and fled to the kitchen. Wiggling her way underneath the sink piping, she waited there, uncertain of who or what would come after her next.

Jahx opened the cupboard doors and looked at her solemnly. "I think there's still a little water coming from this sink. I'll help you get washed, okay?"

"I'm sorry, Jahx!"

Spiraling backward, outward. Triel found herself collapsed on top of Jetta, her mind still stretched between worlds until she felt her friend's biorhythm vanishing beneath her and grounded herself.

"Jetta," Triel whispered. "I saw you. You're not a monster. Your powers are limitless. But right now you draw your talent from your fear."

Triel slipped one hand over the knife wound and laid the other on Jetta's cheek.

"Oh no…"

The Healer couldn't reach her—not like before, at least. *Whatever the Motti did to corrupt Jetta's cellular growth is accelerating,* she thought, unable to isolate any healthy tissue to stimulate regeneration of her injured areas.

Considering her limitations, Triel performed what she could. When she inspected the site, she found an angry lump of scar tissue.

A patch job is the best I can do, she thought, feeling the heat of inflammation and foreign bodies below Jetta's skin. With a fresh wave of fear, she realized the bleak truth: *If Jetta gets hurt again, I might not be able to heal her at all…*

Garbled sounds from behind made Triel whip around.

Amargo! Seeing the blood bubbling out of his mouth, she rushed to his side. Tenderly, the Healer held his head up as he tried to speak. "It wasn't… supposed… to be like this."

Triel felt a hand on her shoulder. Her initial flood of relief dissipated when she saw the bleary-eyed, pale commander bracing her gut as she knelt down beside her.

"He's dying and there's nothing I can do to save him. Whatever you did to him..." Triel began, but Jetta's shame rushed out like a geyser and doused her words.

Amargo's breaths rose to gasps, his pulse uneven.

"Move aside," Jetta said.

Triel didn't know what to expect when Jetta grabbed hold of Amargo's hands and closed her eyes.

Who—or what—is that? she thought, seeing the silhouette flickering inside Amargo. The Healer blinked, disbelieving as Jetta's lips formed words she never spoke. A low hum surrounded them, seeming to originate from somewhere outside the Healer but simultaneously resounding within her. *What is she doing?*

Jetta opened her eyes. The humming stopped. A sad but strangely satisfied look crossed her face as she laid Amargo's body down to rest.

"What happened?"

"He gave me permission to take all his knowledge and memories," Jetta said quietly, sitting back on her heels. "He was... an extraordinary man."

Triel sensed there was something she was leaving out. "But?"

"But despite all of his convictions, he had doubts."

"About what?"

"All of this," Jetta said, her eyes resting heavily on the body of the dead archeologist. "He found flaws, inconsistencies, in the histories and writings of your people. It was because of his belief in the power of his promise to his ancestors and to the Prodgy that he kept them to himself. But now that I see them, I can't ignore them like he did."

Triel was about to say something when she caught a glimpse of the figure carved into the door. *It's like looking into a mirror*, she thought, leaving her frightened and speechless.

315

"Even that," Jetta said, following her line of sight, "isn't what it seems. I think the Temple of Exxuthus has many secrets that not even your highest priests were allowed to know."

Triel's eyes scanned the violence depicted on the wall. "The legend said that this place was built within a tree older than time itself, and that the tree and the Temple had always been on Algar, even before the Prodgies."

"That can't be true," Jetta scoffed.

"They used to say that no man that sought the Temple could find it. The first visitors were in fact three wanderers that chanced upon the Temple during a full moon several thousand years ago."

"That's at least somewhat possible. Amargo learned that the blood flower blooms during the full moon, and if you're covered in the pollen, the tree can't detect your scent. It was possible your ancestors discovered this trick," Jetta said.

"When the priests arrived, the Gods swore them to secrecy about the Temple, but one of the three broke his promise and went back to his village to tell the others of his discovery. That's when the wars started, and my people nearly killed themselves. Then Saol crossed over, and Rion returned."

Jetta nodded. "That was also consistent in his mind, even the part about the Great Mother's sacrifice and the restoration of the tribes. Except for one thing."

Jetta stood up and pointed to an inscription on the wall. The central symbol stood by itself over a triangle within a circle, surrounded by faded, chipping carvings. "This is a symbol for Earth. And it is a warning. There are other places in the Temple inscribed with this same warning, but they're all worn or destroyed. Amargo pieced together what he could and realized that Algar was linked to Earth at about the same time Saol was reborn as Rion. Look here—you can even see a depiction of the Egyptian pyramids on Old Earth"

"I don't understand what that means."

Locking eyes with Triel, Jetta firmed up her voice. "It means that your ancestors might have known when to come rescue the human race because it was forewarned. And from his studies, he believed that it was something that the Prodgies did or didn't do to anger your 'Gods' that caused the destruction of Earth."

"What?" Triel exclaimed.

Jetta squeezed her eyes shut. "I don't know any more than that. I just have his knowledge and his doubts in my head. This place—the stories you were told—may be a smokescreen. I feel like there is much more to this story, and much more linking Earth and Algar than you and I ever knew, and Amargo believed that it was crucial to get to the bottom of it. He just thought he had more time. He didn't think that I would..."

Jetta started to rub the scar on her belly but stopped when she realized what she was doing. Slowly, she picked herself off the ground. "We can't stay here. I believe this Temple *is* a living place. He was right about that. I feel *alive.* More alive than I've ever felt. I feel like I'm close to something familiar—close to home."

Triel's breath hitched. Some part of her feared looking at Jetta, but she forced herself anyway. *She's my friend,* she reminded herself.

Wringing her hands, Jetta stared at the door to the *Diez di Trios* as sweat collected on her brow. "If I am Rion, then this is the last place I should be. Even the walls seem to be watching me, as if they're expecting something from me."

"Okay," Triel said, "but where do we go? We're literally entombed by the tree, and even if we could figure out how to walk out of here, I have no idea when the next full moon is."

Jetta shook her head. "Not necessary. Amargo and Helena used a freight cruiser to transport their group here. The ship is still docked in the courtyard of the temple."

"Then we can get out of here?"

Jetta looked unsure. "Amargo didn't really do a lot of maintenance once they grounded."

The commander surprised her, grabbing onto her as she tried to get up. "Hey—I'm sorry."

"For what?"

Jetta lowered her eyes. "All of this. I'm ashamed of everything. Thanks for healing me and giving me a second chance. Your faith in me makes all of this worth it."

"Jetta…" Triel began, but she couldn't complete her sentence.

Picking up on her uncertainty, Jetta changed the subject. "What did you mean when you said I draw my talent from my fear?"

Triel thought of the mirrored water she had seen in the otherworldly vision and pointed to the wall. "These men—you see how they fight? Knife to knife, fist to flesh. They draw their power from the same place, and look where it leads them. It's the same with you. When you came out of the *Diez di Trios*, you were scared, right?"

Jetta nodded. "I thought I was being attacked."

"And you drew from that fear to attack the Jumaris and the archeologists?"

"Yes."

"You are capable of so much more, Jetta," the Healer said, softening her tone. "I've seen and felt it. That's why I'm still here."

Jetta looked down at the ugly scar across her belly. "I'm sorry, Triel. I won't disappoint you anymore. I promise."

"I know," the Healer said, squeezing Jetta's arm. "Let's get out of here, okay? I don't like this place. I think the walls are watching us, too."

Jetta picked up Amargo's lantern and some of his personal possessions before they ascended the stairs. When Triel reached the top step, they both heard the whisper.

You can't leave.

"Jetta, who is that? What's happening?"

Thief.

Unable to formulate the words to describe her fear, Triel pointed to the walls. Blood seeped from the cracks in the mortar. Jetta took one look and grabbed her hand. "Run."

"What's going on?" Triel said between breaths as they sprinted toward the wolves. Jetta helped Triel on top of Cano before mounting Kiyiyo. A terrible shriek came from the dark staircase leading to the *Diez di Trios*, but neither of them dared to look back.

Jetta didn't have time to answer the Healer as they spurred the wolves and took off, away from the angry cacophony that belled out from the chamber. The walls shook, covering them in white dust as they streaked down the sloped corridors, the weak light from the lantern and the keen nocturnal eyes of the wolves their only salvation.

Thank Gods she has that talent, she thought as the commander guided them through the maze of the Temple using Amargo's knowledge. *I don't want to find out what's after us.*

The Healer crouched low against her wolf as he ducked under a collapsed construction beam and picked his way across the rubble. Small shafts of daylight broke through the ceiling. *We're nearing the apex of the Temple.*

As soon as she felt an inkling of hope, the ground shook, and the wolves had trouble finding their footing on the shifting stonework.

Thief! the unseen voice cried, rising in frequency, bringing a terrible itch to her skin. She looked up to see Jetta bracing her head in her arms, no longer holding onto her wolf. Blood trickled from her ears as she begged for release, flailing wildly.

"Make it stop—make it stop!"

Triel pulled her wolf alongside Jetta's. Without thinking of the consequences, she leapt from her wolf to Jetta's, narrowly avoiding slamming into an archway.

"Stay with me, Jetta," she said, holding tight to her friend as Kiyiyo jumped over a series of felled pillars.

The voice continued to rise, shaking her bones right down to the marrow. It took everything she had to keep her mind focused on the task as they climbed a small mountain of fractured stone. Sticky spider webs clung to her face, but she dared not let go of Kiyiyo or Jetta to wipe them off.

As they crested the mountain of broken stone, Triel saw where a large area of the roof had caved in. Bright beams of daylight shone through, illuminating their path to freedom.

"So close—" she whispered as the wolf veered toward the opening and prepared to jump.

Reality splintered. She was no longer mounted atop a wolf that leapt toward the sunlight. Instead, she stood in a garden that stretched out in every direction toward the turquoise horizon. Massive stone statues marked intervals along the rows of bushes, plants and floral arrangements.

"Welcome, Triel of Algardrien. I've waited a long time for you to arrive."

"Arpethea..."

Triel couldn't believe her eyes. The old Seer hovered before, wrapped in a light, silken cloth. What little skin showed appeared pearlescent, though the markings of their people had turned dark, like the blackest night she could remember.

"Where am I?"

"You are at the crossroads," the Seer said, her eyes shining like the brightest of stars. "I traveled here at a grave cost to warn you."

"Of what?"

Arpethea's voice dropped an octave. "The Apparax."

"Jetta?" Triel said.

"She is not ready for what she must do. She will try and stop you," Arpethea said, her voice continuing to deepen and magnify. "She will not let you fulfill your destiny."

"What do you mean?"

Arpethea's eyes glowed like cinders. "Do not hesitate to end her life to save your own."

Triel backed away from the Seer as the turquoise sky dimmed to the color of engine oil. As the greenery wilted and the statues crumbled, Arpethea's clothes disintegrated, revealing the patches of discoloration creeping across her skin like rust. "End her life to save our people."

Triel screamed as Arpethea's rotting fingers reached for her.
"Kill the Apparax."

***

Jetta came to sprawled on a grassy mound between overturned statues. The sun felt warm on her skin, birdsong and the rustlings of trees a welcome change from the unwanted voices inside and outside her head.

A warm lick and nuzzle got her attention.

"Kiyiyo!" she exclaimed, wrapping her arms around his neck. The wolf whined and then pulled back, trotting over to join Cano as he inspected the Healer lying a few meters away.

Triel—

Amargo's memories stopped her from checking on her friend just yet. *The wolves got us to courtyard at the apex of the Temple, but we're still in danger.*

Jetta crawled over to a break in the wall and peered through. Leafy treetops poked out of a blanket of white mist, reaching for the sun. One tree, much larger than the rest, had grown around the tiered pyramid of the temple, with its young, purple vines snaking up the stone steps toward the courtyard.

"*Chi'Tabalu,*" Jetta whispered, drawing on Amargo's knowledge of the tree. Ancient scribes had given it a name with two meanings, designating it as both "life-reaper" and "guardian of the heavens."

When Amargo and his wife here landed years ago, they used a manufactured version of blood flower pollen to escape detection by the tree while they gained access to the Temple from the roof, Jetta recalled, searching for a starcraft. She spotted the freight cruiser, overgrown with weeds and covered in layers of dirt and grime, still resting between two spires.

Other realizations came through. *Amargo never expected to leave—*

(But he didn't expect to die.)

Awash in guilt, she fell into a conversation held in secrecy between the two archeologists.

"I will follow the Apparax when she crosses over."

"Amargo, no—that is forbidden!"

"Helena, you know how I feel about this. I must keep my oath to preserve the truth of ancient history, not perpetuate deceit based on the fears of our ancestors and allies. It is the only way!"

Triel's moan distracted Jetta from Amargo's memories. She rose on unsteady legs and limped her way over to the Healer.

"Hey—are you okay?" Jetta asked, gently shaking her shoulders.

Triel opened her eyes and looked at Jetta with fear and terrible knowing. Taken aback by the intensity of her thoughts, Jetta dropped to her knees.

"Jetta?" Triel whispered. Her facial expressions relaxed. Propping herself up on her elbows, the Healer turned to her. "We're safe?"

"Not yet. Can you walk?"

Triel used Cano to help pull herself up. "Yes, I'm fine. Just a little shaken. What happened in there?"

The Healer reached for Jetta's left ear and retracted bloody fingertips. Jetta touched the same site and felt gummy, coagulating blood. "It felt like someone was scraping at the inside of my skull." She shook her head and grabbed Triel's hand. "Let's get out of here and worry about it later."

Even with Jetta's augmented strength and Triel's assistance, the cab door to the freight cruiser put up a fight.

"What a piece of *meitka!*" Jetta shouted, veins throbbing in her forehead. Finally, with the help of the wolves pawing and nosing at the door, they managed to pry it open.

"Get in," Jetta said, shooing the animals and helping the Healer step up to the deck.

Triel swiped a hand through the dust lining the interior. "Does it still work?"

"This piece of junk is older than dirt," Jetta mumbled. She slid into the cockpit and flipped on the central processor, but nothing happened. "*Skucheka!*"

"Is there enough fuel?"

"This has got to be a joke." Jetta tapped the gauges and went to the back to find the emergency toolkit. "Gods, I don't even know—who designed this *meitka*? There must be a short in the primary router. Stay here, and when I give you the signal, give the engines a boost."

As soon as her boot touched the soft grass, she sensed a shift in the air. The birdsong stopped and the mist crept higher, spilling over the courtyard walls in slow motion waves.

Jetta passed the toolkit from hand to hand and nervously looked around.

What is that? she thought as her extrasensory perceptions picked up a strange sort of interference, like the white noise on their old television set. Frustrated, she dug at her ear canals in a futile attempt to clear out the din. With her talents dampened, she sensed only the silence in the untended courtyard, and the coolness of the encroaching mist.

"*Mae dereke ni onanosk,*" she mumbled, ducking underneath the hood-access of the freighter. When she looked inside, she found a tangle of weeds, spider nests, and other multi-legged insects. "*Skuchecka...*"

Old fears screamed for her to run, but she bit down on her lip and thrust herself inside. No matter how many times she brushed them off, the tickle of their tiny legs returned as the bugs searched for cover on her body.

"Try that," Jetta shouted, snapping two fixtures together. The engine struggled, then shut off.

Out of the corner of her eye, Jetta noticed a purple creeper slithering through the bushes, root hairs gyrating in its pseudo-oral

323

cavity. *It's orienting itself toward my scent.* She didn't have much time.

"Try that!" Jetta shouted again. The engine whirred and clicked, then hiccupped and died. "*Mugarruthepeta!*"

Jetta rummaged through the tools, desperately looking for something she couldn't find. *Is it a screwgrinder or a hexjack that I need?* Having always relied on her sister's more mechanically gifted mind, she floundered.

"Jaeia," she whispered, "I could really use you right now."

Something hissed to her left, then her right. Jetta heard the wolves whining inside the cabin of the ship, scratching at the windows as she grabbed a lightsaw.

"Jetta!" Triel shouted from the top hatch.

"I know!"

Distracted, she allowed the lightsaw to dip across the top of her finger, giving her a shock.

"*Gorsh-shit!*" she shouted, dropping the tool. Other expletives spilled out of her mouth as she crawled on her hands and knees, searching through the overgrown weeds and grass for the lightsaw.

Something touched the back of her leg, and she hit her head on the hood-access. Wheeling around, she saw a flash of purple disappear into the mist.

"Jetta, get up here!"

But she couldn't. *If I don't get the engine started, we're as good as dead.*

Flexing her fists, she dug into the past. *Think. Remember the basic principles.*

She was four again, with her brother and sister in a mining ship, working on the secondary engine on one of the bigger drills. The rig lay on the deck in pieces, like an intricate puzzle with an infinite number of parts. Worst yet, someone had used lysturil to lubricate the spindles, and the entire fusion core had eroded. Now they were left struggling to refit the engine before their next shift—a purposely

*impossible assignment that would give Yahmen a convenient excuse
to punish them later.*

"We can do this," Jetta remembered her sister saying. *"We just
have to divide this into working sections. Jahx, take the sub-
processor. Jetta, you take the combustion network. I'll take the
oxidizer and cooling control units."*

*Jetta struggled with her assignment, not having grafted enough
knowledge of combustion networks to make sense of the injectors
and propellant mixers.*

I can't do this...

*Jaeia scooted over beside her and showed her the different
support rings. "Don't look at all the pieces. Just think of the first few
steps. Then after that, the next few. Don't think about the end. Just
look at where you are. It will all come together—promise."*

"Just look at where I am," Jetta mumbled. She flipped over the
hydrogen cells and made a few more connections. Gnawing on her
cheek, she didn't allow herself to despair at the shoddy job. *This is
all I can do with these parts.*

"Try it now!" she shouted.

Sputtering, straining; a puff of noxious gas burped out of the
exhaust. Jetta crawled out from underneath the belly of the ship and
away from the growing black cloud, coughing and sneezing as the
engine misfired.

"Turn it off! Turn it off!" Jetta shouted, but Triel couldn't hear
her above the grating of the engine.

Something flitted in and out of the mist to her left. Several
purple vines crept out from around a statue and exposed their pink
buccal linings.

"Jetta!" Triel screamed, popping her head out of the hatch. The
engine turned over. Overjoyed, Jetta ran to the ship and climbed
aboard. As she slid into the cockpit she saw what Triel had been
trying to tell her.

"Oh my Gods..." she whispered.

A huge purple shoot the width of a small building curled over the edge of the courtyard to hover above their ship. Jetta reversed the polarities on the impulse engines and spun them away just as the vine came crashing down on their docking site, slamming into the roof of the Temple and taking out the courtyard.

"I can't see!" Jetta said, wiping away the soot on the visor shield with her sleeve. The laser wipers cleared only half the grime on the outside as she fought to orient the ship.

Another massive purple vine came coiling toward them. Jetta thrust the engines into second gear, and they narrowly averted the attack.

"Triel," Jetta shouted. "Are the jumpdrives online yet?"

"You can't jump here!"

"Why not?" Jetta asked as the ship began to lose altitude. Two alarm lights on the dashboard turned red, warning of a combustion overload.

"Besides the fact that you'd be destroying an important piece of Prodgy history, this clearly isn't a normal juncture of space-time!" Triel said, trying to strap herself in as Jetta banked hard right.

A massive roar shook the freighter. Jetta couldn't believe her eyes. The tree base rose out of the mist, completely encapsulating the Temple of Exxuthus. Her mouth dropped open as teeth and salivary glands exposed themselves at the tree's core. "*Hei Meitka!*"

Jetta looked at her readings. *Primary thrusters are offline, and the jumpdrive are still in precycle.*

As she dodged another vine, Jetta hesitated over the navigational input. *Triel's right. This place is already experiencing space-time disturbances, and creating a rift might have unintended consequences…*

I have to find another way.

Another vine whipped past them, clipping the wing of the ship and sending them spinning out of control.

"Hold on!" Jetta said, her stomach rising in her throat as she wrestled the controls. Once she stabilized the ship, she swallowed hard and glanced to the back of the cab. "Everyone ok?"

Dizzy and disoriented, the Healer and the wolves collected themselves off of the floor.

"Yeah," Triel said, holding her head in her hands.

Reverting her attention back to navs, Jetta tried to boost the gravitational compensators to stabilize the ship. Then she had an idea.

"Stupid launnie," the captain sneered at her as he captured two of her last three battleships. "Always putting yourself in my targeting sights."

Jetta found herself back aboard the Dominion ships, playing one of the Fleet officers in another of the endless rounds of the Endgame. In this scenario, her ships engines had been rigged to fail, exposing her to her opponent's front line. Even after grafting the Sumarese captain's knowledge, she couldn't determine a plan of attack.

He's a good commander, *she thought, squirming in her seat.* And he's right about me. I'm just waiting to be slaughtered...

Then she thought of something that neither the captain nor her predecessors had. A tactic she synthesized from the bits and pieces of knowledge that thousands of Sentients had given her over the course of her short life.

My last remaining battleship is *Marticion* class; I have double the normal reserves of power in that vessel as opposed to my other starcraft—

It's like sitting on a giant atomic bomb.

She smiled.

In a deft maneuver, she ordered her last remaining ships to fly belly up toward the enemy line.

"What in the name of Sukathra are you doing?" the captain said, his many eyes jumping out of his head at the unexpected move.

327

"I will accept your surrender, Captain Daylis," she said, hoping he would fall for her trick. "Accept now or lose your entire Fleet."

The captain bared his teeth and stabbed his console. "All ships, fire at my mark."

Flashing his most arrogant smile, he spoke every word with a superior air as his entire fleet lined up to fire at her ship: "Three... two... one... mark."

This is going to be better than I hoped, *she thought, setting her internal gravitational compensators on a redundant feedback.*

As the captain gave the command to fire, she released the compensators, flushing out her ship at a million parts per nanosecond. When the enemy missiles hit the wall of reversed gravity, they rebounded in the opposite direction.

She never forgot the soul-crushing, defeated look on the captain's face as his ships vanished from the game field.

"Let's hope that would really work," Jetta said, setting the gravitational compensators in a redundant feedback.

As the ship rattled from the overheated compensators, Triel crawled her way back into the nav seat. A nasty bruise, already black and blue, darkened the crest of her cheekbone. "What are you doing?"

Two more vines looped toward them. Jetta put her arm across Triel. "Hold on!"

She reversed the compensators. Bracing for impact, Jetta kept one eye open as the attacking vines came hurtling at her vessel. Instead of crushing the freight cruiser, the strike repelled them in the opposite direction.

Jetta fought with the controls as they flipped over on their broadside and hurtled through the sky. Clenching her teeth, she tried to reboot the thrusters and level out the ship.

"Precycle complete!" Triel shouted as the needles on the altimeter spun around and around.

Looking out the window, she saw the toothy mountaintops they had crossed to escape the Lockheads rising up to meet them. *There is no way we will survive the crash.*

"Jetta!" the Healer cried.

With no time to spare, Jetta typed in the first destination that came to mind. She didn't know why she chose such a dingy, remote planet, but it came through her fingertips before she had time to second-guess her choice.

She looked out the window as she hit the punch. *Too late.*

Time and space split apart as the nose of the ship collided with a snow-capped peak.

Jaeia—

***

Out of the nowhere, Jaeia felt someone or something knock the wind from her lungs and sweep her legs out from under her. She fell to her knees, gripping the railing of the lift as she tried to catch her breath.

"Should I call a medical team?" Admiral Unipoesa asked, slowing their transport.

"No." Jaeia collected herself, pressing her hands against her chest and stomach. "I'm fine. Just haven't been eating enough lately."

It was a lie, and the admiral knew it. But she didn't see how she could possibly get him to understand the truth.

"Is it Jetta?" the admiral inquired, helping her up.

Jaeia decided to give him a chance. "She blocked me out a while ago, but that doesn't mean I can't feel her when something big happens. She's in trouble."

"What kind of trouble?"

Jaeia hung her head. "I don't know. She's not sharing."

"Can you go through with the meeting?" the admiral asked as he opened the lift gate to their destination.

Jaeia straightened out her uniform and rewrapped her hair in a bun. "I don't have a choice," she said, filing in behind the few senior officers left aboard the Alliance Central Starbase.

As she took her seat, Jaeia caught sight of her reflection in the tabletop finish.

Is that me? she thought, pulling down the lower lids of her eyes. Although she had accepted that the Motti modifications made her sick, she never expected her appearance to alter so drastically over such a short period. Her eyes looked bleary and aged, and her skin sagged like she had aged thirty years in a matter of weeks.

Maybe I just need to rest.

No, she quickly corrected herself, touching the cold edge of the reflection. *It's more than just the stress of the situation...*

Chilled by the thought, Jaeia turned her attention to Wren as he took the podium. With his unbuttoned uniform and eyes, ringed with shadows, the CCO looked as if he hadn't slept in days. *I'm not sure who looks worse.*

"This is it," he said, clicking on the holographic projector in the center of the room. The lights dimmed as the picture of the central news anchor for Trigos fanned out into three dimensions.

"Tonight on Channel 97, we are following up on today's disturbing broadcast from President Victor Paulstine of the Galactic Republic. His startling accusations against the Kyron twins and the role of the Alliance in keeping their psychological instability out of the public eye has divided the General Assembly."

The news team played a shortened version of the tape Victor had shown them. Jaeia looked around the room. Even seasoned the war veterans, their faces pinched with concern, could not mask their dwindling hope.

"Public support for the Starways Alliance took a two-thousand-point drop this evening. Forecasters predict the collapse of—"

But Wren clicked off the feed. The projector slid back down into its pod. "It's over. Victor won."

"He said he would give us his demands—" Jaeia said.

Wren kept his head down. "It's over. We are finished. The General Assembly is pulling out all the stops. What we do from here on out is no longer sanctioned by our government."

"What government?" Msiasto Mo exclaimed. "Victor dissolved that, too!"

Shouting and accusations flew across the table. Jaeia sagged in her chair, bewildered and defeated, unable to engage in any form of argument or diplomacy.

The admiral put a hand on her shoulder. "Don't give up. Not now. Please."

He stood up and took the podium from Wren. When the others wouldn't settle, he slammed his fist against the speakers with a thunderous boom that shocked the audience into silence.

"As many of you already know, I've been in close contact with the Liberalist Pancar of Nagoorian for the last several years. Though he is no favorite in the courts or in the eyes of our former Minister Razar, he has been slowly building a following for the last decade. We may no longer hold the favor of the General Assembly, and Victor may now have the funding and the following of a greater army—but we have something more. We have the truth. And when the people hear the truth, Victor's hold on the Starways will crumble."

"What truth?" Commander Rook asked over the hush of the room.

The admiral looked over at the Minister. Eyes cast downward, Wren looked like a man out of options.

"We will tell the worlds the real story of the Kyron triplets. And we will tell them about Kurt Stein."

The room filled with excited chatter. Jaeia spoke up. "But we don't even know if he's alive."

"Yes, but the idea of him will be enough to quell Victor's fear-mongering. It will give the people hope that we can rebuild our worlds, and that we don't have to live under his umbrella of protection to defeat the Deadwalkers."

331

"But even if we *found* Kurt Stein, it wouldn't be enough to stop the Deadwalkers. Victor still has that advantage," Wren pointed out.

"This will give us time; it will be enough of a diversion for us to regroup with Pancar's army and come up with a way to infiltrate Li's army and learn of their countermeasures."

"Collaborate with that Liberalist?" Msiasto Mo said. "As the chief of military intelligence, I can hardly advise this."

Admiral Unipoesa held up his hands. "I understand your reservations, but we are running out of options. The only reason I returned to Alliance grounds is because I believe in universal freedom and a future without fear. I would not have risked refreezing or imprisonment if I didn't have my convictions about the core values and the integrity of the Starways Alliance."

An old, nameless feeling pressed against Jaeia's sternum. As she grappled with her unease, she recalled the time when the admiral first convinced her to challenge Li and then face Jahx.

"Do whatever it takes to win, Jaeia. It's what Jahx would have wanted," she remembered him saying, feeling the shadowed pain behind his words as he asked her to make the choice that would ultimately end her brother.

Memory and emotion conjured other scenes from the past: The broken figure of Tarsha Leone hunched over the Endgame console and the jackal sneering back at her.

"I loved her from the very beginning."

The admiral's own words, spoken in grief, colliding with his action as he picked up a gun and killed Urusous Li's only love in cold blood.

Jaeia rose from her seat. "I stand by you, Admiral."

Nobody said a word. Jaeia didn't break the admiral's gaze. She thought she saw him smile.

"I also stand by you, Admiral," Severn Mallok said, breaking the silence.

"I, too," someone else added.

332

Others joined in steadily until only one remained. Gaeshin Wren walked up to the podium, his emotional turbulence clouding Jaeia's ability to sense what he would do next. Bracing herself against the edge of the conference table, she watched as the COO got in the admiral's face.

"For the Alliance," he whispered. "I too stand by you, Admiral."

Jaeia exhaled, not realizing she had been holding her breath as the Mo proposed that the admiral would deliver the message to the Starways.

That will work, Jaeia thought. *He's the old war hero from the Raging Front, and the best-liked figurehead in the Fleet. Better yet, he'll goad Li into action.*

After the content of the message was decided, the group disbanded to enact the plan's individual components.

Dr. DeAnders stopped Jaeia as she exited. "I wanted to wait for a better time to tell you this, Jaeia, but there really hasn't been a good opportunity."

Leaning against the door frame, Jaeia closed her eyes. "Jahx."

"Yes."

"How long?"

DeAnders shook his head and removed his glasses. "I don't know. A few days. A week or more if we're lucky. But it's inevitable. The Grand Oblin's cellular decay is steadily increasing despite every measure we take. He's dying."

You can't cry now, she told herself, refusing to give in to emotion. Pressing her knuckles into the metal door frame, she thought of her sister. "Thank you for telling me. I'll stop by later this evening."

"Of course. Let me know if there's anything else I can do to help you."

Benumbed by fear, she boarded a lift and directed it to the security and interrogation wing. She couldn't rationalize her feelings, but she couldn't deny the need to see the Spinner named Aesis again.

Jaeia let herself slide down to sit on the lift floor as she cruised down the halls. "Jetta," she whispered, the tears rolling down her cheeks freely. "You have to come back."

CHAPTER VI

Jetta! she heard someone cry. The voice sounded from somewhere overhead, but very far away.

Wheeling back in time, Jetta found herself stuck in a vertical air duct joint.

"Mugarruthepeta," *she muttered. Jaeia had told her to take a tube of engine grease with her in case she got stuck in the c-juncture, but she had left the apartment in a hurry that night. Yahmen had beaten them all pretty badly and there wasn't time to nurse any bumps and bruises at home.*

As she wiggled around the sharp turn, her headlamp sputtered on the last few ounces of juice.

No, no, no— she thought, pushing harder and scraping the skin off of her side.

Even though she and her sister had marked their routes with scratches in case their lamps failed, the last thing she wanted to do was be stuck in the dark. On a place like Fiorah, always suffused by light, the dark became that much more terrifying. Alone and isolated, thoughts became reality, and Jetta's worst nightmares came true.

Jetta! the voice called again.

The headlamp petered out. Darkness prevailed. Jetta swept her hand along the walls, tracing her way back home by the feel of the grooves. Duct rats scuffled in a nearby joint, and she quickened her pace.

Don't think of the rats, *she told herself over and over.*

Passing a slotted juncture, she felt cold, damp fur and exposed bone.

That's a dead cat—

Repulsed, she reared back, only to feel the unfortunate animal's rigid body, postured in sheer panic, fall out in front of her. Unable to see its face, she imagined it's yellow eyes frozen open in a terror-stricken state as the rats ate it alive.

With a scream perched on her lips, she batted away the carcass, trying to ignore the fact that the backside of it had been picked clean.

Jetta focused on the soft light glowing up ahead. When she turned the corner and entered the duct tapping into her apartment, she saw a figure hovering over the opening. A silhouette, larger than a child, but smaller than either Galm or Yahmen, waited for her.

(Jetta,) *the figure cried,* (you have to come back.)

Tiny whiskers tickled her feet. Something furry brushed her toes.

(Climb faster—)

(You have to come back—!)

(Hurry—)

Teeth bit into pink skin—

"Jetta!"

She awoke to the crack of thunder and someone shaking her shoulders. When her eyes converged on the figure overhead, she couldn't believe who she saw.

"Triel?"

"We've got to get out of here," Triel shouted above the fury of the storm. "It's getting worse!"

Holding her aching side, Jetta looked around the ship, trying to assess the situation. Their collision with the peak had horribly buckled the forward cabin, but despite the heavy damage the freight cruiser had sustained during their jump off of Algar, it had somehow landed safely. If the cockpit seats hadn't broken off their pedestal on impact, neither of them would have survived. Jetta's lips twisted in a half-smile at the irony of the poor, antiquated design of the freight cruiser actually saving their lives.

"Where are the wolves?" Jetta asked, picking her way through the wreckage to the door.

Triel looked outside to the wind-whipped terrain. "I don't know. When I came to they were gone."

"*Meitka*," Jetta cursed.

337

She leaned out the door and shielded her eyes. Somehow they had plowed through the most level area in the foothills of a forgotten city. Sand and debris rained from the tortured skies as lightning lit up the wasteland.

"Where are we?" Triel called over the howling winds.

Jetta gestured to a discarded plastic bottle lying in a pile of refuse just outside their cruiser. "Earth."

"What? Why did you jump us here?"

For a moment, Jetta questioned her own judgment, but her resolve only firmed. "Because we haven't found all the answers yet. We need to know why Earth is linked to Algar. Amargo felt it too. The truth was never on Algar."

"Then why did he stay at the Temple of Exxuthus?" Triel shouted over a clap of thunder.

Jetta shut the bay doors as best she could to keep out some of the noise. "Earth is too dangerous; he had enemies—he couldn't go back. Besides, he had to keep his Promise to the Prodgies. He also thought he could get the answers by following me in the *Diez di Trios*, but then… things got confusing."

"And another thing," Jetta said, remembering Admiral Unipoesa's confession to her and Jaeia in the medical bay. "Here we'll also find the answers to a much more serious problem. Answers that can restore the Starways."

Jetta told Triel about Kurt Stein, his work with genetic archiving, and how Admiral Unipoesa believed that the inventor held the key to resurrecting dead planets. She also touched on her encounter with Agracia, and the mission she interrupted when she crash-landed on Old Earth the first time. The Healer listened intently as she explained the importance of the passenger list stored somewhere in a smart server deep in the heart of the Deadzone near Ground Zero, and the odd coincidence that Agracia recognized her tattoo.

"I need to find Agracia—I need her knowledge of the Deadzone," Jetta said.

Not sparing any detail, she went on to tell Triel about Josef Stein, and Edgar Wallace's belief that his laboratory might still be intact somewhere deep in the Deadzone. She also shared her curiosity about the similarities between the teachings of Ramak Yakarvoah and Victor's philosophies, and the possibility that the key to Josef Stein's Smart Cells, and to Ramak, was hidden in the personal journals in his lab.

"Well," Triel said, "what now? Everything that was important on this planet was destroyed centuries ago."

Jetta couldn't outright disagree. From what she grafted, Amargo had fruitlessly searched through the ruins of the pyramids and the ancient cities for years. Then again, Amargo didn't have Agracia and Bossy to help him scavenge.

"I don't know, but I feel like we need to be here," Jetta said. "All the answers are here, I know it. Just trust me."

Peering out the window, Jetta scanned the horizon. Come nightfall, exposure to radiation and the elements would be the least of their concerns. *The surface is dangerous; we need to leave as quickly as possible.*

Jetta bit her lip. Most of the memories she had stolen from Agracia's mind involved wild nights and street brawls. *I need an accessway to a Pit or shelter, not how to pick a fight while drunk.*

Taking a deep breath, she trained her thoughts on Agracia's memories and took another look outside.

"Agracia's been around here before," Jetta said. She tried to bring up the navigational computer, but despite her best efforts the terminal remained dead. A thorough search of the storage compartments turned up a few miscellaneous tools and three lifesuits, though only one seemed to be fully functional.

"What are these?" Triel asked as Jetta handed her the blue suit.

"I'm guessing that this old freighter probably carried starship parts and supplies for booster highway repairs. These suits were used for manual repairs outside the starships if they were too far out for a tow. They have Grade I protection, so we should be okay."

339

"What about you?" Triel said, seeing that Jetta had handed her the only functional one.

Jetta measured the ripped suit against the one missing the radiation sealant. *I'm dying anyway,* she thought to herself. "I'll be fine. You're more important."

"No, please—"

Jetta pressed the suit into her chest. "You can always heal me— I can't return that favor."

With a pinched brow, Triel turned over the suit in her hands. "It's getting harder, Jetta," she said quietly, "whatever the Motti did to you…"

The Healer pointed at her stomach to the scar that hadn't healed, but Jetta didn't look, instead asking, "Hey, what's in that box over there?"

Triel removed some of the fallen debris sitting atop a ration box. "Ugh—old MREs," she said, dusting off the ready-to-eat meals.

Even the mention of stale, dusty food made Jetta's stomach growl. "When was the last time you and I really ate?"

As they suited up and dined on old meat substitute and water pouches, Jetta thought of her dream.

"What's wrong?" Triel asked, seeing the look on her face.

"Just before I woke up I had a weird dream. I was back on Fiorah, mapping the air ducts. I thought I heard Jaeia calling for me. But it didn't feel like a dream. I think Jaeia needs me; I think something's happened."

"What can you feel?" Triel asked.

Jetta shook her head. "No, I can't go there. Not now. I have to complete this. I don't know why, but I feel like everything I've done so far has led me here. I have to stay on this path."

Triel tilted her head. "But what if we need to go back?"

Pursing her lips, Jetta set down her meal. "I'm sure of this. Jaeia is tough. Stronger than me even. She can handle whatever is happening out there."

But the Healer heard the waver in her voice. "What if something's happened to Jahx?"

Jetta stuffed the remaining supplies—the laser bolt gun, socket lugger, flashlight, feather grinder, and the last of the water and MREs—into the other suit and tied it into a sack that she slung over her shoulder. "I *have* to stay on this path."

Swallowing the dry lump in her throat, Jetta tried not to think about Jahx. She had avoided it as best she could while she and Triel searched for answers, but consciously or not, her mind always returned to her brother and sister. Only her fear kept her from running back to them.

(They can't see what I am.)

"Let's go," Jetta said, shoving open the bay door.

She held on to Triel's hand as they bowed to the raging winds. Better outfitted for outer space than a terrestrial storm, Jetta crossed her fingers that the freighter suits would protect them long enough to reach safety.

Jetta remembered her first involuntary visit to Old Earth, when Agracia had wrapped her in a gear bag for protection as they trekked across the exposed terrain of the wastelands. The gales and detritus had torn up her legs, and even the thought rekindled the pain. Heeding the memory, Jetta chose her path as carefully as she could, sticking close to the shelter of fallen rubble and staying out of the direct path of the wind.

I haven't really rested in days, she thought, still fighting the winds for every centimeter of ground gained. As much as she tried to shy away from the truth, she couldn't help but acknowledge that grim reality. *I can't keep pushing myself this way. If we don't stop soon, our entire mission will be compromised.*

Jetta spotted a rundown shelter constructed from steel beams and rusted metal scraps thirty meters ahead between heaps of trash. Digging into Agracia's memories, Jetta learned that Scabbers frequently made temporary safe houses to wait out storms.

It looks new, Jetta thought, her eyes following the series of lightning deterrents running along the patched roof. *I guess it's better than nothing.*

Jetta motioned for Triel to wait outside as she circled the building. Through the gaps in the slats she tried to discern something useful, but the dark interior revealed no secrets. She couldn't sense anything, but with the sheer commotion surrounding them, she didn't entirely trust her senses.

Carefully, she tested the door, but the old metal wouldn't budge.

Hurry, she told herself, sensing not only the wind pick up, but the frequency and proximity of the lightning strikes.

A crack of thunder broke the skies. Adrenaline-spiked, she rammed the door with all her strength. The metal buckled, then flung open, sending her stumbling inside.

Triel's voice crackled over the helmet microphone. "Are you okay?"

Jetta turned to see Triel using her body weight to shut the door against the brutal winds.

"Yeah," Jetta said, flicking on her helmet's night vision mode and picking herself off the dirty ground.

"Wait," Jetta whispered, holding up an arm to halt Triel's advance. In the opposite corner of the shelter lay a curled human figure with a discolored blanket wrapped around his shoulders.

"Don't worry—he's dead."

Jetta didn't doubt Triel's perceptions, but she poked the corpse with her foot before relaxing.

"How did he die?" Triel asked as Jetta overturned the body. The wounds to his chest and thighs answered her question. It looked like someone or something had torn into him with something sharp. When the smell filtered through her helmet, Jetta released him and backed away. After a moment's thought, she covered his head with the blanket, leaving his boots exposed, and dragged him outside.

A quick survey of the building turned up a few useful items the dead man had been carrying.

Three candles, a lighter, a handful of trading caps, and some food rations, Jetta thought, taking a mental inventory as she went through a ratty stuffsack. A dirty medication bottle, marked with skulls and biohazard symbols, caught her attention. Inside, she found several red and black striped capsules. She rolled one of them between her fingers until she found the answer within Agracia's memories. *Anti-radiation pills.*

Given the degradation of the bottle, she doubted the efficacy, but she took them anyway. *Rather have something than nothing.*

Despite carrying a short rifle and a six-shooter, Jetta judged the man grossly unequipped for life aboveground. No hazard suit of any sort, no maps, no medkits, no survival gear. The thin blanket he died in barely covered his large frame.

"What are you doing?" Triel asked as Jetta moved to the center of the room, where a wood composite platform served as the only clean space. Jetta coaxed a few wicks out of the heap of candles melted onto the platform corner before using the dead man's lighter.

"I'm tired," Jetta said, removing her helmet and sliding down the wall nearest the candles. Her breath rose in puffs into the chilly air. "I know you are too. We need to rest, if only for a few hours."

Triel didn't argue but took her helmet off as well.

"Hey—" Jetta protested.

"You took yours off."

Jetta swallowed one of the radiation pills. "I was just testing these out."

"Give me one, then."

"No! Put your helmet back on!"

"Jetta Kyron..." Triel said, crossing her arms.

Mumbling under her breath, Jetta dug a black and red pill out of the bottle and handed it to the Healer. She swallowed it with a disgusted look on her face but said nothing more.

As the wind whistled through the cracks in the shelter, Jetta watched the candle flames, mesmerized by their ocher light. "So, did you get what you needed from the Temple of Exxuthus?"

Triel took a seat opposite of her and leaned against the wall. "I don't know. It certainly wasn't what I was expecting." A troubled look crossed Triel's face, but it passed as quickly as it formed. "What about you—did you find what you needed there?"

Bringing her knees to her chest, Jetta threw a handful of dirt in the opposite direction. "Just more questions."

They sat in silence for a moment, listening to the rampage of thunder and wind. The candlelight lulled Jetta, calming her thoughts until she thought only of laying her head down and closing her eyes.

"I miss my sister."

The words came out of her mouth before she could put thought into them. Triel, who had dozed off, looked up sharply. "Can't you just tell her that?"

Jetta shook her head. "Not right now."

The Healer pursed her lips, her eyes narrowing. "What are you afraid of?"

"It's not that," she said, straightening up. "I just…"

By the uncompromising look on Triel's face, Jetta thought better of lying to her fellow telepath. "I am afraid," she conceded, averting her eyes. "Of a lot of things. Especially of what Jaeia will say when I talk to her. I… hit her."

Triel didn't hide her surprise. "When?"

"After I got into Victor's mind. She was standing in my way so I knocked her out cold. I had to see him. I had to know about those terrible things I saw in his head."

Jetta traced her tattoo in the dirt but quickly wiped it away when she realized what she was doing. Once again, the words left her lips before she had a chance to bite them back. "What am I?"

Triel cautiously stood up. For some reason Jetta thought she might attack and backed up as far as she could against the wall. Instead, the Healer took a seat beside her, sitting close enough that their shoulders touched.

"You're my friend," Triel said, her eyes reminding Jetta of the clearest blue waters.

344

"Do you really believe that?"

"Jetta," Triel said, her voice barely rising above the wind, "if there's anything I've known for certain in my life, it's that nobody—*nobody*—can tell you who you are."

Jetta let her head drop back against the wall. The question she posed came from inside her, from a place she seldom understood. "What did Lady Helena show you in there?"

With a shy smile, the Healer shook her head. "Something unbelievable. Very strange. I'm not entirely sure. It didn't make sense."

Then the troubled look came back.

"What is it?"

Triel wiped her eyes. "Nothing. I'm just confused."

Jetta took her hand. "Tell me."

Chortling, Triel played with Jetta's hand. "Just a vision I had. Very confusing. Nothing I expected. You'll have to excuse me if I digest it a bit longer before sharing."

Jetta made a sour face, not hiding her offense.

"Like you've never kept anything from me," Triel said, raising a brow.

Grumbling, Jetta withdrew her hand.

"Hey," Triel said, looking her over with a serious eye. "You really don't look good."

Jetta picked up the lighter and looked at herself in the reflective finish. The stranger staring back had colorless skin, and eyes deepened into hollows. She put the lighter down in disgust. "Not much either of us can do about that now."

"I wish I could help," Triel replied softly.

Jetta forced a smile. "You've done so much as it is. I can never repay you for all the times you've saved me."

Triel paused before replying. "Yes, you can." The haunting need returned to the Healer's eyes. "I'm your friend. Haven't you always been able to trust me?"

Jetta said nothing, knowing the Healer wouldn't stop there.

"Why won't you open up to me? Every time I've been able to see you—really see *you*—it's been a life or death situation. I don't want that any more. I want to see you, now, without the threat of death, without you running away, without any more diversions."

Jetta didn't look at her. "Why are you asking this of me?"

"Because it's too important to avoid any longer. I need to know, Jetta."

Jetta fumbled with the sleeves of her lifesuit. A ball of emotion grew inside her chest, pushing against her ribs and rising in her throat in an acid wave. Frustration found its way into her words.

"Haven't I shown you enough?" she exclaimed. "How can you ask me that when you already know?"

Triel touched her arm. "Maybe it's not words that I want anymore, Jetta."

"Reht is the love of your life," Jetta whispered, her cheeks and eyes hot with anger. "I murdered your family. I destroyed Algar."

"Reht was my first love, but not my life love," Triel countered. "And the Core destroyed my world, not you. I blamed you at first, but that was before I knew you and saw through your eyes."

"I'm a girl," Jetta said, hiding her face behind her knees.

Triel chuckled. "Really?"

Snapping her head back up, Jetta gave her friend a frown.

The Healer changed her tone. "That doesn't matter."

"Why me?"

"You don't need an explanation. You know the truth. You have always sensed it."

"I know that you're my friend," Jetta said stupidly. Before she could stop them, tears cascaded down her face. Cheeks turning an even deeper shade of red, she hated Triel for making her cry. *Why does this unravel me so quickly?*

"Yes, I am. But look deeper, Jetta," Triel replied, shaking her head. "You can lie to yourself all you want, you can choose not to see what is right in front of you, but what is true will still exist no matter how much you fight it."

Jetta inhaled deeply and shut her eyes, trying to focus on something—anything—else so she could steady her emotions. *Why are we having this conversation now, on Old Earth, as we are exposed to poisonous radiation in the middle of a surface storm?*

Exhaustion ate into the marrow of her bones, further weakening her emotional control. *I can't do this right now.*

But before she could derail her nerves with anger, two soft lips pressed into her cheeks.

"Let go," Triel said, her warm hand cupping the commander's jaw.

"I can't!" Jetta said, pulling away. "It's not right."

"What's not right about it?"

"Jaeia would hate me," Jetta whispered. "She can never find this out about me."

"She's your sister, your twin—more than that, even. She's part of you. Don't you think she wants you to be happy?"

"I'm already a freak—she doesn't need this to worry about too," Jetta said. The same paralyzing fear that kept her silent for so long found its way back into her mind. *This is wrong—all of it. Leeches are abominations, humans are infections, Fiorahians are street rats, and for me to love a woman—*

"Don't do that," Triel said, pinning her wrist against the wall.

"What do you want from me?!" Jetta shouted.

"I want you to kiss me," she whispered back.

As Jetta stammered, Triel let go of her wrist and took her hand. Despite herself, she allowed the Healer to lead her onto the composite platform next to the candles. Every muscle in her body went stiff and numb as the dark-haired woman pulled her down so that she would lay next to her.

"Jetta Kyron," Triel said, tucking the stray strands of hair behind the commander's ear. "You can defeat the Motti, you can lead the Starways Alliance Fleet, you can face your brother and you can save a Fallen Healer countless times—but you can't kiss the woman you love."

"Hey!"

Something inside her snapped, and she leaned over to kiss the Healer. At first she was tentative, but when Triel slipped her tongue into her mouth, the floodgates of uncharted desires broke open. Pushing Triel down onto her back, Jetta laid on top of her and kissed her with a passion she had never expected from herself. After so many months of suppression, what came forth was uncontrollable.

Triel gently slid her hand between them for a moment, trying to catch her breath as she spoke.

"You always were an easy tease."

"That's not funny."

"Don't stop," Triel said, pulling her back on top of her.

The Healer started slowly, kissing her neck and caressing her sides. Unzipping the top of the commander's lifesuit, Triel let her hands slide between her skin and the suit. Jetta hadn't realized how cold it was outside until she felt the warmth of Triel's touch against the biting chill.

As the Healer went back to kissing her lips, her hands moved underneath her shirt. When Triel grazed the underside of her breasts, Jetta gasped. She had never been touched like this before, and even from her borrowed memories, she had never expected the actual sensations to be so powerful.

Triel kissed her mouth lightly and whispered, "Just stop and feel."

"I can't—"

Rolling back onto her side, the Healer rested her head on her arm. "You've never done anything like this before, have you?"

"I haven't exactly had a normal life," Jetta replied, somewhat annoyed, but also intimidated. *Am I doing something wrong?*

Triel shook her head. "I didn't mean to offend you. I just think we should take things slowly."

"This body isn't eight years old," Jetta whispered. "*I'm* not eight years old. I've already grafted more experience than I will ever live out in my own lifetime."

"I know."

Moving her hand to Jetta's stomach, Triel reached under her shirt. Her fingers traced the ugly, self-inflicted scar that wouldn't heal, but didn't linger long before traveling up her chest.

"You know, I'm new to this, too. I've never been with another telepath. It's different, you know," Triel commented as she lightly caressed the curve of Jetta's breasts.

"Yeah?" Jetta replied, only half-paying attention to what she said as Triel's hand moved underneath her lifesuit to her hip, her leg, and then pausing a moment before slipping down to her inner thigh.

"I'm not ready for that—"

"Don't worry," Triel said. Her muscles rippled for a moment but relaxed again as Triel kissed the tender place below her ear. "I wanted to try something else. Prodgies have the ability to enter one another both physically and psionically. It's a more intimate experience. Do you want to try?"

Breathing hard and fast, Jetta barely uttered the word as Triel's hand moved back to her chest and lightly pressed her fingertips above her heart. "Yes."

The Healer, not taking her hand away, moved on top of her and rested her forehead against Jetta's. Again she kissed her, but this time she slipped inside Jetta through her lips. At first the sensation felt similar to all of the other times Triel managed her wounds, but within a heartbeat it transformed from a warm, electric current to something more. Jetta gasped as Triel's inner light filled her soul to the brink, illuminating the totality of her being as something far greater than she could have imagined.

As they overlapped each other on a different plane, Jetta held onto the Healer's body and tried not to cry out. *This is beyond anything I could have ever imagined,* she thought as their minds twined together and physical boundaries fell away, merging them in perfect unity. For the first time in Jetta's life she knew wholeness; every action and reaction made sense to her, her needs and desires not at war with each other but aligning in a harmony that soared toward something high and bright.

Jetta's was still heaving for air when Triel rolled off of her and laid her head on her chest.

"That was better than anything I've known—or could have expected," Jetta said between breaths.

Triel smiled. "I beat out thousands of years' worth of stolen lovemaking?"

Wide-eyed and breathless, Jetta touched the Healer's face, feeling more than the softness of her skin. "Definitely."

Not wanting to move, Jetta laid with Triel for some time. All her worries, even the tempestuous storm outside, fell away, until she heard and felt only the beat of the Healer's heart.

"Do you love me, Jetta Kyron?" Triel asked softly.

Jetta rolled toward her, losing herself in the blue serenity of her eyes. "I always have," she whispered back.

Putting her arm around the Healer, Jetta pulled her close, enwrapped in her warmth despite the barrier of clothing between them. As the winds battered their shelter and the storm raged overhead, Jetta's eyes drifted closed, and for the first time in a long time, she slept.

***

Despite her exhaustion, Triel didn't find sleep as easily as Jetta. She drifted in and out of fitful dreams, never certain what was real and what was nightmare.

The crude walls of the shelter disappeared, replaced by skies swirling with putrid greens and angry streaks of lightning. Trees and bushes, decomposing before her eyes, became oily pools of sludge.

"She is not ready for what she must do. She will try and stop you," she heard Arpethea say, her voice rising from the decaying pits of the stone garden. "She will not let you fulfill your destiny."

Two fiery eyes rose in a swell of dark matter. "Do not hesitate to end her life to save your own."

Jetta materialized in front of her, smiling and laughing with arms outstretched, until a gnarled hand emerged from nowhere and tore into her abdomen.

"Kill the Apparax!"

Triel woke with a start, sitting up straight, disoriented and unsure of where she was. After a moment, she remembered.

Crash-landing. Earth.

More alert, her eyes went to the shelter door as it banged loudly against the wall. At some point the winds had knocked it open, blowing the candles out and leaving them in near darkness.

Something isn't right.

"Jetta," Triel whispered, nudging her sleeping companion. Jetta rolled over with a yawn and sat up.

"What's wrong?" she asked, stretching her neck and back.

"We're not alone."

Snapping to attention, the commander homed in on something moving in the shadows. Triel backed up as Jetta climbed over and put herself in front of the Healer.

"Show yourself!" Jetta demanded.

The thing breathed noisily, sending out curls of vapor into the air. A boot moved into the low light, then a mangled thigh.

"The dead man—"

The words had no sooner left her mouth when the corpse came rushing at them. Jetta angled herself to redirect the attack and threw him against the far wall. The dead man slammed into one of the steel beams only to bounce off seemingly unharmed and rush them again.

"Grab the six-shooter!"

Triel fumbled with her helmet. Using its night vision mode, she dug the gun out of their pile of supplies.

"Kill it!" Jetta said as she wrestled the dead man away from Triel.

Triel took aim but couldn't get a clear shot. The dead man's eyes glowed in the light filter of her night vision, his teeth dripping something oily that didn't look like blood or saliva.

Fearing for their lives, she closed her eyes and squeezed the trigger. Something fell heavily to the ground.

"Nice shot," Jetta said. She rummaged around in the dark until she found her own helmet.

"Right in the head. And I thought you hated guns," Jetta said, kicking the dead man's skull. It bounced limply off her shoe.

Triel threw the gun down. "That's not funny."

Focusing on the attacker, Jetta leaned down and inspected the corpse more closely this time. "I think this is a Necro. Or he became a Necro. These must be bites," she said, overturning his arm and exposing a black and purple patch of skin, "and these are claw marks."

She bowed her head. "This is my fault. I should have checked Agracia's memories. She would have known better than to leave a body unattended on the surface. We should have burned him."

"What are Necros?"

"Infected humans—well, really any living thing. Twenty-first century bioterrorism. 'Dead things that don't die,' as Agracia liked to think of it."

Triel remembered the link she made after healing the twins. "Similar to the plague on Tralora."

Jetta raised a brow. "Yeah, I read your report on that. Very weird. The Deadwalkers must have taken their cue from Earth's past."

Zipping up her lifesuit, Jetta started to gather their things. "It's time we take off anyway. No use staying around here."

"Jetta—I need to tell you something," Triel said as Jetta hoisted their supplies onto her shoulder.

"Can it wait until we reach the nearest Pit?"

Triel played with the webbing between her fingers. She wanted so badly to tell Jetta about her vision with Arpethea, but she didn't know how. The Seer's words still rang in her head—

She will not let you fulfill your destiny

—but when she looked at Jetta, she only saw a young woman who confounded her, sometimes even frightened her, but found undeniably attractive.

Kill the Apparax.

And somehow, through some bizarre intuition, she knew she would have to.

"Y-yes. Yes it can. Let's go."

After gearing up, the two headed back out. The storm had tempered, but no abated, making it a battle to stay upright against the wind and debris that thrashed across the wasteland.

It's getting really dark out, Triel thought, noticing the sun, a pale disc fighting to be seen behind the brown cloud cover, vanishing behind the horizon. *I don't know if we'll be able to see much, if anything, once the sun sets, even with the night vision mode.*

Jetta led the Healer inside a ruined building marked by fallen archways and rusted girders. The wind followed them, keening through the breaks in the walls and sections of collapsed ceiling. Advancing slowly, Triel kept a careful eye on the shifting shadows of the dugout corridor. *The dead man was probably attacked somewhere in the vicinity of the shelter, meaning that there are probably Necros lurking around nearby.*

"Down these stairs," Jetta whispered through the helmet mike. The Healer spotted the staircase up ahead, reinforced by shoddy post-war construction.

Jetta touched Triel's shoulder before handing her the six-shooter. "Hold onto this, okay? We're almost there."

They descended three flights of narrow stairs before entering a subbasement with a carved-out hole near the old sump system. Jetta stuck her head in and listened for a full minute before reemerging.

"I'll go first, okay?"

"Jetta, don't leave me—"

"It's okay," she said, taking the Healer's hand. "This is the passageway to the Pit. It's clean. I'm just not sure about the fall, so let me test it first, okay?"

Jetta dropped the supplies first, and then stuck her feet down the hole. "Wait for my call, okay?"

And then she disappeared.

Completely sheltered from the storm, darkness and quiet pervaded the subbasement. Triel gripped the six-shooter, aiming it at nothing in particular. *This place is empty,* she told herself as the gun shook in her hands.

A noise like the sound of a cockroach skirting across broken tiles pricked her ears. She adjusted the zoom on her visor and shakily aimed the gun at the movement, but nothing was there. Just her imagination.

Maybe Arpethea was my imagination, she thought to herself. *Maybe I'm just afraid of what could be...*

"Triel!"

The Healer looked over the dark lip of the hole and saw the faint glow at the end of a long curve.

"Jetta?"

Nobody called back. The voice was gone, the glow diminishing.

Something scuttered behind her. She whipped her head around. This time, she was sure she saw something in the shadows.

That's not a cockroach—

The sound amplified and transformed, until she covered her ears to protect herself from the tempest of insect wings. "Gods—please," she prayed, trying to adjust the magnification of her visor.

Fingers, petrified and blackened, reached out from the shadows.

Triel, you must obey—

"Father?!"

She glimpsed only a flash of his cerulean eyes before she pitched backward and headfirst into the hole. Panicked, she spread out her arms and legs to slow her descent, but the corrugated, irregular walls gave her no chance.

The curve in the channel lessened the impact of her fall, but she couldn't tell up from down as she shot out the other end to land in a heap.

"Are you okay?" The entire room spun and dipped until Jetta took hold of her hand. "Didn't want to wait?"

"I thought I heard you call my name," Triel said, rising on unsteady legs.

Jetta shook her head and picked up the rifle and gear off the ground. "No. I wasn't done securing the area."

Triel looked around. The concrete hideout seemed to be a staging area for access to and from the surface, its walls lined with the broken-down remains of an old subterranean wastewater management system. Decorative lights hung off the walls and piping, though only a few still flickered.

"I must be going crazy," Triel mumbled to herself.

Jetta lifted her visor and scratched her forehead with the tip of the gun. "I think we might have spent too much time in the Temple of Exxuthus."

"Agreed."

"Come on," Jetta said, helping her up. "I can smell the juke joints from here."

"Jetta, wait," Triel said, stopping her from lifting the decorated cardboard flap hiding the next descent. Under different circumstances, the dirty word, scrawled in red paint over the picture of a nude woman, would have made the Healer blush. "There's something I have to ask you."

Jetta turned around and looked at her curiously. "What?"

"Where do you think this will lead?"

"What?" she repeated, this time confused.

Triel closed her eyes. "I need to know. What's going to happen to us?"

Perplexed, Jetta's dark brows pinched together. "What are you worried about?"

Triel couldn't tell her the truth. How could she possibly impart Arpethea's warning and her spectral father's demands?

It's all nonsense anyway, she told herself. *Ingesting the llalana leaf caused the vision, and my father's ghost is the manifestation of my oldest guilt. No, it isn't real—*

Her subconscious interceded. *(—then how do I know that it is true?)*

Jetta looked at the ground, defeated by Triel's silence. "Honestly?"

Triel hugged her chest to conceal her shivering. Fortunately, Jetta was struggling too much with her own truths to notice her discomfort.

"Somehow, I know that it will be just me and Victor in the end. I don't know why or how, but I'm right. And I have to be ready for that. I have to know what exactly he is—if he's human or something else. But more importantly, I have to know more about myself, about why I am the way I am, to be able to face him. What's inside of him—I don't know how else to say this—but it *likes* me. It understands me. We share the same voice. And I'm worried that when I face him I'll be... tempted."

Unprepared for her startling confession, Triel couldn't accept her friend's truth. "Jetta—from what you told me, he's completely bereft of humanity. You couldn't possibly share anything in common with a beast like that."

Shrugging her shoulders, Jetta let her eyes fall back to the ground. "You know what I'm capable of. I'm ashamed of the things I've done to harm others, but that doesn't make that ugly part of me go away."

Jetta kicked a crumpled advertisement for the fighting rings and looked at her with the gaze Triel knew all too well. "I have no choice. I will have to face Victor, and when I do, no one can come with me. It's something I have to do alone."

"Not alone. Never alone," Triel said, touching Jetta's shoulder. The Healer oved to take her hand, but Jetta shied away. "What about me? What about your sister—and brother?"

Snapping her visor back in place, Jetta turned back toward the entrance to the Pit. "There are some places that good people shouldn't go; they'll just never come back. And where Victor's heart lies is a place that only I can find."

***

As they descended the series of ladders and crudely forged stairs, Jetta sensed a break in the uneasy silence.

"What is it?" Jetta said as Triel stopped at a junction, rigid and hyperventilating.

Concerned, Jetta removed her friend's helmet. The Healer's skin appeared pale and clammy under the dim arrangement of buzzing electric lightbulbs.

"Talk to me," Jetta said, helping her into a sitting position.

"Reht—something is very wrong with Reht."

Without intending to, Jetta's words came out sounding hurt. "I didn't think you two had that kind of connection."

"We don't," she said between gasps. "That's how I know something is wrong."

Jetta closed her eyes and searched Triel's impression, but could gain nothing from it.

"Your sister—ask your sister," the Healer pleaded.

"Triel, I can't—"

Triel grabbed at her chest, the muscles on her neck standing out taut against an invisible force.

"Okay, okay—just hold on," Jetta said, holding the Healer down.

Jetta didn't know how to begin. She had shoved her sister's aura so far out of reach that it rode the edge of her mind's horizon. When

357

she faced it for the first time in days, she winced at what had become of their once unfettered connection.

Fragments of unanswered conversations and unbridled emotion refracted across the mirrored dome of their shared consciousness. Once smooth and electric, their connection had transformed into a tangible, angry thing that bulged in the psionic divide. To breach it would mean more than just a simple "hello" across the schism.

Jetta reached out and touched the smooth surface with her fingers, surprised at how painfully cold it was to touch. (Jaeia, I—)

"Jetta, stop!"

Jetta found herself on her knees, her fists laying waste to a boy that was a good twenty kilos heavier than her. Covered in tan dust and each other's blood, Jetta breathed in hot, thick air that tasted like copper with a jarring tang.

Topitrate. Fiorah. The mining ships.

It was an old memory, one she had carefully tucked away, but she knew exactly where she was and when. Yahmen had sentenced them a few weeks prior to the lead drillship, and their introduction into the ranks of the other child laborers had been unwelcoming and unmerciful. Her siblings still wouldn't let her use her talents and risk them getting reported to the Dominion, so she did what she did best. She fought.

This one was named Sniffer because of his giant aquiline nose. He was a weasel, an opportunist, always picking on the smaller children and getting away with it. Having seen Jetta rightfully win four pieces of bakken in the scramble for food, he had waited until the others had returned to duty before seeking her out on the lower decks the laborminders seldom traversed.

"Hey little rat, little launnie." The way he spat the words made his nostrils flare. "Gimme your bread or I'll break that ugly face of yours."

Jetta had tried to run and hide in the conduit, but Sniffer knew her tactics too well. He was quick, too, grabbing her by the foot as she dived for an open hatch.

"Give me your bakken!" he said, punching her in the back.

Watching street brawls and picking through the minds of thugs taught her where to hit and how to defend herself against a larger opponent. Still, she was new to the idea. She had never physically fought with her siblings, and even when they play-wrestled it always ended in laughter and tickling.

His acne-pocked face got in hers, his yellow and brown teeth showing in a smile that made him look like a toad. "If you wanna play, rat, I'll make it worth your while."

As he cocked his fist, her perception of time slowed. Jetta shivered as she recalled her actions.

I let myself go... she thought, remembering her first step across the line she had feared and anticipated for months.

Sniffer missed her face by centimeters. He yelped when his fist connected with the walkway, breaking his hand.

As he cradled his injury, Jetta rolled away. She could have run. She even spotted an escape route. But she didn't.

Squaring her shoulders, she faced him, and before he could even utter a full sentence—

"Don't even think about—"

—her heel cracked against the biggest target on his face. His nose gave way easily under her strength, sending blood gushing onto his tepper-cloth shirt.

As Sniffer garbled and choked on the blood streaming down his face and flooding his mouth, Jetta rushed him. With all of her strength and force, she slammed him back against the grated floor. He clawed blindly at her, nails scraping at her skin, but she knew nothing of her own pain in the din of his agony as she laid waste to him.

"I hate you—I hate you—I hate you—" she repeated each time her fists struck his mashed face. It wasn't just Sniffer beneath her anymore. She saw all of the other child laborers, the laborminders, the people that spat on them in the street, Mr. Gravesbury, the telepath-hating Dominion Core, Yahmen—*every single person that had hurt or disappointed her. Even Galm and Lohien.*

He had long since ceased to fight back when Jaeia appeared in front of her, panic-stricken and aghast.

"Jetta, stop!"

But she couldn't. Sniffer was a raw, bloody pulp, his features rendered indistinguishable under her fists, but it wasn't enough. She had to end him—she had to erase the torments he inflicted—she had to make the terrible feelings inside herself go away.

"Jetta, stop!" Jaeia put her hand on Jetta's shoulder to try and pull her off, but Jetta didn't understand what her sister was doing.

(I hurt Jaeia—)

It was a memory as painful as it was shameful. Jetta didn't know why it was at the forefront of Jaeia's mind, but it was the gateway back into her consciousness, and she had no choice but to relive the nightmare of turning on her twin.

(Jaeia, I'm so sorry,) *Jetta cried.*

But nothing changed. Jetta backed her sister into the wall and punched her in the chest and face repeatedly. Jaeia fought back, parrying some but not all of her blows.

"Jetta—" she said, spitting blood as Jetta plowed her elbow into her stomach.

(Jetta, stop.)

Jahx appeared, standing over Sniffer's broken body. The memory froze.

Wait—what happened years ago didn't involve him. *Thinking back, she remembered their brother being trapped in the engine room explaining to one of the deckhands why a four-year-old shouldn't be responsible for decompressing an entire drillhead.* Is this real?

(Jahx?)

Breaching the memory, Jetta stepped out from behind the veil and onto the mining ship. As she approached her brother, his form changed, growing older until he matched her enhanced age. His eyes, bluer than she could have imagined in dreams, searched her face.

(I'm glad you came back to her, but you have to realize what you've done.)

Jetta wanted to run away. Her brother never talked like this. Where was his soothing reason? Where was his gentle confrontation?

(I have no time to be your shepherd,) *he said, stepping towards her.* (Where you've gone, what you've done is beyond my help.)

(Jahx, conserve your strength—)

(The Grand Oblin was generous enough to give me the gift of his life, and I'm saddened that this is how I must use what little time he and I have left. Why must it always be like this, Jetta? Why must it always be us running after you?)

(It's not like that,) *Jetta said, tears pricking her sinuses. She fought them back with the unnamed fury that surged in her veins.* (I'm doing this for both you and Jaeia. I will defeat Victor, and I will find a way to save you.)

(Don't lie to me,) *he said, his voice sharp and angry.*

Shaken by his tone, she fell to her knees. (Jahx, you don't know what I am.)

He crouched down, leveling his eyes with her, but she wouldn't look at him. (I know exactly what you are.)

Taking her hand, he unfurled her fingers and placed something in her palm before closing it with his. He tightened his fist around hers.

(Don't you forget.)

The ship, and Jahx, disappeared, leaving only the naked, celestial plane of the world between. No dreams, only the stars and the infinite, versicolor sky.

She looked down at her hand and opened her fist. The rock dice. Jahx's voice came in a whisper that echoed all around and within her. (Find Josef Stein.)

Heart aching, she closed her fist and squeezed as hard as she could.

(So, you've come back?)

Surprised at the voice, Jetta turned around. How did I get here? *she thought, recognizing the decor of her sister's quarters.*

Jaeia sat on the bed, facing the mirror on the dresser. Through her sister's eyes, she saw her own reflection.

(I don't even know where to begin, Jaeia. I'm so, so sorry. I know I haven't been a good sister—or a good friend. I've been so selfish.)

Jaeia nodded.

(I shouldn't have hit you, and I should never have left—not like I did, anyway. What can I do to make this right?)

Gray eyes looked tired, withdrawn. (I don't know anymore, Jetta.)

(Jaeia, I—)

(It doesn't matter,) *she said, folding her arms across her chest. Jetta noticed the way her uniform sagged on her shoulders, no longer stretching against a strong frame but drooping around a sickly husk.* (At least not right now. Things are bad.)

Jaeia told her everything, from Victor's latest move to break apart the Fleet to the death of Reht Jagger.

(But it wasn't confirmed,) *Jetta said.*

(His last known location was on the *Ultio*, which I helped to destroy.)

(But there was a cruiser that ejected—)

(The Handlers' last contact stated that Diawn had imprisoned him with the other humans on the cargo ship.)

(*Skucheka*. We needed him to find the woman that put a memory stain on him,) *Jetta realized,* (the one you thought could be our...?)

(Mother. Yes, I know,) *Jaeia said, not offering anything more.*

A long silence passed between them as fragile hope slipped through their fingers. Jetta didn't know what to say. How am I going to tell Triel?

(Jetta, I don't feel like I can trust you anymore.)

It did no good to tell Jaeia about what she learned on her journey about Josef Stein, Edgar Wallace, the Lockheads, the wolves, the Jumaris, the two human archeologists, or the strange happenings at the Temple of Exxuthus. She even told her about her encounter with Victor in the museum on Jue Hexron and its strange parallels with the otherworldly creatures she encountered in the Diez di Trios, *but it didn't change her mind.*

(Azerthenes?) *Jaeia repeated.*

(That's what Victor called them. The thing that impersonated me said they had many names.)

(What about Triel?)

Jetta didn't hide her frustration. (We both left with more questions than answers.)

Looking at the digital clock on her sleeve, Jaeia sighed. (I have to get back.)

(Why?)

(The only world that hasn't pledged itself to Victor is Trigos, and I intend to defend her. Li said that he won't protect Trigos from the Motti unless we resign our command, and with the Motti so close to the borders, I'm afraid of what will happen after the deadline.)

(How long?) Jetta asked.

(Seven days.)

(That seems very generous,) Jetta commented.

(Victor's very confident. He gave us enough time for the nations to give in to panic and not enough time to evacuate the planet before the Motti's weapon is in range. A smart move.)

(An arrogant one.)

(Yes, but that doesn't change the fact that he's going to win. We have no defense against the Motti's weapon. Whatever Li has is unknown to our technologies.)

363

Jetta turned over the rock dice in her hand. (Jaeia, I have to stop Victor.)

(You can't kill him, Jetta,) *she said, firming her tone.* (He has too much power now.)

(What do you suggest, then?)

(Admiral Unipoesa is serving again, and he and I are collaborating with Pancar of Nagoorian. The Liberalists have quite the army.)

(To do what?)

Jaeia shook her head. (We're still working on that.)

Taking a deep breath, Jetta squeezed the rock dice and decided her next move. (There's some unfinished business I have on Old Earth, and then I will rejoin you. Together we will put an end to this.)

(Why can't you come back now? What in the name of the Gods are you looking for?)

Jetta didn't know quite how to explain it to her sister. Closing her eyes, she allowed her sister her impressions and experience, both gained and borrowed, on Algar. (All the answers—about Victor, about Josef Stein, about the Prodgies, about the humans—about us—everything is here—I *feel* it. You know just as I do that the only thing that will undo Victor's fearful reign is hope.)

Jaeia chortled. (Find Kurt Stein. That's what we need. That, and a way to stop the Deadwalkers.)

(No,) *Jetta said.* (We need to know about his father's Smart Cell experiments, too. Finding Kurt's Ark will be fruitless without his father's nanites. They were a team.)

(A team?) *Jaeia repeated.*

(Yes,) *Jetta said, letting the silence take over their conversation.* (Just like you and me and Jahx. Before the universe decided to pit us against each other.)

Jetta's stomach leapt into her throat. She had been avoiding asking her most important question out of fear, but she could hold back no longer. (Jaeia... how is he?)

(Come home, Jetta,) *Jaeia whispered, the tears making her gray eyes shine like polished silver.* (We both need you.)

He's still alive, *Jetta thought, breathing a little easier. That's all that mattered. She just needed more time, and then she would have all the answers.* (I will. And then you and I can end this. I'll keep the promise I made to you years ago, back under the protection of our cots. We'll find freedom, we'll have a family, and we'll have peace.)

Jaeia smiled hesitantly.

(What?) *Jetta said.*

(Nothing. You just sounded more like the old you.)

Jetta smiled back. (I'll see you soon. Protect Trigos. Keep the Fleet together. I'll get the answers we need and be back so we can finish this once and for all.)

(Jetta—do one more thing for me, okay?) *Jaeia released her memories of Unipoesa's confessional in the intensive care unit.* (There isn't much time for Agracia. Help her remember Tarsha before it's too late, even if you don't get everything you want from her.)

(Why? Is she so important to you?)

Eyes pleading, Jaeia softened her voice. (Just do it. Please.)

Jetta felt her sister's cerebrations across the stars, and couldn't debate the importance of reawakening the Sleeper. (I promise. See you soon.)

Catapulting backwards, Jetta fell out of the connection forged across countless light years. There didn't seem to be an end as she telescoped through time, gaining speed and momentum the longer she spent reconnecting with the threads of her corporeal being. The sense of disconnect brought panic, and she flailed about, trying to gain purchase in an intangible world.

"You okay?" Triel said, crouching over her.

Jetta found herself on the ground, visor up, her head jammed awkwardly against the wall. Feeling something warm trickling from her nose, she wiped her face with the back of her hand, smearing blood across her cheek.

"How long was I out?" she asked. Against better judgment, she tried to rise, even though her arms and legs tingled and refused to coordinate.

Triel helped her into a sitting position. "Ten minutes. Maybe less. I didn't like it—your pulse, your vital signs were dangerously low. I thought I'd have to pull you out."

Jetta couldn't quite understand what had happened. Transactions across the psionic plane happened much more rapidly than in real time. For every minute that passed in telepathic limbo, only fractions of a second went by in the physical world. Even so, she had communicated with her sister at greater lengths before, but not with such intensity.

"Maybe it was the distance. And the type of contact. I was in pretty deep."

"Don't do that again, okay? Not like that. It scared me. I thought I was going to lose you," Triel said, her eyes still piqued with fright.

Jetta removed her helmet to better wipe her face with her sleeve. Her head throbbed and protested with even the slightest movement. "I feel like I got hit with a sledgehammer."

"What did you learn?" Triel asked, sitting back on her heels and raising her own visor. The Healer cradled her hands against her stomach, and her body swayed in nervous anticipation.

Knowing it was impossible to lie to her, Jetta reluctantly told her the truth.

"Reht's dead."

Triel's face crumpled. Doubling over, she looked like she was going to scream, but the sound never came.

"I know we fought. I know he did wrong by me. But I still loved him," she whispered. The tears slid down her cheeks and made dark spots on the collar of her suit.

Guilt and sorrow twisted Jetta's stomach into knots. Reht was her friend, her rescuer, but also her unspoken competition for Triel. She rarely admitted her own jealousy, but faced with his death, she was unfairly confronted with the breadth of emotions she felt for the dog-soldier captain.

A small voice inside her told her she was being unreasonable, but the cauldron of anger in her chest drowned it out. *(Reht is Triel's choice. See? How could she really ever love you? You're a fool for thinking it was possible. She never stopped loving him. He will always have her heart.)*

Jetta caught her own reflection in the tin siding of the tunnel. *(How could she ever love a monster like you anyway? You're worthless. You're disgusting. You're all I've ever hated.)*

Holding her breath, Jetta silenced the voices inside her head. Tears threatened to fall, but she fought them back with the pain that had laid its hooks into her heart.

She did the best she could by laying a comforting hand on Triel's shoulder. "I'm sorry, Triel. I know he was…"

But she didn't finish the sentence. She couldn't have if she wanted to.

"Thanks, Jetta," Triel said, taking her hand. "I know you understand. I never stopped loving him. The Alliance couldn't drive that from me, even if they had driven it from him."

Jetta tried for jocularity, but her words came out sounding strangely hurt. "Who's gonna call you Starfox now?"

Triel's brow pinched in confusion. "No one, I guess. It was silly. But that was always his thing."

Cheeks blooming red, Jetta replaced her helmet so Triel couldn't see her shame. "We should keep moving."

"Okay," she said, her voice wavering. The Healer dabbed her eyes, and then put down her visor, ready for Jetta to make the next move.

I am a fool.

Jetta turned toward the downward slope of the tunnel and continued the descent. After walking for a minute or two, Triel tentatively whispered her name. "Jetta, I—"

She didn't turn around. "What?"

367

There was a long pause, and a heavy weight to the air. "Oh, nothing. Never mind."

Despite the distinct dampness on her cheeks and stinging in her sinuses, Jetta trooped onwards, letting the fresh pain of heartache drown the last few inklings of hope inside her.

Not for me. Never for me.

Jetta's eye caught her warped reflection in the metal siding on the wall, and her mind leapt to the sparkle of Victor's diamond teeth.

Doesn't matter anyway, she thought. Victor materialized beside her, dressed in an expensive white suit, laughing mirthlessly as he twirled his cane around his fingers. *Because where I'm going, I'm not coming back.*

(END OF PART I)

The end is here.

I'm not going to make it much longer.

Jetta slid down the back of the wall and peeked around the corner. She heard the pins being removed from flash grenades and the whine of charging pulse rifles. Somewhere, Victor was laughing at her.

(So weak. So afraid of what you are.)

Jetta hugged her gun against her chest. They were still outnumbered. Only one way to get past their defenses. Only one way to survive another psionic expenditure. The easy way was the only way.

Time was running out.

Only one way.

I have to stop him.

Jetta closed her eyes and dug her fingernails into her own throat. *I'm sorry, Jahx.*

—Triorion: Reborn (part II)

For more information go to: <u>www.triorion.com</u>

369

Acknowledgements

Thanks to all the folks who backed this series and this book in the *Triorion* Kickstarter campaign in January and February of 2013. I am overwhelmed by the show of support and am grateful for all the pledges.

A special thanks to Stopher Wong of Banzai Sushi in Denver, Colorado, who was a top sponsor in the *Triorion* Kickstarter. I'd also like to acknowledge the outstanding support from Dr. David Christopher. Although he declined the ultimate Kickstarter reward of becoming a major character in books five through seven, I have a feeling I'm going to find some way to get him written into the series in more than just the acknowledgements section.

To Denny Greene, the masterful filmmaker and photographer who helped produce the *Triorion* teaser trailer and short video for the Kickstarter campaign: Thank you so much for lending your extraordinary talents. I can't wait to see your work on the big screen.

I'd also like to thank Anthony, my training partner in Eskrima and good friend, who has always been supportive of this series, and has really helped me out behind the scenes.

Finally, thanks to all the folks who pledged "no reward" in the Kickstarter campaign. Your faith in this series, and in me, has made the hardest days worth it.

In no particular order, I'd like to recognize the folks from Kickstarter who helped make this book possible:

Nicci E.M., Jacob Mathews, Denny Greene, Wa!, Cef Grima, Steven Thai, Thomas Krech, Frankie Blooding, Keith Hall, Joshua

Long, Thomas Harrison, Christian Steudtner, Eve & Ryan, Mikael Olsson, Kairam Ahmed Hamdan, Heather Norcross, Stevie Schafer, Tim & Ericka, Jason and Kristina, Jessica Roberts, Will Stone, my dear friend Chrissie D'Alexander, Zoey's Grandma, Nicole "Bitmap" Lorenz, Tabitha Mackin, Jessica Carter, Wolfgirl guitarist Drake Emko, Lori Russell and the Russell family, Jo Ann Gau, Chris N Tracy, Steve Wolk, Janet Davidson, Carol A. Smith, Carly Atencio, JParr, Warden JR, Francis Barbeau, Kyle J. Schnitzenbaumer, Vincent Meijer, Jeannine "J9" Labbe, Earl Anderson, Rasmus Bode, Courtney Allen, Dan Rekeweg, S. K. Stidolph, "Wednesday," Kami Castellano, DawnDawn, Vossie, Dabid Hangmeister and Mystic Shirley, Elizabeth King Ziemann, John Glick, Sara "Schmoopy" Major, Brian and Katrina Hall, Pam Peschel, Robert Hewett, Steve Hochberger, ABC&E, www.gnut.co.uk, Jim Honiotes, Gail & Lawrence Radcliffe, Linzy, Kevin, Mike, JE, the lovely Deana R., Eric, The Wit Theatre Company, Steve P., Erik B., Julie D., Jennifer S., Irene, David, my favorite Auntie in New Hampshire—Roberta! and Melinda B.

About the Author

L. J. Hachmeister is an author and registered nurse from Denver, Colorado. When not writing novels, she enjoys martial arts, music and chasing after her wild mountain dogs.

40256075R00208

Made in the USA
Middletown, DE
25 March 2019

EXERCISING OUR WORLDVIEW